New voices in sci-
ence fiction

New Voices in
Science Fiction

New Voices in Science Fiction

Stories by Campbell Award Nominees

Edited by

George R. R. Martin

Macmillan Publishing Co., Inc.

NEW YORK

Collier Macmillan Publishers

LONDON

Macmillan Publishing Co., Inc.
866 Third Avenue, New York, N.Y. 10022
Collier Macmillan Canada, Ltd.

Library of Congress Cataloging in Publication Data
Main entry under title:
New voices in science fiction.
   CONTENTS: Tuttle, L. The family monkey.—Thurston, R. Kingmakers.—Martin, G. R. R. The stone city. [etc.]
   1. Science fiction, American.   I. Martin, George, R. R.
PZ1.N4445 [PS648.S3] 813'.0876 76-16028
ISBN 0-02-580870-2

FIRST PRINTING 1977

Printed in the United States of America

for my parents
with love

Contents

Acknowledgments

Writers and editors are so often cast as natural enemies that it sometimes becomes difficult to think of them in any other light. But the characterizations are often unfair. Editors are not always monsters. Why, some of my best friends are editors.

So it is with sincere gratitude that I mention the advice, assistance, and encouragement that three such editors gave me at various points along the line. Without it, New Voices would likely have remained only an idle thought. Each editor worked for a different publisher, and each was interested in the book, but their help was given freely, without strings. Nor did it cease, from any of them, when the contracts were signed.

Therefore, many thanks are due to Dave Harris, who helped to start it, and Dave Hartwell, who kept me going, and Ellen Couch, who went through hell and then some.

—G. R. R. M.

Introduction

Ben Bova

YOUTH WILL BE SERVED.

It's a phrase we have all heard countless times. Whenever a smiling young man or woman surprises the world by accomplishing something significant, the elders among us nod knowingly and mutter about youth being served. As if, somehow, being young is what made the accomplishment possible.

Young writers know how tough it is to "be served." An unknown writer must begin his or her career by mailing stories blindly out to publishers, knowing full well that the manuscripts will be tossed onto the publisher's "slush pile," to be read if and when an editor has the time to tackle them. In most cases, the person assigned to reading the slush-pile manuscripts is the lowliest employee on the editorial staff. The more valuable time of the senior editors is reserved for the older, successful, money-making writers.

Young writers have wailed since the days of clay tablets and cuneiform script that it is easier for a camel to pass through an editor's doorway than for a new writer's manuscript to be treated fairly.

Except in certain cases.

In our particular niche in space-time, one of the most notable of those special cases was John W. Campbell Jr.

Briefly, just in case you don't know anything about science fiction, the field as it exists today is almost entirely an expression of John W. Campbell Jr.'s overpowering influence. Campbell was one of the best and most successful of the new young writers during the dreary Depression days of the mid-thirties, when he became editor of what was then called *Astounding Science Fiction* magazine.

He made science fiction what it is today. He lifted the field out of the pulp-magazine category and made it the exciting, thought-provoking, future-scanning, idea-challenging literature that it is now. Not entirely by himself, of course. But close enough.

For thirty-five years, Campbell made *Astounding*—which name he changed to *Analog* in 1960—the premier magazine in the science fiction field. Everybody else either imitated him or reacted against him. You could agree with John or not, but in science fiction he was as dominant a figure as Franklin Roosevelt was in politics.

And how does an editor dominate a field as deep and diverse as science fiction? By seeking, recognizing, and cultivating good new writers, that's how. Far from farming out the slush-pile reading chores to an assistant, Campbell took on the task of reading *all* the incoming manuscripts himself.

"I'll bet I've read more lousy science fiction than anyone in the world," he would boast.

It was true. But buried in the midst of all that useless slag were diamonds.

Isaac Asimov is one of the teenagers that Campbell discovered. He published Robert A. Heinlein's first stories, although Heinlein (like many science fiction writers) was already an adult before he turned his hand to writing. The *Hall of Fame* anthologies produced by Science Fiction Writers of America are a-chock with stories from Campbell's "stable" of writers: Asimov, Poul Anderson, Lester del Rey, Heinlein,

Henry Kuttner, Catherine L. Moore, Eric Frank Russell, Theodore Sturgeon, Jack Williamson, James Blish, James H. Schmitz, Clifford D. Simak, and many others.

Campbell built his career, his magazine, and the entire field of science fiction, on the finding and development of new writers.

When he died in 1971, the publishers of *Analog*, the Condé Nast Publications, Inc., generously agreed to sponsor a John W. Campbell Jr. Award for the Best New Science Fiction Writer of the Year. Only writers whose first published work had appeared no earlier than three years before the award year were eligible. And like the science fiction achievement awards (called Hugoes) the Campbell Award nominations and final selections are voted each year by the science fiction readers. Not the authors or the editors or a panel of "experts." The readers themselves do the voting. Thus the awards reflect the judgment of science fiction's audience, a unique situation among artistic awards.

The purpose of the Campbell Award is twofold: first, to memorialize John in a truly fitting way; and second, to honor the good new writers who enrich the science fiction field.

This first volume of *New Voices* goes a step farther in bringing much-needed recognition to new writers. Conceived by George R. R. Martin (himself one the best new writers of the seventies, and a Hugo Award winner) this anthology consists of original, previously unpublished stories by the nominees for the first Campbell Award. Each story in this volume was written expressly for this anthology by the writers who were nominated for the 1973 Award.

Jerry Pournelle won the Campbell Award in 1973, with George Alec Effinger coming so close in the voting that he received a special runner-up certificate. The following year Lisa Tuttle shared the award with Spider Robinson. Lisa, as a 1973 nominee, is represented in this book. So there are actually four award recipients in this volume of six stories.

Thus the *what* and *why* of this anthology. It is intended to honor the best new writers in this field we call science fiction. Perhaps it will also encourage even younger, newer writers to persevere until they, too, can "be served."

In my own mind, though, the best part of this book is that—like the Campbell Award itself—it helps to perpetuate and honor the memory of the man who spent most of his lifetime helping struggling new writers: John W. Campbell Jr.

BEN BOVA

Manhattan
September 1975

New Voices in
Science Fiction

LISA TUTTLE

*was not yet twenty-one when the nominees were an-
nounced for the first John W. Campbell Award in 1973. She
therefore set an immediate record as the youngest Campbell
Award nominee in history. Not at all satisfied with that honor,
however, she came back the following year and won a second
nomination, thereby establishing a second instant record: the
first (and so far only) person to be up for the Campbell Award
twice.*

*The second time around, she won. Lisa Tuttle has no shame
at all.*

*Young writers come into sf from all sorts of places, but two
of the most dependable breeding grounds are sf fandom and
the Clarion Writers' Workshops. Tuttle is a product of both.
She began when she was a mere child in Houston, editing a
fanzine called* Mathom *which she has refused to show to this
editor on the grounds that it might embarrass her. Much later
(in 1971, actually), she joined the Clarion kids by attending
workshops at Tulane and the University of Washington. As a
result, the second and third Clarion anthologies both contain
lovely Tuttletales.*

She has all the usual credits required of an up-and-coming

1

sf writer: she has published stories in all of the genre magazines, several anthologies, The Last Dangerous Visions, *that sort of thing. She also has some rather more berserk credits. When* New Ingenue *magazine sponsored a teenybopper sf writing contest a few years ago, requiring contestants to write stories around a number of rather strange and arbitrary plot elements suggested by big-name writers, Lisa was right up there among the strange and arbitrary winners. Even for her, the resulting story was unusual.*

Seventeen *magazine profiled her even before the Campbell Award nomination, in an article called "The Uncanny World of Lisa Tuttle."*

Currently her uncanny world is Austin, Texas, where she lives, writes, and edits the TV-entertainment section of the local newspaper. But she has been known to do a fair amount of traveling, and her prior residences include places like Sherman Oaks, California (which she liked), and Syracuse, New York (which she hated).

She is fond of browsing for hours in bookstores, taking long aimless rides in automobiles with the radio playing, and reading. She is allergic to everything. She is short.

Mostly, though, she is just talented. Her fiction runs the gamut: incisive mainstream pieces, nasty little stories about carnivorous dolls, hard sf, soft sf, fantasy. Modesty forbids me to mention "The Storms of Windhaven," a novella of some note which she co-authored with your editor.

Modestly does not forbid me to mention the story that follows, however. It is prime Tuttle, distinctive, delightful. No one but Lisa could have written it. Read it, and find out why this young punk is setting all these records.

—G. R. R. M.

The
Family
Monkey

ॐ

Lisa Tuttle

WILLIAM

I WAS SITTING WITH Florrie on the porch of her Daddy's house,
watching the night get darker and wondering about making
a move. I was at that time living in a boarding house in Nacogdoches, and Florrie's father had made me an offer to work for
him that came complete with a house to live in. I didn't know if
I wanted to be that much obligated to the man: I still thought
I might want to go back to Tennessee, and maybe I'd be better
with nothing to keep me here.

But then there was Florrie. I still can't figure why I was so
interested in that scrawny little old girl, but I was. I guess
there weren't too many women in Texas then, but still—most
of the time Florrie didn't seem more than a child. But it was
those other times that made me wonder, and made me wait,
staying on in Texas, a place I didn't much like and didn't at all
belong.

I was just deciding that moving a little closer to her there
on the porch couldn't do no harm when there was a sudden
flash in the sky, much brighter than any falling star ever was.
It began to drop, leaving a streaky, glowing trail behind as it
blazed brighter and then disappeared into the pines.

"What was that?" Florrie asked, already standing.

"Falling star?" I got up beside her.

"If it was, it must have fallen right over in the graveyard, it was so big and bright," Florrie said. Then: "Let's go see! I'd love to see a star up close!"

I thought I'd like to see a star up close myself, not that Florrie gave me any time to agree or disagree. She just took off into the woods and I followed after as best I could. I ran into a lot of things in those dark woods. I tried to take hold of Florrie's hand, but she was impatient with me and pushed me off, saying there wasn't room for but one on this path, and that was true. It wasn't much of a path, and it must have been made by children, or elves, because below the shoulders I was fine, but I kept running head-on into hanging vines and protruding branches. I scratched my face up pretty good, and I guess I was lucky not to lose an eye. And Florrie really trotted through those woods, although I kept calling to her to slow up.

Halfway there it suddenly dawned on me. "Hey, Florrie, how're we gonna see anything? It'll be pitch-black in that old graveyard, and we didn't bring a lantern."

"If you'll hurry we can get there before the star burns itself out. We'll see by the light of that."

So I saved my breath for keeping up with her, not wanting to be lost in the woods without a light *or* a girl.

"There—is that it?"

I came up close behind her and looked where she was pointing. Whatever it was had sure enough landed right in the graveyard, but if it was a star or not we couldn't tell, for it had burned itself out. The night grew thicker around us and about all you could make out was a big, odd-angled, collapsed shape, like a barn some giant had pitched across a pasture. Whatever it was, it had no business being in that graveyard.

"What is it?" Florrie whispered, but I had no inclination to find out. Because suddenly, maybe foolishly, I was wondering if something might not come crawling out of the wreckage.

"Let's leave it be," I whispered back, "We can come out in the morning and see what it is. It's too dark now."

"If we wait till morning something might happen to it," she

objected. "I'll just run back and fetch a lantern—you stay here and watch it."

"Why don't I go for the lantern?"

"You might get lost. I can go quicker'n you."

"Why don't we both go?"

"Are you afraid?" she asked, suddenly understanding.

"Of course not!" I said, real quick.

"Then wait till I get back." And she took off running, and what could I do but stay? I didn't want her to think me a coward, and, besides, she was right—I would have gotten lost in those woods.

Now, I am not the type who gets nervous about graveyards, after dark or otherwise. I don't believe in ghosts, and back in Tennessee there was a girl I used to take to a graveyard to court, so I have a kind of fondness for the places. The thing that was bothering me was that thing which didn't belong there, that chunk of star or whatever it was that had fallen out of the sky.

And as I sat there, staring at it (I couldn't see anything, but I didn't like the idea of turning my back on it) I started to hear something—a scratchy, grating sound that seemed to poke at the roots of my teeth and needle me just under my skin—and yet, though it didn't seem to make any sense at the time, I wasn't at all sure I was really hearing it. It seemed to be somehow inside me, a noise that my body sensed more than heard, a noise that was somehow a part of me, like the sound of my own blood pounding in my ears when everything else is silent.

I wanted to break and run, but there was something—and it was something more than fearing to look a fool in Florrie's eyes, it was a kind of compulsion—that wouldn't let me leave. So I stood there sweating, and argued with my feet, which seemed bent on dragging me over to that thing.

"Mr. Peacock?" Florrie, with a light, burst out of the brush. "Oh, there you are. You weren't going to explore it without me?"

I looked at where I was: it seemed my feet had done a pretty good job despite my arguing.

"Why, no, ma'am," I said, but she wasn't paying attention. She held the lantern up and away from herself, and we looked.

The thing which had fallen from the sky was of some dull metal. We could feel the heat from it, and the ground around was charred. I couldn't make out what it was, because I'd never seen anything like it, but I thought, it's a flying machine, and it's come from far away. And then forgot it.

"What's that?" Florrie said, whispering again.

There was a hole in the thing, deep blackness that the lantern-light didn't touch against the silvery metal, and I couldn't tell if it was an accidental hole or some kind of door or window. Then I saw that Florrie had seen. Something was moving inside the darkness of the hole, something trying to get out.

You might have expected a woman to go crazy then, and Florrie did, but not at all in the way you'd expect. She didn't grab me, and she didn't scream, and she didn't faint or cry or run for home. She said, "We gotta help him, Billy." Her voice was urgent, and she immediately started towards the hole without any fear or hesitation.

Most of all I noticed that she called me Billy. Next I noticed she'd said "him"—"We gotta help him"—and with that noticing, I hardly paid any attention to the fact that I was agreeing with her, and going with her to the hole, reaching in (carefully, afraid the sides might burn us) and catching hold of something, someone, and pulling it out. I was scared, but I couldn't stop doing what was scaring me so. The flesh beneath my fingers didn't feel like the flesh of any man, but it was not an animal we were grappling with. He was stuck, and we knew we were hurting him, but we knew we had to get him out. It had to be done: the urgency was as much there as if this had been my mother, pinned beneath a rock-slide.

And then we got him out and stretched on the grass. He looked enough like a man—in that he wasn't a dog or a horse —but even in the lantern light it was plain he wasn't human. He was some kind of freak or monster. His skin was too big on him. It hung like a sheet draped over his bones, the way the skin of a fat man, suddenly starved, might hang. It was rough and pebbly to the touch, and later, in daylight, we saw that he was a greenish grey color all over. His eyes were too round, and there was something funny about the eyelids, and he didn't have a regular nose but only a couple of slits with flaps of flesh over them in the center of his face. It gave me a real creepy feeling all over when I saw what he was doing with his throat—blowing out a sort of translucent bubble of skin, the way a certain kind of lizard does.

I wished we hadn't come. I wished like anything we hadn't come.

"We'll have to get him to shelter so we can look after him," Florrie said. She stared down at the creature. I looked at her, not wanting to look at it. I wondered why she sounded so sure of herself, and why she wasn't scared, why she didn't want to run from there the way I did.

Her face was tight, like she was hurting and trying not to let it bother her. "I wish I knew rightly what to do," she said quietly. "I know what's wrong, and I know what would make him worse, but . . . maybe there isn't anything I can do to make it better, maybe there isn't anything anyone here can do for him now. But we can try—we can make him more comfortable, anyway. We'll have to fix up some kind of stretcher, anyway, to bring him up to the house. I'll go—"

"You'll go? Why don't I?"

She looked at me scornfully. "Because you can't just go and get things out of my house without a lot of questions, that's why."

"What does it matter? I could get someone else to help if we're going to take him up there anyway."

"We're not."

"You said—"

"Your house, not mine."

"My house! I don't have a house. If you mean the boarding house, do you intend to carry him into town?"

"The guest house. That's what I meant. You'll be moving in after a few days, and we can keep him hidden there till he gets better."

"What makes you so sure I'm going to move in?"

"Now, Billy, don't be like that. We're just wasting time—somebody might come and see him."

"Well, so what if somebody does come?" I was getting pretty exasperated with her. "So what? Why can't we take him up to your house? We could get a real doctor, since you're so concerned with his health."

I stopped just short of saying what else I believed—that this thing would be better off dead, that it didn't belong and had no right to be here. Something like it would be easier explained away and forgotten, dead. Tuck him down in the graveyard—the other bodies would be too far gone to have any complaints about their company.

Florrie straightened slightly and said flatly, "My daddy shot a nigger once for comin' round on his property. He doesn't hardly think niggers are people, so you can guess what he'd have to say about this one. He'd kill him like an animal and feel less guilt. Now you just wait here, while I go get some things."

"Why should I? Why should I wait here with this old monster?"

"Billy, you just have to." She looked at me with her grey eyes shining in lantern light, and I saw she wasn't a child at all. So I put my arm around her and made to kiss her, and she punched me in the gut.

Then she went off into the woods again while I was still hunched over. I started swearing, but I didn't go after her, and I didn't go off on my own. I stayed there with that thing, just like she wanted me to. Just like it wanted me to.

And we took it up to the guest house, and she tended it and nursed it, and just as she'd said, I moved into the house and went to work for her father, and never made it back to Tennessee. And in time I married her, despite that gut-punch and the way she had of bossing me. Pete—as we called the monster after the only sound, the only real sound, we ever heard him make, a sort of *ppppp-ttttt* sound in his throat—became a part of the family and didn't seem such a monster any more. In time, he looked just as natural to us as any other person did, although he never stopped making me uneasy. It really unsettled me the way he and Florrie seemed to understand each other, whereas he and I were always strangers to each other. Our kids, when they came in time, loved Pete, and he was good with them.

I guess in all it's been good, it's worked out. I've made a home for myself here, and a name, friends and family. I think about the Tennessee hills sometimes—it's too flat here, and too dusty, even in the piney woods, for my taste—and I miss them, and the people I used to know. But they're all dead now probably, or gone away, and if I was to go back there wouldn't be anyone that knew me. This is my place now, even if I still don't much like it.

ADAPTATION

At first it seemed only an oddity that they left him alone during the hours of darkness. At first, he was too immersed in his pain to notice how life around him slowed and consciousness moved to another level.

There was much to learn, once he had mended (as much as he would ever mend) and could turn his attention to things outside his body. Sleep intrigued him—it was strange to him.

Life was very boring here for him, injured and out of touch with his own people. He searched hungrily for new interests, knowing that he must keep himself going, keep himself intrigued, or die. Something had happened to him in the crash which made it harder for him to think. His mind seemed wrapped in gauze now; he was limited. He could not communicate with these creatures, could not understand nor be understood except on the fuzziest, most imprecise and primitive levels. He was frustrated by the multitude of things he could no longer do, some of them simple things learned in childhood. There were ranges and heights now forever barred to him.

He continued his work with the limited mental equipment left to him. He tried to go on being a scholar, to give his life some meaning.

Sleep: it fascinated him. Here was something which might be important, a mental-spiritual state alien to his people. All of these creatures slept: what did it mean? What did they take from their journey through it every night?

To find out, he set about trying to fall asleep, to study the phenomenon at first hand. But he had no experience and no knowledge to draw upon. How to attain it? How to abandon oneself to it? It took him years to learn—but he had years. And when, finally, he had it:

He couldn't get back. It rushed upon him, swallowed him whole; he was wrapped, weighted and sinking, and it was beyond all fighting. He had wanted this: why then did he now want so desperately to fight it? What instinct was this which prompted him to hold it off?

But it was too late. He was lost to sleep, swathed in it like the humans who had rescued him.

If sleep was frightening, the dreams were worse. He could not control them, and they were not his. He'd fallen into a pit, the abyss mankind kept hidden behind the curtain of sleep.

He wandered through the dreams of others, not even of his own kind, was caught in them and forced to play them out. Gave nightmares as well as received them as he shambled through the sleeping world.

Woke to the sun, terrified. Felt pity for the human race, a rush of gratitude for his own mental structure. He would never, he vowed, sleep again.

But the next night the battle began again. Sleep had him now. He'd made the mistake of learning it, and once learned it would not be unlearned. It gripped him already with the force of undeniable habit.

Every night he fought it as long as he could, but it always overpowered him, submerged him, and every morning he dragged himself, shivering, out of the strange and terrifying sea of human sleep.

He was not, and could not be, human. The sharing of humanity's nightmares did not make him more human, yet it made him less than what he had once been. He forgot things; memories were lost, replaced by new learnings and by the useless memories, grafted on during sleep, of others. He changed and adapted, worn down by the numbing effects of day after day of living in this new, limited and limiting world.

EMILY

I looked through the dust-streaked window at the sunlit pine forest and could almost smell the baked resinous scent of the country where I had grown up. New York was far away now. I was bone-weary and longing for the jouncing train ride to end. Just then I didn't care that it was Texas I was going to, not Paris; I simply wanted to be at rest.

My fingers brushed the cover of the book in my lap. The poems of Byron. Paul had given me that book. I heard his voice again, and wondered if anyone would ever again say my name the way he had said it.

I put the book inside the brown valise at my feet. In the bottom of that valise lay two hundred pages written out in my best hand: my unfinished novel. Unfinished, because I felt the hypocrisy of writing about love when I knew nothing about it, yet I wanted to write about nothing else.

The train was crawling along now. The Nacogdoches station would not be far away. It was good that I had come to Texas; it would be better for me—more real, and less romantic—than Paris could have been.

In Texas I would learn to write about something other than love. I would relearn the important things, forgotten since childhood.

When Florrie embraced me, holding me close in her strong, capable arms, it seemed Mama was alive again, and I could become a little girl. Was this my little sister?

"Emma Kate! Oh, honey, how are you? It's so good to have you home again!"

I hugged back, and kissed her, a little awkwardly through being out of practice. "I'm just fine; I'm just fine, Florrie." I felt like crying, and saw there were tears shining in Florrie's eyes, too.

"It's just so good to have you back!" One more squeeze and she moved back reluctantly. "Now, where's the porter with your bags? Oh, Billy's got them. Come on, now—we'll get you home and out of those stiff clothes." It did me good to hear Florrie rattling on. "Now, we'll have a good long talk once you're settled in. I hope you're going to stay a good long while? No, no; we'll talk about all that later."

Billy hugged me, and it seemed strange to me that he was family now. I'd not set eyes on him since the day he and Florrie wed. And their children! It startled me a bit to see their four children. Florrie had been getting on with her life while I had been up in New York, teaching and playing at being an intellectual.

Billy loaded my things into the wagon with the children and helped me into the seat up front, between himself and Florrie. Then he clucked to the horses and we started off, slow and swaying. I looked out at the dusty road, the scrubby pines, the clapboard houses, the poorly dressed people, the animals. It seemed foreign to me after the manmade world of New York City.

The road wound through forest then, and the trees gave shelter from the sun and hid the straggling remains of the town. But the forest wasn't as deep as I remembered it. There were vast bare patches, ugly and denuded of trees: the harvest of the family lumber mill. The land was scarred, as by a forest fire, with tiny saplings pushing up bravely to stitch closed the wound. The old landmarks were gone and I couldn't be certain how far we were from home.

Florrie continued to talk, and sometimes I listened. Finally she patted my knee. "Here. Almost home." The horses tugged us wearily around one last bend. Home. "Ain't it nice?"

I had imagined, somehow, that they would still be living in the old bride's house, although Florrie's letters had been rich with details of the building of their new home.

"It's lovely, Florrie," I said, and hugged her.

The house was large and sturdy, yet managed to have some style, a certain gentle elegance. It was painted white and the windows, upstairs and down, were decorated with green shutters like many of the houses in New Orleans. The little bridal house, a log cabin, still stood, not far across the sloping lawn. It had been Billy and Florrie's first home, but once the children started coming it must have quickly become more cramped than cozy.

A colored woman came out of the side door as we rolled up the looping ribbon of driveway, hurrying towards us and beaming. This was Mattie, who hugged me while Florrie told me what a great help Mattie was with the children and the cleaning.

I looked suddenly from Mattie's dark face to my sister's smile. "Where's Daddy?"

Florrie's smile tightened. "We'll go see him as soon as you get cleaned up." She took my arm and walked me up toward the house, Billy following behind with my bags, the children scattering like a flock of birds uncaged.

"I thought he might have come up here to meet me," I said.

"Well, we asked him to supper, of course, But he won't come up here. He's as stubborn as he ever was. He don't like niggers around the place."

Of course. Why had I thought he would mellow with age?

"It's not so much Mattie and Tom," Florrie said. "They're help—he might get used to ignoring them. But it's Pete he won't forgive us for."

"Who's Pete?" I didn't want to see my father. Every word Florrie said made me more certain.

"Pete," said Florrie. Her voice was odd. "Didn't I tell you about Pete? I suppose I never did. Well, you'll meet him by and by."

We entered by the back door, walking into a warm, good-smelling kitchen. But Florrie didn't give me time to gaze around, walking me quickly through a dark-wood hall and up uncarpeted stairs. "Right now you'd best get freshened up and go over to Daddy's. You know how cranky waiting makes him."

I did know, and I didn't like discovering that I still feared his anger.

My room was fresh and airy-feeling, from the white curtains sprigged with green to the patchwork quilt on the big brass bed. But I couldn't lie down on that bed for a nap; I couldn't even take a bath. Now that I knew Daddy was waiting for me I became rushed and clumsy, knocking over the china pitcher after I had poured water into the washbowl—almost breaking it, but it landed on the rag rug instead of the floor, spilling out the rest of the water but not cracking.

I washed my face, neck, hands—trembling and trying not to tremble as I exchanged my travel-stained dress for a clean one. I was a grown woman. Say what he liked, he would not make me a girl again.

"Emily?" It was Florrie, peeking around the door. She hurried in and embraced me. "Oh, honey, don't be nervous!"

"Isn't it silly?" I said, trying to laugh. "I've faced down angry parents, and the headmaster at my school, but I'm afraid to see my own father. You were always the only one of us who could stand up to him, Florrie. I had to leave the state to be free of him."

We hugged again, and I clung to her a moment, trying to absorb some of her courage before I went to face our father.

He was waiting for me on the porch of the house I had grown up in. It was smaller in life than in memory, but he was not.

"It's about time you got here. Gossiping up there with your sister, I suppose."

"Hello, Daddy."

He got up to embrace me. We held each other awkwardly. I tried to kiss him, and his cheek rasped against mine.

"Come in and take dinner with me."

The kitchen too was smaller than I remembered it, and it

was dirty, as it had never been when my mother was alive. Dinner was cornbread, beans and ham, eaten sitting at the wooden table my father had built. It was much too large for just the two of us, but I suppose he didn't see any need to build himself a smaller one when this would do. He cooked and cleaned for himself now—Florrie might have done more for him, but I suspected it came down to a battle of wills between them.

We didn't speak much while we ate. That was my father's way. But the weight of the things we would say lay heavily on my tongue and I didn't eat much.

He commented on that, of course.

"Find a taste for fancy foods while you were up north?"

"I'm just not very hungry."

He wiped up the last few beans and sauce from his plate with a hunk of cornbread, washed that down with a gulp of iced tea, and settled back heavily in his chair, the wood complaining at his weight.

"Well," he said. "So you've come home. You given up on schoolteaching?"

I had known the question would come, but I had hoped for more time to think about it, time to talk with Florrie.

"I don't know if I've given up," I said. "I might just be here on a visit. Maybe I could see about getting a job near here— maybe do some tutoring." His eyes mocked me. He didn't believe me. He demanded some further explanation of myself and, unnerved, I made a mistake. I blurted out something I had meant to keep secret from him. "I thought I would do some writing while I'm here. I'm writing a novel."

His reaction was what I had known it would be: laughter; an outraged snort of laughter. "So now you want to be a writer. Why didn't you stay in New York with all those other writers, with all those intellectuals?"

"I may go back," I said. "I told you I hadn't really decided yet. I . . ."

But he wasn't listening; he never listened to me. "You thought that since the life you chose for yourself didn't work out that you'd come back here where your family would take care of you and you could play at writing without having to worry about being good or making a living at it. You could play at being an intellectual without having to prove yourself. You're like your mother, Emmie."

There were tears in my eyes, and I concentrated on not letting them fall.

He was silent, as I was—perhaps because he was sorry, or because he was thinking of my mother. Then he sighed and shook his head. "You shoulda got married, Emmie. You scared 'em all off with your learning and your books. Now you know you need a husband—but you might have done better to stay in New York, because there aren't any men in Texas who are gonna want a thirty-two-year-old spinster with too much book learning."

I wanted to refute him. I wanted to be cool and precise and witty—to laugh in his face as I told him how wrong he was, that I had never wanted to marry and that I had known far more of life than he ever had. That I had seen great actors on the New York stage, had been driven about in a motor car, had conversed once at a party with Dr. William James and his brother, the novelist, Mr. Henry James, had heard Samuel Clemens lecture, and had won the love of a fine man who would, I was certain, be known as a writer some day.

But actors, according to my father, were immoral; he wouldn't know who William James or Henry James or Samuel Clemens were; motor cars were a silly fad; and this fine, undiscovered writer who loved me was a married man.

And I was a spinster, as he said, and I was getting old, and I had come back to Texas where my book learning meant nothing and my father was still my father and could preach to me as he chose. I was silent for a long while, on the verge of tears as I stared down at the cold lumps of food on my plate.

He began to feel more kindly toward me in my defeat. "Well, Emmie," he said. "There have been spinsters that lead worthwhile lives before you. Now that you're back home you can make yourself useful by looking after me and caring for this old house. It needs a woman's hand—I can't do woman's work, myself. And your sister and I, we just can't get along in the same house together. She's too strong-willed for a woman." He chuckled, rather pleased. "She's too much like me, I guess."

I no longer wanted to cry. I wanted to scream. Terror crept up into my throat, choking me. Take my mother's place? Be bullied and bossed by my father until that far distant day when he allowed himself to die?

"What d'you say, Emmie? You can move right into your old room—have it to yourself now that Florrie has a house of her own. You can even work on that novel of yours in your spare time if you like." He was growing benevolent, almost jolly, with the prospect of capturing me once again.

I shook my head wildly, unable to speak, and raised my face to his. I suppose the wild animal look in my eyes, my terror, must have shocked him: the smile slid right off his face.

"Now see here, Emily Kate, you're not a child anymore. You've got some duties, and since you never married, your duties are still to me. You can't just flutter through your life like a butterfly—for one thing, you haven't got the looks or the spirit to get away with it. And your sister don't have room for you and she don't need you. She'll have another child one of these days and need your room for it. You don't know nothing about babies, so you won't be any help there." He spoke ponderously, leaning and bumping against me with his words, sure of wearing me down, just as a horse will hit against a door with a worn latch until the door falls open before the animal's dumb persistence.

I clung to the thought that this time I must not give in, I must not let him wear me down. I was not demanding anything from him, only trying to keep my freedom. I would not come back under his roof and be imprisoned; I did not owe him that much.

"Or maybe you plan on trying to teach in town? Well, you could try, but they like to have men—a woman can't handle some of these rough country boys. Also, I think they've got enough teachers in town—they don't need to hire someone who's practically a stranger. And people will talk, they'll sure wonder why this nice maiden-lady is letting her old daddy live alone and uncared for. Maybe, they'll say, she ain't really such a nice—"

I suddenly recalled my last major confrontation with my father. How I had wanted to go to school, to go East and earn a degree, and how my father had cornered me and knocked down every one of my reasons for going, telling me what a fool I was to consider it, telling me there wasn't enough money, telling me I was needed at home, telling me it wasn't fair to my sister, telling me I would never be any good, telling me women didn't need to know much, telling me if I liked to read I could stay home and read, and I, numbed into silence simply by the power of his presence, had begun to nod along with him, seeing my dreams char and burn to ash. And then—

"Harold."

We had both turned at the unfamiliar sound of the name, and the unfamiliar steel in the familiar soft voice. My mother had been unsmiling. "Harold," she said again, she who always called him Darlin' or Husband or Hal-honey. "I want to talk to you. Emma-honey, go help Florrie out in back."

I was slow in doing what I was told, lingering to hear what my gentle mother could do against my powerful father.

"Harold, the girl is going to school. That is already settled. She is going to have a chance. She's smart, and we can well afford to send her and we aren't going to deny her this one thing that she wants. It's her *life* and I won't let you ruin it."

I could hardly believe that was my soft, wheedle-tongued mother speaking. Perhaps my father was as startled as I, for instead of bullying her into tears as I had seen him do so many times before, he let her have her way. I did go to school; my mother had freed me.

But now my mother was dead; she couldn't fight my battles for me.

"And if you want to write a book—why, honey, you can go right ahead and write it. I won't stop you. All I ask is that you keep the house clean, do my mending, and cook meals for the two of us. That's certainly not much to ask." My father was sure this battle was already won.

"It is too much to ask," I said grimly. I moved, rather shakily, out of my chair and away from the table. I had to get out; I was terrified that he would raise his voice to me and I'd start crying. "I won't keep house for you, Daddy. I've got to live my own life—I'm grown up now." I didn't feel grown up at all. "You can get yourself a maid if you want someone to cook your meals. I didn't come back to Texas to be your slave."

"Now, Emma Kate, that's no way to talk to your father—" There was the barest trace of uncertainty beneath the bluster. My rebellion, small as it was, had shaken him.

"I've got to go now," I said "I told Florrie I'd come right back. We have a lot to discuss." I backed toward the door, keeping out of his reach, afraid he might try to stop me physically.

But he had decided to let me go this time. Shaking his head like an old dog bothered by flies, he said, "We'll talk about this some more when you've settled down. You're still tired from your trip and you need a chance to rest and give some thought to your life. There's plenty of time to work things out —you can move in whenever you like. This is always your home, Emma Kate."

The trace of gentleness—which I knew to be a trap—almost undid me, but I managed to get out onto the porch before I tossed my quavering goodbye at him.

And then I ran back through the woods—ran like my father's little girl, and not at all like the aging spinster who had just defied him.

Florrie looked up from the game she played on the lawn with two of her children, concern on her features at the sight of me as I burst through the woods: red-faced, panting, hair straggling like a hoyden's. She got up at once, with a word to her children, and hurried to my side.

"Emmie, honey," she said, gripping my arm.

"I'm all right. I—ran—through the woods—all the way—

back." My panting slowed almost to normal as we walked up the lawn to the house.

"What happened?"

I shook my head. "It was terrible."

Upstairs in my room I washed my face and combed out my hair while Florrie began to unpack my bags, laying out fresh clothes for me.

"Florrie, he wants me to move in with him again. He wants everything to be just as if I had never escaped from him, as if I didn't have all my learning. He thinks I owe my life to him simply because I've never married." I began to pant again, this time with emotion.

Florrie took me in her arms and held me tightly. "Hush, now, honey."

"He—he said you don't have room for me here, and that no one wants me—"

"Emmie, stop it. You know we love you and you'll always be welcome here, just as long as you want. Don't let him scare you so. You're doing just fine with your life, and it's foolish for you to even worry about what he thinks."

I pulled away from her and busied myself unpacking. "I— I know that, Florrie. But he goes on at me so—I'm afraid that one day I'll agree with him—he'll bully me into moving into his house—and then I won't ever be free again. I can't take it, Florrie. I think I've got a life of my own, and a mind of my own, but then he yells at me and I go all over like a little child again."

"You're tired," Florrie said gently. "Just tell yourself that you have your own life to live and it doesn't matter what he says. You'll start believing in it after a while."

"It's hard to do," I said. "I'm not like you, Florrie. I never could stand up to him—I could only run away. I haven't got your backbone. I'm more like Mama—I let him wear me down."

"Emily." I looked at her. "Don't underestimate yourself *or* Mama. You are more like Mama than I am, but Mama was never weak. She was gentle, and she let Daddy have his way when it would keep peace, but for anything important—she wouldn't stop fighting until she had won. Remember how she stood up for you when you wanted to go to college? She faced Daddy down because—"

"Yes," I said. "I thought of that today. But she fought Daddy for *me*. She fought to protect us because she loved us. But she would never fight for something on her own behalf. She'd go without anything, put up with anything, unless it hurt us. And then she'd go to war. But for herself, she wouldn't raise a finger. And I'm afraid that I'm like that. Perhaps I might protect my child, if I had one, but I don't know how to fight to save myself."

Florrie looked at me with love and pain in her eyes, and I looked back. In a moment we might dissolve into tears, I thought, and to break the tension I said briskly, "Come now, Florrie. I need to get these things put away, and then I would love a nice hot bath."

"You could take your bath now," she suggested, "And I could put away the rest of your things."

I shook my head. "No. If we work together, it will give us a chance to talk. Oh, Florrie, I've missed talking with you so! There's so much that never gets said in a letter."

"You're right," Florrie said a little ruefully. "Why, I somehow never could tell you about Pete. Well, you'll meet him later."

"Florrie, don't tease me! Who is this Pete? When will I meet him?"

"In the morning. But now you tell me something. What made you decide to leave New York? You always seemed so happy there—at least, your letters made you sound very happy. Busy, working, meeting people. Did something happen, to change things? Why did you leave?"

As she spoke, by coincidence, I had in my hand the book of Byron's poems Paul had given me, and was casting about for a way of introducing him into the conversation. I turned to face her, and perhaps it was in my face.

"A man, Emily?" she asked softly.

"He was married."

"Oh, Emily . . ." Her arms went around me and again she

held me tightly, comforting me. She drew back and looked at me tenderly. "Poor darling. Do you want to talk about it?"

We sat down side by side on the bed, holding hands, and I was reminded of confidences exchanged in childhood. Many years had passed since then and now, married and the mother of children, Florrie seemed the older sister.

"He was a teacher," I said. "We had similar interests. We met to talk about our work, about poetry and philosophy. We both wanted to be writers ourselves someday, and we showed each other work we didn't dare show anyone else. We criticized each other, both honestly and gently, and helped each other become better writers.

"I thought it was a platonic friendship. I met his wife and she didn't like me—she was jealous of what I shared with her husband. I thought she was foolish to be jealous—Paul and I had the sort of friendship two men would be fortunate to have."

"And then you realized you were in love with him?"

I looked at her without surprise—it was the natural assumption—and shook my head. "No—one evening he confessed his love for me. Of course, I told him I did not return his feelings."

Florrie squeezed my hand.

"I thought we could continue to be friends," I said. "I thought that if I discouraged him, and kept talk away from romance, we could still be friends. I couldn't—perhaps I should have refused to see him, but I didn't like the thought of losing his friendship, and since I didn't love him somehow I didn't really believe that he loved me, either." I didn't feel proud of myself, telling Florrie. My own excuses sounded feeble in my ears. Perhaps I had been leading him on, afraid he might be my last chance for a different kind of life and afraid to let him go.

"Finally he—he offered to leave his wife for me. He wanted to take me with him to Paris. Morality is different there, and it would be easier to live together. And of course, he knew how I wanted to live in Europe. So I left. I gave up my job and came down here because it would have been too easy to give in and go with him—let him ruin his life."

Florrie sighed. "Oh, Emily, how noble of you."

Noble. That was a word Paul had used, too—misunderstanding. I thought coward might be an apter choice.

"But I didn't love him," I said to Florrie. "I wasn't being noble. If I had really loved him"—loved, in the way of the heroine of a novel or play—"really, wholeheartedly loved him, then I wouldn't have hesitated. Then I would have given myself to him, Florrie; I would have run away with him at once."

That is what I believed. And, later, when I was alone, I thought more on my ideal of love, and wondered if I would ever experience anything I would think worthy of the name love. There would be—could be—no questions and no doubts, as there had been with Paul. Neither laws nor morals would keep me from the man I loved; I would stop at nothing, I would do anything he asked, give myself utterly.

I sat up in bed, brooding on the question of love. The house was quiet, everyone asleep. I had thought I would sleep, but although I was bone-weary, my body eager to slide into the healing lake of sleep, my mind was still active, jumping between thoughts of my father, thoughts of the career I had left behind, thoughts of Paul, thoughts of what love would mean to me.

I got up, then, and went to the bottom drawer of the dresser, where I had stored my unfinished novel. I lifted out the manuscript, remembering all the time that had gone into the writing and rewriting of the pages. I carried it to the bedside table and perched on the bed with it in my lap and began to read it by the light of the lamp.

It was the story of a perfect love between a man and a woman: the man an idealized Paul, the woman an idealized Me. I had been halted in my writing because, since I did not intend the novel to be a tragedy, I did not know where to go with this perfect love.

As I read over the pages of my novel, these pages that were the best I could write, my cheeks began to blaze. I felt feverish and unhappy, embarrassed by the prose. I imagined my father coming upon the manuscript and reading it, and laughing. I imagined Florrie being kind. I felt a sudden revulsion toward Paul, who had encouraged me in this sickly, silly fantasy about love.

I knew nothing about love, and probably never would. I was, as my father had said, a thirty-two-year-old spinster, and my ideas about love had come from books. How many of those books had been written by other people who knew as little about love as I?

I put the pages aside, my hands trembling, feeling sick at heart. I could not go on with it. I had thought to build a new life in these pages, and they would be better ash.

This thought firmly in mind, I rose and took the pile of paper to the washstand and there I burnt it, page by page. The sight of the flame licking at the first page, the curling of the paper, the way the writing changed color and disappeared, word by word, invigorated me. I would start fresh, write about something new, but not until I knew something to write about. I would forget this novel as if it had never existed. I would not write something my father could laugh at—until I could write something good and strong and true I would write nothing at all. I would give up my pretensions.

The second page went quickly. I burnt my finger on the third. On the fortieth I felt a sudden sick surge of regret: what if I was wrong? But the fortieth burned, too, and the forty-first —which I paused to read—made me certain again.

Halfway through, a wave of exhaustion made me sway, and I feared I might swoon. But I was determined to see it through. I burnt my fingers again, several times, but I saw every page of my novel become ash.

I woke in the morning feeling hollow inside, with the certainty that something that was important to me was gone forever. I opened my eyes, then, and remembered the novel. It was for the best, I thought. I did not regret it.

I had slept late, being so exhausted from the events of the preceding day, and breakfast had already been cleared away when I came downstairs.

"Mattie will fix you whatever you like for breakfast," Florrie said, kissing me on the cheek. "I thought you needed all the sleep you could get."

"I feel much better," I said, although I didn't. I felt drained and wished I were still asleep.

Florrie joined me in the kitchen for a cup of tea while I ate the scrambled eggs and sausage Mattie had fried up for me. I was just beginning to relax, to consider telling Florrie what I had done with my novel, when the door flew open and Florrie's eldest boy, Joe Bob, burst in.

"Young man, is that any way to come into a house?" Florrie said indignantly.

He grinned engagingly. Then he looked at me. "Grandaddy says whenever you feel like gettin' up he wants you to go over and have a talk with him."

I lost all appetite for breakfast. Florrie looked at me sharply. "Now, Emmie. You eat a good breakfast. You don't have to go hoppin' over there everytime he says 'frog.' You need a chance to relax and get your courage up. And I want you to meet Pete, first, anyway."

"Very well," I said dully. I could not face my father so soon. First, I had to adjust to my life without the novel—my life without writing. I had to build a new life, and it would be fatal if my father began arguing at me again while I was without supports. I had nothing left with which to resist: I could only cling with determination to the idea of not giving in, of not going to live in my father's house, and hope that would be sufficient to carry me through his attacks upon me.

I pushed my eggs around on the plate, then looked up at Florrie. "I can't eat," I said. "Really. I'm too nervous."

She bit her lip, then nodded. "All right. I'll take you to meet Pete. He'll make you feel better."

I laughed, out of nervousness. "Really? I'm intrigued about this Pete-person. Does he have another name?"

"No," she said, with a mysterious smile. "Come."

We went down the wide stretch of lawn dotted with pine trees and scrub oaks to the little cabin where Florrie and Billy had lived when they were first wed.

Florrie rapped sharply on the door once, then opened it, and we stepped into the dark cabin where the sudden change from daylight dimmed my sight. I could make out somebody moving slowly, uncertainly forward from the far corner.

"Pete, it's Florrie. I've brought my sister Emily to meet you."

At that first meeting I thought him very old. He moved with difficulty, shuffling and awkward as if plagued by pain and weakness. He was too small, the way an old man will seem shrunk down to his bones, although he was no shorter than I. I gave him my hand when Florrie pronounced our names, and felt the long, hard, thin fingers move lightly over my palm, as if reading it, the way a blind person might. But I didn't think he was blind, for the big round eyes shone, and looked directly into mine.

Except for those eyes—which were beautiful, but not normal in a human face—he was, I thought, very ugly. I thought at first he had no nose, and revulsion rose within me, only to be smothered at once by pity, or something like it, flowing smooth and heavy as molasses into my mind and drowning the revulsion before it was fully formed. I realized then that he did have a nose, but it wasn't like the noses I was used to: nothing more than a couple of slits with flaps of flesh over them.

The three of us went to the big table beside one window. Florrie and I sat and Pete disappeared into the kitchen. I looked at Florrie but I said nothing. I had questions, but for the moment they didn't matter.

Pete returned with a teapot and three cups and saucers, setting the tray down carefully on the table before Florrie, who poured out the tea and served us all.

I had a chance to examine Pete more closely now. His skin hung in folds and wrinkles from his slight frame, like an exaggeration of the shrinkage of age, but I no longer thought he was old, nor did I think he was ugly. He could not be compared with anyone else within my experience, so he was neither ugly nor beautiful, but only himself.

We sipped our tea and smiled at one another, and after a quarter of an hour Florrie rose and indicated that it was time for us to go. It was only then that I realized we had none of us spoken since the greeting, and Pete had never spoken at all. And yet never had I felt so comfortable, so instantly at ease with a stranger as I had these past fifteen minutes.

Florrie and I said goodbye, and Pete nodded at us and blinked his bright eyes.

"You liked him," Florrie said, as we started back up to the big house.

"Yes. Florrie . . . who *is* he?"

"I don't know," she said, as if it did not matter. "I think Billy and I saved his life. And after that . . . he's just stayed with us." She was silent then, as we passed the two older children who were tumbling about on the grass. Then, just before we reached the house she spoke again. "I would hate to have him leave. He's closer than kin."

I took a nap before supper, and Florrie came upstairs to wake me, sitting beside me on the bed and gently touching my face.

I opened my eyes, feeling the dream fading past recall already. "I dreamed about Pete," I said, struggling to hold it.

Florrie nodded. "We all do. Good or bad?"

"Good." The dream was gone, not even an image remained, but I was left with a feeling of warmth toward him.

"My dreams about him are good ones, too. Sometimes I think—" she broke off.

"That he dreams about us, too?" I ventured.

Florrie nodded. "Mostly our dreams are good—sometimes the others have nightmares. I never do. But Sarah Jane"—that was her four-year-old—"has nightmares all the time about him. For some reason she is terrified of him. The other children love him and always want to play with him, but Sarah Jane cries whenever she sees him. I don't know why that is."

I couldn't understand it either. Pete might be frightening to a child only at first sight—he radiated such an air of harmlessness, of gentleness, that his looks soon become unimportant.

"I wonder if we give him nightmares," I said.

The next morning I did something I had not done since my

college days: took out my sketchpad and went outside to try some sketches. Later, perhaps, I might return to my watercolors as well. Since I had abandoned my novel I needed something to fill in the gap.

I took a canvas chair and set it beneath a large shade tree, not far from Florrie and the baby. I chose to sketch them: mother with child in sunlight.

I had not been long at work when I saw Pete traveling toward me in his slow, painful hobble—as if he fought against great weights with every step. He stood beside me and watched with interest as my fingers—now somewhat crippled by his regard—created penciled figures on the paper.

Mysteriously aware of his presence, the other two children (but not, of course, Sarah Jane) came running around the side of the house to play at being mountain goats upon poor Pete. I saw one of the dogs, a hunting hound who had been running with the children, turn tail at sight of Pete and slink off out of sight.

Wondering a little uneasily why dogs should fear Pete, I continued my sketch until it was done. It was crude, and I was annoyed by my clumsiness, but Pete seemed pleased with it. He indicated that he wanted the pad and pencil, and when I gave them to him he hunkered down in the grass and set to work.

He was not especially skilled, yet I knew the first face for mine; next Florrie's; then his own. They were not technically perfect, nor even very good, yet there was a spark of life there, something which made it obvious what they represented.

Now, as I watched, he began to draw a story. Florrie—a very young Florrie—and a younger Billy; a starry night; a falling star; a crumpled, crashed vehicle—a flying machine—grounded in a graveyard.

I was so absorbed in what he was showing me that I scarcely noticed when Florrie and the baby went back up to the house. He drew me pictures of another land and, with a sudden shock, I recognized the landscape of my dreams the night before. I stopped his hand with mine and made him look at me—but his eyes were not human, and I could read nothing in them.

"Emily Katherine!" Like a whip cracked above my head. I jerked my head up and saw my father standing some yards away. There it was again, that fear out of childhood. My stomach contracted and my mind, in old habit, nervously tried to remember what I had done that he might consider wrong.

"Come here, missy, I want to talk to you."

Whatever I had done, it was very bad indeed. My hands and feet left like blocks of ice as I rose and walked to him. He grasped my arm, not gently, and walked me away.

"I know they preach nigger-loving up north," he said. "But you're a daughter of mine and I won't—I'd a damn sight sooner see you cuddlin' up to the biggest, blackest nigger in Texas than what I just saw." His voice was thick with fury, and his fingers were gouging my arm.

"Daddy, don't!" I tried to pull away. "I don't know what you're talking about!" I knew my voice was too shrill, and I couldn't stop shaking. How I hated him just then, for making me fear him so.

"What I'm talking about is that monster. It's bad enough that Florrie and Billy keep it—it's too much to see you nose to nose and making cow eyes at it. Can't you see that thing ain't human? It's an animal, and it doesn't belong here. It should be killed, just like you'd kill a snake, so it can't spread its poison around."

"Don't you call Pete a monster," I said, nearly in tears, "And don't you insinuate—"

"I ain't insinuating. I'm *telling*. That monster is trouble, and you'd better avoid it. If I ever see you cuddlin' up to that thing again—"

"Stop it!"

He let go of my arm. "Emily, you just do what your Daddy tells you and keep away from that thing. Don't talk to it, don't touch it, and don't sit with it. Or you'll be sorry—I'll make you sorry."

Tears blinded me. He always reduced me to that, the child's refuge. I had never been able to defy my father except by running away to New York. And I was sure he saw it as running away—I would never be an adult in his eyes.

When I walked back towards the house I wasn't thinking of Florrie but of Pete. I wanted the peace his presence gave me, and I wanted to disobey my father at once. So I turned towards the little house where Pete lived, and saw him waiting for me on the porch. And when I saw him—the dear, already familiar, not-human ugliness of him—something like a bolt of pain went through me. And, although I have never fainted in my life, I thought that I would faint then, standing on the wooden porch staring at Pete.

He touched my arm and we went into the house together. I felt dazed and clumsy—I felt too large, as if all my skin had suddenly swollen, and my clothes were painfully constricting. Pete led me out of the main room and into the back room, his bedroom. It was a small room, and familiar. As children, Florrie and I had come here to play games with our dolls. It seemed very bare now, empty of the personal possessions one would expect to find in a bedroom. There was only the bed against one wall, and a chair beside the window, and old rag rug on the floor. I looked at the window which, although screened with vines, let in filtered sunlight. Sensing my concern, Pete crossed to the window and closed the shutters across it. I heard the small, wooden click as they closed together.

I wanted to speak to him. He seemed suddenly a stranger, standing across the room in the sudden darkness. He came close to me, and I could see his features again, and they were as well known as if I had seen them every day of my life. I no longer wanted to break the silence with words.

He placed his hand, palm down, against my bosom, on the stiff, smooth fabric of my dress, meaning: undress.

I could not look at him while I stripped off my clothes: I turned my back and the rustling sounds as we both undressed filled the room with the sound of a flock of birds taking flight.

And my heart beat like a trapped bird's fluttering as I

climbed naked into the bed. Pete laid his head against my breast, listening to it, and he knelt beside the bed and stroked me slowly with the flat of one hand, soothing my shiverings as if they had been those of a horse.

When I was still and breathing only slightly faster than normal, he got into bed beside me, pressing close to me. His flesh was cool, so cool that it frightened me, and peppered roughly all over with what seemed to be goosebumps. I wondered if he was frightened too, and the possibility made me feel better.

He put his face closer to mine, and I closed my eyes, expecting to be kissed. I had been kissed before. But his lips never touched mine: instead, I felt his breath warm against the skin of my face and a gentle fluttering touch which I later realized was his nose—rather, the flaps of skin over his nostrils, moving out and in as he sniffed.

I began to feel warm all over—much too warm—and his cool, pebbly flesh moving against mine was a friction I wanted and needed. I kept my eyes tightly shut: since I had closed them I had not dared to open them again. I had glimpsed something—had glimpsed his male member—sprouting from the juncture of his legs, a frightening purplish vegetable. I felt it, warmer than the rest of his flesh, graze my leg now and again as he sniffed and stroked me.

I lay very still, hands clenched at my sides, clenched with wanting and with terror. I wanted to hold him and was afraid to touch him. I wished I would faint, that it would all suddenly be over with, that I would know what to do.

I made a soft sound in my throat. I thought I might cry. I was excited, desperate and dreadfully confused. I had never before been in such a turmoil of conflicting desires. I moaned again, asking for his help, his pity.

I felt him move away from me suddenly, and my eyes flashed open. "Pete."

He looked at me and I couldn't read his eyes. What was he thinking? I noticed how green his skin was in the dim, filtered light, and saw how the hairless skin hung from his bones. I remembered what he was. Then I didn't faint or run away, but instead, most improbably, I felt a surging of love. It ran through my veins with the blood, heating me and making me brave enough to half sit up—trying desperately to forget my naked-ness—and lean forward, reaching out for his hand, pulling him closer to me. I tried not to see the rising movement, the thing growing between his legs. He took me in his arms and I closed my eyes again, my mind rioting with senseless dream images, my thoughts a pathless jungle.

He parted my legs with his hands and I thought my heart would leap through my mouth. No—I didn't want it—I wanted to be safe and alone again—I did want it—I didn't—

I cried out at the first suggestion of pain—much more loudly than the discomfort warranted—and he stopped hurting me at once.

When he shifted position, my legs fell back together. Tears trickled from beneath my tightly shut lids—tears of fear and shame—and he licked them away.

He began stroking me again, and I realized that his finger-tips had become warmer. They were raspily pleasant, like the tongue of a cat. They moved between my legs, caressing me more and more intimately until my legs fell apart and my body moved and I moaned and thought in strange, rapid, jagged images and my breath came as quickly as my thoughts, and I forgot about him and about my fear, it was as if I were alone with myself in my own bed, and so I clenched my teeth, my back arched, and I screamed silently, silently inside my head, bursting all the brilliant balloons of my thoughts.

Far away, yet very close, I felt him moving, and then the cool, rough length of his body was pressed along the length of mine and as I rocked towards sleep I was content. I seemed to feel Pete with my mind as well as with my body—we ap-proached sleep together and his mind was joined to mine in a way our bodies had not been. His mind, I thought, was sooth-ing mine as his hands had soothed my body. I was very sleepy and it was pleasant, even if utterly foreign to me, to be so close to another. So close, falling asleep together.

Then my father's face—a memory or a dream—shattered the moment, and I struggled to wake.

But I could not move, could not even open my eyes. As I fought it, I was drawn more deeply into the dream.

I saw my father sitting in his kitchen, cleaning out the gun he used for shooting squirrel and rabbit. But I knew, with the absolute certainty we have in dreams, that he did not intend to go hunting for his dinner this evening. His thoughts were open to me: I knew that he would go to some of the local men he knew, men ready to be frightened by the threat different colored skin posed to their property and their women. My father thought of me: a spinster whose virginity had made her crazy, easy prey for the monster he now intended to kill or, at the least, to torture and disfigure and run out of the county.

I was humiliated by the vision my father had of me and, for a moment, I blazed with hatred.

His fingers tightened on the gun in his lap, and his face twitched. Had my hatred done that? He tried to set the gun aside, but could not. Rejoicing in my power, I made him stand.

My father got the bullets and loaded the gun—not at my direction, but of his own accord. I watched, seeing that he was thinking of Pete. His face was ugly with hate and anger, and his eyes whipped around the kitchen in restless search, as if he felt Pete's presence.

The gun moved—seemingly of its own accord—and my father, as his hands turned the gun to point at his own legs, struggled to turn it away.

The struggle was silent and fierce. I had Pete helping me, and his force magnified my own. I won't let you shoot him, I thought grimly at my father. You won't shoot Pete.

The gun barrel shifted, and for a moment I thought my father was winning. I made my father raise the gun. The position he held it in was unnatural and uncomfortable.

"Emily!" He said my name as if it were a curse. He was demanding again, not pleading. He would not acknowledge my power; even when I controlled his movements he still thought he could command me.

The gun was at his heart. I could have killed him if I chose.

"Emily!" The tone that could make me tremble, even in dreams. The barrel shifted slightly, caught in his will to move it, and mine to hold it still. Caught by my indecisiveness.

I shot him, and felt, for one impossible moment, the bullet tearing through his flesh.

I fainted then, or slept.

When I woke—feeling sick and miserable—Pete had already gotten up and dressed and was sitting beside the window. I dressed myself and left the house without speaking to him. He did not once turn to look at me.

I was the one who found my father lying in a pool of his own blood. It is likely that no one else would have stopped by to visit, and if I had not gone when I did, he would have died.

It was natural that I should be the one to stay with him, and look after him until he was completely well again. Everyone said how fortunate it was that I had come home. And, after my father was healed, it seemed for the best that I continue to live in his house. After all, the house was too big for one man, and Florrie, with another baby on the way, could use the room I had been staying in.

My father said that he had accidentally shot himself while cleaning his gun—not knowing it was loaded. He never spoke —to me, or anyone else—of our struggle. Perhaps it was only a dream. I still get dreams from Pete, but that's the only time I am close to him. He makes me uncomfortable now, and I avoid him, except in my dreams. And no one would say that we can control what we do in our dreams.

LIVING AND DYING

The new woman, Florrie's sister, was a surprise to him. She was open and vulnerable, beaming her needs, her wants, her fears at him with more intensity than he thought a human could possess. He didn't have to search at all—she presented everything.

And, he was surprised to realize within moments of meeting her, he could fill her needs.

The understanding shook and intrigued him. Might it be possible that he need not remain a stranger forever? That he could have true communication with some one of these beings?

He both desired and feared the union which might be possible. Like sleep, which had so fascinated him as a key to understanding these aliens, might not this too be a trap? To grow closer to them, to any one of them, was to risk becoming too human, to risk losing all that made him what he was. He might become nothing more than a freakish, incomplete human.

But if he were to spend the rest of his life among humans, never to be among his own kind again, then he must try to build a new life here. He must become as involved with human society as possible. He could read them now with ease, and he could send feelings, but the idea of attaining something more, a more true and equal communication, tempted him strongly. The thought of what might be possible stirred up his loneliness again, and Emily's own open hunger struck a responsive chord within him. How lonely he was. How he missed his own kind. Were he home, he would be choosing his life-mate.

With that thought came an almost undeniable urge, and he resolutely made himself ignore all the things which made her physically strange—almost repugnant—to him, and to concentrate on the likenesses.

He began the task of knowing her by making himself known to her. First he sent a dream, then followed that up with pictures when she was waking, to let her know, most basically, that he came from another world.

But there was not time for the courtship to make its leisurely progress. She came to him one afternoon desperately in need and also projecting the idea that he was danger from her father. There was no time for the courtship, no time to learn about each other, no time to grow naturally into a physical union.

Still, things were different on this world—events moved rapidly, these people lived their lives out so soon. He would adjust to this different pace—perhaps they might be mated in body and later in mind.

It might have worked; it might still have worked; but for Emily's fear. The fear rolled off her like a dreadful stench and it bewildered him, confused him and made his genitals shrink. Fear had no place in lovemaking, and although with the room dim and his vision relaxed she might have been one of his own people, and although her desire for him aroused desire in him for her, her fear overwhelmed all desire and incapacitated him.

Yet she needed him—he could feel that—and when she reached out for him (bravely, against her own fear) he tried, his limbs trembling with confusion, to ignore her fear. But then he hurt her, and the pain and fear undid him completely.

What sort of creature was this to feel pain and fear and still desire? He suddenly saw her as if in a blaze of light, body and feelings all joined and hideously clear. She was an alien, a beast, a monster, unnatural and loathsome.

Yet he had hurt her, even if she was a monster, and he responded almost instinctively to stop her pain. He brought her to orgasm with his hand, meanwhile holding his emotions firmly in check. He wanted to run, to panic, to flee this revolting imprisoning planet.

He pushed her into deep sleep, knowing that he would have to follow, and cast about in search of her father, in search of the danger, wanting to think of anything but what he had just done with this alien creature. He wouldn't think of what he had almost shared with her and he would never again consider mating with a human. He would deal with these creatures, his unsuspecting jailers, only as was necessary to sustain his life. He was a castaway, and had better get used to the life of a hermit and not think of coupling with beasts.

And so the years passed in solitude of his own choosing. He saw few humans and cared for none of them. Billy died, and Florrie after him, and he mourned neither of them. Others were born who continued to let him live in the little house and brought him food and occasional company, thinking of him as a strange old relative or family servant—an odd responsibility, but not very interesting. So he lived out his life like the days of a prison sentence and struggled against the involvement of dreams—knowing more about these people than he cared to, involved more than he wanted to be—and the tyranny of sleep every night.

And then one was born who, even in infancy, was different, who made herself felt. She had a potential he had seen in none of the humans he had encountered. She stirred something in him, an interest he had thought dead. And perhaps because he was of an age to be raising a child of his own, were he home, he cared for this child and began to teach it, to nurture its strange talent.

He wove dreams for her. He gave of himself to her, spending his nights in her dreams, becoming teacher and spiritual father to this strange child who became, under his care, something less or more than human.

JODY

As soon as I got off the bus I threw my thoughts on ahead to Pete, to see where he was and what he was feeling. And because it was a beautiful, blue-skyed day and I felt itchy and cramped and grouchy from sitting in school with a bunch of stupid kids and teachers—none of whom knew nearly as much as I did—I started to run just as soon as my feet hit the dusty side road which led off the highway and into the woods toward home.

But something was different. I found Pete's mind, like always, but he pushed me away. His thoughts were all agitated and rolling around. I couldn't understand it, and he wouldn't help me. I tried to get hold of something underneath all his thoughts. Was it fear? Anger? Suddenly I recognized it: joy. He was feeling joy, an almost unbearable excitement, and he didn't even want me around to share it.

I realized I had stopped stock-still in the road, my mouth probably hanging open. I started myself up again. My heart was lurching around like a dying fish. I didn't know what was going on, but it had to be something terrible. I couldn't even remember the last time Pete had pushed me out of his mind.

The walk down that interminable dusty road, striped with pine-shadows and blazing sunlight, was the most painful I ever took. I don't think I was reacting just to his pushing me away —I think I knew already, knew without understanding just why, that this was the end of Pete and me.

There were a whole bunch of strange cars pulled up on the circular gravel drive and when I walked into the front hall the air was blue with smoke and ringing with voices.

They were all in the living room. They went on with their talking at first, not noticing me in the doorway. My folks were there, and my sister and her junior politician boyfriend had driven in from Austin, and there were reporters with cameras and tape recorders and some senior politicians and some very quiet men who couldn't be anything but plainclothes police. And Pete was there, the center of it all, sitting in the antique Italian chair that nobody but company ever got to sit in, with reporters buzzing like flies around a cow pattie.

I sent a cry out to Pete, but his wall was still up. My sister Mary Beth quit chatting to some woman, turned, and saw me.

"Jody!" She hurried toward me. "Thank goodness you're finally here—I was thinking of sending Duane in his car up to school to fetch you." Even while she was glad to have me here, I could feel her automatic assessment and disapproval of the way I looked. She couldn't understand how I could be so tacky as to wear baggy blue jeans, a shirt with a rip under one arm, and dusty boots to school. I made a face at her for her thoughts, and she looked a little shook-up. She gripped my arm too tightly and whispered at me, "Jody, behave! There are some very important people here today and they're interested in Pete."

"So what?" Inside I felt like being sick. This was it. This was finally it. Somehow the government had found out about Pete and they had come to take him away. And Pete was just sitting there, stone ignoring me. He was going to let them take him away.

"Honey, are you all right?"

I must really have looked terrible for Mary Beth to ignore my rudeness.

"Yeah," I said. "What's going on?"

Instead of answering me, Mary Beth addressed the room at large. "Everybody," she said brightly, the sorority girl at a club meeting, "Jody's come home from school! She's always been able to communicate with Pete better than anyone else can— it's a special talent of hers."

They were all staring at me. A flash bulb flared.

"You can all go to hell," I said, but I said it so low, my chin down, blinking from the flash, that I don't think anyone but Mary Beth heard me. Her long nails pressed warningly into my skin.

I stared at the ground. I wasn't going to help them take Pete away. Mary Beth would have to do a lot more than pinch me to get me to talk, I thought.

"Jody," my mother said, her voice threatening in the most civilized manner. "No one is going to hurt Pete. We have just learned that Pete comes from another planet. And his friends—"

"You aren't his friends!" I cried. "None of you are! Pete doesn't have any friends except me!"

My mind was running around like a hamster on a wheel, trying to think of a way to get Pete and myself away from here. We had to get away. I knew how to drive, although I wasn't old enough for a license, and if I could get somebody's keys away from them—

Pete came into my mind then—maybe he'd been watching my thoughts all along and knew where I was headed—and ended it. He showed me himself surrounded by others who looked like him. They were his own people, his friends, and they had found him and come to take him home. And Pete was happy. Overwhelmingly, unbearably happy to be leaving the planet he'd been exiled to and to be going home again.

He was leaving *me*. Not simply a strange planet, but *me*. And he was happy.

Pete laid a comfort-touch on me, but I evaded it easily, his heart not being in it. He was so consumed by his own joy that he didn't have time for me. My sadness only irritated him.

My mother and Mary Beth's officious boyfriend were taking it in turns to tell me what I already knew. I was too numb to tell them to save their breath, that I didn't care about any of it. Pete had told me all I needed to know, and I didn't care about the details of the landing and the discovery. I didn't care what had been seen on TV or how the rest of the world was reacting.

"Mary Beth and I just happened to have the television on while we were having breakfast this morning—" Duane stopped suddenly, blushing. The biggest event in history had just happened and that fool thought people cared if he and Mary Beth had spent the night together.

"And there they were," Mary Beth said quickly, filling in for him. She would make a good little wife. "There they were on TV. We couldn't believe it at first—Duane thought it was a hoax, but I said, "Why that looks like Pete! Our funny old Pete!"

"So Duane, after I'd told him about Pete, and after what the announcer said on the TV about these alien visitors looking for a lost comrade, well, Duane said that maybe he should call up his friend in the governor's office, and maybe also call up the newspaper, and . . ."

I turned around and started to leave. I wanted to be by myself.

"Jody, we haven't finished," Mary Beth said.

"I already know what you're saying," I said.

"But everyone's been waiting for you," Duane said. "Isn't there something Pete would like to say to all of us? Can't you tell us how he feels?"

I looked back at them all for a moment, at all of them and at Pete who was bobbing gently in the good chair like a slightly dotty old man. The membrane at his neck was billowing gently and flaring orange. Since the photographer wasn't going crazy I gussed this was nothing new to him, although it was to me. It was a sign of extreme emotion, I knew, but I had never seen it before.

"He's very happy," I said finally. "He's very, very happy that his friends have come for him at last, and he can't wait to go home again. That's all. He doesn't have anything he needs to say, except to his friends." Then I want upstairs to my room and closed the door.

My mother came up a few hours later with some sandwiches and a piece of cake and glass of milk on a tray.

"I thought you'd like something to eat," she said, setting the tray down on my dresser.

"Thanks," I said, scooting across the bed to reach the food on the dresser. I was hungry and wished I wasn't. It didn't seem right that my whole life could be breaking up and I was still getting hungry at the usual times. I broke off a piece of the cake and tasted it.

My mother sat down on the bed beside me. "Jody," she said carefully. "You understand Pete awfully well. Do you—that is, I heard that his friends all speak, uh, with their minds. They don't make a sound that can actually be recorded, but to us it seems as if they are talking. At least, that's what I've heard. Can you—when you know what Pete wants, do you read his mind?"

"When he lets me," I said. My mother has been frightened of me since I was just a baby, although that's not something she will admit even to herself.

"Can you—" she stopped. She would never believe me if I answered her now, so I waited. "He speaks to you through, um, telepathic conversation?" She gave the word an odd emphasis, and I suspected she had heard it for the first time today.

"Yeah. I guess. Sort of," I said.

"Why can't he talk to the rest of us like that, then? These other aliens talk to everyone mind-to-mind. Why do you sup-pose Pete can't?"

I looked at her in surprise. I'd always taken it for granted that I was special in being able to understand Pete.

She steeled herself. "Jody, can you read our minds, too?"

"No," I said. "Look, I can only read Pete's mind when he lets me. He sort of gives it to me. I send my thoughts back to him. I don't know how I do it—I guess he taught me how when I was such a little baby that I just can't remember it. But when he doesn't want me to, I can't. And I can't read anyone else. It's like I can hear Pete, but nobody else is talking the way he is."

"I see." My mother bent her dark head to examine her well-kept nails. "I thought—well, you sometimes seem to know what I'm thinking or what I'm going to say, and I thought that maybe—"

"I can't read your mind," I said. "I guess I'm just real observant. I sort of put things together from how you move and what I know about you." This was true, but I wasn't going to tell her about the dreams. I wasn't going to tell her I could go into her dreams at night, or that it was her dreams which let me know so much about her.

"These aliens," I said, wondering about these creatures who could talk to everyone when Pete couldn't. "When are they getting here?"

"They'll arrive sometime tomorrow," she said. "They're all being flown in with a lot of government people, secret service, reporters—that whole lot. This is a big deal, you realize." She looked at me curiously. "Have you always known what Pete is?"

"Sure."

"And you never told anyone. Why?"

"Why should I?"

She looked at me in silence, looking like she might be feeling sorry for me.

"Poor Jody," she said, confirming my thought. "Pete's always been very special to you, hasn't he?"

That didn't even deserve an answer.

My mother looked at me like she wanted to put her arms around me, like she wanted to get into my mind. "Try not to take it so hard," she said. "Of course you'll miss him, but it's really for the best. You know he's never been entirely happy here—he wants to go home, where he belongs, to be among his own people. Think of how he feels."

I tried to block out her voice. I closed my eyes. I wished she would shut up and go away; she didn't know anything. There was no way she could understand how I felt. I was beginning to hate her.

I heard her sigh, and get off the bed. "Okay. Try to get some sleep, Jody. You'll feel better after some rest."

I twisted my head away when she bent down to kiss me, and she went out of the room without another word. I was already going away myself, reaching out for Pete. He was in his house and, I thought, by himself. His thoughts were strung taut and vibrating slightly. I couldn't get ahold of anything. He wasn't pushing me away, he just wasn't paying attention to me.

Then there was something—a little like static and a little like an electric shock—and I sat up in bed, trembling. I was nowhere near Pete. I was all alone in my room and I felt boxed in. And I knew what had just happened. I knew what it meant even though I had never encountered it before. Pete had been talking with someone else.

I didn't want anyone to see me and stop me, try to interfere or to help, so I was very careful as I crept down the backstairs and out the kitchen door. To get to Pete's little house I had to pass in front of the lighted living room window. It was early twilight, and I might be seen, so I ran and cast the image of a dog about me so that anyone looking out the window would think that one of the dogs had run past.

I found Pete where I expected he would be: in his bedroom, sitting on the cane-bottom, straight-backed chair beside the useless window. The window was a mass of vines and I could barely make out Pete's shape in the darkness.

"Pete?" I didn't try to touch his mind, knowing he'd probably still be locked in communication with some of his people. I hadn't liked the feeling when I'd bumped into it before. I hadn't liked it one little bit.

I waited in the dark for Pete to respond. I didn't mind the

wait. I was starting to feel better, calmer. I was fooling myself, of course, since nothing had changed, but just being in the same room with Pete was a tremendous relief after the confusion and loneliness of the afternoon.

He touched my mind with a question. A familiar touch, but strange. He was different: he was happy. I felt uncomfortable, wondering if what I had always thought normal for him had been a constant state of unhappiness, or loneliness, or sickness. I felt guilty. I had never been able to make him happy.

But that wasn't my fault; I couldn't be expected to do that— he sent impressions rapidly into my mind. He had been lonely, physically sick as a reaction to our atmosphere and psychically sick with longing for home and friends. I could do nothing— I had made him as happy as it was possible for him to be on this strange planet. But all that I had done wasn't enough— now he was going home, to be among his own kind again.

"What about me?" I demanded, so upset that I spoke to him in words. "I'm like you—you *made* me be like you. I'm different from everybody else. I can't stay here if you're gone. You know what it's like to be lonely; think of how it will be for me! It isn't fair, it isn't right for you to go off and leave me after you've turned me into some kind of monster."

He tried to calm me—this was always his first defense against the destructive emotions of humans. But I wasn't just another human, and I didn't let it work on me.

"Don't leave me," I said. "I can't stand it if you go. I'll be all alone; I won't have anybody. I won't even be able to wait and hope that someday my people will come for me because there's only you. There's only you and me, Pete. We belong together. Don't leave me here with strangers. Take me with you. Please, Pete. We need to be together."

He did love me; I know he did. And he must have seen what it would be like for me if he left me. He couldn't condemn me to a loneliness worse than the one he had been rescued from. I would be a stranger among his people, but I was a stranger among my own. If I stayed with him I would have only what I had always had.

He accepted me; he agreed. Pete would take me home with him.

By first light, the place was like a fairground or the site of a rock concert. Newspeople and security guards littered the grounds around the house, and there were plenty of gawkers who made their way down from the highway only to be run off again by police. I was up early after spending the night with Pete. He had shared vivid memories of his home planet with me, something he had done before, and this time they were even more real and special to me because I would soon be going there myself. Finally, despite my excitement, I had drifted off to sleep. But I dreamed alone that night, for Pete only held me in his arms and lay wakeful on the bed all through the night.

I hung around with my mother in the kitchen while I waited for the motorcade bearing the aliens to arrive from the airfield. I helped her and Mary Beth make sandwiches and coffee to feed the visitors, and hoped they wouldn't guess that my mood had changed from sorrow to excitement. Because of course they would try to stop me. I knew I couldn't even say goodbye —I would have to slip away somehow—because if I did they would never let me go.

I saw the short strand of black cars from the window, and bolted out the door, taking a short cut that zig-zagged through the woods and running hard, suddenly afraid that I still might get left behind, despite Pete's promise.

The porch and grounds around Pete's little house were swarming with people, and just as I got there I heard them all exclaiming, and the motorcade pulled up in a fine mist of dirt and gravel.

I was craning as eagerly as everyone else to see the first alien step out of a car—but they weren't aliens, I chided myself. They were people, my people, and I would have to get used to them.

When the first one came out through the car door I reacted as if it were Pete, my mind leaping forward in greeting. But what I found was not Pete. My mind encountered something cold and unintelligible. I felt my mind touched in response, and then I was rebuffed.

There were two more of them, and they all looked the same to me. This might be expected from the rest of the humans, but I felt that I, at least, should be able to tell them apart. But I could see no individual differences among them, and they wore form-fitting skin-like suits which hid their sexual differences and protected their bodies from the poisons in the atmosphere which irritated Pete's skin.

Pete came out of the house, moving slowly as always, his neck-membrane flaring brightly with his emotions at being reunited with his people after so long a time. He came down the porch steps, the onlookers moving away before him, as much to avoid his touch as to clear a path for him, and his alien brothers came forward and all four merged together in a large embrace which lasted long minutes. I felt very strange: uncomfortable, unhappy, left out, repelled.

Then one of the aliens spoke, and it was strange because I knew I was hearing it in my mind, the way I had heard Pete so many times, but this was not private or personal—I knew that everyone else was hearing it, too.

"We thank you people for your hospitality and kindness in caring for our injured brother. We will take him home with us now, and trouble you no further."

I felt a hand on my shoulder and twisted around to see my parents and Mary Beth and Duane. I shrugged off my father's hand.

Pete? I thought at him fiercely, but he wasn't looking at me or responding. Pete, tell them I am coming with you. I ran to him and threw my arms around him, hugging him tightly. Pete, you aren't going to leave me?

I felt the cold touch of one of the other aliens, and then he mind-spoke, not bothering to speak directly to me, letting everyone know: "You can't come with us. You must stay here with your own kind, child."

I was outraged and betrayed. Pete, tell them! "Pete," I said aloud, pleading.

And, reluctantly, he gave me his thoughts: he had asked, but the others were displeased by the very idea. They didn't want me; they refused to take me.

Pete was docile and bending before their wishes. He hadn't insisted, I realized. He was as weak and uncertain as a hospital patient. He seemed to have given up all his own wants and powers of decision in order to let them do all the deciding. He was as helpless before them as I was but, it seemed to me, of his own choice.

My mother touched my shoulder. "Darling. Let us all say goodbye to Pete; we'll miss him too, you know."

I resented her words, but I loosened my hold on Pete and stepped back. No one could miss Pete the way I would.

My mother hesitated a moment, a little timid now that Pete was an alien instead of an old member of the family. But he *had* been a member of the family, and so she conquered her fear and hugged him. My father shook Pete's hand and patted his shoulder as if he were one of the men who worked for him, about to leave on a long journey. My sister looked a little sick but made herself do the proper thing as she saw it, and hugged Pete for the first and last time in her life. Pete put his hands out to them as if he wanted to talk to them, to express something important before he left. Then he looked at me, and I saw the wattles of skin at his neck darken and wave slightly, about to flare.

That terrified me, that sight of emotion, for I knew it meant Pete was saddened by having to leave me. And that meant that he *was* leaving me, and this was the end with no escape.

Suddenly I was crying, for the first time in years, and I threw myself at Pete. "Take me with you . . . Oh, please, take me with you." I was crying and begging with mind and voice, with all of me. I didn't want to be alone. All my life, I had never been alone, and I couldn't bear the thought.

My mother tried to pull me away, but she was too gentle,

feeling sorry for me. Pete stood still, simply suffering my embrace. I stopped crying with an effort because I had thought of another chance. I wouldn't give in as Pete had; I would not be meek, I would keep trying. I released Pete and turned to my family.

"Look," I said, as calmly as I could. "Just let me go with him. Just in the car. Just up to the highway. I need to say goodbye to him, I need more time. Please. Let me. Please. Just to the highway—the driver can let me out there." If I could get in the car I might have half a chance to make the human driver forget to stop, forget I was there.

My mother looked very unwilling—she must have known I would desert her and all the earth for Pete.

"I'll come back, I will," I said. "I just want to drive with Pete up the road to the highway. Then—I need to be alone, to think for awhile by myself. So I'll walk in the woods for awhile. OK?"

The need I projected got to her and she relented, nodding at the driver and the government security man who stood by the car. "It's up to them," she said. "If there's no room, or they don't have time . . ."

I looked at the man I figured to have the most power—it showed in the way he held himself—and gave it everything I had. I tried to fix in his mind the idea that it would be a good idea to take me, and stupid to leave me; that in fact they must take me, it was already decided, they would take me—

One of the aliens—I couldn't even tell which one—intercepted my projection, snapped it up, and nullified it just like a frog taking a fly from the air. They all three looked at me with their unreadable, alien expressions, and for just a moment they didn't look like Pete at all, and I was afraid of them.

"Ma'am," said the man I'd meant to aim my plea at, "I don't think it would be a good idea." He looked at my mother. "There's no point in dragging out these goodbyes—it only makes the final parting more painful. And there'll be a lot of sightseers up by the highway—it might not be safe or wise to stop. I'm afraid I'm going to have to say no." He smiled.

I turned and ran back to the house, hating the tears that

stung my eyes, hating the aliens, hating the man who smiled, hating my parents, hating Pete for doing nothing at all. I would have fought to keep him with me, I wouldn't have given in as he did. I would have fought all the armies of Earth for him, and he wouldn't even argue with his friends.

And that was the last of Pete for me. He was soon too far away for me to reach, although I'm sure that if he'd wanted to he could have reached *me* with his mind. But he didn't. And when they took him into space I knew it because I felt it, like a numbing shock. And then I knew about being alone. No more Pete. No more mind-talk. Ever.

I'm all alone among these humans I can communicate with no better than Pete ever could. At night I wander through their dreams, oppressed by their limited range, missing Pete beside me to show me things I cannot see alone.

And Pete is out there somewhere. If only I could reach him. I wonder if he's as lonely as me. Sometimes I believe he will come back for me. It's not something I should count on or believe in, but I do sometimes because it's all I have. I'm just afraid that if he does come back it may be too late. I may spend my life waiting for him, and die before he comes. But that is all I can do. He made me into his companion because he was lonely on this strange planet, but then his friends came and he left me here alone.

My parents are waiting for me to get over my misery. They think I miss Pete the way I would miss a friend or relative who died or went away. They think that I will get over it in time. They don't realize I am in mourning for my lost life.

They bought me a monkey, a bribe to cheer me up. What a joke. It almost makes me cry to look at it, sitting there on my bed and picking at things with its tiny hands, wearing a face no animal should wear, staring at me with those sorrowful, wise and stupid eyes, wishing I'd pretend to be its mother and teach it the ways of our tribe.

REUNION

He was not accustomed to such excitement, not such excitement bursting from the inside to the outside, its source within himself. It had been so long, and he had become resigned to his way of life. Now—now he could barely control his thoughts and some of the more embarrassing body functions evaded control: limbs twitched or spasmed at moments, the neck membrane bloomed and sank in meaningless indications. Worst of all, he still had the embarrassing habit of sleep which he could not conquer. But his fellows assured him that all would be well, he could be cured and made whole again, once he was safely home.

And he was grateful to his fellows, for he knew he embarrassed them. Easier for them all if he'd had the grace to be dead. They had a defective on their hands now, a defective long presumed dead, to take home. But he thought of his friends waiting for him at home. They would be glad. They would welcome him in and cure his sick, weak body. His thoughts turned more and more toward home.

He had no time for the humans now. They could, at last, be shed. Jody embarrassed him—she clung so hard, making his leavetaking ambivalent at a time when he should be feeling only joy. Jody made his fellows feel scorn for him, he knew. There was a suggestion that such a close relationship with an alien creature was perverted and shameful. True, he must have been lonely. They expressed understanding and compassion, but he knew they did not understand at all, and for a moment he feared that Jody was right, that they both were monsters, alienated from their own races, at home only with each other.

He didn't like feeling uneasy; he wanted to return to the life he had known so long ago, the proper life for him. And so he submerged his will and let the others tell him what do and what to think. He was, after all, an invalid; badly injured in the crash and seriously malformed by the years of living on this unhealthy planet.

The humans, seen now through the eyes of his fellows, began

to look ugly again. They were unfamiliar, and their ugly plump-almost-to-skin-bursting bodies made him curl with distaste. He was seeing them for the first time. He saw only Jody still with his own eyes—she was still Jody, and he couldn't help regretting that he had to leave her. But she would be miserable on his planet—it would be harder for her to learn to survive there than it had been for him to adapt to her world. Her life span was too brief for such changes.

The others noticed Jody, too, for she was more noticeable than the other humans, made more like them than the others by her association with one of their kind. But their interest was only a passing spark—she made them uneasy, like an animal dressed in clothes to amuse or frighten.

He tried to make them see that she was different—but they responded that she was not different enough. She was a freak among her own people, but she was still only a human.

He was saddened by leaving Jody, but there was never any question but that he would leave her, never any question of his not going away with his own people. Although he quickly realized that he was almost as out of place among them as he was among the humans, still he had faith that soon everything would be as it had been. Soon, he would be home among friends and family, he would be cured, and he would live out a proper life in comfort among his own kind. Jody, he thought to ease his mind, would find the same. She was young and would adjust. It was right and proper for a being to be among its own kind.

So he went away and never came back to Earth again.

BOB THURSTON

was a reluctant candidate for the 1973 John W. Campbell Award. When Condé Nast first announced the award, to be given that fall at the Toronto World Science Fiction Convention, various fan magazines began to speculate immediately as to who the contenders would be, or should be. Thurston's name was frequently mentioned. In the short time since his first story had broken into print, he had already acquired a reputation as one of the field's most promising talents.

In response to the speculation, Thurston wrote a letter to LOCUS (the newspaper of science fiction), asking that his name be withdrawn from consideration and giving his reasons. LOCUS printed the withdrawal, but not the letter.

The fans and voters nominated Thurston anyway, and his name appeared on the ballot with the other five finalists.

The Campbell Award nomination that he did not want was not Thurston's first experience with awards. Three years earlier, his story "Wheels" had taken the first NAL-Clarion prize for the best story to come out of the 1970 Clarion Workshop, beating out fine stories by writers like George Alec Effinger and Vonda N. McIntyre. The following year, another Thurston piece finished second in the same competition.

Since then Bob's career has rolled merrily—if a bit unpre-dictably—along. His stories appear regularly in Damon Knight's Orbit *anthologies, in* The *Magazine of Fantasy & Science Fiction, in* Amazing, *in Robert Silverberg's* New Dimensions *series, and elsewhere. His stories are read and noticed and talked about. Fans mention them when they're thinking about Hugo awards; other writers mention them when they are thinking about Nebulas. If Thurston continues to produce work like his recent, highly acclaimed novelette "Under Siege"—and like the story you are about to read, for that matter—then it's only a matter of time until he gets a Hugo or a Nebula, or both. Whether he wants them or not.*

That is, of course, presuming that Thurston continues to write sf. He is not, nor has he ever been, a genre writer pure and simple. He does mainstream and experimental fiction with equal skill, and is endlessly mixing elements of this and that and the other thing to come up with something that is pecu-liarly his own.

The story that follows is a case in point. It's a time travel story. It's about politics. It's about people. It's . . . no, you decide what it is.

It's by Robert Thurston, mostly.

—G. R .R. M.

Kingmakers

Robert Thurston

1

THOMASON FIRST MET Ludvik in 1953, on an unusually cool August day. For Ludvik this was their last meeting. It took place in the study of the Thomason home, the site of all their meetings. At that time the Thomason home was in the last years of its era of pleasant suburban respectability.

Thomason, who had just acquired a pair of black pegged pants and white ducks, came to the study to provoke his father's disapproval of the new clothes. Ludvik sat behind his father's desk, a massive piece of furniture that dominated the room and allowed only narrow passing space between it and both walls. Whoever sat behind the desk automatically appeared important. Ludvik looked especially authoritarian. He had recently, in a giant step, grown old. His eyes had become black dots.

"Who the hell are you?" Thomason asked.

Ludvik, not interested in the question, picked up a paperweight—a snow globe that made snow fall upon a gliding sleigh. He held it up and shook it. "This is new," he said. "It was never here before."

"It's always been here. Long as I can remember. Dad won it

at an Old Home Week, target shooting or throwing darts or something."

"They're lovely, these reminders of old times, artifacts. My son hates my interest in them. He refuses to go to museums. Whatever happens to this, I hope it won't be thrown out or packed away and forgotten."

"What are you talking like that for about a stupid paper-weight?"

"At my age, it is easy to be sentimental over a paperweight."

"Well, Jeez, don't make a federal case out of it."

Ludvik smiled affectionately, as if he were about to produce a secret present. "Right," he said. "Sentimentality—that is perhaps the one fault that's prevented me from becoming a first-rate scholar. They don't realize—it is *so* easy to get sentimental over history you can touch. They believe in the cold objectivity of a Belliveau. Belliveau, hah! Sneaking behind the closest arras to watch the Kennedys squabble. That's *their* kind of historian."

Thomason walked to the desk, to look at the old man's face in a better light. "What?" he said. "We buy gas down at the Kennedys' station because they give stamps, but I don't know any Belliver. Is he a new history teacher at school or what?"

Ludvik did not acknowledge the fact that Thomason had spoken. He was more interested in the movement of the snow as he slowly revolved the globe with his hand.

"You punctured my sentimentality first chance. Typical of you. I did not know that you and my son were so alike. I should have seen it. Maybe I brought him up that way, spent so much time on you that unconsciously I molded him into something of a replica. A walking footnote to my study, as it were. I have admired your belligerence, but I was really not prepared for it this time. Not this time. You must have been born belligerent, William."

"How do you know my name? You a friend of Dad's?"

"I never met your father, sorry to say. A pity, really. I imagine that, if I'd been able to come back here during the preparatory period of my work, I wouldn't've made the early chapter mistakes."

"You don't sound right, your voice and all. You sound like you got marbles for brains."

"I'm not being careful any more, am I? Why should I? There's no more research to do, no more questions to ask. This is, in a way, just a nostalgic visit. Nothing can be hurt by it—my life is proof of that."

"You are out of your everlovin' mind. I'm going to get' my dad."

"No. Wait!"

Thomason's flight was stopped by the authority in the man's voice.

"Forgive me, William. I have looked forward to this particular meeting for such a long time—even knowing that it would be a disappointment. And I know that you will not leave me yet."

"Oh, yeah? I'll go if I want to when I want to."

Ludvik smiled, pleased about something. He turned over the globe and watched the snow fall from the ground.

"Just who are you and where did you come from?"

Since the only other access to the room was through the dormer window, Thomason feared that the stranger might be a gentleman burglar, a suspicion he found attractive. What a write-up he'd get in the paper if he captured a thief.

"I don't answer that question now. Not in full, anyway. I can tell you my name is Fritz Ludvik, and I can tell you a few things about your future."

Convinced the man was a lunatic, Thomason made another move toward the door, but was stopped as he reached for the doorknob by Ludvik's dropping of the snow globe. It rolled a half revolution and came to a halt lying sideways, its snow stirring in all directions as if disrupted by a sudden gale.

"You're full of guff," Thomason said. One of his father's favorite expressions. "You flipped your lid."

"Yes, you told me you thought I was a madman."

"I know I did. Just now."

"That you would think of me as a madman for several years. Whenever you recalled this incident, anyway."

"That what you meant when you said you'd see into my future? Big deal! Anybody with half a brain could *pre-dict* I'll think you're nuts from now on. Hell, for the rest of my life I'll think you're nuts."

"No, you won't, I'm afraid. Actually we become pretty good friends. As much as is possible within the severely limited contexts of our encounters. That's why this time—now—is so sad for me. Perhaps because I go on to a less certain but at least not overlong future."

Thomason was about to protest again, but a gesture from Ludvik interrupted him before he started. Ludvik appeared quite unhappy. Eyes narrowed, hiding the black dots.

"God, this is more frustrating than I'd expected. I knew you wouldn't know me or understand me, but I failed to foresee the tension in it. Suddenly it seems that I've done so little, and here's my last chance and nothing I can do with it."

The stranger stood up, fitted himself in the narrow area between the side of the desk and the wall. His movement caused Thomason to retreat a couple of steps.

"Being here now makes me realize how time, measurable time, cannot be stretched or filled properly or mutilated. I've become old, and for what? For you."

"Mister, you can't—"

"I'll tell you what I've learned, though it will not mean anything to you. Nor, apparently, do you ever realize its meaning. You see, you told me I would reach—that in your terms I *had* reached—this moment. You said to me that I was strangely morbid. And I never really believed it. With the knowledge that each of us had, we could not bring ourselves to quite believe the prophecies we made for each other's future. But what of it? Should a prophet listen to what another prophet tells him?"

Thomason looked around the room for a possible weapon to use on this maniac. Maybe he could find a way to get to his room and his rifle.

"To business. Strange, I thought I'd want to prolong this last meeting. Instead, I'd rather it be perfunctory. I am pressed by the foreordained, I suppose. But I must accomplish the minimum. To wit—you, William Thomason, are destined for greater things than you imagine."

"Did you see that in your crystal ball or what?"

Ludvik, his eyes glazed, gazed through the window. He came away from the wall, sat on the front corner of the desk. This is my chance, Thomason thought. Eyeing the globe on the floor as the best makeshift weapon, he edged closer to the stranger.

"All right," Ludvik said, weariness in his voice, "I suppose I was sounding a bit like an oracle. What I'm trying to tell you is that soon you're going to be snapping out of that adolescent haze you're in now and—"

"What the hell do you mean, haze? Who do you—"

"Okay, I'm sorry. This is so hard, try to understand. Excuse an old man for incoherence, it's a privilege of age. Listen. You'll come out of your—intellectual doldrums and discover that you have a power to sway others."

"You don't say!"

"You'll have more of a way with words than you apparently do now and you'll find in yourself a strong desire to use them. First for your own good, later for more humanitarian motives. The thing to remember, and one of the few things that will stick with you from this meeting, is that in spite of self-doubt, you must retain confidence in yourself and—"

"Cripes! You sound like one of my teachers."

"I am your *greatest* teacher!" Ludvik almost shouted.

"You are my greatest *nut*." Thomason did shout—as loud as he could. He hoped the noise would rouse his dad. All he had to do was keep needling this man. Someone would hear the commotion and come.

"What do I have to do, beat you into listening?"

"Just try it."

Ludvik appeared willing to try. Veins in his forehead became darker blue, sentinels of danger. "This can't happen," he whispered, struggling for control of his emotions. "Must—must remember not to hold you responsible for not exhibiting your future self at the fifteen-year-old stage. I just—just didn't expect you to be such a tedious little son of a bitch."

"Such terrible language. Tsk-tsk." Thomason exulted over his clever retorts. He was beginning to lose his fear and enjoy himself. The stranger's hands curled, as if they had a desire to strangle. Well, just let him try it.

Ludvik stood up and walked to the window, looked out on the serene summer day. Again Thomason eyed the paperweight. As long as the man was looking away, there was a chance to zonk him. Thomason took a step toward the potential weapon.

"Some day, William Thomason, you won't be such a tedious little son of a bitch."

"I'll be a tedious *big* son of a bitch."

That remark scored, too. Ludvik looked away from the window for a brief scornful glance. Shouldn't rile this guy up too much, keep his attention fixed on the view outside.

"By some historical assessments, yes," Ludvik said, "a big, a monumentally tedious son of a bitch."

When Ludvik looked away again, Thomason took another step toward the paperweight.

"But I could not agree with such an assessment. That's what put me on to you in the first place. The records didn't seem straight, too much vehemence in them that didn't agree with the facts. My duty, I thought, was to investigate and set things straight. Which I did."

Thomason now stood over the paperweight. Ludvik continued to talk but Thomason, intent on his master plan, no longer listened carefully. The man's talk made little sense. There was something about Thomason and his misunderstood powers, something else about corruption being more a matter of the times than the men, something sounding vaguely Communistic about Thomason's shrewd understanding of the masses and their motivations. The stranger really got carried away with a bunch of terse remarks about the scope of Thomason's abilities. It all sounded something like a funeral oration.

Although parts of the stranger's speech came back to him

later—at odd times—at that moment he was more concerned with working up the necessary courage. He must have stood over the paperweight five minutes before he finally stooped down awkwardly and picked it up. As soon as he had it in his hand, snow swirling beneath his fingers, he knew he must act fast or he would not act at all. While the man was spouting off something about the historical significance of compassionate justice, Thomason threw the paperweight as hard as he could. It bounced off Ludvik's head without a sound. He seemed to speak at least two more words before he fell. Thomason cautiously walked over to the man and peered at his head for signs of blood. He could see none. He looked around for the weapon and found it lying where it had rolled by a window curtain, a furious storm raging within the globe. He was about to pick it up when he realized that he should get help before the man regained consciousness. Before going out the door, he took one last look at the man, who lay still and unmoving, his body curled. The only movement in the room was the whirling snow of the paperweight.

When he returned—charging into the room ahead of his scowling father, who was on the verge of a sarcastic expletive—the man was gone. Thomason realized immediately that the paperweight was no longer by the curtains, so he looked around for it. What he found were its pieces—shards of glass, a bent cardboard sleigh, and flecks of white plastic arranged within a wet spot on the rug—all lying next to the wall against which it had been hurled. His father was momentarily heartbroken about its loss and did remark that he could not believe his son was strong enough to throw it so hard that its thick glass could be shattered. He told Thomason that there must be a fierce amount of hatred in him if he would destroy such an important—even historical—object.

2

Cautiously Thomason pressed his hand against his bandaged thigh, testing to make sure that no new blood had started flowing. For hours he had ignored the throbbing pain, ever since he first sat down behind the desk in his father's old study. It had been bright daylight then—he had been blinded by the glare and had difficulty finding his way around a room that was no longer familiar—but now it was dusk, his headache was gone, and he could see the room in dim but precise detail. It hadn't changed much. Mother said that she had been keeping the room pretty much intact since Dad died. Everything certainly appeared the same. But it had been so long since Thomason had been here that he could not be sure. It fit his fuzzy memory, and that was all.

All he could think of as his eyes scanned the shelves of books was that he had lived in this house all those years, among these volumes, and he had never bothered to open one. There were so many years of learning here. What if he had read them? Would he have advanced upon his awkward path more quickly, become more of a scholar? Or would he have reached the same stupid point that he'd achieved in so blissful an ignorance?

He stretched his wounded leg. It felt much better, just a slight twinge of pain. They said it was just a superficial wound, a bullet passing through a fleshy part of the thigh. In the first hours it had seemed like a mortal blow.

He stood up, used the desk as a crutch to get around it to the open part of the room, and started to limp delicately about. The leg felt okay; he should be able to go anywhere in a short time, an hour or two.

"Maybe it would be safer to stay right here," he said aloud. He never usually talked to himself, and he was surprised by it. He was even more surprised when he received a response.

"Nobody's coming after you. They haven't even thought of this place."

Thomason whirled around. A bit too fast, for he felt a massive spasm of pain in his leg. He winced.

The man behind the desk stood up and came toward him.

"You should rest," he said, taking Thomason's arm. "Sit down."

"I've been sitting for hours." But he let himself be led to the chair behind the desk. "Who the hell are you? How did you get in here? How *could* you get in here? Did I fall asleep on my feet or something? You couldn't get past me."

"Save the distress. We'll work all that out in a minute."

He sat Thomason down on the chair. Thomason put his head back against the leather and closed his eyes. Superficial wound or not, he certainly felt like hell.

When he again opened his eyes, he saw his helper sitting casually on a corner of the desk and gazing down at him. There was something familiar about his face, something comfortably familiar about the gentle way he smiled.

"You've nothing to worry about. The fact that nobody knows you still hold the deed on your family home works out as an advantage to you. They're scouring the big cities for you. You've been away from your hometown so long that it never occurs to anybody as a hiding place."

"I'm supposed to believe that? Man, you are out of your gourd."

As he thought about how weird this man was, he remembered when he had seen him before. This was the mysterious intruder from, oh, how many years ago—fifteen or sixteen at least. But he looked somehow different. Younger than he should be, younger than he was then. He must be some close relative of that stranger, one in whom the family madness had been passed on by heredity.

Thomason tried to remember the incident from his forgotten past. He could recall the man and some of the conversation, and that he had brained him with a paperweight of some kind. He shut his eyes again and tried to see the old stranger's face. At first the mental image was indistinct; then he opened his eyes again and mentally drew age lines on this vigorous-looking middle-aged man's face. Yes, the resemblance was extraordinary. The only difference seemed to be age and degree of vitality.

"You seem to be remembering me."

"Yes—no. Not you. I don't remember you. I remember some-body else, an older man. Your father, maybe, or an uncle or something . . ."

"No, it was me, no doubt."

"If it was, you've found a fountain of youth, or have a real great cosmetics specialist giving you treatments."

"Nothing of the kind."

"Suit yourself." He tried to force his slightly blurry vision to focus more clearly on the man's face. "Say, I remember that day better. What the hell happened to you?"

"I'm sure I haven't the slightest idea. And I doubt that I'll receive firsthand knowledge very soon."

"What are you talking about?"

"I'll explain later. First, you tell me all you can remember about our first meeting."

"It couldn't've been you. Anyway, why should I tell you any-thing? What right have you got to give me the third degree?"

"The right of a scholar to an unhindered path of research."

"I don't get that."

"I'm sure you don't. Just tell me about our first meeting. We have plenty of time. It's not only desirable that you tell me, I already know that you will."

"Yeah, well, maybe I'll just get you thrown off my property."

"By whom? With what?"

"No, you're right. Ah, what the hell, pass the time. I don't remember too much, but I'll do what I can."

Once he started relating the incident, Thomason was sur-prised at how much he did remember. Details that he had not thought of in years came back to him. The passing of years did give the events a different sort of character, and he depicted himself as a rather tough and courageous young man. Caution made him skip the part about hitting Ludvik with the paper-weight; he said instead that he had run out of the room while Ludvik was distracted.

"That's about it," he said, after he described returning to the room with his father. "Like I say, I was pretty rough on you and you didn't seem to like it one damn bit."

"I can hardly accept that. I'm sure that you misunderstood me in some way. I can't believe that I would turn on you so coldly. You were just a child, really, and I suppose that fact distorts your memory."

"Suit yourself. I thought you said you were there, so— Well, anyway, that's what I remember."

"Well, we'll see." The gentleness in Ludvik's voice seemed almost patronizing. Thomason chose to ignore it.

"I'm pleased to see you looking so vigorous."

"Me? There's a goddamned bullet wound in my leg and you say I'm vigorous? I'm getting less sure about you by the minute."

"I realize your physical weakness, but that's a temporary condition. All I mean to say is that I'm happy to see you not looking drawn and worried. I'm talking about the health in your face. And your youth, I suppose."

"Look, I'm twenty-nine, I was only fourteen when you saw me last, how can you say—"

"I'm sorry. I forgot that there's some explanation due this time around. You told me this was the time I did that. I merely had forgotten I hadn't done it yet."

"Do you do Danny Kaye imitations or something? I can't understand a word you say."

"Be calm. You're as nervous as an android at Checkup Center."

"What in the hell did you just say?"

"I'm sorry. Another slip-up. One of your favorite phrases, but it didn't occur to me that, of course, this would be the first time you heard it."

"Mister, you may have gotten younger somehow, but you're sure as crazy as you were before. Crazier."

"No. Listen to me, we'll get through this as smoothly as possible." Ludvik began to walk around the room. Certain books appeared strange to him and he examined them while he talked.

"The reason the words I just used sound so strange to you is that they come from the future. *I* come from the future, where we use androids for a number of tasks. The ones I deal with mainly do research for me. They have become more and more humanoid over the years, and exhibit a quite humanlike nervousness when they have to go to the center for a checkup—they treat repairs the way humans do operations, and they know there's a statistical chance that, if some of their workings are unrepairable, they might be switched off, although that rarely happens. I'm sorry—you do know what I mean by android?"

"Sure. It's more or less common knowledge—you really expect me to believe you come from the future?"

"Not only expect, I *know* you'll believe. It's a characteristic of my kind of time travel."

"Time travel and androids. Neat."

"Quite. You see, we've met before not only in your past, but in your future."

"Well, if you're hopping through time—"

"Kindly do not interrupt. I am easily impatient."

"Yes, I've seen."

"I don't know about that. You see, we do not *hop* through time, although a later era may master that ability. What you have already experienced, meeting me in your past, may represent the furthest limits of time travel for my time, as this visit now represents the furthest point backward in time we could travel at this point in my subjective time—or therefore the year in which I left to visit you here in 1968. Am I getting too complicated for you?"

"No, I follow most of it. I've been in one or two bull sessions about time travel. Paradoxes and that sort of thing."

"We don't worry about paradoxes, since we're pretty sure they do not occur. There's some discussion of it, but we're all of us, those allowed the time travel privilege, very careful. We wouldn't have the privilege if we were not trustworthy."

Thomason leaned his head against the back of the chair and smiled. "This is all very . . . restful," he said.

Ludvik approached the desk.

"My time has been experimenting with time travel for only

a few decades—of our time, of course. All the experiments have been strictly controlled. Early jumps back into time were only to fairly recent times. Later, equipment improved and we could jump back further. This, as I said, is the earliest point in time we have so far reached, though I've known from my other visits that I've eventually come back as early as the 1950's. I believe other travelers have received similar hints, but great control is placed upon the information each of us receives. I, for example, am not allowed to say anything about my own personal time travel experiences in the works I publish."

"And what works do you publish?"

Ludvik seemed pleased by the question. "My whole scholarly life has been devoted to assembling and writing material about you."

"Me? Why me?"

"You told me that when you asked that question, all kinds of possible glory passed through your mind."

"This is like a goddamned magic act. Okay, you're right. That's exactly what I was thinking just now. And, okay, you couldn't know it unless there's something in what you've been saying. Okay, screw that, tell me why you are—have been—will be—writing stuff about me."

"Sorry. Forbidden."

Thomason's disappointment was clear.

"One of the rules, one you told me you were glad of eventually. I *can* tell you that you're an important historical figure around whom controversy collects. My theory had been that you were misunderstood by your contemporaries and by later historians who followed their lead, and I was given a grant to amplify this theory. I can't discuss my findings in detail, but I can say your image in my time has been, shall we say, improved by my time research."

Thomason and Ludvik stared at each other for a very long time.

"I feel cold, right down to my bones," Thomason said.

"Why is that?" Ludvik's voice now had a scholarly tone.

"For very complicated reasons. First, the whole idea of becoming an historical figure is scary. Both exciting and scary."

"Funny—you already have a certain amount of reputation in your own time. As a national figure, you shouldn't be especially frightened of an even larger reputation."

"Well, yeah, I'd like to be somebody, no doubt about that. My ambition is already a prime topic in a number of publications—God, I'm beginning to sound like you."

"You're choosing your words. A good sign, means you're beginning to believe me."

"Don't get messianic."

"Sorry. Problem of the profession."

"I'll bet. So—I'm both attracted and repelled by what you've suggested about my own future. I have a very thin skin, in spite of the toughness that's attributed to me. In my own mind, I'm a Nixon of the left—by the way, is he—"

"Yes, by a narrow margin."

"I was afraid of that." Thomason became silent.

Ludvik prodded: "Go on about why you're repelled by your future."

Thomason almost whispered. "There are a lot of things I want to do. With my own life and for others. And—this may sound funny—I want to do them *right*."

Ludvik nodded, but Thomason did not notice.

"Nobody seems to understand that. Nobody seems to care. So many people around me each have their own axes to grind, and for their own selfish purposes—they only smile secretly or mutter 'right on' or some other dumb thing when I try to discuss larger motives. They only understand larger motives as generalizations. They seem to have so little commitment in them. You can't even use the word commitment around them without drawing a sarcastic, all-knowing chuckle. I mean, it's not true of all of them, I know—it can't be—but I don't know for which of them it *is* true."

Thomason laughed. "We all look alike, I guess. Ah, hell, I don't know what it is. Maybe we're all niggers to each other— not seeing anybody else as a thinking, feeling human being just as complex as we are; instead, seeing each other as ciphers behind big smiles, or something like that. I'm sorry, I'm rambling."

"It's . . . useful rambling."

"For you or for me?"

"Both of us, perhaps."

"I feel like I'm talking to a notebook."

"You never quite lose that feeling with me, I'm afraid. A pity, in that it is not necessary."

"Well, tell me, what year do you come from?"

"Sorry—"

"Forbidden."

"Yes."

"I guess I just wanted to know how many years I'll be remembered."

"Enough."

"You're getting cryptic."

"My time is limited, so I want *you* to talk."

"Go screw. I don't think I like being a, uh, a *subject*."

Thomason felt a sudden pain in his thigh. It felt like a big hand had grabbed the core of the wound and squeezed.

"Your wound?" Ludvik asked.

Thomason nodded.

"I've been wanting to ask you about it. There's nothing in your known history about a leg wound during this time period."

"Odd, I thought I made a pretty big thing out of it when it happened."

"And when was that?"

"Yesterday. I was well, working at *instigating* a riot at a plant that manufactures napalm for 'Nam. We'd gone through all the proper and legal avenues of dissent and were getting exactly nowhere. So I thought a little action might stir up things. I set up this great master plan, got the cameras there and everything. I even discovered who, among the security force we were harassing, could be made to attack us first. Unfortunately, the plan worked a little too well. A couple of shots were more or less accurate, including this one."

"Yes, I have some information on the riot and about your

escape here. But, well, the wound is one of those little surprises that delight a historian."

"Jesus, I'm just thrilled about that, man."

"You should be. Now, my time is limited, and I have a few questions I'd like to ask right now." Ludvik did not wait for a response. "I want to ask about certain gaps in your past."

"Hell, go ahead. Anything to take my mind off the pain."

The gaps concerned Thomason's college years, his emergence in the mid-sixties as a radical activist, his climb to the pantheon of nationally known antiestablishment figures.

"Wait a minute there, not exactly the *pantheon.* I've got something of a rep, yes—a few lines in *Time* and *Newsweek*—but I'm not even in the top forty of leading activists."

"Really? Interesting. Doesn't jibe with the information I have. Perhaps there's been a little myth-making along the way. I'll have to research this aspect a bit more."

Thomason continued to supply detailed answers to Ludvik's obviously prepared questions. All the talk about his "historical role" made him feel increasingly uncomfortable. He wondered how his decidedly minor-league achievements would lead to anything that could possibly justify this strange man's visits.

The tone of Ludvik's voice became more intense as he switched the focus of his inquiry from the basic facts of certain events to Thomason's feelings and motivations during them. Ludvik's knowledge of the incidents was so precise that he seemed to know more about them than his subject.

Gradually Thomason became irritated. "Hey," he finally said, "when you juxtapose all those things, I start sounding like a first-rate heel."

"Why's that, William?"

"I—well—I seem to have failed my goals and, damn it, hurt a lot of people doing it. Self-seeking's the word, I guess."

"It's the word, all right."

"Look, I'm willing to let you ask your dumb questions, but I don't have to take judgments from you."

"I'm sorry. I was being more objective than it sounded. Many of the people to whom you refer did later write about you. 'Self-seeking' is the word they used."

"Bastards—"

"Well, one of the things we can do here is correct their mistakes, so to speak. Your former cohorts have passed on a rather harsh image of you to history. Maybe we can ameliorate that, to some extent."

"I'm for that, God damn it."

"I'm not surprised."

Thomason put extra effort into answering Ludvik's next questions. Halfway through his memories of a march on Washington, Thomason broke off suddenly.

"What's bothering you, William?"

"I'm starting to sugar-coat things. I'm treating my life like a faked grade-school history book. What kind of a scholar are you? You told me too much, made me too self-conscious. How do you hope to achieve anything if you let me portray myself in superhuman proportions?"

Ludvik seemed pleased at the outburst.

"Be more honest then. Tell me the worst about yourself."

"Don't be so smug. You know more than you say. I think you know all too well that I am also not the type to blow a golden opportunity to set records straight just for a diverting side-trip into my heart of darkness."

"I'm not all that conniving, I'm afraid. You have the advantage in all meetings between us. My time is limited. I take from you whatever I can get, whatever you wish to supply."

"God, you're like all goddamned academics—a leech sucking the blood out of their subjects."

The calm disappeared from Ludvik's dark eyes. For a moment he could not speak.

"You are not merely a *subject* to me," he finally said. "All the energies of my adult life have been directed toward, *absorbed into,* my study of you. Years of intense preparation, more years of angling with blind committees trying to get this project approved according to *my* terms and *not* those currently applying to time-travel-based research—I did not give up those years for a mere cold analysis of a *subject,* even though I'll grant you that analysis is an obvious goal of the project. I knew, *knew*—in my unobjective heart, if you will—that history had been mistaken about you, in its assessment of you and your activities. My primary goal has been to square that account, and I've worked damned hard at it. You look as if you don't believe me."

"No, I'm willing to believe you all right. This ain't disbelief, it's shock."

"Shock?"

"It's such a . . . well, such a terrible life, yours is. So—so *passive.* I mean, all that effort put into studying me."

"Your importance—"

"I don't give a damn about my importance. I feel—I don't know—angry. Angry that you should waste so much of your time justifying a man's life, a man's principles, when—when you should be out fighting for them or something—"

"You're arrogant."

Thomason smiled. "Well, I thought by now you'd know that about me."

Ludvik returned the smile. "You make your point. Anyway, there's no need to work actively for your kind of *principle* in my time. We are a more or less passive society, you see."

"Utopian?"

"Not exactly Utopian, no. We have our share of trouble. Now and then our younger generations erupt, much as it is doing here in your time, but things are worked out reasonably. The World Council is able to take care of matters with—"

"World Council. You mean the one-world concept has been achieved?"

"Well, not precisely. National boundaries are preserved, but government is in the hands of the council rather than power-hungry national leaders. A nation is administered rather than led."

"Sounds like a bureaucratic hell. Is that what my activities are working toward? I'd rather not, thank you kindly."

"I'm sorry, I've gone too far. It's a peaceful time—you might even approve of it—but perhaps we should talk no more about it."

"C'mon, let me have some fun, some secret information I can enjoy as, say, a fruit of your visits. Tell me more about your time. Things are pretty well straightened out then?"

"Pretty well."

"And one-world?"

"Not really. Perhaps you could say two-thirds world. There are segments that do not go along, but they have caused only minimal trouble and are kept almost completely in check by the council's power."

"Segments, hey? What are they? Black? Yellow? Women, maybe?"

"That is as much as I plan to tell you. We must get on with proper business."

"You are really spoiling my fun, Ludvik. But, anyway, it's comforting to know about your segments. Man, I wish I could travel ahead to your time. I'd get out into those *segments* and get them organized with dispatch, believe me."

"Yes, I can believe you. But, uh, I don't think we need you in my time. The council, I'm sure, can handle things without you."

"By oppression, no doubt. You know, Ludvik old cracker, when you get back there, you should trip out to the field— you know, shuck this dry old thesis about me into the fireplace and establish a base in one of your segments. Take a few tips from your subject."

"I'll . . . I'll think it over."

"You do that."

"I have more questions."

"Shoot."

Ludvik delivered his questions so quickly that the interview began to feel more like a grilling by a tough detective. But Thomason picked up the rhythm and provided his answers just as quickly.

"I think that should do it," Ludvik announced suddenly. "I've about exhausted my questions, if you don't have anything more to add."

"Not me, I'm just plain exhausted."

They were silent for a moment.

"Thank you," Ludvik said. "You never disappoint me."

"As the hooker said after giving a freebie to her true love."

"What was that?"

"Sorry, just a remark. You irked me for a second there. I sensed warmth and I'm always uptight around warmth."

"I meant it. Warmth was intended."

"Then that's why I feel like a whore."

"I'm afraid I don't understand." In addition to lack of understanding, Ludvik's face showed some pain.

"Forget it. I didn't understand it either. I didn't mean to bug you."

"Surely."

"But I didn't mean to say that with warmth."

"Whatever you say, William."

"Damn it, you can be goddamned patronizing, you know that, man?"

"It's something of a disease with scholars, I'm afraid."

"God, you sound so worldly-wise that—"

Ludvik abruptly disappeared.

"—for the moment everything ahead of me seems empty, lacking in potential."

Thomason continued to stare at the chair.

"*A demain,* Ludvik, you old bastard."

3

Thomason watched Ludvik materialize between the V of his two feet propped on the front of his father's ancient desk. First there was a suggestion of an aura, then Ludvik quickly, almost instantly, taking shape.

"Ludvik, you old bastard, hello."

Ludvik seemed surprised. Thomason studied his face. Again younger, about early middle age—a bit younger than Thomason, perhaps—a little fleshier, the future harsh worry lines only sketched in now, his eyes apparently bigger without the weight of age around them. His body also seemed larger.

"Don't worry about that spare tire around your middle," Thomason said, "you'll be losing it."

"You know me, do you? I wasn't sure whether—" Ludvik's voice seemed higher-pitched, perhaps a result of his confusion.

"Sure. Fritz Ludvik, visitor from the future."

Ludvik blinked his eyes a couple of times and looked around the room. "Excuse me," he said. "This will take a minute."

"Be easy. Far as I'm concerned, you're in control of time here, no joke intended."

Ludvik stood up and walked about the room. Thomason swung his feet off the desk to watch. The man glanced idly at the few volumes left on the bookshelves. He seemed most interested in the titles. He glanced out the window, but the afternoon's heavy fog obscured most things.

"Looking for something?" Thomason asked.

"Yes—a building . . . out there."

"It's there, all right. Beyond the fog. Well, not exactly there. You can sometimes see the framework from here, and that they've started some of the other work. It's going to be an impressive building, from the looks of it."

"Yes. It'll be named after you."

Thomason exploded with laughter. "After me? That's hilarious. They wouldn't give you two rusted girders for my name right now. They're furious with me. They wanted to build here, on this property, but I wouldn't let them."

"Yes, I know."

"And all because of you I refused them. I had to preserve this house, *this room,* so that we could have these tête-à-têtes whenever they come. You don't know how much money I passed up."

"Yes, I do." Ludvik named the figure.

"Of course you know. What am I saying? Anyway, I would never've bet they'd come around so much as to name the goddamned structure after me."

"They will. But not for a while yet, not for a long while. This is still the eighties, isn't it?"

"1988."

"Mmmmm, yes, I see. No, there's some time before you get connected with the building. There'll be a long delay when the whole affair will be abandoned, and it's some years before it's actually finished."

"That's pleasant to hear. Are you acclimated now, ready to get to business?"

"Business?"

"Yes, sit down again."

Ludvik returned to the chair behind the desk. From a file tray, Thomason pulled a cardboard folder and presented it to him.

"What is this?"

"A report."

"A report on what?"

"On me, of course. I thought I'd be prepared for you this time, save you a few minutes of interrogation, etcetera. I assume you can't take it back with you."

"Correct, unfortunately."

"Thought so, so I've made the thing as concise as possible. Lots of short sentences, and I've been updating it regularly, since I didn't know exactly when you'd be showing up again."

"How could you be sure you would be here when I came?"

"I was beginning to wonder, since it's been almost twenty years since we last got together. But, well, you said we had a couple more meetings here, so I figured I could come here at will, and eventually hit the time you materialized. I check in here a couple of times a year. Man, I was really hoping this would be the right time. But go ahead, read the report. I want to get this research part over with, because I've got some tough questions to ask you."

Ludvik read through the material quickly, his eyes frequently scanning a page in just a few seconds. Thomason kept sneaking looks to see what part of the report Ludvik had reached. He successfully resisted interrupting the reading with supplementary remarks. When he had finished, Ludvik looked up, an odd smile on his face.

"Well?"

"Very efficient. Informative. But I have, well, reasons not to be surprised, William."

"I figured I knew the kind of thing you'd want, and I've gotten pretty good at shortcuts."

"Yes, that is obvious. But, before you . . . *guide* me to the next stage of your plans here, let me ask a few questions. To clarify."

"Sure, that's your trade. Shoot."

Ludvik leaned back in the chair, the report in his hand, and riffled to a certain page. "You say here you became involved with organized politics because it seemed the only sane thing to do."

"Right. For a few years there, when everything in politics was especially mad and bizarre, I began to wonder. But my kind of sanity was making attacks, and it tended to work as a strategy. I'm glad I took my time. After the madness and all its contradictions, things did work a lot better for me and the party, for everybody. But I suppose you know the historical side of this."

"To a certain extent, though there are some missing links."

Ludvik introduced some questions about the previous decade and a half that seemed tedious to Thomason, but he answered them as well as he could.

Then Ludvik said, "About the campaign—"

"I've been waiting to get to that. But first, you've got to answer a question for me this time. You owe me."

"Well, I'll see . . ."

"You'll see. Well, okay. This is it: I've got a long autumn ahead and I want to know one thing—are we going to win?"

Ludvik frowned.

"Look, this is desperate. I need a bending of the rule."

"I can bend rules, that's no problem. I just don't know if it's wise."

"Damn, that sounds like we're going to lose."

"No, forget that, I shouldn't have—well, I was warned that people from the past play tricks. I just hadn't wanted to diminish your excitement by telling you—but, yes, William Thomason, you are going to win. Cameron Brooks will be elected president this fall."

Thomason sprang out of his chair. "Really? And you think that'd *diminish* my excitement? Fritz my friend, I've been sitting in this godforsaken room for hours in mortal fear that you might show up and tell me we were going to lose. God, this is the best news possible. Wait a minute. I bought something just in case I could trick you out of some information."

"I suppose I should have expected something this diabolical from you, William."

From next to his chair Thomason lifted a bucket containing a champagne bottle. Water sloshed over the sides of the bucket. "It's a little warm, of course; the ice has melted. C'mon, Ludvik old stiff, let's celebrate."

Ludvik hesitated. "Later, maybe," he finally said. "Some questions of my own to ask. I don't come back to your time for the parties, you know."

"Always businesslike. You must be a credit to the academia of your times."

An uncharacteristic burst of laughter erupted from Ludvik. "Hardly," he said. "I'm regarded as a nonconformist eccentric for my study of you and this particular period. Especially because I felt mistakes had been made."

"Mistakes?"

"The smug scholars of my time have made their usual sweeping judgments. Yet I treat your era as something of a mystery. Even those that agree are not engaged by it. So much so that I had to pull all kinds of strings just to get the necessary grant to continue my work."

"The old World Council's not supporting your kind of work?"

Ludvik raised his eyebrows in surprise. "The World Council? That aging bunch of fascists and reactionaries! Bad enough that they put down every expression of important human spirit that rises to the surface—I wouldn't take a cent of their blood-stained money for my studies, it just wouldn't be worth it. My funds are from a private foundation. What are you chuckling at?"

"I'm sorry, Fritz my friend, but I would guess that that's forbidden for me to tell you."

"You can't make me curious. Let's get to things. I want to know more about why and how you entered organized politics."

Thomason had anticipated the question, and he set off on the long monologue he'd rehearsed in his mind several times. He told Ludvik about the two years of writing his book *Catering to a Selfish America,* a *J'accuse*-style book that detailed the ways that the country had been plunged into a moral, sociological, and political morass through the selfishness of its citizens. It was not a very profound thesis, but the book was published at the right time and got Thomason "one hell of a lot of notice." At the time, his contention that it was imperative to return to the original American ideals hit the right note with people desperate for reasonable patriotism.

The book had been an easy springboard into active politics, and Thomason toiled in the electoral fields for a long time before he found a candidate he could support, Cameron Brooks. Brooks was the ideal fusion candidate. He agreed with Thomason's ideas and supported his programs. Also, he had the appeal to voters that Thomason, who tended to be abrasive in public appearances, so regrettably lacked.

From his own intensive study of disastrous national campaigns, Thomason worked out a political strategy designed to avoid previous mistakes. They had almost succeeded four years ago, but it was too soon and there was too much division at the convention. Since then Thomason had systematically made Brooks more visible to the public and more acceptable to party leaders. He was especially good at buttering up the feudalists who still maintained regional power. At the same time he concocted speeches, which Brooks delivered splendidly, about how "the people" needed to be freed from the elitism that had eroded national politics for so long. After a cautious and successful preconvention campaign, playing down the primary results and courting all the right people, he and Brooks came to the convention with what appeared to be small support. In reality they were in the string-pulling position. Brooks seemed to be in a contest with a Southern senator with solid antebellum credits and a dashing liberal from the good old Eastern Establishment. However, each of the opposing candidates bowed out gracefully—at Thomason's orders—at the right moment and Brooks won what looked like a hard-fought third ballot victory.

But in the weeks since the convention, Brooks had been running seriously behind the incumbent opposition in the polls, which was the reason for Thomason's present anxiety.

"Actually, I've been sitting here as nervous as—"

"An android at the Checkup Center?"

Thomason laughed and told Ludvik how the simile had come up at their last meeting. Ludvik then commenced his usual barrage of direct questions about Thomason's emotional and mental states during certain specific occasions, and his private opinions about subjects he dared not discuss publicly or write openly about.

"You can really make me squirm, Fritz," Thomason said when Ludvik appeared to be finished with his inquiries.

"I don't mean to. I'm just trying to accumulate as much useful and pertinent historical information as the time will allow."

Thomason hunched his shoulders. "There you go again, making me shiver. As usual."

"Why's that?"

"Each time I realize that this is history we're talking about, I get frightened, that's all. Never mind, if I remember correctly I tell you a lot about that the next time around. Anyway, history or no, I've learned a lot from these—"

"Learned?"

"Yes. Is that so strange? Every time we've encountered each other, even the very first time, I've come out of it all having learned something important about myself. Not only that, it's stuff which I have—consciously or, as more usual, unconsciously—applied to my subsequent actions."

Ludvik scowled.

"What's the matter, Fritz? You seem disturbed."

"I am, frankly. In my profession one gets very apprehensive about influence. I am a studier, an observer—ideally I am not supposed to influence the subject."

"Well, you have, so live with it. You've taught me a great deal about myself, especially the last time we met. I came out of that really shaken, you'd be surprised."

"I'm surprised enough right now, I'm afraid."

"Forget it. It's all for the good, you'll see. I've never been able to open myself up to anyone. That's why I'm a lifelong bachelor, I suppose. The late-forties playboy of Washington, D.C. Are you married, Fritz? No, of course you are. Or at least you have a son, anyway. I have an astonishingly vivid memory of your complaining about a son and comparing me to him. It's one of the things I've remembered for all— Why are you laughing?"

For a moment, after their eyes had met, Fritz could not control his laughter. Finally he said, "I laughed because, you see, I do not have a son. You've told me something in my future. I am not myself married and have not the slightest idea upon whom I will father this progeny. What you said about yourself is so right for me—I can't talk intimately to people either, colleagues or friends. I'm an outsider, something like yourself."

"I see, then—"

"And furthermore. Furthermore"—Ludvik started to laugh again, this time more heartily—"*your* long-established bachelor state is about to spectacularly end. You'll be married sooner than you think, and you don't know to whom—none of the ladies you are now thinking about, certainly."

"How did you—never mind, I don't want to know anything more on this subject. Whatever, it is an even more important occasion for champagne, don't you agree?"

"Certainly."

Thomason popped the cork. The warmth of the liquid caused quite a lot of it to bubble over, but there was plenty left and Thomason uneasily poured two rather large glasses.

Ludvik raised his glass in toast. "To all that you have provided for my quest for significant historical accuracy."

"Glad to drink to that."

They each took sips, then smiled at each other.

"Now my turn," Thomason said. He raised his glass. "To all that you have taught me, Fritz Ludvik." After Thomason had taken his sip, he said, "You didn't drink on that one. Why not?"

Embarrassed, Ludvik took a quick swallow, spilling a bit of the champagne in the process. "I'm sorry," he said. "It was just the word 'taught.' That I taught you—it is an idea I cannot easily accept."

"I think you will, Fritz. I do believe you will."

Ludvik vanished some time after they had finished several glasses of champagne. Thomason was too cockeyed drunk to notice exactly when.

4

Thomason sensed Diana hovering somewhere outside the study door. He imagined her squatting, ear next to the door, straining to hear his infrequent movements. Ever since she had turned sixteen, she had become a confirmed snooper. He could not be mad at her for it, because it derived from the protective instinct she had shown ever since Laura had died. Diana, so unlike her mother in matters like decorum and patience, had nevertheless inherited from Laura the need to watch over his welfare.

He wished he could somehow contact the Ludvik he'd last encountered so that they could again discuss marriage. Especially how love had meant significant sacrifices from the obdurate side of his character. Ludvik, when he next arrived, would probably want to know about the marriage, and Thomason had prepared some protective platitudes. There was no need to mar her image in history by revealing her final obsessions. It had been bad enough that she had died so suddenly, before each of them had been able to forgive. Laura had always been treated well by contemporary sources and by the media; let that suffice for history.

Glancing at the cot which Diana had (with complaints)

helped him drag into the study, he considered taking a nap. Let her sit outside that door and listen to him snore. She was already furious that he spent most of the time in this room, which she had termed filthy, unhealthy, and aesthetically unappealing. Every day she begged him to return to their Florida home where, she insisted, she could take better care of him. He tried to console her by promising that they'd go soon, as soon as he got something accomplished. He even considered telling her that the something was his final meeting with Ludvik, but he was afraid that Diana might use that as psychiatric evidence for his forcible removal from the house.

As soon as he made himself comfortable on the cot, he dozed off. His dreams were filled with quiet seascapes, soothing colors, and Laura. He woke up gradually, opening and closing his eyes as if the lids had been pasted together. It was a moment before he noticed Ludvik standing by the desk looking down at him. The awe in his face discomfited Thomason.

Ludvik was young. Too damned young, Thomason thought. A face remarkably free of character lines and a general cast of boyish innocence that set Thomason on edge immediately.

"You look like a grinning idiot, Fritz," he said, and was immediately angry with himself for being gruff.

Ludvik was obviously surprised. And not just surprise—shock. "You know me?"

"Of course. Find yourself a place to sit, we've got a lot to do."

Ludvik responded to the order like an automaton. He sat on the arm of a cushioned chair, as if ready to spring at any attack. "Is this a joke? Did Belliveau set something up?"

"Calm down. I don't know any Belliver. Who's he?"

"Just another person in . . . in my line of work."

"A fellow historian and scholar?"

Again Ludvik seemed amazed. "You know who I am then?"

"Of course. Could we dispense with all this—"

"No. Emphatically not! I need my questions answered so I know where I—"

"Same old Ludvik. Well, you can just—" Thomason laughed. When he spoke again, his voice was softer. "No, I'm sorry, I see I have you at a disadvantage. My impatience shouldn't preclude the necessary rituals. You were patient with me once, I can certainly do you the same favor."

Thomason told Ludvik a little, but not much, about their previous encounters. He spoke quickly, concisely—for him this was just another of thousands of briefings he'd given in his lifetime. While Ludvik listened, his wide eyes fixed on Thomason, he fidgeted incessantly. He could not seem to keep his hands still. Twice he stood up, walked nervously to the desk and back, then abruptly sat down again.

"So you see," Thomason concluded, "there's a certain amount of destiny hanging like crepe streamers over this particular meeting. For me, at least, since it has been the focal point of my life for a good long time now. I look older than I am because these age lines are the direct result of years of anticipation."

Ludvik strode to the window. When he spoke, it was in a crisp, distant voice: "I should have expected something like this. I did not see this as anything more than a single trip to the past. There did not seem reason for more than that. Certainly those tight-fisted World Council cretins seemed unlikely to allow me any more than what they've already given me. Especially on a project involving this period of history. And there seems so much more to do, so many more projects I want to get to, so much need to—"

"I didn't expect you to be so disturbed."

"I don't care what you expected. I am disturbed."

"Hey, calm down, young man." Thomason almost choked on the words "young man." "Listen to me. You—that is, your future self—seemed mightily pleased at the way things worked out. You said—"

"I can hardly believe that."

"Well, you'll just have to. Your future is a fact to me, remember."

"That is absolutely chilling to—"

"Sorry, I'll try to watch what I say, but—"

"Belliveau hinted to me that there might be some shock when

I arrived at my destination point. This, I suppose, is what he meant. That building out there. That is the Thomason Building, named after you, isn't it?"

"Yes, surprisingly enough. Though I understand there's a move on to take my name off it. By some of my more zealous opponents."

"The name will stay. In my time, my office is in that building."

"That does surprise me. Very impressive."

"Not so impressive. It is a wretched office, and the building is an eyesore which should be torn down. I signed a petition to that effect some time ago."

"Oh. I think I feel disappointed."

Ludvik began to pace. As he walked he performed small, fluttery gestures with his fingers.

"Take it easy, Fritz. You're as jumpy as an android at the—"

"Androids, there are androids now? That is not so, it could not be. Androids don't—"

"Calm, calm. You dropped the phrase at another of our meetings. I just picked it up because I liked it."

"I see." He stopped pacing and stared at Thomason.

"Well," Thomason said, "shouldn't you be getting on with it? Your study?"

"You affect my concentration. This is not cat and mouse, it is research. I need for you to be cooperative."

"You say 'need' as if you mean 'demand.' "

"That is what I mean. Now you are ready to argue irrelevantly with me."

Thomason took a deep breath. "I am deeply sorry. Go on with whatever procedure pleases you."

"I would like to begin with the particular question I came here for. Why—"

"Why did I betray Cameron Brooks?"

"You know the questions before I ask them! How can I conduct any sensible inquiry if you are going to be coy and clairvoyant with me?"

Thomason laughed. "You're very touchy."

"Touchy? I am frustrated."

"We can cooperate, don't fly off the handle. I'm not any more used to you like this than you are comfortable in the situation. But we will accomplish a great deal, I promise you. But first, though, I want to tell you that I've prepared somewhat for you."

"And just how did you do that?"

"Knowing you can't carry material back to your time, ten years ago I buried a lead-lined strongbox. It contains all of the records, documents, and other data covering my years with Brooks and later. I put in everything I thought you might be able to use for your study. Plus three memoir-essays from my aborted autobiography. Which, incidentally, I could never finish because of you, since I was sure that no autobiography of mine could have survived into your time, else why'd you be visiting me in the first place? The memoirs, especially, since no one of my time would dare publish them, are pertinent to the incidents involving Cameron Brooks. The strongbox is buried beneath the cornerstone of this house. The northwest corner, if the house still stands. You can work it out through old documents if it doesn't. All you have to do, then, is return to your own time, dig the stuff up, and you will have it made with your research. That can be done, can't it?"

"Easily. I even own the property. But I must know now! I've expended too much time and energy for this moment; I will hear it from your lips."

"It's all right with me, I'd like you to understand. You, particularly."

Thomason stood up and put a hand on Ludvik's shoulder. Ludvik not only seemed younger, Thomason could have sworn that he was taller. He began to walk about the room as he talked. His walk was slow, a contrast to the way Ludvik had paced.

"'After inauguration, Brooks and I got right down to business. There were so many mistakes to correct from previous administrations. So many compromises dictated by limited ideology or too-strict partisanship. The beauty of everything, I thought, was that we were free from such debts. But we faced a hell of a job, I can tell you. I became Special Advisor with Cabinet rank, just the sort of schtick I could handle."

"Schtick?"

"Not enough time to provide glossaries, Fritz. Look it up in an Old American dictionary. The position allowed me to comfortably work out all the behind-the-scenes stuff, while at the same time accomplishing many goals as a public figure. The influence was enormous! I could present my programs along with a solid political philosophy—it had been a long time since Washington had seen anything like it. I cut a wide swath and kept things boiling, and was able to take care of most matters without involving Brooks until the proper times. Brooksie liked that—he was not much for tarnishing his image with public controversy. We established reforms like we were planting trees, one right after the other. It was perhaps the fastest rate of executive and legislative achievement ever. Certainly made Johnson's ramming through of the Kennedy programs look minuscule by comparison.

"But all of that was just foundation—the first steps toward the *really* controversial reforms which Brooks had insisted must wait until the middle of his term. Well, the middle of the term came, and Brooks still counseled delay. I had faith in him, I didn't realize the sonofabitch was blocking me. I displayed some impatience, but the kind I thought allowable between friends. What I didn't realize was my mistake in calling that sonofabitch a friend."

Thomason spoke quietly as he described the strategy used against his power. He did not enjoy talking of the slanted newspaper and TV stories, followed by the use of journeyman politicians to drop hints that Thomason was too much of an extremist for the good of the country, and then the seamier hints that he was involved in hushed-up scandals.

"Well, that was partly true. There were a few peccadilloes, but I doubt they could have destroyed me with them. Don't get anxious, I've even included that type of information in the strongbox."

"You needn't worry—I'll keep such information secret, even from the eyes of Belliveau."

"Finally I got fed up. I went to Brooks and laid it on the line. He played clean-handed statesman, said he could think of no reason why there was such antagonism to me. 'But take it easy, Billy,' he said, 'I won't let 'em scare me. I'll stick by you. I owe you everything, and couldn't dump you without a thought.' All this, of course, while the sonofabitch was engineering the whole strategy.

"Later things got worse. Polls were against me, more politicos spoke out against me. Some even spoke for me. Brooksie vowed his support publicly, with his good old pat-of-the-hand sincerity. Privately he was trying to plant the idea of resignation in my head. You know, I could sacrifice for *his* sake. He knew that loyalty's a fatal disease with me, so I almost did re—"

"Dad!" Diana's voice. "Dad!" She knocked tentatively. "What's going on in there?"

"Go away!" Thomason shouted.

"I can hear you talking."

"So you can hear me talking. Go away!"

"Are you talking to yourself out loud?"

"Yes, God damn it! Go away!"

"I will not!"

"My daughter," Thomason said to Ludvik, then shouted toward the door: "Scrunch down and listen then!" He led Ludvik to an area between the window and desk. "She won't be able to hear much of what we say from here. What if she does, she'll just think I'm crazy and talking in two different voices."

Ludvik glanced toward the door. "That is Diana, eh?" he said. "I wish we could invite her in."

"What the hell good would that be? I wouldn't invite her in on this on a bet. Settle your mind about that, my dear Fritz."

Ludvik grinned. It was a smile Thomason could not interpret.

"Go on," Ludvik said.

"Well, my staff submitted a report—they'd been investigating for me—and I wanted to kill myself. Imagine, kill myself over that bastard Brooks. I'd expected to have to tell myself that Brooks was weak, even that he was stupid, but not—well, not what he was in all its stark raving complexity. He had never been my friend or my candidate or almost anything he had seemed to be. He was—hell, I thought I could talk about this rationally, but I keep calling up mental pictures of Brooks, implanted memories that're vivid and never change in detail. Look, what do you know about Manstead?"

"Manstead? Something, but not much in relation to Brooks or you."

"That's not surprising. He kept himself secret. He was one of many clandestine figures with whom Brooks had some connection. But I've always believed he was the most influential, particularly in bringing about my downfall. Manstead was an A-one bastard, but he had more power than a man could use. The irony I've always seen is, he and I were the same age and had each managed to reach a certain power level, only his was in shadow and mine was public. While I thought I had the harness on Brooks, it seemed it was Manstead who was doing most of the pulling of the reins. Manstead was a sort of central clearing agency for most of the forces I was working against. Resource exploiters, big business, corrupt democracies and republics and dictatorships of the world—he even had a direct line into the Mafia. Perhaps he originated there, I don't know. Anyway, he and his group had Brooks by the short hairs, and they were beginning to pull them out strand by strand. Funny, I might have forgiven Brooks simple corruption. Anybody who could swindle a few bucks off the top without my awareness was welcome to them. My particular monomania had to do with my social and political programs—some I'd already set in motion, some I was setting, some planned for the future. These last were especially advanced; I describe them in detail in some of the strongbox papers. But when I read in the staff report of the extent to which Brooks was controlled by Manstead and the rest, I could almost see all the programs, past and future, fading in front of my eyes. It was horrible."

Ludvik was leaning so close, he looked as if he could easily be pushed over at a touch. "I can practically see your mental note pad being scribbled upon, Fritz."

"Let's say you've caught my attention. Go on."

"This part is painful, more painful even than what happened later—what I imagine has been my historical legacy. I could not get to Manstead and his organization. Even the few public mentions I made of them later drew only disbelief—I had to drop them as an issue. I considered compromise, but the only compromise I could make was to stay in office and let Brooks call the shots, cancel all I'd worked for. Even if I played my cards closely and allowed some postponements of certain reforms until I could obtain an advantage, the postponements would be *too* disastrous and could have set back important progress by too much. Like, say, environmental reform, which Brooks had so enthusiastically collaborated with me on during the campaign years—it was our biggest pet project, and it would have been virtually destroyed if I'd knuckled under to Brooks and the forces behind him. It makes me furious to think of all the time the sonofabitch spent brainstorming the environmental stuff with me. All sham just to keep me content so I could engineer the big victory.

"Well, one of the strongbox memoirs covers most of this. The extent of his deceptions, his goddamned opportunism, it was all too much of a shock to me at first. I thought I'd known Brooks so well. Hell, it was my past played out over again. Every time I put faith in something, it turned up empty. All things I could trust floated on muck, it seemed. I confronted Brooks. He tried to ease his way out of it. Lie, make excuses— but I had too many facts and figures, and eventually he had to admit it. Easier to tell me the truth than some congressional committee. He tried to put himself and his actions in the best possible light. 'All I require is your cooperation!' he shouted. 'Cooperation!' I shouted back at him. 'You mean corruption.' He looked at me as if the words were synonyms.

"Anyway, I couldn't stand him any more and I stormed out of the Oval Office, out of the White House, out of the Northwest Sector, eventually out of Washington altogether. I came back here and sat in this room for days. I don't know, I suppose I hoped you would show up and solve my problem for me."

"Impossible."

"In time I realized that. And I also came to the conclusion that I had to resign. Resigning left me free. I had to take the risk of giving up both hope and power in order to be able to function freely. Freedom was all I ever wanted. Always want what you can't have, they say. But—the moment I knew I would definitely resign, I also knew exactly what I was going to do to Brooks."

Thomason looked out the window at the building named after him. It looked so shiny and solid now, it was hard to envision it as rundown in the future.

"I see no reason to go into details over my 'betrayal.' Over the years I'd made valuable connections in both parties. I went to those I could trust and enlisted their aid. The day after my resignation went into effect, I called a press conference and announced I would switch parties and work against the renomination and reelection of Cameron Brooks. I refused to say why. Since the press had treated us as being as close as Damon and Pythias or Tweedledee and Tweedledum, as they sometimes called us, my announcement was the kind of bombshell they loved. A bombshell which, I expect, has been well enough recorded in your time."

"Well enough."

" 'Unprecedented' was what everybody said at the time. They also said that, whatever the machinations behind my surprising maneuver, whether it was politics or pique, I could not possibly succeed in marshaling enough forces to defeat a popular president like old dear Brooksie. But they didn't know me. I'd thought all that out while in retreat, knew the risk, and— perhaps because of some prescience or something, or perhaps some sense that my role in history would be based on something more than I'd already done—whatever the reason, I was confident I had a good shot at manipulating everything.

"Brooks's countermoves were predictable. I let him put me down, criticize me, with all the condescending politeness at his command. He did it well, I'll give him that. He was smooth and clever, quite admirable in his restraint. But—but I'd drawn him out into the open early, just short of two years before election year. Whatever he gained through vilification of me had been dissipated long before the election itself. And I had accomplished my initial purpose, my defection planting a seed of doubt in the apparent flowering of politics' golden age.

"I was then able to fade from public notice, while at the same time working closely with my cohorts, most of whom formerly had been the opposition. They were desperate to regain power. Absolutely desperate. Even before my resignation I'd selected their best young comer, a man they'd not even considered yet for major office—George Hartog. He was not particularly bright and he was something of a simp in private, but he could talk as long as somebody wrote the words for him or gave him a good briefing. So I became that somebody. Hartog, though not gifted with political or social insight in any great proportions, was nevertheless easily convinced of the need for my kind of programs. Well, I'd had a good press in all the best and most respectable places, and *they* liked my ideas, so it was easy for Hartog to like them. He was quite sensitive to that kind of influence. I figured that Hartog was the only one I had a chance with, and I knew further that he would finish the work I'd started in Brooks's administration. As indeed he did. His campaign is, I imagine, well recorded?"

"Well enough."

"It was brilliant, if I may say so myself—and I may say so, since I put it all together. Hartog, dumbass that he was, would have gone to the people—to the 'people,' for God's sake, with appeals and reason. I talked him out of that fast enough. Appeals and reason would've earned him a place in history beside Goldwater, McGovern, and Landon. No, we worked like a good boxer. Not really dirty, keeping the blows above the belt, but working on the other guy's cuts and bruises methodically, wiping away old blood with our gloves and at the same time encouraging the flow of new blood. We hit away especially on doubts we'd created about Brooks's competence. His angry, overemotional reactions made our job only that much easier. Before he knew it, and before we even expected it, we'd pulled nearer him in the polls. During that era it seemed quite easy to convince people of the incompetence of politicians. Then we started dragging out the good issues—the scandals and the misguided decisions. Hartog could explain a Brooks mistake with so much conviction that people had to believe him. At least, as I'd written it, it lent itself to his brand of conviction. We still might not have made it if Brooks hadn't kept blundering in public outbursts. Even his attempted defamation of my character backfired, since people just were not aware, or willing to believe, the extent of my influence on Hartog. They began to think that Brooks was raving, overdoing his attacks out of some personal revenge motive. Which was somewhat true, of course.

"By election time, we'd pulled even. After what I can assure you was a nerve-racking night, the surprise of the California vote, favoring Hartog so heavily in what we'd regarded as an iffy situation, gave us that narrow electoral edge, and the presidency. If the public could've seen the drunken and hysterical victory scene between Hartog and me just after his public victory speech, they might have had some morning-after doubts. It was a brilliant campaign, Fritz, brilliant and insidious."

Ludvik smiled. His body, which had been tense most of the time since his arrival, relaxed.

"Hartog tried to find a way to put me on the Cabinet, but it would have caused too much friction at the wrong time. I didn't mind, I didn't want any more of it. Hell, most of the Cabinet that did serve were my choices, anyway. They and the president, all they had to do was follow guidelines which I'd already set up, for domestic programs, anyway. And they were all so well chosen, they met all the new crises reasonably and with great intuitive foresight. Hartog's administration, all eight years of it, certainly has been treated well by most historians so far. I mean—well, they do go on at length about his drinking problem and some of his foreign policy and the collapse of his political influence later, but nobody can take away all that he accomplished in those two terms. I still hear from him on occasion. He rails at me some, and goes on self-pity binges, but—well, at least he still calls me.

"And that was pretty much the end of my public life. I retired to here. In spite of my later successes, my career in general has been somewhat in shadow. It's not easy to forgive a turncoat. A few articles came out about me, attempting feebly to analyze my betrayal. It was fun for them, I suppose, and I did get something of a kick out of the ineptitude of their analyses. Not everybody who retires with a cloud around him can sit back knowing that the cloud will be dispersed by a future historian. You seem annoyed, Fritz. Why?"

Ludwig turned away, looked down at the scarred ancient desk. "You are smug," he said. "You seem to think I will do your bidding. I have more . . . more integrity than that."

Thomason patted his shoulder. "I know you have, Fritz, I know you have."

"I will use what you've told me for study, along with the strongbox material you've buried for me, and I will make my own conclusions based on the evidence."

Thomason nodded.

"You didn't say anything about Charlotte Brooks," Ludvik said quietly.

Thomason's turn to retreat. "I know. I hoped that subject wouldn't come up. Didn't seem—seem pertinent."

"Some letters have survived. Apparently they were discovered by someone, a functionary of some sort, after Brooks's death. He kept them hidden away for four decades. After his death, they came into the hands of a newsman—that would be a few years from now. The letters are signed Charlotte Brooks, with no indication of forgery. Some are addressed to you, but apparently were never sent. Others are to her husband, others have unspecified addresses. In them she says some—some rather affectionate things about you."

"Rather affectionate—you are so goddamned polite, Fritz."

After the elation Thomason had felt describing his political success, Ludvik's revelation made him feel old and sad. He looked for a place to sit. Ludvik blocked the way to the cot, and it would be awkward to twist his way around to the chair behind the desk. Instead, he leaned against the wooden frame of the window. "And I suppose you want to know the truth about Charlotte—among your other, well, research needs?"

Ludvik nodded. "It's history," he said.

"History, damn it, it's backstairs gossip."

"Backstairs gossip, history—same thing, sometimes."

"What a cynical, priggish bastard you are!"

"My duty is to investigate the scandal as well as the—"

"Oh, shut up, God damn it, shut up!"

Ludvik seemed indignant. Well, let him have his scandal, see how he'll like it. "There was—there was something between Charlotte Brooks and me, yes. It wasn't much. One rather pleasant evening—and don't look eager, you get no more details than that about it. It happened at a time when I was most confused and despondent about what Brooks was doing to me, and I suppose that any psychological coloring you put on my motives will at least partly be accurate. I bargained for a second night with Charlotte, but it turned out I was not too good at —at country ways. My wife, Laura, somehow found out about the first evening, which canceled out the second. Laura was not too good at forgiving, and our marriage, though splendid in many ways and much better after the birth of Diana, was never quite the same after her discovery. And that's all I will give you on that, my dear friend."

Ludvik had walked closer. Their bodies almost touched. "And the letters?" Ludvik asked.

"You never goddamn let up, do you?"

"I have very little time left."

"I—ah, forget it. I'll try to imagine you as somebody I've never met before. Put us on equal footing, anyway . . . The letters. I know so little about the letters. I didn't get them, remember, the ones that were addressed to me. But she did manage to send out one or two that your little man of history, your little nobody lurking around the leftover artifacts, did not of course discover. They were very—very loving letters, and so, I imagine, were the ones she didn't send. Are you satisfied?"

"I see. Then you know nothing of why she wrote them, or of her fantasies of running off to you, or of—"

"You know about the fantasies, then. God, I hate to think of that having been bequeathed to history. But—well, she would call me at night and tell me she was on her way and I had to talk her out of it. It was so damned hard to talk her out of it. She was so lovely, Charlotte Brooks. Have you seen pictures of her?"

"Yes."

"She had the face of a twenty-year-old. Beautiful. And she was something like forty-nine when I knew her. Her cheeks were often red, as if she'd just come from exercise, or love-making—but, well, why should I get sentimental with you around to take it down?"

"Do you have any idea why she never sent the majority of the letters?" Ludvik's tone was so eager. He seemed more interested in this phase of his inquiry than in the political information.

"I don't have to guess, damn you, Ludvik, I don't have to guess. I know why she didn't send them. I was around for that."

Ludvik's eyes clearly said, tell me, please tell me. For a moment Thomason considered keeping this one scrap of information for himself. Cheating history for once. But all the years, and the other meetings with this strange visitor, had created within him an inability to cheat, of all things, history.

"You're not very insightful, Fritz, you and your time. Didn't it ever occur to you how curious it was that you found these oh-so-damaging letters in the effects of Cameron Brooks and not Charlotte?"

"Well—yes, that does not seem so difficult. It must have been because she died first and possession passed to—"

"No, it was because Brooks found them and stole them from her. When it happened, she called me and told me about it. She was afraid even to tell him that she knew they were missing. I don't know why she couldn't confront him, since he'd broken something like three locks to get at them—I mean, including the door to her room and all. I asked her why—if she had not intended to send the letters—she kept them around at all. She couldn't answer that. She didn't know why. Might have been psychological, she said; maybe she wanted Cameron to find them. Whatever her reason or how deep-seated it might be, she said, the letters were terribly important to her. If they were so goddamned important, I asked, why didn't she send them in the first place? She just said she didn't know. Myself, I don't know whether she could ever have sent them. I don't know what the letters were about exactly, but I suspect they were cries for help. Disguised, of course, and polite. And Charlotte was not one to ask for help. Brooks's mind was gone, and she could no longer live with him. He called me, too, a day or so after Charlotte."

Thomason hated the way Ludvik's eyes brightened further at each new detail, so he turned away from him. "He called me around three in the morning. He'd apparently been brooding about the letters ever since he'd stolen them. He threatened me, tried to blackmail me, wound up crying about how we'd been such good friends back in the old days. I reminded him what kind of a friend he had been. He said he'd had the best intentions, he'd meant to do something wonderful for me in return for my giving up my plans. I told him that would have been unnecessary, that he'd already worked enough wonders. He got angry and hung up. Less than a year later, both he and Charlotte were dead. I can't cast any light on the circumstances."

"Some of my colleagues have published studies suggesting that Brooks killed himself."

"I doubt that, but perhaps. His mind was in bad shape. Anything was possible. Too bad he didn't leave you any letters."

Ludvik grimaced. No wonder—it was a pretty low blow. Neither man said anything for a long time.

"Sorry, Fritz. You always said I was arrogant—actually 'belligerent' was your word for me. I thought I'd mellowed, but I guess I just rusted. Would you like a drink? I've saved some good brandy."

"No, there's not enough time. I have to go. I—I am sure that what you have told me and left me will be extremely useful. I am cognizant of all that you've done. And its value."

He said it as if he were not all that certain. Thomason nodded anyway.

"Farewells are awkward," Thomason said. "I'm not much good at them, never have been. There were things I'd planned to say, but—"

"Father! What's happening in there?"

Whenever Diana addressed him as "Father," it meant that she was about to do something. Ludvik glanced toward the door.

"Diana can be very impatient," Thomason said.

"Yes," Ludvik said, smiling.

"You say that as if you know something about *her*, too."

"I do."

"You look almost moonstruck, as if you are in love with her."

"In a way, I am."

"Wait a minute. There's not something you've never told me, something about you and Diana—some connection that brought you to be interested in me in the first place."

"Connection?" Ludvik laughed. "I see. You think that my interest in your daughter has something to do with something more personal?"

"Something like that."

"No, you're wrong. My interest in her, in just standing here and listening to her voice, is much akin to my interest in you. Diana is also a part of the past to me. She was a mysterious and lovely woman, your Diana."

"*My* Diana? That bitchy, nagging girl is—"

"—is to be quite something. You don't imagine . . ."

"Damn right I don't imagine. Why is she so important? How is she so important?"

Ludvik's knowing smile seemed downright arrogant. He

backed away from Thomason, saying, "In my time your daughter's name will be as well known as yours, and as interesting to history, though in a quite different way than you. She will re—"

Abruptly Ludvik disappeared. Even after Thomason had stared for a while at the empty air, he listened for the end of a sentence. She will re. She will re. Re.

Suddenly he realized that, with the change of subject to his daughter, he had let Ludvik leave without saying all of those valedictory things that he'd been planning for so many years. The farewells he had mentioned a minute ago. He took the brandy bottle from the shelf, the shelf which had once been overflowing with books, and carried it with him to his cot, where he laboriously sat down. He opened the bottle and took a swig from it, then sat still for a long, quiet time.

"Father, I've found the spare key, and I'm going to open this door if you don't let me in."

"Go away!"

"What's the matter with you? With your voice? You sound as if you've been crying." The ensuing silence ended with the sound of a key being fumbled into the lock.

Thomason took a deep breath. "Don't be a goddamned idiot. Get away from the goddamned door. I'll come out when I'm goddamned good and ready."

GEORGE R. R. MARTIN

is me, your editor.

I've always felt that editors who bought their own stories for the books they edited were playing dirty. I still feel that way. A writer can't really edit himself; he is in no position to be an objective judge of his own work. There is simply too much emotional involvement.

Nonetheless, here you find my story.

Well, I have an excuse.

I was, after all, one of the nominees for the first John W. Campbell Award. And since New Voices *is a showcase anthology, set up to give the reader a sampler of the literary wares offered by each of the finalists, it would be cheating to omit myself.*

So I had to do it.

Didn't I?

At any rate, I did. There was only one thing that I could do by way of atonement, so I did it; I tried like hell to make sure that the George R. R. Martin story I included was one of his best.

Of course, a writer can't judge his own work, so you'll have to decide. But for what it's worth, the editor liked this story.

—G. R. R. M.

The Stone City

George R. R. Martin

THE CROSSWORLDS HAD A thousand names. Human starcharts listed it as Grayrest, when they listed it at all—which was seldom, for it lay a decade's journey inward from the realms of men. The Dan'lai named it Empty in their high, barking tongue. To the ul-mennaleith, who had known it longest, it was simply the world of the stone city. The Kresh had a word for it, as did the Linkellar, and the Cedrans, and other races had landed there and left again, so other names lingered on. But mostly it was the crossworlds to the beings who paused there briefly while they jumped from star to star.

It was a barren place, a world of gray oceans and endless plains where the windstorms raged. But for the spacefield and the stone city, it was empty and lifeless. The field was at least five thousand years old, as men count time. The ul-nayileith had built it in the glory days when they claimed the ullish stars, and for a hundred generations it had made the crossworlds theirs. But then the ul-nayileith had faded and the ul-mennaleith had come to fill up their worlds, and now the elder race was remembered only in legends and prayers.

Yet their spacefield endured, a great pockmark on the plains, circled by the towering windwalls that the vanished engineers had built against the storms. Inside the high walls lay the port city; hangars and barracks and shops where tired beings from a hundred worlds could rest and be refreshed. Outside, to the west, nothing; the winds came from the west, battering against the walls with a fury soon drained and used for power. But the eastern walls had a second city in their shadows, an open-air city of plastic bubbles and metal shacks. There huddled the beaten and the outcast and the sick; there clustered the shipless.

Beyond that, further east: the stone city.

It had been there when the ul-nayileith had come, five thousand years before. They had never learned how long it stood against the winds, or why. The ullish elders were arrogant and curious in those days, it was said, and they had searched. They walked the twisting alleys, climbed the narrow stairs, scaled the close-set towers and the square-topped pyramids. They found the endless dark passageways that wove mazelike beneath the earth. They discovered the vastness of the city, found all the dust and awesome silence. But nowhere did they find the Builders.

Finally, strangely, a weariness had come upon the ul-nayileith, and with it a fear. They had withdrawn from the stone city, never to walk its halls again. For thousands of years the stone was shunned, and the worship of the Builders was begun. And so too had begun the long decline of the elder race.

But the ul-mennaleith worship only the ul-nayileith. And the Dan'lai worship nothing. And who knows what humans worship? So now, again, there were sounds in the stone city; footfalls rode the alley winds.

The skeletons were imbedded in the wall.

They were mounted above the windwall gates in no particular pattern, one short of a dozen, half sunk in the seamless ullish metal and half exposed to the crossworlds wind. Some were in deeper than others. High up, the new skeleton of some nameless winged being rattled in the breeze, a loose bag of hollow fairy bones welded to the wall only at wrists and ankles. Yet lower, up and to the right a little from the doorway, the yellow barrel-stave ribs of a Linkellar were all that could be seen of the creature.

MacDonald's skeleton was half in, half out. Most of the limbs were sunk deep in the metal, but the fingertips dangled out (one hand still holding a laser), and the feet, and the torso was open to the air. And the skull, of course—bleached white, half crushed, but still a rebuke. It looked down at Holt every dawn as he passed through the portal below. Sometimes, in the curious half-light of an early crossworlds morning, it seemed as though the missing eyes followed him on his long walk towards the gate.

But that had not bothered Holt for months. It had been different right after they had taken MacDonald, and his rotting body had suddenly appeared on the windwall, half joined to the metal. Holt could smell the stench then, and the corpse had been too recognizably Mac. Now it was just a skeleton, and that made it easier for Holt to forget.

On that anniversary morning, the day that marked the end of the first full standard year since the *Pegasus* had set down, Holt passed below the skeletons with hardly an upward glance.

Inside, as always, the corridor stood deserted. It curved away in both directions, white, dusty, very vacant; thin blue doors stood at regular intervals, but all of them were closed.

Holt turned to the right and tried the first door, pressing his palm to the entry plate. Nothing; the office was locked. He tried the next, with the same result. And then the next. Holt was methodical. He had to be. Each day only one office was open, and each day it was a different one.

The seventh door slid open at his touch.

Behind a curving metal desk a single Dan'la sat, looking out of place. The room, the furniture, the field—everything had been built to the proportions of the long-departed ul-nayileith, and the Dan'la was entirely too small for its setting. But Holt had gotten used to it. He had come every day for a year now, and every day a single Dan'la sat behind a desk. He had no idea whether it was the same one changing offices daily, or a different one each day. All of them had long snouts and darting eyes and bristling reddish fur. The humans called them foxmen. With rare exceptions, Holt could not tell one from the other. The Dan'lai would not help him. They refused to give names, and the creature behind the desk sometimes recognized him, often did not. Holt had long since given up the game, and resigned himself to treating every Dan'la as a stranger.

This morning, though, the foxman knew him at once. "Ah," he said as Holt entered. "A berth for you?"

"Yes," Holt said. He removed the battered ship's cap that matched his frayed gray uniform, and he waited—a thin, pale man with receding brown hair and a stubborn chin.

The foxman interlocked slim, six-fingered hands and smiled a swift thin smile. "No berth, Holt," he said. "Sorry. No ship today."

"I heard a ship last night," Holt said. "I could hear it all the way over in the stone city. Get me a berth on it. I'm qualified. I know standard drive, and I can run a Dan'lai jump-gun. I have credentials."

"Yes, yes." Again the snapping smile. "But there is no ship. Next week, perhaps. Next week perhaps a man-ship will come. Then you'll have a berth, Holt, I swear it, I promise you. You a good jump man, right? You tell me. I get you a berth. But next week, next week. No ship now."

Holt bit his lip and leaned forward, spreading his hands on the desktop, the cap crushed beneath one fist. "Next week you won't be here," he said. "Or if you are, you won't recognize me, won't remember anything you promised. Get me a berth on the ship that came last night."

"Ah," said the Dan'la. "No berth. Not a man-ship, Holt. No berth for a man."

"I don't care. I'll take any ship. I'll work with Dan'lai, ullies, Cedrans, anything. Jumps are all the same. Get me on the ship that came in last night."

"But there *was* no ship, Holt," the foxman said. His teeth flashed, then were gone again. "I tell you, Holt. No ship, no ship. Next week, come back. Come back, next week." There was dismissal in his tone. Holt had learned to recognize it.

Once, months ago, he'd stayed and tried to argue. But the desk-fox had summoned others to drag him away. For a week after-wards, *all* the doors had been locked in the mornings. Now Holt knew when to leave.

Outside in the wan light, he leaned briefly against the wind-wall and tried to still his shaking hands. He must keep busy, he reminded himself. He needed money, food tokens, so that was one task he could set to. He could visit the Shed, maybe look up Sunderland. As for a berth, there was always tomorrow. He had to be patient.

With a brief glance up at MacDonald, who had not been patient, Holt went off down the vacant streets of the city of the shipless.

Even as a child, Holt had loved the stars. He used to walk at night, during the years of high cold when the iceforests bloomed on Ymir. Straight out he would go, for kilometers, crunching the snow beneath until the lights of town were lost behind him and he stood alone in the glistening blue-white won-derland of frost-flowers and icewebs and bitterblooms. Then he would look up.

WinterYear nights on Ymir are clear and still and very black. There is no moon. The stars and the silence are every-thing.

Diligent, Holt had learned the names—not the starnames (no one named the stars any more—numbers were all that was needed), but rather the names of the worlds that swung around each. He was a bright child. He learned quickly and well, and even his gruff, practical father found a certain pride in that. Holt remembered endless parties at the Old House when his father, drunk on summerbrew, would march all his guests out onto the balcony so his son could name the worlds. "There," the old man would say, holding a mug in one hand and point-ing with the other, "there, that bright one!"

"Arachne," the boy would reply, blank-faced. The guests would smile and mutter politely.

"And there?"

"Baldur."

"There. There. Those three over there."

"Finnegan. Johnhenry. Celia's World, New Rome, Cathaday." The names skipped lightly off his youthful tongue. And
his father's leathery face would crinkle in a smile, and he would
go on and on until the others grew bored and restive and Holt
had named all the worlds a boy could name standing on a balcony of the Old House on Ymir. He had always hated the ritual.

It was a good thing that his father had never come with him
off into the iceforests, for away from the lights a thousand new
stars could be seen, and that meant a thousand names to know.
Holt never learned them all, the names that went with the
dimmer, far-off stars that were not man's. But he learned
enough. The pale stars of the Damoosh inwards toward the
core, the reddish sun of the Silent Centaurs, the scattered
lights where the Fyndii hordes raised their emblem-sticks;
these he knew, and more.

He continued to come as he grew older, not always alone
now. All his youthful sweethearts he dragged out with him,
and he made his first love in the starlight during a SummerYear
when the trees dripped flowers instead of ice. Sometimes he
talked about it with lovers, with friends. But the words came
hard. Holt was never eloquent, and he could not make them
understand. He scarcely understood himself.

After his father died, he took over the Old House and the
estates and ran them for a long WinterYear, though he was
only twenty standard. When the thaw came, he left it all and
went to Ymir City. A ship was down, a trader bound for
Finnegan and worlds further in.

Holt found a berth.

The streets grew busier as the day aged. Already the Dan'lai
were out, setting up food stalls between the huts. In an hour
or so the streets would be lined with them. A few gaunt ul-
mennaleith were also about, traveling in groups of four or
five. They all wore powder-blue gowns that fell almost to the
ground, and they seemed to flow instead of walking—eerie,

dignified, wraithlike. Their soft gray skin was finely powdered, their eyes were liquid and distant. Always they seemed serene, even *these,* these sorry shipless ones.

Holt fell in behind a group of them, increasing his pace to keep up. The fox merchants ignored the solemn ul-mennaleith, but they all spied Holt and called out to him as he passed. And laughed their high, barking laughs when he ignored them.

Near the Cedran neighborhoods Holt took his leave of the ullies, darting off into a tiny side street that seemed deserted. He had work to do, and this was the place to do it.

He walked deeper into the rash of yellowed bubble-huts and picked one almost at random. It was old, its plastic exterior heavily polished; the door was wood, carved with nest symbols. Locked, of course—Holt put his shoulder to it and pushed. When it held firm, he retreated a bit, then ran and crashed against it. On his fourth try it gave noisily. The noise didn't bother him. In a Cedran slum, no one would hear.

Pitch-dark inside. He felt near the door and found a coldtorch, touched it until it returned his body heat as light. Then, leisurely, he looked around.

There were five Cedrans present: three adults and two younglings, all curled up into featureless balls on the floor. Holt hardly gave them a glance. By night, the Cedrans were terrifying. He'd seen them many times on the darkened streets of the stone city, moaning in their soft speech and swaying sinister. Their segmented torsos unfolded into three meters of milk-white maggotflesh, and they had six specialized limbs; two wide-splayed feet, a pair of delicate branching tentacles for manipulation, and the wicked fighting-claws. The eyes, saucer-sized pools of glowing violet, saw everything. By night, Cedrans were beings to be avoided.

By day, they were immobile balls of meat.

Holt walked around them and looted their hut. He took a hand-held coldtorch, set low to give the murky purple half-light the Cedrans liked best, plus a sack of food tokens and a clawhone. The polished, jeweled fighting-claws of some illustrious ancestor sat in an honored place on the wall, but Holt was careful not to touch them. If their family god was stolen, the entire nest would be obliged to find the thief or commit suicide.

Finally he found a set of wizard-cards, smoke-dark wooden plaques inlaid with iron and gold. He shoved them in a pocket and left. The street was still empty. Few beings visited the Cedran districts save Cedrans.

Quickly Holt found his way back to the main thoroughfare, the wide gravel path that ran from the windwalls of the space-field to the silent gates of the stone city five kilometers away. The street was crowded and noisy now, and Holt had to push his way through the throng. Foxmen were everywhere, laughing and barking, snapping their quick grins on and off, rubbing reddish-brown fur up against the blue gowns of the ul-mennaleith, the chitinous Kresh, and the loose baggy skin of the pop-eyed green Linkellars. Some of the food stalls had hot meals to offer, and the ways were heavy with smokes and smells. Holt had been months on the crossworlds before he had finally learned to distinguish the food scents from the body odors.

As he fought his way down the street, dodging in and out among the aliens with his loot clutched tightly in his hand, Holt watched carefully. It was habit now, drilled into him; he looked constantly for an unfamiliar human face, the face that might mean a man-ship was in, that salvation had come.

He did not find one. As always, there was only the milling press of the crossworlds all around him—Dan'lai barks and Kresh clickings and the ululating speech of the Linkellars, but never a human voice. By now, it had ceased to affect him.

He found the stall he was looking for. From beneath a flap of gray leather, a frazzled Dan'la looked up at him. "Yes, yes," the foxman snapped impatiently. "Who are you? What do you want?"

Holt shoved aside the multicolored blinking-jewels that were strewn over the counter and put down the coldtorch and claw-hone he had taken. "Trade," he said. "These for tokens."

The foxman looked down at the goods, up at Holt, and be-gan to rub his snout vigorously. "Trade. Trade. A trade for you," he chanted. He picked up the clawhone, tossed it from one hand to the other, set it down again, touched the coldtorch to wake it to barely perceptible life. Then he nodded and turned on his grin. "Good stuff. Cedran. The big worms will want it. Yes. Yes. Trade, then. Tokens?"

Holt nodded.

The Dan'la fumbled in the pocket of the smock he was wearing, and tossed a handful of food tokens on the counter. They were bright disks of plastic in a dozen different colors, the nearest things to currency the crossworlds had. The Dan'lai merchants honored them for food. And the Dan'lai brought in all the food there was on their fleets of jump-gun spacers.

Holt counted the tokens, then scooped them up and threw them in the sack that he'd taken from the Cedran bubble-hut. "I have more," he said, reaching into his pocket for the wizard-cards.

His pocket was empty. The Dan'la grinned and snapped his teeth together. "Gone? Not the only thief on Empty, then. No. Not the only thief."

He remembered his first ship; he remembered the stars of his youth on Ymir, he remembered the worlds he'd touched since, he remembered all the ships he'd served on and the men (and not-men) he had served with. But better than any of them he remembered his first ship: the *Laughing Shadow* (an old name heavy with history, but no one told him the story until much later), out of Celia's World and bound for Finnegan. It was a converted ore freighter, a great blue-gray teardrop of pitted duralloy that was at least a century older than Holt was. Sparse and raw—big cargo holds and not much crew space, sleep-webs for the twelve who manned it, no gravity grid (he'd gotten used to free fall quickly), nukes for landing and lifting, and a standard ftl drive for the star-shifts. Holt was set to working in the drive room, an austere place of muted lights and bare metal and computer consoles. Cain narKarmian showed him what to do.

Holt remembered narKarmian too. An old, *old* man, too old

for shipwork he would have thought; skin like soft yellow leather that has been folded and wrinkled so many times that there is nowhere a piece of it without a million tiny creases, eyes brown and almond-shaped, a mottled bald head and a wispy blond goatee. Sometimes Cain seemed senile, but most often he was sharp and alert; he knew the drives, and he knew the stars, and he would talk incessantly as he worked.

"Two hundred standard years!" he said once as they both sat before their consoles. He smiled a shy, crooked smile, and Holt saw that he still had teeth, even at his age—or perhaps he had teeth *again*. "That's how long Cain's been shipping, Holt. The very truth! You know, your regular man never leaves the very world he's born on. Never! Ninety-five per cent of them, anyway. They never leave, just get born and grow up and die, all on the same world. And the ones that do ship—well, most of *them* ship only a little. A world or two or ten. Not me! You know where I was born, Holt? Guess!"

Holt shrugged. "Old Earth?"

Cain had just laughed. "Earth? Earth's nothing, only three or four years out from here. Four, I think. I forget. No, no, but I've seen Earth, the very homeworld, the seeding place. Seen it fifty years ago on the—the *Corey Dark*, I'd guess it was. It was about time, I thought. I'd been shipping a hundred fifty standard even then, and I still hadn't been to Earth. But I finally got there!"

"You weren't born there?" Holt prompted.

Old Cain shook his head and laughed again. "Not very! I'm an Emereli. From ai-Emerel. You know it, Holt?"

Holt had to think. It was not a world-name he recognized, not one of the stars his father had pointed to, aflame in the night of Ymir. But it rang a bell, dimly. "The Fringe?" he guessed finally. The Fringe was the the furthest *out*-edge of human space, the place where the small sliver of the galaxy they called the manrealm had brushed the top of the galactic lens, where the stars grew thin. Ymir and the stars he knew were on the other side of Old Earth, inward toward the denser starfields and the still-unreachable core.

Cain was happy at his guess. "Yes! I'm an outworlder. I'm near to two hundred and twenty standard, and I've seen near that many worlds now, human worlds and Hrangan and Fyndii and all sorts, even some worlds in the manrealm where the men aren't very *men* any more, if you understand what I'm saying. Shipping, always shipping. Whenever I found a place that looked interesting I'd skip ship and stay a time, then go on when I wanted to. I've seen all sorts of things, Holt. When I was young I saw the Festival of the Fringe, and hunted banshee on High Kavalaan, and got a wife on Kimdiss. She died, though, and I got on. Saw Prometheus and Rhiannon, which are in a bit from the Fringe, and Jamison's World and Avalon, which are in further still. You know. I was a Jamie for a bit, and on Avalon I got three wives. And two husbands, or co-husbands, or however you say it. I was still shy of a hundred then, maybe less. That was a time when we owned our own ship, did local trading, hit some of the old Hrangan slaveworlds that have gone off their own ways since the war. Even Old Hranga itself, the very place. They say there are still some Minds on Hranga, deep underground, waiting to come back and attack the manrealm again. But all I ever saw was a lot of kill-castes and workers and the other lesser types."

He smiled. "Good years, Holt, very good years. We called our ship *Jamison's Ass*. My wives and my husbands were all Avalonians, you see, except for one who was Old Poseidon, and Avalonians don't like Jamies much, which is how we arrived at that very name. But I can't say that they were wrong. I was a Jamie too, before that, and Port Jamison is a stulty priggy town on a planet that's the same.

"We were together nearly thirty standard on *Jamison's Ass*. The marriage outlasted two wives and one husband. And me too, finally. They wanted to keep Avalon as their trade base, you see, but after thirty I'd seen all the worlds I wanted to see around there, and I hadn't seen a lot else. So I shipped on. But I loved them, Holt, I did love them. A man should be married to his shipmates. It makes for a very good feeling." He sighed. "Sex comes easier too. Less uncertainty."

By then, Holt was caught. "Afterwards," he'd asked, his young face showing only a hint of the envy he felt, "what did you do then?"

Cain had shrugged, looked down at his console, and started to punch the glowing studs to set in a drive correction. "Oh, shipped on, shipped on. Old worlds, new worlds, man, not-man, aliens. New Refuge and Pachacuti and burnt-out old Wellington, and then Newholme and Silversky and Old Earth. And now I'm going in, as far as I can go before I die. Like Tomo and Walberg, I guess. You know about Tomo and Walberg, in here at Ymir?"

And Holt had only nodded. Even Ymir knew about Tomo and Walberg. Tomo was an outworlder too, born on Darkdawn high atop the Fringe, and they say he was a darkling dreamer. Walberg was an Altered Man from Prometheus, a roistering adventurer according to the legend. Three centuries ago, in a ship called the *Dreaming Whore,* they had set off from Dark-dawn for the opposite edge of the galaxy. How many worlds they had visited, what had happened on each, how far they had gotten before death—those were the knots in the tale, and schoolboys disputed them still. Holt liked to think that they were still out there, somewhere. After all, Walberg had said he was a superman, and there was no telling how long a superman might live. Maybe even long enough to reach the core, or beyond.

He had been staring at the console, daydreaming, and Cain had grinned over at him and said, "Hey! Starsick!" And when Holt had started and looked up, the old man nodded (still smiling), saying, "Yes, you, the very one! Set to, Holt, or you won't be shipping nowhere!"

But it was a gentle rebuke, and a gentle smile, and Holt never forgot it or Cain narKarmian's other words. Their sleep-webs were next to each other and Holt listened every night, for Cain was hard to silence and Holt was not about to try. And when the *Laughing Shadow* finally hit Cathaday, as far in as it would go, and got ready to turn back into the manrealm towards Celia's World and home, Holt and narKarmian signed off together and got berths on a mailship that was heading for Vess and the alien Damoosh suns.

They had shipped together for six years when narKarmian finally died. Holt remembered the old man's face much better than his father's.

The Shed was a long, thin, metal building, a corrugated shack of blue duralloy that someone had found in the stores of a looted freighter, probably. It was built kilometers from the windwall, within sight of the gray walls of the stone city and the high iris of the Western Door. Around it were other, larger metal buildings, the warehouse-barracks of the shipless ul-mennaleith. But there were no ullies inside, ever.

It was near noon when Holt arrived, and the Shed was almost empty. A wide columnar coldtorch reached from floor to ceiling in the center of the room, giving off a tired ruddy light that left most of the deserted tables in darkness. A party of muttering Linkellars filled a corner off in the shadows; opposite them, a fat Cedran was curled up in a tight sleep-ball, his slick white skin glistening. And next to the coldtorch pillar, at the old *Pegasus* table, Alaina and Takker-Rey were sharing a white stone flask of amberlethe.

Takker spied him at once. "Look," he said, raising his glass. "We have company, Alaina. A lost soul returns! How are things in the stone city, Michael?"

Holt sat down. "The same as always, Takker. The same as always." He forced a smile for bloated, pale-faced Takker, then quickly turned to Alaina. She had worked the jump-gun with him once, a year ago and more. And they had been lovers, briefly. But that was over. Alaina had put on weight and her long auburn hair was dirty and matted. Her green eyes used to spark; now amberlethe made them dull and cloudy.

Alaina favored him with a pudgy smile. " 'Lo, Michael," she said. "Have you found your ship?"

Takker-Rey giggled, but Holt ignored him. "No," he said.

"But I keep going. Today the foxman said there'd be a ship in next week. A man-ship. He promised me a berth."

Now both of them giggled. "Oh, Michael," Alaina said. "Silly, silly. They used to tell *me* that. I haven't gone for so long. Don't you go, either. I'll take you back. Come up to my room. I miss you. Tak is such a bore."

Takker frowned, hardly paying attention. He was intent on pouring himself a new glass of amberlethe. The liquor flowed with agonizing slowness, like honey. Holt remembered the taste of it, gold fire on his tongue, and the easy sense of peace it brought. They had all done a lot of drinking in the early weeks, while they waited for the Captain to return. Before things fell apart.

"Have some 'lethe," Takker said. "Join us."

"No," Holt said. "Maybe a little fire brandy, Takker, if you're buying. Or a foxbeer. Summerbrew, if there's some handy. I miss summerbrew. But no 'lethe. That's why I went away, remember?"

Alaina gasped suddenly; her mouth drooped open and something flickered in her eyes. "You went away," she said in a thin voice. "I remember, you were the first. You went away. You and Jeff. You were the first."

"No, dear," Takker interrupted very patiently. He set down the flask of amberlethe, took a sip from his glass, smiled, and proceeded to explain. "The Captain was the first one to go away. Don't you recall? The Captain and Villareal and Susie Benet, they all went away together, and we waited and waited."

"Oh, yes," Alaina said. "Then later Jeff and Michael left us. And poor Irai killed herself, and the foxes took Ian and put him up on the wall. And all the others went away. Oh, I don't know where, Michael, I just don't." Suddenly she started to weep. "We all used to be together, all of us, but now there's just Tak and me. They all left us. We're the only ones who come here any more, the *only* ones." She broke down and started sobbing.

Holt felt sick. It was worse than his last visit the month before—much worse. He wanted to grab the amberlethe and smash it to the floor. But it was pointless. He had done that once a long time ago—the second month after landing—when the endless hopeless waiting had sent him into a rare rage. Alaina had wept, MacDonald cursed and hit him and knocked loose a tooth (it still hurt sometimes, at night), and Takker-Rey bought another flask. Takker always had money. He wasn't much of a thief, but he'd grown up on Vess where men shared a planet with two alien races, and like a lot of Vessmen he'd grown up a xenophile. Takker was soft and willing, and fox-men (some foxmen) found him attractive. When Alaina had joined him, in his room and his business, Holt and Jeff Sunderland had given up on them and moved to the outskirts of the stone city.

"Don't cry, Alaina," Holt said now. "Look, I'm here, see? I even brought food tokens." He reached into his sack and tossed a handful onto the table—red, blue, silver, black. They clattered and rolled and lay still.

At once, Alaina's tears were gone. She began to scrabble among the tokens, and even Takker leaned forward to watch. "Red ones," she said excitedly. "Look, Takker, red ones, meat tokens! And silvers, for 'lethe. Look, look!" She began to scoop loose tokens into her pockets, but her hands were trembling, and more than one token was thrown onto the floor. "Help me, Tak," she said.

Takker giggled. "Don't worry, love, that was only a green. We don't need worm food anyway, do we?" He looked at Holt. "Thank you, Michael, thank you. I always told Alaina you had a generous soul, even if you did leave us when we needed you. You and Jeff. Ian said you were a coward, you know, but I always defended you. Thank you, yes." He picked up a silver token and flipped it with his thumb. "Generous Michael. You're always welcome here."

Holt said nothing. The Shed-boss had suddenly materialized at his elbow, a vast bulk of musky blue-black flesh. His face looked down at Holt—if you could call it looking, since the being was eyeless, and if you could call it a face, since there was no mouth either. The thing that passed for a head was a flabby, half-filled bladder full of breathing holes and ringed by whitish tentacles. It was the size of a child's head, an infant's, and it looked absurdly small atop the gross oily body and the rolls of mottled fat. The Shed-boss did not speak; not Terran nor ullish nor the pidgin Dan'lai that passed for cross-worlds trade talk. But he always knew what his customers wanted.

Holt just wanted to leave. While the Shed-boss stood, silent and waiting, he rose and lurched for the door. It slid shut behind him, and he could hear Alaina and Takker-Rey arguing over the tokens.

The Damoosh are a wise and gentle race, and great philosophers—or so they used to say on Ymir. The outermost of their suns interlock with the innermost parts of the ever-growing manrealm, and it was on a time-worn Damoosh colony that narKarmian died and Holt first saw a Linkellar.

Rayma-k-Tel was with him at the time, a hard hatchet-faced woman who'd come out of Vess; they were drinking in an enclave bar just off the spacefield. The place had good manrealm liquor, and he and Ram swilled it down together from seats by a window of stained yellow glass. Cain was three weeks dead. When Holt saw the Linkellar shuffling past the window, its bulging eyes a-wobble, he tugged at Ram's arm and turned her around and said, "Look. A new one. You know the race?"

Rayma shrugged loose her arm and shook her head. "No," she said, irritated. She was a raging xenophobe, which is the other thing that growing up on Vess will do to you. "Probably from further in somewhere. Don't even *try* to keep them straight, Mikey. There's a million different kinds, specially this far in. Damn Damos'll trade with any*thing.*"

Holt had looked again, still curious, but the heavy being with the loose green skin was out of sight. Briefly he thought of Cain, and something like a thrill went through him. The old man had shipped for more than two hundred years, he thought, and yet he'd probably never seen an alien of the race *they'd* just seen. He said something to that effect to Rayma-k-Tel.

She was most unimpressed. "So what?" she said. "So *we've* never seen the Fringe or a Hrangan, though I'd be damned to know why we'd *want* to." She smiled thinly at her own wit. "Aliens are like jellybeans, Mikey. They come in a lot of different colors, but inside they're just about the same.

"So don't turn yourself into a collector like old narKarmian. Where did it ever get him, after all? He moved around a lot on a bunch of third-rate ships, but he never saw the Far Arm and he never saw the core, and nobody ever will. He didn't get too rich, neither. Just relax and make a living."

Holt had hardly been listening. He put down his drink and lightly touched the cool glass of the window with his fingertips.

That night, after Rayma had returned to their ship, Holt left the offworld enclave and wandered out into the Damoosh home-places. He paid half-a-run's salary to be led to the underground chamber where the world's wisdompool lay: a vast computer of living light linked to the dead brains of telepathic Damoosh elders (or at least that was how the guide explained it to Holt).

The chamber was a bowl of green fog stirring with little waves and swells. Within its depths, curtains of colored light rippled and faded and were gone. Holt stood on the upper lip looking down and asked his questions, and the answers came back in an echoing whisper as of many tiny voices speaking together. First he described the being he'd seen that afternoon and asked what it had been, and it was then he heard the word Linkellar.

"Where do they come from?" Holt asked.

"Six years from the manrealm by the drive you use," the whispers told him while the green fog moved. "Toward the core but not straight in. Do you want coordinates?"

"No. Why don't we see them more often?"

"They are far away, too far perhaps," the answer came. "The whole width of the Damoosh suns is between the manrealm and the the Twelve Worlds of the Linkellar, and so too the colonies of the Nor T'alush and a hundred worlds that have not found stardrives. The Linkellars trade with the Damoosh, but they seldom come to this place, which is closer to you than to them."

"Yes," said Holt. A chill went through him, as if a cold wind blew across the cavern and the flickering sea of fog. "I have heard of the Nor T'alush, but not of the Linkellars. What else is there? Further in?"

"There are many directions," the fog whispered. Colors undulated deep below. "We know the dead worlds of the vanished race the Nor T'alush call the First Ones, though they were not truly the first, and we know the Reaches of the Kresh, and the lost colony of the gethsoids of Aath who sailed from far within the manrealm before it was the manrealm."

"What's beyond *them?*"

"The Kresh tell of a world called Cedris, and of a great sphere of suns larger than the manrealm and the Damoosh suns and the old Hrangan Empire all together. The stars within are the ullish stars."

"Yes," Holt said. There was a tremor in his voice. "And beyond *that?* Around it? Further in?"

A fire burned within the far depths of the fog; the green mists glowed with a smoldering reddish light. "The Damoosh do not know. Who sails so far, so long? There are only tales. Shall we tell you of the Very Old Ones? Of the Bright Gods, or the shipless sailors? Shall we sing the old sing of the race without a world? Ghost ships have been sighted further in, things that move faster than a man-ship or a Damoosh in drive, and they destroy where they will, yet sometimes they are not there at all. Who can say what they are, who they are, where they are, if they are? We have names, names, stories, we can give you names and stories. But the facts are dim. We hear of a world named Huul the Golden that trades with the lost gethsoids who trade with the Kresh who trade with the Nor T'alush who trade with us, but no Damoosh ship has ever sailed to Huul the Golden and we cannot say much of it or even where it is. We hear of the veiled men of a world unnamed, who puff themselves up and float around and around in their atmosphere, but that may be only a legend, and we cannot even say *whose* legend. We hear of a race that lives in deep space, who talk to a race called the Dan'lai, who trade with the ullish stars, who trade with Cedris, and so the string runs back to us. But we Damoosh on this world so near the manrealm have never seen a Cedran, so how can we trust the string?" There was a sound like muttering; below his feet, the fog churned, and something that smelled like incense rose to touch Holt's nostrils.

"I'll go in," Holt said. "I'll ship on, and see."

"Then come back one day and tell us," the fogs cried, and for the very first time Holt heard the mournful keen of a wisdompool that is not wise enough. "Come back, come back. There is much to learn." The smell of incense was very strong.

Holt looted three more Cedran bubble-huts that afternoon, and broke into two others. The first of those was simply cold and vacant and dusty; the second was occupied, but not by a Cedran. After jiggling loose the door, he'd stood shock-still while an ethereal winged thing with feral eyes flapped against the roof of the hut and hissed down at him. He got nothing from that bubble, nor from the empty one, but the rest of his break-ins paid off.

Toward sunset, he returned to the stone city, climbing a narrow ramp to the Western Iris with a bag of food slung over his shoulders.

In the pale and failing light, the city looked colorless, washed-out, dead. The circling walls were four meters high and twice as thick, fashioned of a smooth and seamless gray stone as if they were a single piece; the Western Iris that opened on the city of the shipless was more a tunnel than a gateway. Holt went through it quickly, out into a narrow zigzag alley that threaded its way between two huge buildings—or perhaps they were not buildings. Twenty meters tall, irregularly shaped, windowless and doorless; there could be no possible entrance save through the stone city's lower levels. Yet this type of structure, these odd-shaped dented blocks of gray stone, dominated the easternmost part of the stone city in an area of some twelve kilometers square. Sunderland had mapped it.

The alleys here were a hopeless maze, none of them running straight for more than ten meters; from above, Holt had often imagined them to look like a child's drawing of a lightning bolt. But he had come this route often, and he had Sunderland's maps committed to memory (for this small portion of the stone city, at any rate). He moved with speed and confidence, encountering no one.

From time to time, when he stood in the nexus points where several alleys joined, Holt caught glimpses of other structures in the distance. Sunderland had mapped most of them, too; they used the sights as landmarks. The stone city had a hundred separate parts, and in each the architecture and the very building stone itself was different. Along the northwest wall was a jungle of obsidian towers set close together with dry canals between; due south lay a region of blood-red stone pyramids; east was an utterly empty granite plain with a single mushroom-shaped tower ascending from its center. And there were other regions, all strange, all uninhabited. Sunderland mapped a few additional blocks each day. Yet even this was only the tip of the iceberg. The stone city had levels beneath levels beneath levels, and neither Holt nor Sunderland nor any of the others had penetrated those black and airless warrens.

Dusk was all around him when Holt paused at a major nexus point, a wide octagon with a smaller octagonal pool in its center. The water was still and green; not even a ripple of wind moved across its surface until Holt stopped to wash. Their rooms, just past here, were as bone-dry as this whole area of the city. Sunderland said the pyramids had indoor water supplies, but near the Western Iris there was nothing but this single public pool.

Holt resumed walking when he had cleaned the day's dust from his face and hands. The food bag bounced on his back, and his footsteps, echoing, broke the alley stillness. There was no other sound; the night was falling fast. It would be as bleak and moonless as any other crossworlds night. Holt knew that.

The overcast was always heavy, and he could seldom spot more than a half-dozen dim stars.

Beyond the plaza of the pool, one of the great gray buildings had fallen. There was nothing left but a jumble of broken rock and sand. Holt cut across it carefully, to a single structure that stood out of place among the rest—a huge gold stone dome like a blown-up Cedran bubble-hut. It had a dozen entrance holes, a dozen narrow little staircases winding up to them, and a honeycomb of chambers within.

For nearly ten standard months, this had been home.

Sunderland was squatting on the floor of their common room when Holt entered, his maps spread out all around him. He had arranged each section to fit with the others in a patchwork tapestry; old yellowed scraps he'd purchased from the Dan'lai and corrected were sandwiched between sheets of *Pegasus* gridfilm and lightweight squares of silvery ullish metal. The totality carpeted the room, each piece covered with lines and Sunderland's neat notation. He sat in the middle of it all with a map on his lap and a marker in his hand, looking owlish and rumpled and very overweight.

"I've got food," Holt said. He flipped the bag across the room and it landed among the maps, disarraying several of the loose sections.

Sunderland squawked, "Ahh, the *maps!* Be careful!" He blinked and pushed the food aside and rearranged everything neatly again.

Holt crossed the room to his sleepweb, strung between two sturdy coldtorch pillars. He walked on the maps as he went and Sunderland squawked again, but Holt ignored him and climbed into the web.

"Damn you," Sunderland said, smoothing the trodden sections. "Be more careful, will you?" He looked up and saw that Holt was frowning at him. "Mike?"

"Sorry," Holt said. "You find anything today?" His tone made the question an empty formality.

Sunderland never noticed. "I got into a whole new section, off to the south," he said excitedly. "Very interesting, too.

Obviously designed as a unit. There's this central pillar, you see, built out of some soft green stone, and surrounded by ten slightly smaller pillars, and there are these bridges—well, sort of ribbons of stone, they loop from the top of the big ones to the tops of the little ones. The pattern is repeated over and over. And below you've got sort of a labyrinth of waist-high stone walls. It will take me weeks to map them."

Holt was looking at the wall next to his head, where the count of the days was scored in the golden stone. "A year," he said. "A standard year, Jeff."

Sunderland looked at him curiously, then stood and began gathering up his maps. "How was your day?" he asked.

"We're not going to leave this place," Holt said, speaking more to himself than to Sunderland. "Never. It's over."

Now Sunderland stopped. "Stop it," the small fat man said. "I won't have it, Holt. Give up, and next thing you know you'll be drowning in amberlethe with Alaina and Takker. The stone city is the key. I've known that all along. Once we discover all its secrets, we can sell them to the foxmen and get out of this place. When I finish my mapping—"

Holt rolled over on his side to face Sunderland. "A year, Jeff, a year. You're not going to finish your mapping. You could map for ten years and still have covered only part of the stone city. And what about the tunnels? The levels beneath?"

Sunderland licked his lips nervously. "Beneath. Well. If I had the equipment on board the *Pegasus*, then—"

"You don't, and it doesn't work anyway. Nothing works on the stone city. That was why the Captain landed. The rules don't work down here."

Sunderland shook his head and resumed his gathering up the maps. "The human mind can understand anything. Give me time, that's all, and I'll figure it all out. We could even figure out the Dan'lai and the ullies if Susie Benet was still here." Susie Benet had been their contact specialist—a third-rate linguesp, but even a minor talent is better than none when dealing with alien minds.

"Susie Benet isn't here," Holt said. His voice had a hard edge to it. He began to tick off names on his fingers. "Susie vanished with the Captain. Ditto Carlos. Irai suicided. Ian tried to shoot his way inside the windwalls and wound up on them. Det and Lana and Maje went down beneath, trying to find the Captain, and they vanished too. Davie Tillman sold himself as a Kresh egg host, so he's surely finished by now. Alaina and Takker-Rey are vegetables, useless, and we don't know what went on with the four aboard the *Pegasus*. That leaves us, Sunderland, you and me." He smiled grimly. "You make maps, I steal from the worms, and nobody understands anything. We're finished. We'll die here in the stone city. We'll never see the stars again."

He stopped as suddenly as he had started. It was a rare outburst for Holt; in general he was quiet, unexpressive, maybe a little repressed. Sunderland stood there, astonished, while Holt sagged back hopelessly into his sleepweb.

"Day after day after day," Holt said. "And none of it means anything. You remember what Irai told us?"

"She was unstable," Sunderland insisted. "She proved that beyond our wildest dreams."

"She said we'd come too far," Holt said, as if Sunderland had never spoken. "She said it was wrong to think that the whole universe operated by rules we could understand. You remember. She called it 'sick, arrogant human folly.' You remember, Jeff. That was how she talked. Like that. Sick, arrogant human folly."

He laughed. "The crossworlds *almost* made sense, that was what fooled us. But if Irai was right, that would figure. After all, we're still only a little bit from the manrealm, right? Further in, maybe the rules change even more."

"I don't like this kind of talk," said Sunderland. "You're getting defeatist. Irai was sick. At the end, you know, she was going to ul-mennaleith prayer meetings, submitting herself to the ul-nayileith, that sort of thing. A mystic, that was what she became. A mystic."

"She was wrong?" Holt asked.

"She was wrong," Sunderland said firmly.

Holt looked at him again. "Then explain things, Jeff. Tell me how to get out of here. Tell me how it all makes sense."

"The stone city," Sunderland said. "Well, when I finish my maps—" He stopped suddenly. Holt was leaning back in his web again and not listening at all.

It took him five years and six ships to move across the great star-flecked sphere the Damoosh claimed as their own and penetrate the border sector beyond. He consulted other, greater wisdompools as he went, and learned all he could, but always there were mysteries and surprises waiting on the world beyond this one. Not all the ships he served on were crewed by humans; man-ships seldom straggled in this far, so Holt signed on with Damoosh and stray gethsoids and other, lesser mongrels. But still there were usually a few men on every port he touched, and he even began to hear rumors of a second human empire some five hundred years in toward the core, settled by a wandering generation ship and ruled from a glittering world called Prester. On Prester the cities floated on clouds, one withered Vessman told him. Holt believed that for a time until another crewmate said that Prester was really a single world-spanning city, kept alive by fleets of food freighters greater than anything the Federal Empire had built in the wars before the Collapse. The same man said it had not been a generation ship that had settled her at all—he proved that by showing how far a slow-light ship could get from Old Earth since the dawn of the interstellar age—but rather a squadron of Earth Imperials fleeing a Hrangan Mind. Holt stayed skeptical this time. When a woman from a grounded Cathadayn freighter insisted that Prester had been founded by Tomo and Walberg, and that Walberg ruled it still, he gave up on the whole idea.

But there were other legends, other stories, and they drew him on.

As they drew others.

On an airless world circling a blue-white star, in its single domed city, Holt met Alaina. She told him about the *Pegasus.*

"The Captain built her from scratch, you know, right here.

He was trading, going in further than usual, like we all do"—
she flashed an understanding smile, figuring that Holt too was a
trading gambler out for the big find—"and he met a Dan'la.
They're further in."

"I know," Holt said.

"Well, maybe you don't know what's going *on* in there. The
Captain said the Dan'lai have all but taken over the ullish stars
—you've heard of the ullish stars? . . . Good. Well, it's because
the ul-mennaleith haven't resisted much, I gather, but also because of the Dan'lai jump-gun. It's a new concept, I guess, and
the Captain says it cuts travel time in half, or better. The standard drive warps the fabric of the space-time continuum, you
know, to get ftl effects, and—"

"I'm a drive man," Holt said curtly. But he was leaning forward as he said it, listening intently.

"Oh," Alaina said, not rebuked in the least. "Well, the Dan'lai
jump-gun does something else, shifts you into another continuum and then back again. Running it is entirely different.
It's partly psionic, and they put this ring around your head."

"You *have* a jump-gun?" Holt interrupted.

She nodded. "The Captain melted down his old ship, just
about, to build the *Pegasus*. With a jump-gun he bought from
the Dan'lai. He's collecting a crew now, and they're training
us."

"Where are you going?" he said.

She laughed, lightly, and her bright green eyes seemed to
flash. "Where else? In!"

Holt woke at dawn, in silence, rose and dressed himself
quickly, and traced his path backwards, past the quiet green
pool and the endless alleys, out the Western Iris and through
the city of the shipless. He walked under the wall of skeletons
without an upward glance.

Inside the windwall, in the long corridor, he began to try
the doors. The first four rattled and stayed shut. The fifth
opened on an empty office. No Dan'la.

That was something new. Holt entered cautiously, peering

around. No one, nothing, and no second door. He walked around the wide ullish desk and began to rifle it methodically, much as he looted the Cedran bubble-huts. Maybe he could find a field pass, a gun, something—anything to get him back to the *Pegasus*. If it was still sitting beyond the walls. Or maybe he could find a berth assignment.

The door slid open; a foxman stood there. He was indistinguishable from all the others. He barked, and Holt jumped away from the desk.

Swiftly the Dan'la circled around and seized the chair. "Thief!" he said. "Thief. I will shoot. You be shot. Yes." His teeth snapped.

"No," Holt said, edging towards the door. He could run if the Dan'la called others. "I came for a berth," he said inanely.

"AH!" The foxman interlocked his hands. "Different. Well, Holt, who are you?"

Holt stood mute.

"A berth, a berth, Holt wants a berth," the Dan'la said in a squeaky singsong.

"Yesterday they said that a man-ship would be in next week," Holt said.

"No no no. I'm sorry. No man-ship will come. There will be no man-ship. Next week, yesterday, no time. You understand? And we have no berth. Ship is full. You never go on field with no berth."

Holt moved forward again, to the other side of the desk. "No ship next week?"

The foxman shook his head. "No ship. No ship. No man-ship."

"Something else, then. I'll crew for ullies, for Dan'lai, for Cedrans. I've told you. I know drive, I know your jump-guns. Remember? I have credentials."

The Dan'la tilted his head to one side. Did Holt remember that gesture? Was this a Dan'la he'd dealt with before? "Yes, but no berth."

Holt started for the door.

"Wait," the foxman commanded.

Holt turned.

"No man-ship next week," the Dan'la said. "No ship, no ship, no ship," he sang. Then he stopped singing. "Man-ship is *now!*"

Holt straightened. "*Now?!* You mean there's a man-ship on the field right now?"

The Dan'la nodded furiously.

"A berth!" Holt was frantic. "Get me a berth, damn you."

"Yes. Yes. A berth for you, for you a berth." The foxman touched something on the desk, a drawer slid open, and he took out a film of silver metal and a slim wand of blue plastic. "Your name?"

"Michael Holt," he answered.

"Oh." The foxman put down the wand, took the metal sheet and put it back in the drawer, and barked, "No berth!"

"No berth?"

"No one can have two berths," the Dan'la said.

"Two?"

The deskfox nodded. "Holt has a berth on *Pegasus.*"

Holt's hands were trembling. "Damn," he said. "Damn."

The Dan'la laughed. "Will you take berth?"

"On *Pegasus?*"

A nod.

"You'll let me through the walls, then? Out onto the field?"

The foxman nodded again. "Write Holt field pass."

"Yes," Holt said. "Yes."

"Name?"

"Michael Holt."

"Race?"

"Man."

"Homeworld?"

"Ymir."

There was a short silence. The Dan'la had been sitting there staring at Holt, his hands folded. Now he suddenly opened the drawer again, took out an ancient-looking piece of parchment that crumbled as he touched it, and picked up the wand again. "Name?" he asked.

They went through the whole thing again.

When the Dan'la had finished writing, he gave the paper to

Holt. It flaked as he fingered it. He tried to be very careful. None of the scrawls made sense. "This will get me past the guards?" Holt said skeptically. "On the field? To the *Pegasus?*"

The Dan'la nodded. Holt turned and almost ran for the door.

"Wait," the foxman cried.

Holt froze, and spun. "What?" he said between his teeth, and it was almost a snarl of rage.

"Technical thing."

"Yes?"

"Field pass, to be good, must be signed." The Dan'la flashed on its toothy smile. "Signed, yes yes, signed by your captain."

There was no noise. Holt's hand tightened spasmodically around the slip of yellow paper, and the pieces fluttered stiffly to the floor. Then, swift and wordless, he was on him.

The Dan'la had time for only one brief bark before Holt had him by the throat. The delicate six-fingered hands clawed air, helplessly. Holt twisted, and the neck snapped. He was holding a bundle of limp reddish fur.

He stood there for a long time, his hands locked, his teeth clenched. Then slowly he released his grip and the Dan'la corpse tumbled backward, toppling the chair.

In Holt's eyes, a picture of the windwall flashed briefly.

He ran.

The *Pegasus* had standard drives too, in case the jump-gun failed; the walls of the room were the familiar blend of naked metal and computer consoles. But the center was filled by the Dan'lai jump-gun: a long cylinder of metallic glass, thick around as a man, mounted on an instrument panel. The cylinder was half full of a sluggish liquid that changed color abruptly each time a pulse of energy was run through the tank. Around it were seats for four jump-men, two on a side. Holt and Alaina sat on one flank, opposite tall blond Irai and Ian MacDonald; each of them wore a hollow glass crown full of the same liquid that sloshed in the gun cylinder.

Carlos Villareal was behind Holt, at the main console, draining data from the ship's computer. The jumps were already planned. They were going to see the ullish stars, the Captain had decided. And Cedris and Huul the Golden, and points further in. And maybe even Prester and the core.

The first stop was a transit point named Grayrest (clearly, by the name, some other men had gone there once—the star was on the charts). The Captain had heard a story of a stone city older than time.

Beyond the atmosphere the nukes cut off, and Villareal gave the order. "Coordinates are in, navigation is ready," he said, his voice a little less sure than usual; the whole procedure was so new. "Jump."

They switched on the Dan'lai jump-gun.

darkness flickering with colors and a thousand whirling stars and Holt was in the middle all alone but no! there was Alaina and there someone else and all of them joined and the chaos whirled around them and great gray waves crashed over their heads and faces appeared ringed with fire laughing and dissolving and pain pain pain and they were lost and nothing was solid and eons passed and no Holt saw something burning calling pulling the core the core and there out from it grayrest but then it was gone and somehow Holt brought it back and he yelled to Alaina and she grabbed for it too and MacDonald and Irai and they PULLED

They were sitting before the jump-gun again, and Holt was suddenly conscious of a pain in his wrist, and he looked down and saw that someone had taped an i.v. needle into him. Alaina was plugged in too, and the others, Ian and Irai. There was no sign of Villareal.

The door slid open and Sunderland stood there smiling at them and blinking. "Thank God!" the chubby navigator said. "You've been out for three months. I thought we were finished."

Holt took the glass crown from his head and saw that there was only a thin film of liquid left. Then he noticed that the jump cylinder was almost empty as well. "Three months?"

Sunderland shuddered. "It was horrible. There was nothing outside, *nothing*, and we couldn't rouse you. Villareal had to play nursemaid. If it hadn't been for the Captain, I don't know what would have happened. I know what the foxman said, but I wasn't sure you could ever pull us out of—of wherever we were."

"Are we there?" MacDonald demanded.

Sunderland went around the jump-gun to Villareal's console and hooked it in to the ship's viewscreen. In a field of black, a small yellow sun was burning. And a cold gray orb filled the screen.

"Grayrest," Sunderland said. "I've taken readings. We're there. The Captain has already opened a beam to them. The Dan'lai seem to run things, and they've cleared us to land. The time checks, too; three months subjective, three months objective, as near as we can figure."

"And by standard drive?" Holt said. "The same trip by standard drive?"

"We did even better than the Dan'lai promised," Sunderland said. "Grayrest is a good year and a half in from where we were."

It was too early; there was too great a chance that the Cedrans might not be comatose yet. But Holt had to take the risk. He smashed his way into the first bubble-hut he found and looted it completely, ripping things apart with frantic haste. The residents, luckily, were torpid sleep-balls.

Out on the main thoroughfare, he ignored the Dan'lai merchants, half afraid he would confront the same foxman he had just killed. Instead he found a stall tended by a heavy blind Linkellar, its huge eyes like rolling balls of pus. The creature still cheated him, somehow. But he traded all that he had taken for an eggshell-shaped helmet of transparent blue and a working laser. The laser startled him; it was a twin for the one MacDonald had carried, even down to the Finnegan crest. But it worked, and that was all that mattered.

The crowds were assembling for the daily shuffle up and down the ways of the city of the shipless. Holt pushed through them savagely, toward the Western Iris, and broke into a measured jog when he reached the empty alleys of the stone city.

Sunderland was gone; out mapping. Holt took one of his markers and wrote across a map; KILLED A FOX. MUST HIDE. I'M GOING DOWN INTO THE STONE CITY. SAFE THERE. Then he took all the food that was left, a good two weeks' supply, more if he starved himself. He filled a pac with it, strapped it on, and left. The laser was snug in his pocket, the helmet tucked under his arm.

The nearest underway was only a few blocks away; a great corkscrew that descended into the earth from the center of a nexus. Holt and Sunderland had often gone to the first level, as far as the light reached. Even there it was dim, gloomy, stuffy; a network of tunnels as intricate as the alleys above had branched off in every direction. Many of them slanted downward. And of course the corkscrew went further down, with more branchings, growing darker and more still with every turn. No one went beyond the first level; those that did—like the Captain—never came back. They had heard stories about how deep the stone city went, but there was no way to check them out; the instruments they had taken from *Pegasus* had never worked on the crossworlds.

At the bottom of the first full turn, the first level, Holt stopped and put on the pale-blue helmet. It was a tight fit; the front of it pressed against the edge of his nose and the sides squeezed his head uncomfortably. Clearly it had been built for an ul-mennalei. But it would do; there was a hole around his mouth, so he could talk and breathe.

He waited a moment while his body heat was absorbed by the helmet. Shortly it began to give off a somber blue light. Holt continued down the corkscrew, into the darkness.

Around and around the underway curved, with other tunnels branching off at every turning; Holt kept on and soon lost track of the levels he had come. Outside his small circle of light there was only pitch-black and silence and still hot air that was increasingly difficult to breathe. But fear was driving him now, and he did not slow. The surface of the stone city was deserted, but not entirely so; the Dan'lai entered when they had to. Only down here would he be safe. He would stay on the corkscrew itself, he vowed; if he did not wander he could not get lost. That was what happened to the Captain and the others, he was sure; they'd left the underway, gone off into the side tunnels, and had starved to death before they could find their way back. But not Holt. In two weeks or so he could come up and get food from Sunderland, perhaps.

For what seemed hours he walked down the twisting ramp, past endless walls of featureless gray stone tinted blue by his helmet, past a thousand gaping holes that ran to the sides and up and down, each calling to him with a wide black mouth. The air grew steadily warmer; soon Holt was breathing heavily. Nothing around him but stone, yet the tunnels seemed rank and thick. He ignored it.

After a time Holt reached a place where the corkscrew ended; a triple fork confronted him, three arched doorways and three narrow stairs, each descending sharply in a different direction, each curving so that Holt could see only a few meters into the dark. By then his feet were sore. He sat and removed his boots and took out a tube of smoked meat to chew on.

Darkness all around him; without his footsteps echoing heavily, there was no sound. Unless. He listened carefully. Yes. He heard something, dim and far-off. A rumble, sort of. He chewed on his meat and listened even harder and after a long while decided the sounds were coming from the left-hand staircase.

When the food was gone, he licked his fingers and pulled on his boots and rose. Laser in hand, he slowly started down the stair as quietly as he could manage.

The stair too was a spiral; a tighter corkscrew than the ramp, without branchings and very narrow. He barely had room to turn around, but at least there was no chance of getting lost.

The sound got steadily louder as he descended, and before long Holt realized that it was not a rumble after all, but more a howl. Then, later, it changed again. He could barely make it out. Moans and barking.

The stairway made a sharp turn. Holt followed it and stopped suddenly.

He was standing in a window in an oddly shaped gray stone building, looking out over the stone city. It was night, and a tapestry of stars filled the sky. Below, near an octagonal pool, six Dan'lai surrounded a Cedran. They were laughing, quick barking laughs full of rage, and they were chattering to each other and clawing at the Cedran whenever it tried to move. It stood above them trapped in the circle, confused and moaning, swaying back and forth. The huge violet eyes glowed brightly, and the fighting-claws waved.

One of the Dan'lai had something. He unfolded it slowly; a long jag-toothed knife. A second appeared, a third; all the foxmen had them. They laughed to each other. One of them darted in at the Cedran from behind, and the silvered blade flashed, and Holt saw black ichor ooze slowly from a long cut in the milk-white Cedran flesh.

There was a blood-curdling low moan and the worm turned slowly as the Dan'la danced back, and its fighting-claws moved quicker than Holt would have believed. The Dan'la with the dripping black knife was lifted, kicking, into the air. He barked furiously, and then the claw snapped together, and the foxman fell in two pieces to the ground. But the others closed in, laughing, and their knives wove patterns and the Cedran's moan became a screech. It lashed out with its claws and a second Dan'la was knocked headless into the waters, but by then two others were cutting off its thrashing tentacles and yet another had driven his blade hilt-deep into the swaying wormlike torso. All the foxmen were wildly excited; Holt could not hear the Cedran over their frantic barking.

He lifted his laser, took aim on the nearest Dan'la, and pushed the firing stud. Angry red light spurted.

A curtain dropped across the window, blocking the view. Holt reached out and yanked it aside. Behind it was a low-roofed chamber, with a dozen level tunnels leading off in all directions. No Dan'lai, no Cedran. He was far beneath the city. The only light was the blue glow of his helmet.

Slowly, silently, Holt walked to the center of the chamber. Half of the tunnels, he saw, were bricked in. Others were dead black holes. But from one, a blast of cool air was flowing. He followed it a long way in darkness until at last it opened on a long gallery full of glowing red mist, like droplets of fire. The hall stretched away to left and right as far as Holt could see, high-ceilinged and straight; the tunnel that had led him here was only one of many. Others—each a different size and shape, all as black as death—lined the walls.

Holt took one step into the soft red fog, then turned and burned a mark into the stone floor of the tunnel behind him. He began walking down the hall, past the endless rows of tunnel mouths. The mist was thick but easy to see through, and Holt saw that the whole vast gallery was empty—at least to the limits of his vision. But he could not see either end, and his footsteps made no sound.

He walked a long time, almost in a trance, somehow forgetting to be afraid. Then, briefly, a white light surged from a portal far ahead. Holt began to run, but the glow had faded before he covered half the distance to the tunnel. Still something called him on.

The tunnel mouth was a high arch full of night when Holt entered. A few meters of darkness, and a door; he stopped.

The arch opened on a high bank of snow and a forest of iron-gray trees linked by fragile webs of ice, so delicate that they would melt and shatter at a breath. No leaves, but hardy blue flowers peeked from the wind-crannies beneath every limb. The stars blazed in the frigid blackness above. And, sitting high on the horizon, Holt saw the wooden stockade and stone-fairy parapets of the rambling twisted Old House.

He paused for a long time, watching, remembering. The cold wind stirred briefly, blowing a flurry of snow in through the door, and Holt shivered in the blast. Then he turned and went back to the hall of the red mist.

Sunderland was waiting for him where tunnel met gallery, half wrapped in the sound-sucking fog. "Mike!" he said, talking normally enough, but all that Holt heard was a whisper. "You've got to come back. We need you, Mike. I can't map without you to get food for me, and Alaina and Takker . . . You must come back!"

Holt shook his head. The mists thickened and whirled, and Sunderland's portly figure was draped and blurred until all Holt could see was the heavy outline. Then the air cleared, and it was not Sunderland at all. It was the Shed-boss. The creature stood silently, the white tentacles trembling on the bladder atop its torso. It waited. Holt waited.

Across the gallery, sudden light woke dimly in a tunnel. Then the two that flanked it began to glow, and then the two beyond that. Holt glanced right, then left; on both sides of the gallery, the silent waves raced from him until all the portals shone— here a dim red, here a flood of blue-white, here a friendly home-sun yellow.

Ponderously the Shed-boss turned and began to walk down the hall. The rolls of blue-black fat bounced and jiggled as it went along, but the mists leeched away the musky smell. Holt followed it, his laser still in his hand.

The ceiling rose higher and higher, and Holt saw that the doorways were growing larger. As he watched, a craggy mottled being much like the Shed-boss came out of one tunnel, crossed the hall, and entered another.

They stopped before a tunnel mouth, round and black and twice as tall as Holt. The Shed-boss waited. Holt, laser at ready, entered. He stood before another window, or perhaps a view-screen; on the far side of the round crystal port, chaos swirled and screamed. He watched it briefly, and just as his head was starting to hurt, the swirling view solidified. If you could call it solid. Beyond the port, four Dan'lai sat with jump-gun tubes around their brows and a cylinder before them. Except—except —the picture was blurred. Ghosts, there were ghosts, second images that almost overlapped the first, but not quite, not completely. And then Holt saw a third image, and a fourth, and suddenly the picture *cracked* and it was as though he was looking into an infinite array of mirrors. Long rows of Dan'lai sat on top of each other, blurring into one another, growing smaller and smaller until they dwindled into nothingness. In unison— no, no, *almost* in unison (for here one image did not move with his reflections, and here another fumbled)—they removed the drained jump-gun tubes and looked at each other and began to laugh. Wild, high barking laughs; they laughed and laughed and laughed and Holt watched as the fires of madness burned in their eyes, and the foxmen all (no, *almost* all) hunched their slim shoulders and seemed more feral and animal than he had ever seen them.

He left. Back in the hall, the Shed-boss still stood patiently. Holt followed again.

There were others in the hall now; Holt saw them faintly, scurrying back and forth through the reddish mist. Creatures like the Shed-boss seemed to dominate, but they were not alone. Holt glimpsed a single Dan'la, lost and frightened; the foxman kept stumbling into walls. And there were things part-angel and part-dragonfly that slid silently past overhead, and something tall and thin surrounded by flickering veils of light, and other presences that he felt as much as saw. Frequently he saw the bright-skinned striders with their gorgeous hues and high collars of bone and flesh, and always slender, sensuous animals loped at their heels, moving with fluid grace on four legs. The animals had soft gray skins and liquid eyes and strangely sentient faces.

Then he thought he spied a man; dark and very dignified, in ship's uniform and cap. Holt strained after the vision and ran toward it, but the mists confused him, bright and glowing as they were, and he lost the sight. When he looked around again, the Shed-boss was gone too.

He tried the nearest tunnel. It was a doorway, like the first; beyond was a mountain ledge overlooking a hard arid land, a plain of baked brick broken by a great crevasse. A city stood in the center of the desolation, its walls chalk white, its buildings all right angles. It was quite dead, but Holt still knew it, somehow. Often Cain narKarmian had told him how the Hrangans build their cities, in the war-torn reaches between Old Earth and the Fringe.

Hesitant, Holt extended a hand past the door frame, and withdrew it quickly. Beyond the arch was an oven; it was not a viewscreen, no more than the sight of Ymir had been.

Back in the gallery he paused and tried to understand. The hall went on and on in both directions, and beings like none he had ever seen drifted past in the mists, death silent, barely noticing the others. The Captain was down here, he knew, and Villareal and Susie Benet and maybe the others—or—or perhaps they *had* been down here, and now they were elsewhere. Perhaps they too had seen their homes calling to them through a stone doorway, and perhaps they had followed and not returned. Once beyond the arches, Holt wondered, how could you come back?

The Dan'la came into sight again, crawling now, and Holt saw that he was very old. The way he fumbled made it clear that he was quite blind, and yet, and yet his eyes *looked* good enough. Then Holt began to watch the others, and finally to follow them. Many went out through the doorways, and they did indeed walk off into the landscapes beyond. And the *landscapes* . . . he watched the ullish worlds in all their weary splendor, as the ul-mennaleith glided to their worships . . . he saw the starless night of Darkdawn, high atop the Fringe, and the darkling dreamers wandering beneath . . . and Huul the Golden (real after all, though less than he expected) . . . and the ghost ships flitting out from the core and the screechers of the black worlds in the Far Arm and the ancient races that had locked their stars in spheres and a thousand worlds undreamed of.

Soon he stopped following the quiet travelers and began to wander on his own, and then he found that the views beyond the doors could change. As he stood before a square gate that opened on the plains of ai-Emerel, he thought for a moment on Old Cain, who had indeed shipped a long ways, but not quite far enough. The Emereli towers were before him, and Holt wished to see them closer, and suddenly the doorway opened onto one. Then the Shed-boss was at his elbow, materializing as abruptly as ever in the Shed, and Holt glanced over into the faceless face. Then he put away the laser and removed his helmet (it had ceased to glow, oddly—why hadn't he noticed that?) and stepped forward.

He was on a balcony, cold wind stroking his face, black Emereli metal behind and an orange sunset before him. Across the horizon the other towers stood, and Holt knew that each was a city of a million; but from here, they were only tall dark needles.

A world. Cain's world. Yet it would have changed a lot since Cain had last seen it, some two hundred years ago. He wondered how. No matter; he would soon find out.

As he turned to go inside, he promised himself that soon he would go back, to find Sunderland and Alaina and Takker-Rey. For them, perhaps, it would be all darkness and fear below, but Holt could guide them home. Yes, he would do that. But not right now. He wanted to see ai-Emerel first, and Old Earth, and the Altered Men of Prometheus. Yes.

But later he would go back. Later. In a little bit.

Time moves slowly in the stone city; more slowly down below where the webs of spacetime were knotted by the Builders. But still it moves, inexorably. The great gray buildings are all tumbled now, the mushroom tower fallen, the pyramids blown dust. Of the ullish windwalls not a trace remains, and no ship has landed for millennia. The ul-mennaleith grow few and strangely diffident and walk with armored hoppers at their heels, the Dan'lai have disintegrated into violent anarchy after a thousand years of jump-guns, the Kresh are gone, the Linkellars are enslaved, and the ghost ships still keep silent. Outwards, the Damoosh are a dying race, though the wisdompools live on and ponder, waiting for questions that no longer come. New races walk on tired worlds; old ones grow and change. No man has reached the core.

The crossworlds sun grows dim.

In empty tunnels beneath the ruins, Holt walks from star to star.

RUTH BERMAN

is a short, quiet young woman of eclectic tastes. One of six children, she was corrupted quite early, when older siblings read to her from Alice in Wonderland *and the* Oz *books. Today she boasts of the finest* Oz *collection in Minnesota. As well as being a science fiction writer and fantasist of great promise, she is also a poet, and has published poetry in* Saturday Review, Toronto Life, Texas Quarterly, *and a dozen little magazines.*

Her fiction also gets around. She has been in all the usual sf markets, of course, but she's also been in places like Jewish Frontiers *and* Cats Magazine, *places your run-of-the-mill sf writer has never heard of. As if that wasn't enough, Berman has been active for a long time in the frenetic world of science fiction fandom. Among her prior credits is a Hugo nomination as Best Fan Writer.*

Ruth lives in Minneapolis, and in years past she has been a teacher, a secretary, an editor, and sundry other things. Currently she's a graduate student in English, working on a doctoral dissertation. Of the story to follow, she writes:

"One of the points in J. M. Barrie's Peter Pan *which has always fascinated me is the fact that Wendy daydreamed Peter*

and told stories about him before she ever met him. What was it like for her to see her private imaginings turn into tangible— and dangerous—reality? Barrie doesn't say directly.

"The problem becomes even more convoluted if the hero of the fantasy world is an extension of the author. This world of Ceremark is based on a world called Coventry (named in an unlikely fashion after Heinlein's 'Coventry'), which was created by a group of Los Angeles area science fiction fans and populated by their alter egos. Not living in the area, I couldn't see directly how the interactions among characters and authors affected each other (a battle between characters could perhaps either reflect or provoke a quarrel between authors). Still, I was so taken by the situation that I wrote a version of 'To Ceremark' using Coventranian characters and creators, even though I knew that I was hampered by not having full knowledge of either of the levels of reality involved.

"In this version, I solved that problem by creating anew both world and creators . . . that is, if it's fair to say I created Ceremark. Philip and Jim Hatchman wouldn't take very kindly to letting someone else claim credit for their world, I fear, but as they're not in this level of reality, they can't stop me . . . can they?"

Nor would they want to, I suspect . . .

—G. R. R. M.

To Ceremark

Ruth Berman

THE U.'s MINIVER CHEEVY CLUB's fall jousting went off well. Holding it early in September, before the university was in session, they were able to reserve the entire mall for the tournament, and half the upper basement of the Student Union Building for the party afterwards.

The weather was cooperative, although somewhat muggy during the afternoon. The various history majors, classicists, Old and Middle English lits, theater students, and eccentrics who went in for the "fun" of padding themselves in thick quilts and walloping each other with wooden swords all got their turns at walloping. The *Daily* photographers had a fine time getting picturesque shots in the heavy light, and the typical Minnesota late-summer electric storm held off until after twilight. They had gathered up the last of the fragile pavilions and transferred to the Union before the first sheet of lightning blasted the western sky open.

Once inside, they had to readjust to their costumes, which had started to look normal on grass under sky. On concrete under neat rows of electric lights, with green walls and a line of sandwich/candy/milk machines for background, the oddity of all the costumes and the attractiveness of the better-constructed ones became once more apparent.

Corey and Marv Atwood, choosing to illustrate the line "He dreamed of Thebes," showed up morbidly as Semele inflamed (a gauzy arrangement of red and orange pointed trim over a white dress) and a blind Oedipus. The Hatchman brothers, of course, had come as the heroes of the stories they'd been writing for the club bulletin, Hatch as Earl Philtron and Jim as Veris of Lujan. They'd built the characters on their own looks and thus looked richly authentic: Jim with his spectrally elongated face and body in Veris' black cloak and gold kilt, and Hatch in the Ceremarkian white uniform of mourning, with his beard trimmed short.

Once the party began, Marv cornered the brothers for a progress report on the current adventure.

"We haven't finished plotting it out," said Hatch.

"I don't think we'll make the deadline," Jim added.

"Traitors." Marv shrugged resignedly. "What's the trouble, can't decide how the Earl's going to get his lands back without Veris there to help? Or are you going to pull a Reichenbach and bring Veris back alive after all?

"Well . . . actually," said Hatch, "Jim thought we should end it where it was, but I told him it wasn't fair to the characters."

"I think we should start writing something different, is all," said Jim.

"Sure," said Hatch. "We will, kid. But later."

"Meanwhile," said Marv, "we're on the hook. *Is* Veris alive?"

Hatch started to admit that they hadn't worked it out that far, but Jim straightened up to his full height and loomed over Marv with a look of exaggerated mystery.

"Okay, okay!" Marv said, giving a chuckle which cracked his makeup. "Ugh," he said, touching his face gingerly. "I'd better go wash this guck off."

"That'll disappoint our resident camera bugs," Hatch said, "unless they've already been at you."

"Sure, when we were out on the mall. Didn't they shoot themselves out then?"

"Nope," said Hatch, pointing.

Marv looked around involuntarily into the explosion of a flash bulb. "Hey, you guys trying to blind me for real?" he said. He groped off toward the men's room, expecting his eyes to clear as he went. It took him a moment to realize that the lights were actually out. He heard someone yelling something about getting the fuses changed in just a moment. "Must be quite a storm," Marv said over his shoulder in what should have been the Hatchmans' direction. "Let me know if you want a ride home."

The walls of the room where the brothers stood glowed softly, but the light seemed dim compared to the flash. At first they saw nothing.

Slowly they became aware of a large grey cauldron in the middle of the floor. It gave off a green light, illuminating a childish face which just barely topped the rim.

The face regarded them with a happy smile, which gradually grew wider and then turned into choked giggling.

"What the hell are you doing?" said a suspicious voice. A thin young man peered in at the door of the room. "Oh, God," he added. He walked swiftly to the girl's side. He bent over the cauldron, and the green light turned into shades of turquoise as it hit the silk of his robes. "Oh, God," he repeated. He went to a low divan in the corner of the room and dropped into it, then stretched his legs out in front and his arms out over the back, and sucked his cheeks in.

The choked giggles had turned to hiccups.

"Oh, most excellent of pupils," he said mournfully, "why do you do these things to me?"

"I did it right, didn't . . . I, Uncle . . . Bvalir?" she demanded, in between hiccups.

"You did it right." He smiled reluctantly. "You remind me of me."

She grinned. "I found the cal . . . culations in your book."

Bvalir took his arms off the back of the couch so that he could drop his head into his hands. He sat that way for some time, hooting with laughter.

The girl walked around Hatch and Jim, surveying them with pride.

"Stop that!" said Jim, grabbing her as she started the circuit a second time. He set her down as far away as his reach allowed, and stomped over to confront her preceptor. "What *is* all this?"

The girl looked up into Jim's face as if delighted to have acquired something so large, and then danced back a pace to see how the other looked and what he would say. Hatch said nothing, but stared intently at the strange child and man and the room around them.

Bvalir held his breath and managed to stop laughing. "A moment," he said to Jim, and turned to the girl. He held out one hand to her. "Give."

She scampered back to the cauldron and picked up a book bound in blue leather from the floor beside it, then brought the volume over and placed it in the outstretched hand.

He checked the first page. "Oh, yes. *That* cycle. And how much did you read?"

"Up to page 136. It was interesting."

"No doubt."

"Yes, like the time you and Father—"

"Quiet, littling. Go tell your father you're in disgrace. And tell him why. But I think," he added, "for his peace of mind, you'd better say you read up to page 40 . . . or so. I didn't set up the programming for all that stuff by myself!"

"Yes, sir." She lingered, gloating over her catch.

"Outgoing, child."

She waved to them, and darted out the door.

"My apologies," said Bvalir. "I hope you will forgive her misuse of the skills of magic."

"Magic! There's no such thing," Jim said belligerently.

Bvalir looked surprised and looked them over again. "I could give you a lecture on the physics of psionic manipulation of continua, if that means anything to you—and if you have the math—but it'd take a good while. And I think it'd be more to the point if I just sent you home. Where do you belong?"

"Valleyride in Ceremark," said Hatch softly.

Jim's head reared up, lengthening his frame even beyond its normal height, but he said nothing.

"Oh? But there's magic—so to speak—in that continuum." He grinned suddenly. "And healthy skepticism in every continuum, too, of course." He stood up and went to the cauldron. "Give me a hand with this."

"What?" said Jim.

"This," he said, struggling to overturn the cauldron.

"Oh, okay," said Jim, glancing at his brother. Hatch nodded, and the three of them upended the cauldron. A shiny, viscous liquid slid out and poured down the drain in the floor beneath.

The drain filled, almost backed up, then gave an obscene gurgle and let the slimy liquid fall through. They lowered the cauldron, and Bvalir pointed his hand at the ceiling and snapped his fingers twice. A jet of water fell into the cauldron. They dumped that out, too, leaving the metal inside clean again.

Bvalir waved them to the divan to sit and rest. Then he went to the wall and ran his finger down it from eye level to the floor. A crack opened in the smooth, glowing substance and irised out to reveal a set of shelves holding an assortment of flasks and canisters and crystals, as well as a stack of paper, and a few sticks which proved to be pencils. Bvalir took one and a sheet of paper, and leaned against the wall for a few minutes, making quick calculations and drawing what looked like doodles. At last he stopped and drew the side of the pencil down the paper. The writing disappeared, and he put both back in the cabinet, then took out an armload of assorted substances, took them back to the cauldron, poured or dropped them in, and called down another blast of water to mix them.

As the powders and crystals dissolved, they streaked the water with intersecting planes of many colors, but the final result was a clear, colorless liquid, like water, except that it gave off a heavy, drowsy scent. Jim and Hatch had to sit bolt upright and keep their eyes staring-wide to stay awake, but Bvalir seemed unaffected.

Finally he turned to them, leaning on the edge of the cauldron to steady himself, and said, "It's all right now. Jump in."

"Now, wait a minute," said Jim.

"This isn't easy to hold. Hurry up."

Jim hesitated, but Hatch rubbed his hand through the short hairs of his beard, bounced to his feet, and began shoving the divan up against the cauldron. Thus bulldozed, Jim gave way and helped move the couch into position to use as a diving board.

Hatch clambered up, turned a last-second look of panic on his brother, and hopped over the edge. He sank out of sight without a splash.

"I can't keep this much longer," Bvalir told Jim. His face was turning pale, and the lines of it stood out sharply even in the dim light.

Jim took a breath, then climbed up, closed his eyes and jumped.

Hatch found himself standing on firm ground with sunlight on his back. By the time his eyes adjusted he found he was staring at a wall, and between him and it were his younger brother's boots. Even as he watched, the long legs came into view on the boots, then hands and torso and arms, and at last the head. He felt oddly embarrassed, as if it was somehow indecent to see his brother half embodied. He looked away, not quite trusting the reality of even Jim's full length. His mouth dropped open at sight of their surroundings.

They were standing in front of a wall, with the ground sloping down from there to a river. The entire slope, up to a few feet of where they stood, was littered with a crowd of people, all dressed in variations of doublet and hose or kilt. Some of them were cheering (mostly the ones at the river's edge), and most were leaning on staffs or sitting on the ground, talking and picnicking. Hatch spotted a couple of pickpockets, a small boy with red hair wandering around with a purposeful air as if playing Master Spy, an assortment of peddlers trying to sell goods to the crowd, and a few herdsmen trying to sell livestock to the peddlers.

Beyond the river a field of improbably green grass stretched up over low hills.

A large blue ship, sail furled, was being rowed upriver by a double row of oarsmen.

A gray-haired man, almost as short as Hatch, was standing on one side of the dock. He was dressed in ceremonial silver, obviously heading an official delegation of welcome. A tall young man was at his side, holding his hand tightly. A group of soldierlike men in red and black stood on the other side of the dock, across from him, and a few men in gray stood at various points between the dock and the wall to keep a path clear to the city gate.

"Good lord!" said Hatch, staring at the gray-haired man. "It's the king."

"And an important occasion," Jim said in an undertone. "He's got the prince out."

Hatch nodded, and stared at the vacant-faced young man, who never let go of his father, except to beg candy from a soldier.

"And . . . that's the Smokewater?" said Jim. He looked doubtfully at the smooth, dark water, as if he'd never seen a river before.

"I suppose it has to be," said Hatch.

Jim put one hand on his brother's shoulder. "Philip Hatchman," he said, using the full name the better to make him squirm, "I'm not sure I like your idea of fun."

Hatch shrugged the hand off. "Sorry." He began to smile. "Calm down, little brother. We know our way around here, don't we?"

"I suppose so."

Hatch tapped the nearest of the crowd of bystanders on the shoulder. "Excuse me, isn't that—"

"Gods, Tarn, look!" The man slugged Hatch, landing his blow squarely on the chin.

"Hey!" Jim yelled as Hatch fell back against him. He struck out over Hatch at their assailant. His blow landed, and the man fell against his companion, the one he had called Tarn. Both were dressed in a candy-cane mixture of pink and silver. "Soldiers," Jim thought, and knew that he knew the uniform, if only he had time to think about it. But he didn't.

Tarn was trying to strike him, but he missed Jim and his fist landed in the small of his comrade's back. "Idiot!" Tarn said. "If you can't stay out of his way, you could at least stay out of mine. And hit low!"

He shoved the first soldier at Hatch.

"But—" said Hatch, thought better of it, and tried to run into the crowd. That turned out to be impossible, but by pushing, squirming, and wriggling, they managed to keep going.

Suddenly they stumbled into the clear. They had reached the aisle between the gateway and the dock.

They tugged at the gate and found it locked, just as the two soldiers burst out into the aisle. The brothers dodged them and went plunging down the hill, their pursuers close behind them.

They were nearly to the bottom of the slope before even the people along the aisle had quite realized what was happening, except for the red-headed boy Hatch had seen from above. The boy was standing in the aisle, and for a moment Hatch thought he was going to run him down. He was running too fast to control his direction well. But the child hopped nimbly aside as he streaked by. A thud, crash, and cursing followed, and he realized that the boy had tripped one of the soldiers.

As they clattered over the dock, Hatch caught a glimpse of the king, colorless with his gray hair and beard, silver suit, and pale face. He seemed to want to speak to them, but there was no time. They skidded to a halt at the end of the dock, with one soldier close behind them, and the ship's gangplank coming down on top of them.

They jumped, one off each side of the dock.

"Stop them!" yelled Tarn.

"Too late for that," said the king.

Tarn was elbowed off the dock by a parade of black-cloaked

men in red doublets and kilts, who came marching off the ship, while the red-and-blacks on the dock pulled out swords and held them over the heads of the newcomers. Somewhere at the back of the crowd two bands began to play, somewhat out of tune with each other.

The king of the Lujanir, brilliant in red and gold, followed his guard off the ship and embraced King Tolemos of Ceremark. Together, the gaudy figure and the pale one marched up the hill.

The two bands got into tune and managed to blow an impressive fanfare.

The door to the High City was flung open from within, and the two kings entered, followed by the Lujan guardsmen, followed in turn by the crowd. In that press of bodies it was hard to do anything but go along with the mob, and the field was empty in a few minutes.

Or almost empty. The red-and-black who had headed the group on the dock was still there, helping the ship's crew raise the gangplank. Once it was freed and well on its way back up over the side of the ship, he knelt down on the upstream side of the dock and stretched his arm out. "Here, sir, let me help you."

Jim had been thrown back against the posts by the river's current. Half-stunned, he accepted the help without question and allowed himself to be pulled onto the dock, where he crouched, cold and dripping.

"Come this way, sir," said the red-and-black, pulling him to his feet. "It's good to see you. Why were you away so long? We thought you were dead!"

The door in the wall had been left open, and they went up the slope and into the City.

"Me, dead?" said Jim. "Not to my knowle—" He caught his foot on a stone and swayed. "Oh, my head!"

"I know what you need, sir—a hot drink."

"A drink at the Gateway!" Jim said derisively. "It isn't real."

"It's right ahead of us," said the red-and-black encouragingly. Across the first street inside the wall stood the Gateway Inn, with its sign showing a gate in a wall, and a bunch of grapes hanging from the arch.

The red-and-black pulled Jim into the inn. "Two mulled ciders," he called.

"Coming, sir," said the innkeeper mildly.

"What . . . who . . ." said Jim.

"Wait till Marek sees you!" the red-and-black said, dropping into a chair at an empty table. Then his face grew sober, and he said, "Don't hold it against me for saying so, but . . . well, he can't control the company. Coldhells know, he's a good soldier, but when it's a—"

"Thanks, soldier, that'll do," said a new voice.

"Marek!" The soldier bumped his chair away from the table and scrambled to his feet. He bowed, and before the reproof he expected could begin, said, "Look, sir! The captain's back!"

Marek's face lit up, and despite himself he began to bow toward Jim. But he straightened with a jerk and stubbornly held his face turned away. "You're drunk, soldier. Can't you tell a fake when you see one?"

"But—"

"Pay your score and get out."

"But we haven't even had one—" The soldier looked up, craning his neck to face Marek, and instantly gave it up. He flinched away, then shrugged, dropped a purse on the table beside Jim, bowed in a direction halfway between Jim and Marek, and marched out of the tavern as if to drums.

Marek watched him go and kept his eye on the door as he said, "Would you care to tell me what the pox you're up to?"

Jim stared at the tall, gaunt man whose face echoed his own, except for the lighter brown of the hair and the absence of a beard. "Marek," he said, enjoying the sound of the spoken name. "And you really do look like him."

"Don't try to be funny," Marek said, turning to glare at him. The glare didn't survive the turn. He looked directly at Jim for the first time, with blank astonishment. "Ver! I thought—" He stopped short and tried to recapture the glare. He failed, but said quietly, "Listen, friend. Don't think you can get past me.

You'd hold it against me yourself if you did." One side of his mouth quirked up. "And I've got enough trouble without that." He took a deep breath, let it out in a sigh, and left without another word.

The drinks came.

"Where'd your friend go?" said the innkeeper suspiciously.

"Ordered back to quarters," said Jim. "Don't worry, he left money to pay for the drinks."

"Did he so? Then, if you please, master—"

Jim handed him the purse. The innkeeper took out two coins. He bounced one on the table and bit at the other. He pocketed both and returned the purse to Jim. "Begging your pardon, master," he said.

"Yeah, sure," said Jim. He wondered what was going on. And where Hatch had disappeared to. And what he ought to do about it. After a moment he decided that the first thing to do, assuming the Ceremarkian landscape around him was not a hallucination, was to find Hatch. He stood up, and his head began throbbing where he'd hit it against the dock. His eyes would not focus, and he gripped the table, afraid of falling. He sat down again and his vision cleared, but he still felt more like someone who was having a hallucination than like someone who was really there. He considered getting in contact with Veris' friend the tobacconist, but then remembered that the only description he and Hatch had given of the shop's location was "halfway up the High in the center of a maze of old alleys built and rebuilt over the years till not a path of it ran straight for more than five yards."

He revised his decision. The first thing to do was to drink the hot cider.

Hatch coughed and sputtered and flailed his arms in a manner which did not do credit to his lifelong residence in a city of lakes, and finally got himself into a definite crawl stroke which took him out of the swift current in the middle of the stream into the shallows. From there he was able to scramble ashore, and he squelched across the bank to a dusty road, where he stood shivering in the light breeze. He saw a familiar black and gold figure trudging up the road. "Hey, wait up!" he yelled.

Veris of Lujan spun around, then relaxed as he saw Hatch's face. "Phil! Good to see you. What's been going on?"

"I'm soaked through."

"I can see that much," Veris said. "Never mind, you'll dry soon enough. Where are we, near the High City?"

"Well, yes. I don't see how it can be anything else. Just back upstream."

"Good enough." He started off, smiling back at Hatch. "Going my way?"

"Right." Hatch came up alongside, feeling relieved that Jim was evidently not angry at having been dragged into a scrape. So his use of Hatch's first name was just teasing, Hatch concluded.

They walked along in silence and soon reached the city wall. Hatch looked around nervously, but there were no soldiers in sight, and very few people of any sort to be seen outside the wall, except the sailors unloading cargo from the riverboat. Then something pulled at his sleeve. He jumped away, then laughed nervously at himself and looked down at cool gray eyes under a familiar flop of red hair.

"Who's this?" said Veris.

"Hi," said the boy. "I got some apples. Want any?"

"Yes, thanks,' said Hatch, suddenly realizing that exercise had made him hungry. Both men accepted an apple. Hatch ate his quickly, looked around for a wastebasket, realized he wasn't likely to find one, and forced himself to eat the core, too. "Where'd these come from?" he said, spitting out the seeds.

"Stole them off the ship yonder, the way you showed me."

"Me?" said Hatch.

"Well, I was hungry, and I didn't know what else to do. I'm sorry. Anyhow," the boy went on, in a practical sort of voice, "you'd best go look for a hide-hole. The High's full of Lord Odander's men, bouncing about like carnival candies. I thought maybe the king'd hide you, though they say he's watched, but—"

"Yes, he's bound to be the best chance," Veris interrupted.

The boy looked to Hatch for confirmation.

Hatch rubbed his forehead. Events were moving too fast for him to follow. He and Jim had always had to chart out Ceremarkian politics and keep the chart up on the wall. Still, the king was supposed to be trustworthy. "All right."

"Come on, then," said the boy. He shoved his hair off his forehead and trotted up the slope.

They entered the gate safely, but as they turned inside the boy suddenly dived into a doorway, pulling Hatch along. Veris followed automatically. "What is it?" he asked.

"Inside!" said the boy.

They slipped through the door and found themselves in a crowded, noisy inn.

"Well, what's the matter?" said Hatch.

"I saw my father coming." The boy's face hardened as much as it could. "I hate him."

"You do?"

"Well . . . well"—the defiant expression melted, and the boy stared down at the floor—"no. But he hates you. And he says my uncle Brin is a coward because he doesn't hate you. And that's not true. Brin sono' Connor is no more a coward than he is. So . . . so there it is . . . I wish Father liked you."

Hatch wanted to demand a more coherent explanation, but the boy was near crying. "We'll work things out somehow," he said, wondering what he was promising.

The innkeeper bustled up to them, chanting his formula like a spell. "If the gentlemen will be gracious enough to wait a moment, it will be my pleasure—" He broke off and peered at Veris, away, and back again. "Amazing!" he murmured. "—to serve them as soon as a little space is free," he finished up.

"As you will," said Veris, cocking his gaunt head back to inspect the innkeeper, who bobbed them a half-bow and vanished into a ring of impatient customers. "I think good business is addling his brain, such as it is."

"No, he's confused over that guy in the corner there," said Hatch. "From the back he looks like you."

"True enough. It's not Marek, though. I wonder if he's a cousin." Veris started toward the corner.

Hatch caught at his arm, suddenly hearing a familiar and unwelcome voice.

"—so we're on duty," it said from just outside the door. "But searching's hot work, Tarn, and I need a drink to carry me through. After all, it wasn't our fault he got out."

"No, but it's your fault we didn't get him when we had the chance."

Hatch edged past the first rows of tables, taking his companions with him, as the door opened.

"Besides, the place's too crowded," Tarn said.

"It isn't. And what do you mean, my fault? You weren't so much help as that comes to."

"Ahhh, tell it to Odander's ass," said Tarn. "Now you've got me thirsty, too."

"Innkeeper!" they bawled in unison.

"Don't look now," said Hatch, "but I think we're about to be in trouble."

The boy looked. "Right enough. They're the same two as tried to nab you by the Smokewater. We'd best get out."

The movement of the boy's bright hair caught Tarn's eye.

Veris was just saying, "Our best chance is the cellar—" when the two soldiers sprang on them. Veris somersaulted, bringing his tacklers along with him. He found himself upright, sitting on top of a groggy soldier. He rubbed at his head impatiently, to clear away dizziness, then pulled himself up with the aid of a chair. He pulled the chair out from under its startled occupant and used it as a cudgel to knock out the other soldier.

Tarn, still half conscious, struggled to roll over and get to his feet, but the boy grabbed a plate and smashed it on his head. Tarn groaned and collapsed.

"Good lad," said Veris. "Let's move." He took the boy's hand and led the way to the bar, ducked behind it, ran down the steps there, and through the racks of barrels till he found a small room at the end of the cellar, half lit by a dirty window at the top of the wall. He darted in and held the door open for the others, and only then realized that he had lost one of his companions. "Phil?" he called in the strained voice of one who shouts but does not want outsiders to hear it.

"He's still upstairs!" said the boy, and turned to run back

"Hey, none of that," said Veris, blocking his way. "He probably went out the front." He scooped the boy up and stood him on his shoulder. "See anything?"

The boy pushed open the cellar window and looked out, blinking at the light. "I see him. My lord Phi–i–ltron!" His voice was lost in the clatter of street traffic. He pulled his head in. "He's round the corner. Come on, or we'll lose him."

Veris set the boy down and shook his head. "No. If he gets to the king he'll be safe enough, and I doubt we can be any help to him in getting there." Veris looked out the door back into the cellar. There was so far no sign of pursuit. He murmured a small thank you to the gods, closed the door, and leaned the full weight of his body against it. "Maybe we can meet him at Kingshall later. But, just for the moment, by your leave, I want to find out what the hell is going on. What's Lord Odander up to? And who are you? One of Phil's Cliff-dwellers, I gather."

"I'm Rvadrin sono' Duonal and Mag."

"R—" Veris could not shape the sounds.

"Rory, for short," the boy said scornfully.

"All right, Rory. And Odander?"

"He captured Lord Philtron and tried to take over his lands —including the Cliffs. Well, my father doesn't like the earl, but he wouldn't stand for that, so he raised the tribes, and got me out of the Croftcenter before Odander took it over, and then he was going to try to win the Cliffs from him, but meanwhile he got away—I mean . . ." Rory lost track of his pronouns and trailed off.

"All right," said Veris. "I get the idea."

Jim stood up with careful dignity and looked around in time to see Hatch charging out the front door. "Hatch!" he yelled. "Hey, Phil!" But his voice went unheard. He steadied himself on the chair back, and reflected that the cider was considerably more potent than it had tasted. He knew he had no chance of catching up to his brother, and he felt some doubt of his ability to balance at all. Meanwhile, there were two unpleasantly familiar candy-cane uniforms stretched out on the floor.

The innkeeper ran past him, heading after the intruders who had gone in back of his own bar into his cellars without so much as a begging-your-pardon.

"Hey!" said Jim, buttonholing the little man and looming over him in a spectral sort of way.

"One moment, honored sir, if you'll excuse me—"

"No," said Jim firmly. "Where's a back room?"

"Sir?" said the innkeeper. "Ah . . . there's an outhouse in the courtyard, but if you want a tub, I—"

"No, no, no. Not a *bath*room. A back room. Front room's too noisy. People jumping all over the place."

"Oh. Yes, indeed, sir. It's bad for the trade. And will you be having another of the same there?"

"I guess so."

"I will be just one moment, dear sir—"

"No," said Jim, putting one hand on the innkeeper's shoulder to steady himself. "Now."

The innkeeper looked down at the hand, then up at Jim. "This way, sir," he said, and led Jim up half a flight of stairs. Where the stairs turned, to continue on to the building's second floor, there was a landing which extended far across the wall. Heavy curtains made a set of quiet alcoves there.

Jim thrust the purse toward the innkeeper. The little man hesitated, obviously weighing his right to compensation for the disturbance and the stranger's ignorance against the stranger's height and strength. Then he dug a handful of silver coins out and scurried back down the stairs, saying over his shoulder as he went, "One cider, coming instantly, sir."

At the bottom of the stairs, he ran into the two soldiers, now muzzily conscious.

"Where'd they go?" said Tarn, grabbing the innkeeper's shoulders and leaning on them.

The innkeeper's control finally gave way. "If you mean, honored sirs, the custom-bringers you jumped on without any provocation a decent body could see, let me tell you, sirs, that I don't know. They left. Suppose you do the same?" He twisted free and went to the fire to set a long-delayed order of mulled wine to mull. He stood shivering there, despite the heat of the fire, and waited to see how the soldiers would react to his outburst.

The soldiers looked at each other and shrugged simultaneously. "Oh, come on," said Tarn. "Maybe we can still catch him." They stomped out and tried to bang the door behind them, but it was too heavy and thick to be pulled shut in a hurry, so they simply glared back with expressions as terrifying as they could manage and disappeared into the street's traffic.

The innkeeper thanked all the gods he could think of, a task that kept him occupied for some time, and then decided to complete the soothing of his nerves by having a cider himself before serving the stranger abovestairs and the other waiting customers. And routing out the intruders below could certainly wait a bit.

"So Philtron escaped before going through a formal surrender?" said Veris. "Well, that's typical. And it explains why Odander's men are after him. Strange, though." He rubbed his forehead, frowning. "Last I remember hearing, the king had Odander under control."

"He stole a magic sword from the Summer's Temple," said Rory.

"Did he!" Veris frowned yet more deeply, then shrugged it off. "And now your people are up in arms?"

Rory shook his head. "I don't think so. Not after Philtron got out. My uncle swore faith to the earl, you see. My father says that that doesn't bind him—my father, I mean—and he was going to lead the Cliffdwellers in my name—"

"In your name?"

"Uncle Brin doesn't have any children, and I'm his sister-son, so . . . But I don't think they'd follow unless my uncle said they could."

"Maybe not," said Veris. "By the way, what's your objection to the scheme?"

"I inherit the oath, too," Rory said, straightening his back in a conscious effort at a noble pose. Then he shrugged and settled down, adding gloomily, "Besides, I like Lord Philtron. He was nice to me when I was at his court in the Croftcenter. And the king's his cousin. We'd have to fight off the whole country to get free of the earldom."

Veris raised his eyebrows. "I wish some of my colleagues had your grasp of the realities, my boy. Well." He went to the window and held out his arm. "Let's go."

"And meet Lord Philtron at Kingshall?"

"No. No, I think we'll go to the Lujan office and see if enough of my men are at hand to make it worth while for us to try a raid—wouldn't any army want to get hold of a magic sword?"

Rory grinned. "I wouldn't doubt it."

Veris boosted the boy out the window, then hoisted himself up and squirmed through, with a helping hand from Rory. The passers-by in the street made no comment. It was only the Gateway Inn again, after all.

The wooden hall was large, rectangular, and unassuming. Only the crystal gate, gleaming in sunlight, gave away its identity as the home of the kings of Ceremark during the past seven generations. Hatch grinned, recalling his descriptions of Philtron's half-snobbish, half-aesthetic sneers at Kingshall as a mere upstart among seats of power. It couldn't compare with the Croftcenter, the stone tower which had been the capitol, back in the days when king of Ceremark and earl of Ceremark were the same title. But though Kingshall was less magnificent, it was better guarded. Hatch wondered if he dared walk in under Philtron's name, but, after dithering a few moments, decided to give the alias Philtron sometimes used. It would be equally good at getting him to Tolemos and less likely to get him spotted by the earl's enemies.

He took one more admiring look at the shining gate, then marched up and announced himself as Ormraven, requesting audience with the king. His white uniform drew odd looks, the more so as it was stained and crumpled, but he was brought in as far as the small room behind the main hall. There he was told to wait.

The chairs were of oak, beautifully carved and polished, just as he had described them. He discovered, however, that they were also very hard and built to the shape of a man of average height. For a short man, like Hatch, they were a pain in the neck, the small of the back, and across the middle of the calves. Hatch wondered how Tolemos could stand it, and decided the answer must be cushions. But there didn't seem to be any around at the moment, so he gave up on the chairs and stretched out flat on the wood floor. It was just as hard, but not quite as uncomfortable.

"——n't that the Earl of Ceremark?"

The startled voice woke Hatch.

"No, that's a cousin's bastard, Ormraven. A clown."

"You mean a spy?"

"If you caught him in Lujan and chose to say so, I'd have no power to say you were lying."

Hatch opened his eyes and was disappointed to discover that both kings had changed out of their ceremonial robes into comfortable but dull robes of gray wool. "Hello," he said.

Tolemos shook his head sadly. "Orm, you have no sense of courtesy. In fact," he added, "you have no sense. I'm busy. Go away and come back later."

"Go away?" said Hatch, trying to clear the remains of the nap out of his thinking.

"Yes, that's the idea," said Tolemos encouragingly. He turned to the visiting king. "Pardon me, if you will——"

"Of course."

"Would you go on ahead and tell Earl Odander I will be with you both shortly? Many thanks." He waited till his guest was out of the room, then dragged Hatch to his feet. "Come on, then. Clown, I said, and maybe I was right, too."

Hatch stumbled after him into the private Littlecouncil's room, across that and into the king's bedroom, and across that to the bolt-hole in the wall.

"What the plague are you doing out, anyway?" said Tolemos, as angrily as he could and still whisper. "Don't you realize Odander's men are hide-and-go-seeking all over town for you? And I've got our good cousin here in the castle right now, negotiating with me and the Lujan besides for permission to keep troops in Old Ceremark."

"Are you going to let him?" said Hatch curiously.

"How should I know?" Tolemos opened the panel. "I don't know what kind of power he has to bargain with—yet. Now hurry up!"

Hatch stepped inside the panel, and Tolemos slid it shut, leaving him in a musty-smelling darkness. He slid one foot around warily, and came to a sheer drop-off.

A little more investigation revealed that the drop-off ended six inches down in a narrow stair tread. Hatch picked his way down and came at last to a dirt floor. He followed the wall to one side for a few paces. The room was evidently narrow; when he tripped on something soft he bumped his head on the stone of the adjoining wall, lost interest in trying to explore where he couldn't see, and decided to resume his interrupted nap. The stuff he had tripped on turned out to be a little heap of cushions, which he spread out beneath him. The cushions made a soft enough surface, and his body's clock was telling him that it was long past bedtime, even the bedtime on the night of a party.

When he woke, the room was partly lit by an oil lamp perched precariously on a torch sconce at the foot of the stairs. King Tolemos was there, talking to a young man dressed in a dirty tunic and hose of faded green.

"But I haven't been outside," the young man was saying. He shook his head with a look of disbelief.

Hatch caught a glimpse of his own face and pinched himself —not so much to be sure of being awake as to be sure that he was still where he thought he was and not on the other side of the bolt-hole. Then he realized that he was looking at Philtron, the earl of Ceremark in the kingdom of Ceremark.

"In fact," said Philtron, "I was asleep most of the day, until you came down singing alarums. Gods! Tom, what sort of fool do you think I am?"

For a moment Tolemos grinned.

"Don't answer that," said Philtron hastily.

Sighing, Tolemos sat down on the lowest step. "Let's say that I think you have faults. But I prefer you to Odander. At least after I'm dead you'll probably keep my boy alive when you take over the throne."

"What?" Philtron's head jerked back, and he surveyed the king's face. "I don't want to be king. I have enough troubles."

"Of course. But I doubt that what you want will matter very much when the time comes. In the meantime, do me a favor and stay alive, will you?"

"Believe me, I'm not fool enough to go for a swim in the Smokewater when our dear Dandy's men are swarming in the High. Not unless I'm turning into a sleepwalker in my old age."

"My reports agree that you were there. I saw you myself."

Hatch picked himself off the floor, groaning at the stiffness in his legs and back. "I think I'm the problem."

Philtron and Tolemos whirled on him, both drawing knives out in the same motion.

"Who's here?" Philtron asked quietly.

Hatch stepped into the light to show his face. "Hi, I . . . I happen to look like you. I'm Philip Hatchman. Hatch for short." He held out his hand and tried to look trustworthy.

Philtron sucked his lower lip in and raised his eyebrows, producing an exaggerated look of surprise that made Hatch chuckle and Tolemos groan. Philtron flipped his knife in the air and sheathed it. "Oh, calm down, Tolly. So now we know that the problem's a double-walker. There's no harm done, and all we have to do is keep him locked up."

"Now, wait a minute!" said Hatch.

Philtron went on, paying no attention to him, "In fact, he may have done some good. My gentle cousin must be in a frenzy by now."

"Who, Odander or me?" said Tolemos.

Philtron gave him an angelic smile. "And you can drive a better bargain with Dandy when he's in a frenzy. He doesn't think clearly when he's angry, poor fellow."

A smile escaped on one side of the king's face. "How true! He even conceded neutrality to me and my guards just now."

"Did he indeed?" Philtron's smile became, if anything, even sweeter, and he started to ask for more details on the cousins' talks.

But the panel at the top of the stairs slid aside, letting a little window light from the room above spill down into the bolt-hole.

Philtron grabbed Hatch's arm and spun him off into the shadows of one corner, spinning himself off into the opposite shadows at the same time.

"Are you down there, sir?" a voice called, striking a neat balance between enough volume to carry down the stairs and not enough to carry outside the walls of the bedroom.

Tolemos relaxed and nodded to Philtron. "Yes, I'm here, Crosskeys. What is it?"

A round-faced king's guard with two crossed scars on his forehead, belying the innocence of his expression, came down the stairs in three jumps, and launched into his report. "Lord Odander's men are fighting a band of Lujanir, and there's a horde outside the High trying to storm the gate. The Lujan leader *looks* like Captain Veris—"

"His half-brother," Tolemos said.

"No, sir, Marek's in attendance with their king here, and they both claim it's an imposter."

Tolemos looked at Hatch. "Another double-walker?"

"Yes, sir."

Philtron chuckled suddenly and stepped into the light. "What about the bunch at the gate? Where're they from?"

Crosskeys gaped as he realized he was seeing two out of three with the same face, then recovered himself, shrugged, and said, "I don't know. Their horses look like that kind of shaggy little pony I've seen on your land, sometimes, sir."

"Ponies!" Philtron let out a whoop and went bursting up the stairs before they could stop him, filching Crosskeys' sword out of its scabbard on the way.

"Phil! you whoreson crazy fool, wait!" Tolemos ran after him, tripped on the bottom step, and gave it up. "He moves too fast when he gets in that mood. So. What's Odander doing about all this, by the way?"

Crosskeys frowned, wrinkling the double scar on his forehead. "He charged off, sir. Meaning to get his magic sword and join his men, if guessing's in order."

"Oh, yes, very much so." Tolemos sighed and combed at his beard with his fingers. "Master Hatchner."

"Yes, sir?" Hatch felt foolish calling anyone sir, but he found it was not too difficult in front of Tolemos. He felt he could almost have brought out a "Your Majesty" without stumbling on it, but he knew that Tolemos disliked ceremony.

"Could you impersonate Philtron, at need?"

"I suppose."

Tolemos turned to the guard. "Get Master Hatchner a hood and a sword, and keep him out of sight till his face is under cover. Then get him out of the Hall. And then bring the guardsmen out—staffs only, no edged weapons. Push that fight out of the High. Once you get them through the gate, Phil's Cliff-dwellers should be able to finish off Odander's lot. And the king will have been neutral throughout, doing no more than to keep the peace with the High."

Crosskeys looked startled, then chuckled. "Yes, sir."

Tolemos said to Hatch, "Find Philtron and Veris . . . the double . . . if you can, and tell them the Cliffdwellers are outside. And tell Phil to get outside and keep those barbarians of

his off the walls. They can wait to fight until the enemy's outside. If you can't find him, try to hold them back yourself."

"Yes, sir," said Hatch. His stomach cringed at the idea, but
he tried to ignore his feelings.

Crosskeys clambered up the steep staircase, waited just long
enough for Hatch to reach the top behind him, and then set
off at a brisk, businesslike trot. Hatch followed directly behind,
his face hidden by the taller man's bulk.

Crosskeys took him to the guardroom. The watch, a tall
young woman playing a lap-sized keyboard, looked up at their
entrance and nodded a welcome without missing a beat. "What
news of the brawl?" she asked as she played.

"As in dance, or in battle?" Crosskeys pulled out a plain
gray cloak with no embroidery of rank, and a sword belt from
the racks.

"Battle, my lad, battle," she said, although the notes from
her fingers seemed to belie her.

"Little enough. We're to get them outside the walls. With
luck, that'll do it. Staffs only." He tapped his chin thoughtfully,
then added a helmet and handed the lot over to Hatch.

"I'll pass the word," said the woman. She ended the piece
with an elaborate, trilling flourish, set down her keyboard, and
ran lightly from the room.

"Do you know the way out?" Crosskeys asked.

Hatch nodded.

"Good. Till we meet, then." Crosskeys turned away and
began laying out helmets and quarterstaves.

Hatch started to protest, then realized that Crosskeys was
paying him the compliment of considering him able to take on
a delegated responsibility. Tolemos' own habit of assuming self-
reliance in his own men had evidently spread among them.
Hatch took a deep breath which was half a shiver, put on the
gear Crosskeys had assigned him, and marched himself out of
Kingshall.

The street was as jammed as the river dockside had been,
but this crowd was not an audience. It was struggling to flee
and could not, for no one knew precisely where the danger lay

or precisely what it was, except that it came from Odander of Meadale's soldiers. Shouts of "To me! Get the Dalians!" or more simply "Dalians! Get 'em!" indicated attempts to rally the city people to fight, but the shouts came from different parts of the crowd, and the segments trying to rally kept colliding with the segments trying to get to safety.

Hatch tried to squirm through, but fell and was caught among trampling feet. He could not find room to stand up in, so he crawled, trying to follow the flow of his particular section of crowd so as not to be stepped on. But even so booted feet kept slamming against his sides and his rear, and the dust and the smell of horse dung got into his nose and throat, choking him. He was half unconscious when someone's stumbling shoved his head and chest into a clear, dark space. He knocked against something steady, grabbed it, and heard a woman's startled cry somewhere far above him.

Hands grabbed him and pulled him out and up, into light and clean air. "Thanks," Hatch managed to get out.

"You!" said an unfamiliar voice.

"No, I'm not," said Hatch in what was becoming a reflex, "I only look like him." He tugged at his cloak, trying to get the hood back in place. He found that he was leaning against a wall of a house, supported on one side by a burly, red-haired man and on the other by the woman whose wide skirts had formed the space where he'd found shelter from the crush of frightened townsfolk. The couple looked vaguely familiar.

"Now, Duonal—" said the wife. Something in the timbre of her voice and the man's red hair suddenly told Hatch who they were.

"Oh! you're that kid's parents!" he said unspecifically, but they understood anyway.

"You've seen Rory?" Duonal's voice was so thunderous that it actually silenced the crowd for several yards around them.

"Clear the way from the Hall!" yelled Hatch, taking advantage of the lull. "Clear the way! The guardsmen are coming to stop the fighting!" He turned to Duonal. "I saw him, but I don't know where he is now. Help me yell."

"Help you?" Duonal snorted at the idea.

"It's either that or be squashed like berries in a jam pot," said his wife. "Clear the way!" she called, aiming her voice to bounce off the upper windows of the buildings near them.

Duonal frowned, but began to do the same. Hatch tried, but could not catch the knack of the echoes, so he simply followed downhill in their wake, shouting as loud as he could. The crowd slowly shifted before them and melted down side streets.

By the time the guardsmen came charging out of Kingshall, Hatch was halfway down the hill and could see the bright colors of the knot of Lujanir and Meadale soldiers struggling in front of the gate. He could hear the noises of the Cliffdwellers beyond the wall.

"Wait," he said, catching at the shoulders of Duonal and his wife. "I've to get over the wall."

"Why?" said Duonal.

"To warn the Cliffdwellers not to break in. The guardsmen are going to get that lot outside, and they can fight them then."

Duonal turned to his wife. "Mag, your damned fool of a brother has raised the folk to come help Philtron!"

"I expect so," she agreed. "Would you rather have Dalians in charge?"

Duonal made an exasperated growling noise and said, "True. Come on." He and Mag set off along a side street, and Hatch followed after them. They detoured past the main area of the brawl and made it easily to the city's edge. The two Cliffdwellers pulled out their ropes and picks and began scaling the wall.

A harassed guard atop the wall spotted them as they neared the top, and she complained to the clouds, "Gods! They're coming and going!" She stretched out her pike to knock a climber off the outside of the wall and then turned to deal with the two on the inside.

"No!" Hatch called up, throwing back his hood. "We've got to get over to make them wait outside."

She stared, then shrugged one shoulder and knelt to give Duonal and Mag a hand.

Once up, the two Cliffdwellers dropped down a rope, and Hatch tried to climb up. In street clothes plus a cape and sword, the process was not as simple as it had been in gym classes. Mag and Duonal exchanged a shocked look, then lowered a loop for him to sit in and pulled him up.

From atop the wall he could see the Meadale and Lujanir soldiers fighting, one street over, and the king's men pressing in around them. A flashing red streak of light shone in the middle of the brawl, and he suddenly realized that it was a flaming sword, in Odander's hands. He shuddered and turned away quickly. "Do you see Brin?" he asked Mag.

She gave him yet another surprised look, and waved to a tall redhead who, along with half a dozen others, was swinging a log against the gate. "Hey! Brother!" she called, cupping her hands to aim her voice at him. "Stop! Wait!" Meanwhile, Duonal had set out a rope, and Hatch began shinnying down. He managed not to take the skin off his hands in the process.

Brin left the log and loped along the wall. His face brightened as he saw who was there. "Good to see you alive. What's the news?"

"Get your men lined up around the gate and keep them still. The Dalians are about to get thrown out of town. But there'll be Lujanir mixed in with them, so watch where you hit. And Lord Odander has a flame-sword."

Duonal and Mag finished climbing down, and embraced Brin —Mag cordially, Duonal not.

Brin laughed and pulled the rope off the wall for them. "Duonal, will you help?" he said.

"I . . . yes."

Brin and Duonal raced back to the main crowd of Cliffdwellers, and set about ranging them in ambush. Hatch looked around for some safe place to hide himself, but the open hillside down to the river offered no cover, and the ponies had scattered far up and down the stream as they grazed. He looked to see what Mag was doing, and discovered that she was trotting matter-of-factly into a place among the soldiers, her pick held ready to double as battle-ax.

Hatch pulled out the sword he had been given, sighed, and skittered into line beside her.

The gates opened, and the seething masses of combatants spilled through and were shoved out. Hatch watched stupidly, looking for familiar faces. Odander stood out, the flame sword clearing a wide space around him and scorching the grass at his feet, so that his path was marked by a brown stain. Hatch could see Jim's face and his own . . . Philtron's, he corrected himself. A bright flash of red hair down around the level of Philtron's chest told him that Mag's son was there, too. And then Cliffdwellers were charging forward, and Hatch found himself with his sword held out, running at a Meadale soldier's back.

The sword went in and stuck, jarring him to a halt. The man screamed, and blood spurted out on the pink cloth of his uniform.

Hatch tugged at the sword.

It came free, and the man fell, still bleeding.

Someone else's sword slammed down into his shoulder. Hatch screamed and doubled up, vomiting. He remembered to roll, and so fell downhill, out of the area where he could be trampled by the combatants. As soon as he had finished throwing up, he tried to move on, in case the motion of the fight brought it down on him, but his shoulder hurt too much. Besides, the space around him was still clear.

Then he felt a warmth coming towards him.

He struggled up to an unstable crouch, on knees and one good hand, and saw Odander running at him.

Hatch managed to raise his head. "I'm not Philtron," he said as loudly as he could over the sour, scratchy taste in his mouth. "Look behind you."

"That's an old trick," said Odander. He raised his sword.

Rory tackled his legs from behind, and the two of them fell

and rolled. The boy wailed as his sleeve and the grass caught fire.

Then Veris and Philtron were up with them, beating out the flames. Philtron snatched up the flame-sword and held it high in the air.

"Yield, Odander," he said, "or I'll bring this down."

Odander said nothing. Philtron hesitated and looked at Veris, who jerked off Odander's helmet and struck him on the head with the flat of his blade, knocking him out.

"Meadale, yield yourselves!" called Philtron. He had learned the echo trick from the Cliffdwellers, and his voice came rolling back from the city walls. "The earl is down, Dalians! Put down your swords!"

A few obeyed. For the rest, the battle turned into a rout, with Meadale soldiers fleeing to either side, up and down the river, pursued by Lujanir and Cliffdwellers.

Philtron started to kneel by Rory; then, remembering the sword, he cursed and remained standing, arm up in the air. "Mag! Duonal!" he called.

They were already running to meet him, and they knelt by their son.

"How is he?" said Philtron.

Mag, tearing part of her skirt into a bandage, made no answer, but Duonal said, "He'll do, Lowlander."

"Thanks," said Philtron. He turned away, looking for Veris.

"Lowlander," said Duonal.

"Yes?" Philtron turned back.

"My wife's fool brother has pledged you his faith, I understand."

"Yes."

"I don't pledge mine—but I'll let well enough alone."

"Thanks, Duonal," said Philtron. The two men held each other's gaze for a moment.

"If anyone had the sense to bring salve and proper bandages in their packs," Mag said, "someone should be calling the ponies in."

Duonal nodded and went loping down the hill.

Veris finished tying up Odander (using the earl's belt and cloak) and came back to Philtron. "Isn't your arm getting tired?" he said, grinning at the statue pose.

"Yes. Want to take it?" said Philtron.

"I thought I did, but on second thought . . . no."

Philtron rubbed his free hand across his forehead. "Well, I'll think of some way to handle it, I suppose. Gods, Veris, is it really you? I thought you were dead."

"He is," Hatch said feebly. The river, the hillside, and the city wall were fading out around him, and he wondered if he was fainting or dying.

The blackness lifted, and he was lying on a stone floor in a dim room. Bvalir's face loomed into view. "You're not Philtron and Veris," he said reproachfully.

"No," said Hatch. He could hear Jim's voice saying no at the same moment, but his brother was not in his field of vision, and he felt too tired to look around.

"Where do you really belong?"

"In the Student Union at the U.," said Jim.

"The what?"

"The U. of M. The University—"

"Well, never mind. I suppose we can figure it out." Bvalir was holding a staff with a crystal on the end. The crystal lit as he spoke, throwing miniature rainbows about the room as he moved the staff back and forth. "And how did you like Ceremark?" he asked.

"Aren't you going to help my brother?" Jim said angrily.

"What? Oh, the shoulder. No, I'll just be a moment, and you can bind it when you're back. I don't want to start this spell all over from the beginning. You had an interesting time, evidently."

"Yeah," said Hatch.

"I didn't see much of anything," said Jim. "I got trapped in the Gateway Inn and . . . well, I drank myself under the table waiting for the coast to clear."

"You're crazy!" Hatch said. "You were . . ." The effort of contradiction was too much for him, and he felt himself blacking out again.

When he woke again he was sitting on a tile floor, supported by someone who held him up from behind. The neon lights of the Student Union hung over him in their orderly rows. Cory, still in her silken flames, and Jim were binding up his shoulder with bandages from the club's first-aid kit. "Hi, Cory," Hatch said.

"Hey, hold still," said Marv's voice from behind him. "I can't keep you steady if you squirm. What'd you guys run into, anyway? I thought everyone'd left when that guy in the dragon suit finally finished getting it off of him and took off. Then I start to go around and see if people left stuff, and I find you two still here, with old Hatch bleeding all over the floor."

"I dunno," said Hatch, more or less honestly.

"He must've run into something," said Jim cautiously.

"Well, you probably ought to stop by the Health Service," said Cory practically. "That bandage looks pretty professional, if I do say so, but I suppose they can fix it better." She started packing up the kit.

"Yeah, I guess so."

"Think you can stand up?" said Marv.

"Uh-huh."

Marv helped him up, steadying him from the side. "How do you feel?"

"Okay. Dizzy."

Jim added support from the other side, and they moved slowly toward the back door of the Union.

"Well," said Marv, "I guess that settles the question of whether you're going to finish your stuff in time for the next bulletin."

"Oh, I think we'll manage to finish the story, one way or another," said Jim.

They emerged into dawnlight. The grass in back of the Student Union was silvered with leftover raindrops, and sunlight came edging back from the river along the quiet street as the sun rose over the hospital.

"We'll finish the one story," Hatch agreed. He looked down at the torn and dirty cloth of his formerly white Philtron-outfit. "Be good to get out of costume."

GEORGE ALEC EFFINGER

is unique. There has never been another writer quite like him in science fiction; in fact, there has never been another writer even remotely like him. I'm not entirely sure that I believe in George Alec Effinger.

Writers make their debuts in various ways. Some toil for years before anyone notices them sitting there and sweating over the typewriter. Others become stars with a single story. Effinger—well, Effinger became an sf star virtually overnight, though he didn't limit himself to one modest little mind-blowing story. No. When he broke into print in early 1971, he did it with a whole bunch of stories, coming out onetwothree right after one another in magazines and anthologies and more magazines and more anthologies. In June of 1971—the same year Effinger's first story came out, remember—your editor attended a regional sf con in Washington, and there was Effinger, a celebrity already, signing autographs, fighting off groupies, and sitting on panels behind a sign that proclaimed him to be the Stanton A. Coblentz of his generation.

Simply looking at Effinger gives no clue as to the reasons for his instant popularity, his record transformation from an unknown to a Name to Be Reckoned With. He is a short, slight dark-haired young fellow, very gaunt, and he looks as though he desperately needs a meal or two or ten. Sometimes he wears a beard and sometimes he does not; when he does, he looks vaguely like a miniature of Robert Silverberg. But that doesn't account for his success.

Talking to him doesn't explain anything either. In person, Effinger is shy and soft-spoken, with a mildly distracted air and a self-effacing manner. He smiles and jokes a lot, and he loves baseball and his pachinko machine and his private recipe for peach soup.

So why were all the editors and readers so excited?

Ah . . . the stories.

Effinger's stories are wry and black and savage. They are a hundred times funnier than the output of most of the genre's self-proclaimed humorists, but it's not quite safe to laugh at them—there's a knife behind every smile. He is the author of two decidedly odd novels, What Entropy Means to Me *and* Relatives. *The former earned a Nebula nomination; a section of the latter, published as an independent novelette, was a Hugo finalist. He is also the author of a whole slew of deftly insane short fictions, some of which have also earned him awards nominations.*

No one else could possibly have dreamed of some of the stories he writes. No one else could have told us of the quiet cataclysm that began when all the mollies in all the world's fish tanks died at once. No one else could have introduced pollution to the world of The Wind in the Willows. *No one else could have invented the one-legged horse that won the Kentucky Derby.*

And no one besides George Alec Effinger, I think, could have told this story.

—G. R. R. M.

Mom's Differentials

George Alec Effinger

LES GREUN HAD A small cubicle for an office, a long walk from the elevators. His little space was bounded by three thin plasterboard walls and a rectangular hole; the walls were nose-high and painted the same light green that walls in elementary schools are painted. From where Les sat at his desk he could look out through the hole, or doorway, at the green partition across a narrow corridor. The smallness of his own cubicle did not bother him; it seemed appropriate, after all. Les was not a leader. He was a member of a team, and not a particularly important one, at that. He was not entitled to much more. He certainly hadn't earned a nose-high door with a panel of frosted glass. But Les was content. He did not lust or grasp for objects beyond his means, things that were symbols of a status he did not seek. Among his associates it was unusual to be content. It surely was not expected, and Les had learned to hide his feelings of satisfaction and join his co-workers in frequent demonstrations of group frustration.

His job consisted of planning interchanges and cloverleaves for superhighways. In the cubicle directly east of his worked a woman who had much the same job. Her name was Judy Nominski, and one of her chief complaints was that in all likelihood she would never get to see the very cloverleaves that she had designed, nor on the roadways themselves would there be little bronze plaques proclaiming the interchanges to be the creative product of her talents. Les tried to ease her anger, at least in the early days of their friendship; he soon learned that quieting her anxiety entirely was impossible. He gave that up, and just nodded and smiled whenever she began the familiar conversation.

Les spent his workday composing equations that, when plotted on a graph by means of a computer, would produce curved lines which met specifications given him by various highway commissions in various places. Sometimes the cloverleaves or the bypasses were of a standard variety; in these cases there were reference manuals in which he could find the precise equations he needed. That part of his job bored him a little. There was no need to check the plotting on the computer, no need to stand by the terminal and watch the graceful arcs grow from the electronic roots of the machine. Using the preplotted data in the manuals was like being back in high school, doing simple problems in trig class, copying methods and values from the tables in the back of the book. But frequently enough he had to improvise, which meant estimating and hedging and fiddling until the plotted graph looked more and more like the required model. He thought that part was actually fun; he could never get Judy to agree.

On this particular day, Les had designed a small section of an exit ramp for a proposed superhighway; the road was to be built between Lemontier and Claybury, Montana, a total distance of one hundred and twenty-five miles, over which Les would have almost complete control. The equations for the exit ramp were pleasing to him: precise, neat, and clean in their lack of detail; no service roads, no special U-turn islets, no tangential minor arteries. Les left his desk at five o'clock with the feeling of having filled a day as well as he could. He was satisfied.

At home, the mail was waiting for him, and the afternoon newspaper. Les's wife, Charlotte, hadn't come home yet; her blue Dodge Dart was missing from its parking place. Les picked up the newspaper, the five magazines, the bills, and the letters, and pushed the button for the elevator. He waited, and after a short while the elevator arrived. He rode up and unlocked the door to his apartment. His cats were waiting expectantly to be fed. There was no cat food in the kitchen, so Les went back toward the front door, thinking to go across the street to buy the animals some food. He saw a piece of notepaper taped to the inside of the front door. He took it down and read it. It said:

Dear Les:

When you read this note I'll already be gone, of course, so it isn't a matter of me wanting to leave you and you trying to talk me out of it, like the other times. I have decided that being a teacher is not wonderful. At least, not for me. For other people, terrific, I guess. For me, lacking in joy. I am going to California, where I can live like I was intended to live. You know what I mean, we've argued about it enough. I want a more natural life. I want to unfold. At thirty-three, I think it's about time.

It's nothing personal, you know. I love you and I'll always remember you special. I'll think of you whenever I see a highway, which will be pretty often. I'm sure you'll do all right. You're intelligent. You can just pretend that the last twelve years never happened. I'm going to. I'll handle the divorce in California; I know how much you hate bothering with things like that. But in a couple of months, when my W-2 form comes, you'll have to take care of the income tax, okay?

Anyway, I hope you find true happiness and don't think too badly of me. This is something I just have to do.

Love,
Charlotte

From that moment, Les Greun began wondering about the purpose of life in general, and the meaning of his in particular.

"You know, Judy," said Les the next morning at work, "my wife has left me and I'm beginning to question the very basis of everything I've ever believed."

"You'll get the hang of it after a while," said Judy. "You probably won't be very good at first. I could give you a few pointers."

"I'd appreciate that," said Les. "I really would."

Judy began to speak, stopped, shook her head, then shrugged and went back into her own cubicle. Les went into his and looked at the work he had to do. He had to finish off the exit ramp and begin planning an access ramp from a small road near the town of Kerrigan. At nine-thirty the company began piping in music. A study had been made several years before that indicated that up-tempo music at nine-thirty might encourage sleepy employees to get right to work. The music stopped after a short time, because the study proved that uninterrupted music began to lose its effectiveness. Then after a brief interval it started again. This continued until lunch, the selections changing in mood and tempo according to the peaks and valleys of the charts made by the efficiency survey. After lunch the music came on more sprightly than ever to help overcome the loginess that lunch brought on.

About three o'clock, Les put down his pencil, stood up, and walked to Judy Nominski's cubicle. "Judy?" he said softly.

"Hmm?" she said.

"You know what? My wife's gone."

"I know," said Judy, looking up at Les and sighing. "You told me this morning. You're going to keep realizing it, over and over. You'll get used to it."

"You know what really bothers me?"

"How could I?"

"I don't seem to care," said Les, just a little astonishment in his voice. "That worries me."

"Either you're in a kind of shock, or you really don't care," said Judy.

"Isn't that a symptom of insanity?" asked Les.

"You're talking about planing of affect," said Judy. "My analyst went through all that with me. Don't worry about it. You're not that sophisticated. I'll tell you when you can start worrying."

"Thanks, Judy," said Les. "I just need someone to talk to. My job doesn't seem very important any more, not after all this."

"You're making progress, Les," she said. Then she turned back to her work, and Les went back to his cubicle.

A short time later, on the way home, Les saw an elderly woman screaming on the sidewalk. She seemed to be arguing with someone who, to Les's perception, wasn't there. She was a crazy lady. "There's a lot of that going around," thought Les. "I wonder how I can sit in my cubicle day after day, plotting abstract curves on a computer, when there's so much in the world to be concerned about. It doesn't make any sense any more. That's what Judy's been saying right along." He picked up some strawberries and some half-and-half at the store, and some tuna-and-egg cat food, and went up to his apartment. His pets were glad to see him.

That night, sitting alone in his living room, he felt a growing, objectless anxiety. The room was dimly lit and quiet; the cats were sleeping under chairs; nothing moved except Les's own reflection in the glass of the Leroy Neiman print. The fear, if that was what it was, became so strong that Les was tempted to telephone someone. He resisted the impulse because he had nothing specific to say, and he didn't want to feel even more like a fool. Instead, he put on a stack of records and tried to interest himself in a book. The records helped a little, but not enough to relax him completely, and the book was not very good. He remembered that Charlotte had claimed that one of her vitamins had tranquilizing capabilities; he couldn't remember which one. The inside of the refrigerator used to look like a pharmacy. Les hadn't noticed whether or not Charlotte had taken the pills with her, but he guessed that she had. He did not feel like checking. Instead, he decided to go for a short walk in the cool night air.

In the elevator, surrounded by the Muzak provided by the real estate management company, Les felt a little better. He closed his eyes, and he could almost pretend that he was in his office at work. Then he thought about how little his collection of curves and graph paper related to his problems, and again he experienced a wave of anxiety. There were people starving and crying out and dying, and he spent his time unconcerned, juggling variables in cryptic equations. The equations were often so complex that they masked whatever reality might exist beneath them. He could get lost in that complication. He could also get lost just as easily in the simplicity of the final, perfect curve. It was his way of hiding from the world. Charlotte had been right. Judy Nominski was right. There were people hungry in Asia, and he was hiding. There were people hungry in America, right where the damned highways were going. Les shuddered and listened to the Muzak. The elevator doors opened and he saw the outside. It didn't look particularly beautiful. Les waited, then pushed the button for his floor. The elevator's doors closed. The Muzak continued to play tunes from everyone's favorite hit shows, and the car climbed slowly upward; Les again felt just a little bit better.

The next day, although it was a Saturday, Les saw a physician. The doctor was a very thorough, very expensive doctor, whom Les trusted absolutely. "While you're here," said the doctor, "I want to take a urine specimen, and I want to have you run up and down the little stairs for me. Take this glass into the bathroom."

Les did as the doctor told him. The gentle music played in the office, even in the lavatory where Les was producing the urine specimen. He had a sudden feeling of panic, though, the same one he always felt in doctors' lavatories. Les never knew how much. If he gave just a little, a modest amount, a careful response, it might not be medically sufficient. On the other hand, if he filled the glass to the very brim, how would the nurse feel? He compromised, while the Muzak played a slow, muted trumpet version of a generally sprightly tune from a twenty-year-old Broadway show.

Afterward, the doctor gave him some advice which Les found unpleasant. "This is a prescription for some pills to raise your spirits," said the doctor. "And this is a prescription to help reduce your anxiety."

"I'm grateful," said Les, "but I hate the idea of being one of those people on drugs. I've always thought of myself as more self-reliant."

"I hear that from a lot of patients," said the doctor wearily. "Let me tell you, I'm getting pretty sick of it. If you have an infection, you come in here and the nurse gives you a shot. If you have a pulled muscle or a broken bone, you come in here and I do what I can for you. But when you're going through a crisis like you're going through, when your whole life is being turned upside down, and you're feeling a little strange, you come in here and *ignore* me. These drugs were developed precisely for situations like this. That's what they're *for*. Here, take them."

"Okay," said Les, reluctantly taking the prescriptions. Later, with the prescriptions filled, Les went home unafraid of the empty apartment.

"And what do you think of life now?" asked Judy Nominski the following Monday at work.

"Not too bad," said Les. "My apartment is very clean."

"Well," said Judy, "you're well rid of her. Ask around. They'll all say the same thing."

"Of course they will," said Les. "What else do you think they'd say?"

"Never mind," said Judy. "The sooner you realize that you have to adjust, the sooner the rest of us can stop sympathizing."

"I've already gone quite a ways down the road," said Les. "Look." He poured out several yellow tablets into his hand.

"Wonderful," said Judy, pushing the pills back into the bottle. "I used to take those myself. I've gone on to better ones."

"I can hardly wait for that to happen to me," said Les. "Meanwhile, I'll be satisfied with these."

"Slow and sure wins the race."

"Yes," said Les. "Yes. Of course."

"By the way," said Judy, "I've been thinking about your ex-wife. Charlotte? Was that her name?"

"Oh, God, Judy," said Les, "you were at the damned wedding. You've known her for years."

"I was just thinking that all this time, there might have been more going on than met the eye. Your eye."

"You mean Charlotte and some mystery lover?"

Judy shrugged her shoulders and gave Les a small smile, but she said nothing. She turned and walked away. He turned also and began studying one of the graphed curves he had just completed. It was one of his favorites. He looked at it in silence for a while, then picked it up and took it to the Xerox machine. He made a copy and tacked it up on a wall of his cubicle, beside many others of his previous successes.

This time, though, when he put the curve on the wall he noticed something odd. He couldn't quite decide what the strangeness was, or its significance; but then he had little capacity to appreciate mysteries. He went to lunch.

An hour later Les decided to decorate his cubicle, his meager realm. He chose to take three or four of his favorite graphs, look up their original equations in his old project manuals, extend their parameters beyond those that had been required by the old jobs, and see what lovely things developed as a result.

The graphs came to be quite an unexpected thrill for Les. The isolated curves had been governed by highway necessities before; now they were limited only by his imagination. This was a quality or attribute that Les believed to have fled from him a number of years before. These new curves were in many ways more attractive than the originals, being larger, more graceful, and somehow warmer in their expanded versions.

The area around the computer terminal was as filled with Muzak as his work cubicle. The sound made Les feel whole and healthy. It made him feel darkly tanned, which in point of fact he was not. When he finished plotting his graphs, he decided to do something about his physical appearance. He went to his cubicle and sat down at his desk; until quitting time he thought about being darkly tanned. He resolved to get through the rest of the week by an effort of pure will. Then he would start a program of self-improvement, delayed to begin with the first of the month. At five o'clock he took one of the yellow pills, stood up, and went home.

Les drove the five miles along the interstate and the two and a half miles from the main highway to his apartment building. Then he parked his car in the protected parking area, experiencing an anxiety attack that felt precisely like what he had always imagined madness to be like. He found it difficult to keep a single thought coherently in mind. His head was light and there was a loud buzzing in his ears. His hands tingled. His abdomen was tight. He wanted to lie down but he was too upset. He wanted to work off the great nervous energy that possessed him, but there was no way for him to do so in the apartment building. He wanted to lift great weights, but next to the parking area there were only a few old, broken bricks. Les turned away and went back toward the rear of the building. There was a small swimming pool and a barbecue on the patio. There was also a black wrought-iron table and three matching chairs. A fourth chair was at the bottom of the pool. Les looked around nervously. There was nothing to do. He was panicking, and there was nothing to do. He reached into one of his pockets and took out a plastic vial; in it were the pills which the doctor had said would help him to control his anxiety. He swallowed one; it tasted terrible and seemed to stick in his throat, so that he had to swallow forcefully three times afterward. A minute later he swallowed another. He glanced over the pool again. Dead leaves floated on the greenish water. Les left the patio and went back toward the elevator.

In his mailbox was a note from Charlotte. "Terrific," he thought. "Just what I need." He pushed the button for the elevator and tore open the envelope. On the outside, where a return address would normally be, there was the trademark of a large international airline. Beneath that were the words *In Flight*. As the elevator doors opened, Les glanced at the first sentence of the letter. It said:

Dear Les:
Pat and I have decided to live in Hong Kong for a year.

Les shoved the envelope into his pocket and entered the elevator. The speakers offered him a violin and cello transcription of Sousa's "National Emblem" march. Les decided that he was very definitely depressed. The two pills might help him with his anxiety—they had yet to show any sign of doing so, though it was still early—but it was the yellow tablets that would help raise his spirits. He recalled the doctor using those very words. He had one of the tablets in his hand even before he had taken the keys from his pocket. He held the pill while he opened his front door. He brushed by his mewing cats and hurried to the kitchen, where he swallowed the tablet and a long drink of cola. Then he went into the living room and fell down on the couch.

He didn't stay there more than fifteen seconds. He felt unbearably edgy. In his mind he knew that there was nothing to be afraid of. Emotionally, though, it was another matter. His heart was pounding blood through his body as though Les were preparing for escape or battle. He started into the bedroom. He sat down on the bed. He got up. He decided that he had to go downstairs and go to the store, but he didn't want to face anyone yet. He didn't want to do anything. He just wanted to feel normal.

He went into the spare bedroom and looked at the pile of bills on the desk. He sat down and took out his checkbook. He paid all of the bills, addressed the envelopes, and stamped them. He wrote short notices canceling memberships in three book clubs that Charlotte had belonged to. He canceled four magazine subscriptions. Then he looked in the drawers of the desk. There were quite a few things that Charlotte had left. Les took all of these things and threw them into the wastebasket. He felt bitter. He had noticed that when Charlotte left, she hadn't taken a single photograph of him. She hadn't taken any of the jewelry he had given her, or even any of the funny little odd things. He went through the apartment with a shoping bag and filled it with all of these items. Then he went downstairs and put the shopping bag in the garbage. Les felt depressed, panicky, and very angry. He went across the street to the grocery store. He could taste blood where he had bitten his lower lip.

Judy Nominski was very concerned when Les arrived at work. "How are you?" she asked. "I called about three or four times last night. I was worried about you. There wasn't any answer."

Les looked down at the floor, embarrassed. "I wasn't home," he said.

"Where did you go?"

"Not very far," said Les. "I was feeling pretty rocky. I realized that the yellow tablets were making me really nervous. I couldn't keep still. I went through my apartment like a team of commandos. God, I thought it was clean *yesterday*. You should see it today. I even vacuumed my Persian cat."

"Then where were you?" asked Judy.

"I felt frightened," said Les. "I spent the night in the elevator."

"In the elevator?"

"The Muzak made me feel better," said Les.

"Did you sleep okay?" asked Judy.

"No," said Les. "People kept coming in and waking me up. They couldn't just let me sleep. They had to ask questions. You'd be surprised how many people get home between midnight and six."

"Did you stop taking the yellow tablets?" she asked.

"Yes," said Les. "I put them away until my apartment gets messy again."

"Go to work, Les," said Judy. "These are all stations along the way." She smiled briefly and touched his arm briefly, and walked along the corridor toward her cubicle. Les, finding peace in the prospect of his own work and the sound of the morning's recorded music, went to his office.

Nonetheless, there was something disturbing, something that intruded into the Muzak's rendition of "Clair de Lune." "What could it be?" thought Les. "Everything here looks exactly like it did last night." He stared at the wall with its display of curves. Thoughtfully he stepped closer. Then, moved by a sudden inspiration, he changed the position of three of the sheets of computer print-out paper. He had been correct; they now formed a legible word—OTTO.

Otto? thought Les. He didn't know anyone named Otto.

One of the disconcerting things about the OTTO was that it was written in script, rather than lettered, and the writing—the handwriting—was familiar. The loops in the Os and the way the Ts were crossed were distinctive and tantalizing. He tried rearranging other portions of the graphs. Sometimes these connected, too. That made Les even more uneasy. He found three pieces that spelled MOTH when they were put together. More combinations seemed to form pairs or triplets of letters, but no more words. And they were all written in a handwriting that was somehow well known to him.

The rest of the day Les spent digging out his old favorite equations and expanding them within the same parameters he had chosen the day before. Then he put these on the wall, too. By quitting time he had done none of his day's work, but he had covered two entire walls with sheets of print-out paper. He stared and stared. He shuffled them around. Nothing more presented itself to him. Finally, frustrated, he left his cubicle and went home for the night. It was a trip and a destination for which he had little enthusiasm.

To delay his arrival, Les stopped at a small shopping center at the interstate exit just before his usual one. He parked his car, feeling more than usually upset. Even though he had judiciously not taken any of the yellow pills—or even any of the others, the anxiety controllers, just in case—he was not feeling well. The car's radio was tuned to an AM station that played soft instrumental music; it made him feel almost as good as the Muzak at work and in his elevator at home. But whenever an announcer or a commercial interrupted the music, Les had difficulty avoiding a traffic accident. Now, with the engine off and the radio silenced, Les felt his panic state returning. He opened the car door and stepped out. He hurried across the crowded parking lot toward a squat, rectangular department store.

Les didn't really need anything in the store. But he was pleasantly surprised to find that the store, too, supplied its shoppers with piped-in music. It made him feel better immediately. In a kind of analgesic haze, Les bought an expanding curtain rod and a rusty-red shower curtain. Then he bought three black-and-white-striped cushions. He had no more cash, not even enough for dinner. He took his purchases back to the car, turned on the radio, and drove home.

Les had no intention of going to his apartment. He pushed the button for the elevator. While he waited he looked at his day's mail. There were two bills, three magazines, and another letter postmarked from Hong Kong. When the elevator arrived, Les kicked his packages inside. He put the shower curtain on the expanding rod and installed it about two feet from the back of the elevator. The Muzak blessed him with serenity as he worked. He was pleased to see that the curtain matched the elevator's carpet very well. He put the cushions down on the floor behind the curtain. Then he pushed the button for his floor. When the elevator's doors opened, he threw the empty paper bags out. Les went back behind the shower curtain and sat down on his cushions. The elevator's doors closed with a satisfying sound, and Les leaned back and listened to the Muzak that restored his soul.

That night, he had a date, the first since Charlotte had left him. "It's about time," he thought. "I have to make some attempt to normalize my life. Things go on. I can't just keep feeling sorry for myself. I have to go out. I have to have fun. Maybe then I won't feel so terrified." These were all things the doctor had told him when Les telephoned him that evening. Les had little confidence in their validity.

Naturally enough, the only woman he felt able to invite out was Judy Nominski. He planned a nice dinner at a moderate restaurant, an enjoyable movie, some drinks, and pleasant conversation. If the evening developed beyond that, Les would be surprised. He didn't know if it would be pleasant or not. He called her up shortly after he finished speaking to his doctor. She had already eaten dinner, but she sympathized with his feelings. "Sure, Les," she said, "I'd be happy to go out with you. It would be—what?—medicinal. It would make me feel good to ease your pain."

"I don't want you to ease my pain," said Les. "I just want us to go out and have a good time."

"Sure, Les," she said in a soothing voice. The entire conversation irritated him. They agreed that he would pick her up at her apartment in half an hour and then they would go see a new film, reportedly a screwball comedy. Judy thought that, too, would ease his pain. Les bit his lower lip again, and it hurt even more.

After the movie, after the drinks, after the short, tense conversation, Les realized that their date had reached a kind of silent moment of decision. A great deal depended on what Les said next. Suddenly he felt like he was back in high school. He felt unutterably stupid. "Uh," he said, "would you, uh . . ." Judy wasn't helping at all, and she was the one who claimed to understand everything so well. Maybe she thought it was important that he do it himself. "Would you like to stop off at my apartment before I take you home?" he asked. "Then I could show you the, uh, the . . ."

"Sure, Les," said Judy, swirling the ice cubes in her glass. Her voice was unnecessarily innocent, he thought.

A short time later, they were in his apartment. Not long after that, they were in the bedroom. Les thought that this was the first time that he had tried to have sex with anyone since Charlotte left. And it was in their bed, too. Everything seemed loaded with more meaning than was possible. In the silence, Les longed for the Muzak. His panic grew until he discovered that it was impossible for him to unzip his trousers. Previously, he had spent nearly three minutes trying to unsnap Judy's bra, before he remembered that they didn't snap, they hooked. Judy had been very kind and not said anything. Les damned her for that.

They attempted to make love. In Les's grotesquely frightened state of mind, it was impossible. The two of them tried and tried. Judy was so understanding that Les wanted to strangle her.

"Listen," he said. "It's not you."

"I know," she said. "I know."

"No," he said, pleading. "Listen. I'm sure we can do it. But not here."

Judy smiled. She thought that she understood.

"Put on a robe and come with me," said Les. "Charlotte left some of her things in the closet. I haven't finished tossing it all out yet." Judy did as he said, and followed him; he dressed in a blue flannel bathrobe and led her out into the hall.

"Where are we going?" she asked, the first note of doubt entering her voice.

"The elevator."

"*What?*"

Les pushed the button, the elevator arrived, and the doors slid almost silently open. "Come on," said Les, taking Judy by the arm and urging her into the elevator.

"What's that shower curtain, Les?" she asked, a little frightened herself.

"That's my little refuge," he said. The Muzak lulled him. For the first time, he noticed the shape of Judy's breasts as they pushed against the thin robe. He felt himself becoming aroused.

"You come in here and feel all right?" asked Judy. "You feel sane in here? You've built yourself a little island of peace and solitude in a world that's driving you insane?"

"Now you really do understand, Judy," said Les, his voice hoarse. He reached for her, he tried to kiss her. She pushed him away.

"I understand," she said. "Really I do. And I can't tell you how happy I am for you. I feel a warm glow when I think about the progress you've made. You've carved out a place of security, the kind of niche that most people never have."

"Then what's the matter?" he asked.

"It's disgusting," she said, and left the elevator. Les stared after her. He thought about women for a moment. Then he thought that it wasn't his life that was meaningless, after all. It really was the universe's fault.

At work the next day, Les met Judy in a corridor. He looked away, trying to pretend that he didn't see her, but it was a pitiable ruse in the narrow passageway. She spoke up. "Look, Les," she said, "I want you to know about last night. It really isn't you. Really. You have to believe that. I'm sure there are plenty of women who would enjoy having sex with you like that, in the elevator. You just have to find one, that's all. It's the same problem we all face, no more, no less. I could even ask around, if you like." She looked at him, unable to read anything in his expression.

There was nothing in his expression and there was nothing in his thoughts. He wanted desperately to say something cinematic, something final, cutting, devastating. He couldn't think of anything. Rather than end with "Sure" or "No hard feelings" or "All right by me," he said nothing. He passed her and went into his cubicle.

The graphs on the wall surprised him. The events of the day before had made him forget the mystery that had grown around his curves and the overpasses and cloverleaves they represented. Now they occupied every bit of his attention. Judy Nominski was forgotten for good. Les made a few experimental movements of the paper sheets. The first five were failures; the sixth brought curves together that formed an H and part of an I. Like the day before, he spent the morning hours piecing together what had become a gigantic and strangely obsessive jigsaw puzzle. By lunchtime he had put together several more letters. The Is were dotted with little circles; it occurred to Les whose handwriting it was. It was a crazy idea, but it somehow fit into his situation. The Muzak made him feel calm and receptive to new ideas; the incident with Judy had triggered his sudden success in assembling the fragments. Les was certain that if it hadn't been for the nourishing music, or for Judy's abrupt rous-

ing him from his psychological nightmare, this message would
have been forever hidden from him. It was indeed a message,
and by the handwriting it seemed to be from his mom. Les
didn't have the curiosity to wonder if during all the years he
had held his job, he had subconsciously constructed highways
whose parts, if distorted in just the right way, would speak to
him. Perhaps it was an unexplainable supernatural event—after
all, his mother had been dead for several years.

Les didn't take a lunch hour. When the Muzak cut off, he felt
a return of his intense fear; but now he had the strength to ignore it and continue with his project. By three-thirty he had
the entire message complete. It stood thumbtacked against the
plasterboard of his cubicle. It said:

OKAY. YOU'VE HIT BOTTOM. YOU'LL BE ALL RIGHT NOW. LISTEN.
THIS IS YOUR MOTHER TALKING.

Les laughed. Even the double underlinings were his mom's.
When the Muzak started again, he sat in his chair and felt so
self-assured and balanced that he wished that Judy Nominski
would come into his cubicle. But she didn't.

The drive home was just as horrifying as usual; the radio
station lessened some of his terror, but he was still shaking and
stiff from grasping the steering wheel. He parked his car and
opened the mailbox. There was no mail. What did that mean?
Les was puzzled, but the bewilderment began to vanish as he
pushed the button for the elevator. The lack of mail reminded
him that he hadn't read the letter from Charlotte that he had
received the day before. He took it out of his pocket, opened it,
and read it. It said:

Dear Les:
Well, here we are at the Hong Kong Breezeway Inn. We'll
be staying here until we find an apartment. I guess it's more
difficult to find an apt here than it is in the US. It's really
exciting and different. I couldn't tell you all the things we've

seen, just since we've been here. I guess you'll just have to come here, yourself.

At that point the handwriting changed. Les was mildly curious, and he read on.

Hello. My name is Pat Colerra. We've never met, but I suppose that Charlotte told you something about me. She started this letter this morning. I thought I'd finish it; I think you have a right to know.

We went to a Japanese restaurant for lunch. Charlotte was very excited; you know how she likes Japanese food. She said that she didn't think she'd ever get a better chance to try more or less legitimate Japanese food than while we're here, across the Pacific. She laughed about how you hated raw fish, and the hotel recommended a restaurant that was noted for its *sashimi.* I'm not crazy about raw fish, either, so I didn't have any. Charlotte had heard a lot about this special *sashimi,* made from a blowfish called a *fugu.* I remember reading about them in the *Time/Life* Japanese cookbook. Parts of the *fugu* are so poisonous that if the venom is allowed to touch the edible parts, during inept cleaning and preparation, the diner will just drop his chopsticks and fall to the floor, dead. The poison acts in a matter of seconds. The *fugu* has a special attraction, then. It is supposed to have some superior taste, I imagine, or else all the Japanese who make a ritual of eating the fish are just playing some kind of suicidal game. I mean, even when the *fugu* is perfectly prepared, the diner's lips and tongue become numb from the tiny amount of poison present. The chefs who prepare *fugu* must be licensed; they pass exams and have cards with their pictures on them, just like cabdrivers in New York.

Well. Anyway. Charlotte

The elevator arrived and opened its doors. The Muzak begged Les to enter. He jammed the letter back into his pocket; indeed, he never finished reading it. He settled down on his cushions behind the shower curtain, listening to a melody he recognized but could not name. He was very content. His mom, although she was dead, was right. Just as importantly, his highways were right.

Evidently someone on one of the upper floors had pushed the button, because the doors closed and the elevator began to climb. Les pushed himself even deeper into the cushions. He took a long breath and closed his eyes.

"Listen," the Muzak seemed to sing. "This is your mother talking."

JERRY POURNELLE

was the winner.

The final ballots were issued, along with the 1973 Hugo Award ballots, in the spring of 1973. The voting went on all summer. On Labor Day weekend in Toronto, the verdict of the fans and readers was announced.

It had been a two-man race, which surprised no one, since each of the two leaders alone had more fiction in print than the other four nominees combined. Between the top two, the race was very close. George Alec Effinger received a special plaque as runner-up after losing by a handful of votes.

And Jerry Pournelle, Ph.D., won the first John W. Campbell Award as the best new writer in sf.

Pournelle was in many ways a fitting victor, for he was per-haps the last major talent discovered by John W. Campbell Jr. No less than five of Pournelle's stories had been purchased by Campbell just before his death, and it was those stories—ap-pearing in the pages of Analog, *Campbell's magazine, during 1971 and 1972—that earned Pournelle his reputation, a Hugo nomination, and eventually the Campbell Award.*

If that was his first award, it is unlikely to be his last. He has had five Hugo nominations by now, and each year he seems to pick up a few more. His major novel, The Mote in God's Eye, *written in collaboration with Larry Niven, was an sf event of the first magnitude when it appeared late in 1974, and at this writing it is a strong contender for the Nebula Award. Other novels sit beside it on the stands; still others are forthcoming. And Pournelle is still a regular in* Analog, *where his tales of futuristic warfare consistantly finish high in the magazine's readers' poll.*

Pournelle's stories of mercenaries and military men have a solid grounding: a former soldier with the U.S. Army in Korea, he has kept in close contact with career officers throughout the world. He knows his science and his politics as well, and uses that knowledge to good effect in his fiction. For more than ten years a space scientist, he worked on Projects Mercury, Gemini, and Apollo. He has also been a successful political campaign manager, and served briefly as executive assistant to the mayor of Los Angeles. He holds advanced degrees in psychology, operations research, and political science.

As if all this wasn't enough, Pournelle is also a former (recent) president of the Science Fiction Writers of America. He was a strong *president—that is, people are still* arguing *about some of the things he did.*

A full-time writer since 1971, his output is not limited to sf by any means. He is co-author with Stefan Possony of The Strategy of Technology, *a textbook employed in the War College, USAF, and he currently writes the monthly science column for* Galaxy *magazine. When he's not writing, Pournelle is an enthusiastic sailor and outdoorsman. He lives in Southern California with his wife, four sons, and a husky named Klondike ("Unlike most science fiction writers," he says, "I do not keep cats.")*

Of the story that follows, Pournelle writes: "It is the last thing Mr. Campbell rejected. He also sent his customary nine-page letter telling why. I have not had the heart to revise the thing until now, but it seemed appropriate for this book that I do it. I don't know if John would have liked it as it now is, but I do know there's a lot of his advice in it."

—G.R.R.M.

Silent Leges

Jerry Pournelle

I

EIGHT THOUSAND YOUNG BODIES writhed to the maddening beat of an electronic bass. Some danced while others lay back on the grass and drank or smoked. None could ignore the music, although they were only barely aware of the nasal tenor whose voice was not strong enough to carry over the wild squeals of the theremin and the twang of a dozen steel-stringed guitars. Other musical groups waited their turn on the gray wooden platform erected among the twentieth-century Gothic buildings of Los Angeles University.

Some of the musicians were so anxious to begin that they pounded their instruments. This produced nothing audible because their amplifiers were turned off, but it allowed them to join in the frenzied spirit of the festival on the campus green.

The concert was a happy affair. Citizens from a nearby Welfare Island joined the students in the college park. Enterprising dealers hawked liquor and pot and borloi. Catering trucks brought food. The Daughters of Lilith played original works while Slime waited their turn, and after those would come even more famous groups. An air of peace and fellowship engulfed the crowd.

"Lumpen proletariat." The speaker was a young woman. She

stood at a window in a classroom overlooking the common green and the mad scene below. "Lumpen," she said again.

"Aw, come off the bolshi talk. Communism's no answer. Look at the Sovworld—"

"Revolution betrayed! Betrayed!" the girl said. She faced her challenger. "There will be no peace and freedom until—"

"Can it." The meeting chairman banged his fist on the desk. "We've got work to do. This is no time for ideology."

"Without the proper revolutionary theory nothing can be accomplished." This came from a bearded man in a leather jacket. He looked first at the chairman, then at the dozen others in the classroom. "First there must be a proper understanding of the problem. Then we can act!"

The chairman banged his fist again, but someone else spoke. "Deeds, not words. We came here to plan some action. What the hell's all the talking about? You goddamned theorists give me a pain in the ass! What we need is action. The Underground's done more for the Movement than you'll ever—"

"Balls." The man in the leather jacket snorted contempt. Then he stood. His voice projected well. "You act, all right. You shut down the L.A. transport system for three days. Real clever. And what did it accomplish? Made the taxpayers scared enough to fork over pay raises for the cops. You ended the goddamn pig strike, that's what you did!"

There was a general babble, and the Underground spokesman tried to answer, but the leather-jacketed man continued. "You started food riots in the Citizen areas. Big deal. It's results that count, and your result was the CoDominium Marines! You brought in the Marines, that's what you did!"

"Damned right! We exposed this regime for what it really is! The Revolution can't come until the people understand—"

"Revolution, my ass. Get it through your heads, technology's the only thing that's going to save us. Turn technology loose, free the scientists, and we'll be—"

He was shouted down by the others. There was more babble. Mark Fuller sat at the student desk and drank it all in. The wild music outside. Talk of revolution. Plans for action, for making something happen, for making the Establishment notice them; it was all new, and he was here in this room, where the real power of the university lay. God, how I love it! he thought. I've never had any kind of power before. Not even over my own life. And now we can show them all!

He felt more alive than he had ever had in his twenty years. He looked at the girl next to him and smiled. She grinned and patted his thigh. Tension rose in his loins until it was almost unbearable. He remembered their yesterdays and imagined their tomorrows. The quiet world of taxpayer country where he had grown up seemed very far away.

The others continued their argument. Mark listened, but his thoughts kept straying to Shirley: to the warmth of her hand on his thigh, to the places where her sweater was stretched out of shape, to the remembered feel of her knees against his back and her cries of passion. He knew he ought to listen more carefully to the discussion. He didn't really belong in this room at all. If Shirley hadn't brought him he'd never have known the meeting was happening.

But I'll earn a place here, he thought. In my own right. Power. That's what they have, and I'll learn how to be part of it.

The jacketed technocracy man was speaking again. "You see too many devils," he said. "Get the CoDominium Intelligence people off the scientists' backs and it won't be twenty years before *all* of the Earth's a paradise. All of it, not just taxpayer country."

"A polluted paradise! What do you want, to go back to the smog? Oil slicks, dead fish, animals exterminated, that's what—"

"Bullshit. Technology can get us *out* of—"

"That's what caused the problems in the first place!"

"Because we didn't go far enough! There hasn't been a new scientific idea since the goddamn space drive! You're so damned proud because there's no pollution. None here, anyway. But it's not because of conservation, it's because they ship people out, because of triage, because—"

"He's right, people starve while we—"

"Damn right! Free thoughts, freedom to think, to plan, to do research, to publish without censorship, that's what will liberate the world."

The arguments went on until the chairman tired of them. He banged his fist again. "We are here to *do* something," he said. "Not to settle the world's problems this afternoon. That was agreed."

The babble finally died away and the chairman spoke meaningfully. "This is our chance. A peaceful demonstration of power. Show what we think of their goddamned rules and their status cards. But we've got to be careful. It mustn't get out of hand."

❀   ❀   ❀

Mark sprawled on the grass a dozen meters from the platform. He stretched luxuriantly in the California sun while Shirley stroked his back. Excitement poured in through all his senses. College had been like this in imagination. The boys at the expensive private school where his father had sent him used to whisper about festivals, demonstrations, and confrontations, but it hadn't been real. Now it was. He'd hardly ever mingled with Citizens before, and now they were all around him. They wore Welfare issue clothing and talked in strange dialects that Mark only half understood. Everyone, Citizens and students, writhed to the music that washed across them.

Mark's father had wanted to send him to a college in taxpayer country, but there hadn't been enough money. He might have won a scholarship, but he hadn't. Mark told himself it was deliberate. Competition was no way to live. A lot of his friends had refused to compete in the rat race. None of them ended here, though; they'd had the money to get to Princeton or Yale.

More Citizens poured in. The festival was supposed to be open only to those with tickets, and Citizens weren't supposed to come on the campus in the first place, but the student group had opened the gates and cut the fences. It had all been planned in the meeting. Now the gate control shack was on fire, and everyone who lived nearby could get in.

Shirley was ecstatic. "Look at them!" she shouted. "This is the way it used to be! Citizens should be able to go wherever they want to. Equality forever!"

Mark smiled. It was all new to him. He hadn't thought much about the division between Citizen and taxpayer, and had accepted his privileges without noticing them. He had learned a lot from Shirley and his new friends, but there was so much more that he didn't know. I'll find out, though, he thought. We know what we're doing. We can make the world so much better —we can do anything! Time for the stupid old bastards to move over and let some fresh ideas in.

Shirley passed him a pipe of borloi. That was another new thing for him; it was a Citizen habit, something Mark's father despised. Mark couldn't understand why. He inhaled deeply and relished the wave of contentment it brought. Then he reached for Shirley and held her in his warm bath of concern and love, knowing she was as happy as he was.

She smiled gently back at him, her hand resting on his thigh, and they writhed to the music, the beat thundering through them, faces glowing with anticipation of what would come, of what they would accomplish this day. The pipe came around again and Mark seized it eagerly.

"Pigs! The pigs are coming!" The cry went up from the fringes of the crowd.

Shirley turned to her followers. "Just stay here. Don't provoke the bastards. Make sure you don't do anything but sit tight."

There were murmurs of agreement. Mark felt a wave of excitement flash through him. This was it. And he was right there in front with the leaders; even if all his status did come from being Shirley's current boyfriend, he was one of the leaders, one of the people who make things happen . . .

The police were trying to get through the crowd so they could stop the festival. The university president was with them, and he was shouting something Mark couldn't understand. Over at the edge of the common green there was a lot of smoke. Was a building on fire? That didn't make sense. There weren't supposed to be any fires, nothing was to be harmed; just ignore the cops and the university people, show how Citizens and students could mingle in peace; show how stupid the damned rules were, and how needless—

There *was* a fire. Maybe more than one. Police and firemen tried to get through the crowd. Someone kicked a cop and the bluecoat went down. A dozen of his buddies waded into the group. Their sticks rose and fell.

The peaceful dream vanished. Mark stared in confusion. There was a man screaming somewhere, where was he? In the burning building? A group began chanting: *"Equality now! Equality now!"*

Another group was building a barricade across the green. "They aren't supposed to do that!" Mark shouted. Shirley grinned at him. Her eyes shone in excitement. More police came, then more, and a group headed toward Mark. They raised aluminum shields as rocks flew across the green. The police came closer. One of the cops raised his club.

He was going to hit Shirley! Mark grabbed at the night stick and deflected it. Citizens and students clustered around. Some threw themselves at the cops. A big man, well-dressed, too old to be a student, kicked at the leading policeman. The cop went down.

Mark pulled Shirley away as a dozen black-jacketed Lampburners joined the melee. The Lampburners would deal with the cops, but Mark didn't want to watch. The boys in his school had talked contemptuously about pigs, but the only police Mark had ever met had been polite and deferential; this was ugly, and—

His head swam in confusion. One minute he'd been lying in Shirley's arms with music and fellowship and everything was wonderful. Now there were police, and groups shouting, "Kill the pigs!" and fires burning. The Lampburners were swarming everywhere. They hadn't been at the meeting. Most claimed to be wanted by the police. But they'd had a representative at the planning session, they'd agreed this would be a peaceful demonstration—

A man jumped off the roof of the burning building. There was no one below to catch him, and he sprawled on the steps like a broken doll. Blood poured from his mouth, a bright-red splash against the pink marble steps. Another building shot flames skyward. More police arrived, and set up electrified barriers around the crowd.

A civilian, his bright clothing a contrast with the dull police blue, got out of a cruiser and stood atop it as police held their shields in front of him. He began to shout through a bull horn:

"I READ YOU THE ACT OF 1991 AS AMENDED. WHENEVER THERE SHALL BE AN ASSEMBLY LIKELY TO ENDANGER PUBLIC OR PRIVATE PROPERTY OR THE LIVES OF CITIZENS AND TAXPAYERS, THE LAWFUL MAGISTRATES SHALL COMMAND ALL PERSONS ASSEMBLED TO DISPERSE AND SHALL WARN THEM THAT FAILURE TO DISPERSE SHALL BE CONSIDERED A DECLARATION OF REBELLION. THE MAGISTRATES SHALL GIVE SUFFICIENT TIME . . ."

Mark knew the act. He'd heard it discussed in school. It was time to get away. The local mayor would soon have more than enough authority to deal with this mad scene. He could even call on the military, US or CoDominium, for help. The barriers were up around two sides of the green, but the cops hadn't closed off all the buildings. There was a doorway ahead, and Mark pulled Shirley toward it. "Come on!"

Shirley wouldn't come. She stood defiant, grinning wildly, shaking her fist at the police, shouting curses at them. Then she turned to Mark. "If you're scared, just go on, baby. Bug off."

Someone handed a bottle around. Shirley drank and gave it to Mark. He raised it to his lips but didn't drink any. His head pounded, and he was afraid. I should run, he thought. I should run like hell. The mayor's finished reading the act . . .

"EQUALITY NOW! EQUALITY NOW!" The chant was contagious. Half the crowd was shouting.

The police waited impassively. An officer glanced at his

watch from time to time. Then the officer nodded, and the police advanced. Four technicians took hoses from one of the cruisers and directed streams of foam above the heads of the advancing blue line. The slimy liquid fell in a spray around Mark.

Mark fell. He tried to stand and couldn't. Everyone around him fell. Whatever the liquid touched became so slippery that no one could hold onto it. It didn't seem to affect the police.

Instant banana peel, Mark thought. He'd seen it used on tri-v. Everyone laughed when they saw it used on tri-v. Now it didn't seem so funny. A couple of attempts showed Mark that he couldn't get away; he could barely crawl. The police moved rapidly toward him. Rocks and bottles clanged against their shields.

The black-jacketed Lampburners took spray cans from their pockets. They sprayed their shoes and hands, and then got up. They began to move away through the helpless crowd, away from the police, toward an empty building—

The police line reached the group around Mark. The cops fondled their night sticks. They spoke in low tones, too low to be heard any distance away. "Stick time," one said. "Yeah. Our turn," his partner answered.

"Does anyone here claim taxpayer status?" The cop eyed the group coldly. "Speak up."

"Yes. Here." One boy tried to get up. He fell again, but he held up his ID card. "Here." Mark reached for his own.

"Fink!" Shirley shouted. She threw something at the other boy. "Hypocrite! Pig! Fink!" Others were shouting as well. Mark saw Shirley's look of hatred and put his card back into his pocket. There'd be time later.

Two police grabbed him. One lifted his feet, the other lifted his shoulders. When he was a couple of feet off the ground the one holding his shoulders let go. The last thing Mark heard as his head hit the pavement was the mocking laughter of the cop.

❖   ❖   ❖

The bailiff was grotesque, with mustaches like Wyatt Earp and an enormous paunch that hung over his equipment belt. In a bored voice he read, "Case 457-984. People against Mark Fuller. Rebellion, aggravated assault, resisting arrest."

The judge looked down from the bench. "How do you plead?"

"Guilty, Your Honor," Mark's lawyer said. His name was Zower, and he wasn't expensive. Mark's father couldn't afford an expensive lawyer.

But I didn't, Mark thought. I didn't. When he'd said that earlier, though, the attorney had been contemptuous. "Shut up or you'll make it worse," the lawyer had said. "I had trouble enough getting the conspiracy charges dropped. Just stand there looking innocent and don't say a goddamn thing."

The judge nodded. "Have you anything to say in mitigation?"

Zower put his hand on Mark's shoulder. "My client throws himself on the mercy of the court," he said. "Mark has never been in trouble before. He acted under the influence of evil companions and intoxicants. There was no real intent to commit crimes. Just very bad judgment."

The judge didn't look impressed. "What have the people to say about this?"

"Your Honor," the prosecutor began. "The people have had more than enough of these student riots. This was no high-jinks stunt by young taxpayers. This was a deliberate rebellion, planned in advance.

"We have recordings of this hoodlum striking a police officer. That officer subsequently suffered a severe beating with three fractures, a ruptured kidney, and other personal injuries. It is a wonder the officer is alive. We can also show that after the mayor's proclamation the accused made no attempt to leave. If the defense disputes these facts . . ."

"No, no." Zower spoke hastily. "We stipulate, Your Honor." He muttered to himself, just loud enough that Mark could hear. "Can't let them run those pix. That'd get the judge *really* upset."

Zower stood. "Your Honor, we stipulate Mark's bad judgment, but remember, he was intoxicated. He was with new friends, friends he didn't know very well. His father is a respected taxpayer, manager of General Foods in Santa Maria.

Mark has never been arrested before. I'm sure he's learned a lesson from all this."

And where is Shirley? Mark wondered. Somehow her politician father had kept her from even being charged.

The judge was nodding. Zower smiled and whispered to Mark, "I stroked him pretty good in chambers. We'll get probation."

"Mister Fuller, what have you to say for yourself?" the judge demanded.

Mark stood eagerly. He wasn't sure what he was going to say. Plead? Beg for mercy? Tell him to stick it? Not that. Mark breathed hard. I'm scared, he thought. He walked nervously toward the bench.

The judge's face exploded in a cloud of red. There was wild laughter in the court. Another balloon of red ink sailed across the courtroom to burst on the high bench. Mark laughed hysterically, completely out of control, as the spectators shouted.

"EQUALITY NOW!" Eight voices speaking in unison cut through the babble. "JUSTICE! EQUALITY! CITIZEN JUDGES, NOT TAXPAYERS! EQUALITY NOW! EQUALITY NOW! EQUALITY NOW! ALL POWER TO THE LIBERATION PARTY!"

The last stung like a blow. The judge's face turned even redder. He stood in fury. The fat bailiff and his companions moved decisively through the crowd. Two of the demonstrators escaped, but the bailiff was much faster than his bulk made him look. After a time the court was silent.

The judge stood, ink dripping from his face and robes. He was not smiling. "This amused you?" he demanded.

"NO," Mark said. "It was none of my doing!"

"I do not believe the outlawed Liberation Party would trouble itself for anyone not one of their own. Mark Fuller, you have pleaded guilty to serious crimes. We would normally send a taxpayer's son to rehabilitation school, but you and your friends have demanded equality. Very well. You shall have it.

"Mark Fuller, I sentence you to three years at hard labor.

Since you have renounced your allegiance to the United States by participating in a deliberate act of rebellion, such participation stipulated by your attorney's admission that you made no move to depart after the reading of the act, you have no claim upon the United States. The United States therefore renounces you. It is hereby ordered that you be delivered to the Co-Dominium authorities to serve your sentence wherever they shall find convenient." The gavel fell to the bench. It didn't sound very loud at all.

II

The low gravity of Luna Base was better than the endless nightmare of the flight up. He'd been trapped in a narrow compartment with berths so close together that the sagging bunk above his pressed against him at high acceleration. The ship had stunk with the putrid smell of vomit and stale wine.

Now he stood under glaring lights in a bare concrete room. The concrete was the gray-green color of moon rock. They hadn't been given an outside view, and except for gravity he might have been in a basement on Earth. There were a thousand others standing with him under the glaring bright fluorescent lights. Most of them had the dull look of terror. A few glared defiantly, but they kept their opinions to themselves.

Gray-coveralled trusties with bell-mouthed sonic stunners patrolled the room. It wouldn't have been worthwhile trying to take one of the weapons from the trusties, though; at each entrance was a knot of CoDominium Marines in blue and scarlet. The Marines leaned idly on weapons which were not harmless at all.

"Segregate us," Mark's companion said. "Divide and rule."

Mark nodded. Bill Halpern was the only person Mark knew. Halpern had been the technocrat spokesman in the meeting on campus.

"Divide and rule," Halpern said again. It was true enough. The prisoners had been sorted by sex, race, and language, so that everyone around Mark was white male and either North American or from some other English-speaking place. "What the hell are we waiting for?" Halpern wondered. There was no possible answer, and they stood for what seemed like hours.

Then the doors opened and a small group came in. Three CoDominium Navy petty officers, and a midshipman. The middie was no more than seventeen, younger than Mark. He used a bull horn to speak to the assembled group. "Volunteers for the Navy?"

There were several shouts, and some of the prisoners stepped forward.

"Traitors," Halpern said.

Mark nodded agreement. Although he had meant it in a different way from Halpern, Mark's father had always said the same thing. "Traitors!" he'd thundered. "Dupes of the goddamn Soviets. One of these days that Navy will take over this country and hand us to the Kremlin."

Mark's teachers at school had different ideas. The Navy wasn't needed at all. Nor was the CD. Men no longer made war, at least not on Earth. Colony squabbles were of no interest to the people of Earth anyway. Military services, they'd told him, were a wasteful joke.

His new friends at college said the purpose of the Co-Dominium was to keep the United States and the Soviet Union rich while suppressing everyone else. Then they'd begun using the CD fleet and Marines to shore up their domestic governments. The whole CD was nothing more than a part of the machinery of oppression.

And yet—on tri-v the CD Navy was glamorous. It fought pirates (only Mark knew there were no real space pirates) and restored order in the colonies (only his college friends told him that wasn't restoring order, it was oppression of free people). The spacers wore uniforms and explored new planets.

The CD midshipman walked along the line of prisoners. Two older petty officers followed. They walked proudly—contemptuously, even. They saw the prisoners as another race, not as fellow humans at all.

A convict not far from Mark stepped out of the line. "Mister Blaine," the man said. "Please, sir."

The midshipman stopped. "Yes?"

"Don't you know me, Mister Blaine? Able Spacer Johnson, sir. In Mister Leary's division in *Magog*."

The middie nodded with the gravity of a seventeen-year-old who has important duties and knows it. "I recall you, Johnson."

"Let me back in, sir. Six years I served, never up for defaulters."

The midshipman took papers from his clipboard and ran his finger down a list. "Drunk and disorderly, assault on a taxpayer, armed robbery, third conviction. Mandatory transportation. I shouldn't wonder that you prefer the Navy, Johnson."

"Not like that at all, sir. I shouldn't ever have took my musterin'-out pay. Shouldn't have left the Fleet, sir. Couldn't find my place with civilians, sir. God knows I drank too much, but I was never drunk on duty, sir, you look up my records—"

"Kiss the middie's bum, you whining asshole," Halpern said.

One of the petty officers glanced up. "Silence in the ranks." He put his hand on his night stick and glared at Halpern.

The midshipman thought for a moment. "All right, Johnson. You'll come in as ordinary. Have to work for the stripe."

"Yes, sir, sure thing, sir." Johnson strode toward the area reserved for recruits. His manner changed with each step he took. He began in a cringing walk, but by the time he reached the end of the room he had straightened and walked tall.

The midshipman went on down the line. Twenty men volunteered, but he took only three.

An hour later a CoDominium Marine sergeant came looking for men. "No rebels and no degenerates!" he said. He took six young men sentenced for street rioting, arson, mayhem, resisting arrest, assault on police, and numerous other crimes.

"Street gang," Halpern said. "Perfect for Marines."

Eventually they were herded back into a detention pen and left to themselves. "You really hate the CD, don't you?" Mark asked his companion.

"I hate what they do."

Mark nodded, but Halpern only sneered. "You don't know anything at all," Halpern said. "Oppression? Shooting rioters? Sure, that's part of what the CD does, but it's not the worst part. Symptom, not cause. The cause is their goddamn so-called intelligence service. Suppression of scientific research. Censorship of technical journals. They've stopped even the pretense of basic research. When was the last time a licensed physicist had a decent idea?"

Mark shrugged. He knew nothing about physics.

Halpern grinned. There was no warmth in the expression. His voice had a bitter edge. "Keeping the peace, they say. Only discourage new weapons, new military technology. Bullshit, they've stopped everything for fear somebody somewhere will come up with—"

"Shut the fuck up." The man was big, hairy like a bear, with a big paunch jutting out over the belt of his coveralls. "If I hear that goddamn whining once more I'll stomp your goddamn head in."

"Hey, easy," Halpern said. "We're all in this together. We have to join against the class enemy—"

The big men's hand swung up without warning. He hit Halpern on the mouth. Halpern staggered and fell. His head struck the concrete floor. "Told you to shut up." He turned to Mark. "You got anything to say?"

Mark was terrified. I ought to do something, he thought. Say something. Anything. He tried to speak, but no words came out.

The big man grinned at him, then deliberately kicked Halpern in the ribs. "Didn't think so. Hey, you're not bad lookin', kid. Six months we'll be on that goddamn ship, with no women. Want to be my bunkmate? I'll take good care of you. See nobody hurts you. You'll like that."

"Leave the kid alone." Mark couldn't see who spoke. "I said, let go of him."

"Who says so?" The hairy man shoved Mark against the wall and turned to the newcomer.

"I do." The newcomer didn't look like much, Mark thought. At least forty, and slim. Not thin though, Mark realized. The man stood with his hands thrust into the pockets of his coveralls. "Let him be, Karper."

Karper grinned and charged at the newcomer. As he rushed forward, his opponent pivoted and sent a kick to Karper's head. As Karper reeled back, two more kicks slammed his head against the wall. Then the newcomer moved forward and deliberately kneed Karper in the kidney. The big man went down and rolled beside Halpern.

"Come on, kid, it stinks over here." He grinned at Mark.

"But my buddy—"

"Forget him." The man pointed. Five trusties were coming into the pen. They lifted Halpern and Karper and carried them away. One of the trusties winked as they went past Mark and the other man. "See? Maybe you'll see your friend again, maybe not. They don't like troublemakers."

"Bill's not a troublemaker! That other man started it! It's not fair!"

"Kid, you better forget that word 'fair.' It could cause you no end of problems. Got any smokes?" He accepted Mark's cigarette with a glance at the label. "Thanks. Name?"

"Mark Fuller."

"Dugan. Call me Biff."

"Thanks, Biff. I guess I needed some help."

"That you did. Hell, it was fun. Karper was gettin' on my nerves anyway. How old are you, kid?"

"Twenty." And what does he want? Lord God, is he looking for a bunkmate too?

"You don't look twenty. Taxpayer, aren't you?"

"Yes—how did you know?"

"It shows. What's a taxpayer kid doing here?"

Mark told him. "It wasn't fair," he finished.

"There's that word again. You were in college, eh? Can you read?"

"Well, sure, everyone can read."

Dugan laughed. "I can't. Not very well. And I bet you're the only one in this pen who ever read a whole book. Where'd you learn?"

"Well—in school. Maybe a little at home."

Dugan blew a careful smoke ring. It hung in the air between them. "Me, I never saw a book until they dragged me off to school, and nobody gave a shit whether we looked at 'em or not. Had to pick up some of it, but—look, maybe you know things I don't. Want to stick with me a while?"

Mark eyed him suspiciously. Dugan laughed. "Hell, I don't bugger kids. Not until I've been locked up a lot longer than this, anyway. Man needs a buddy, though, and you just lost yours."

"Yeah. Okay. Want another cigarette?"

"We better save 'em. We'll need all you got."

A petty officer opened the door to the pen. "Classification," he shouted. "Move out this door."

"Got to it pretty fast," Dugan said. "Come on." They followed the others out and through a long corridor until they reached another large room. There were tables at the end, and trusties sat at each table. Eventually Mark and Dugan got to one.

The trusty barely looked at them. When they gave their names he punched them into a console on the table. The printer made tiny clicking noises and two sheets of paper fell out. "Any choice?" the trusty asked.

"What's open, shipmate?" Dugan asked.

"I'm no shipmate of yours," the trusty sneered. "Tanith, Sparta, and Fulson's World."

Dugan shuddered. "Well, we sure don't want Fulson's World." He reached into Mark's pocket and took out the pack of cigarettes, then laid them on the table. They vanished into the trusty's coveralls.

"Not Fulson's," the trusty said. "Now, I hear they're lettin' the convicts run loose on Sparta." He said nothing more but looked at them closely.

Mark remembered that Sparta was founded by a group of intellectuals. They were trying some kind of social experiment.

Unlike Tanith with its CoDominium Governor, Sparta was more or less independent. They'd have a better chance there. "We'll take Sparta," Mark said.

"Sparta's pretty popular," the trusty said. He waited expectantly for a moment. "Well, too bad." He scrawled "Tanith" across their papers and handed them over. "Move along." A petty officer waved them through a door behind the table.

"But we wanted Sparta," Mark protested.

"Get your ass out of here," the CD petty officer said. "Move it." Then it was too late and they were through the door.

"Wish I'd had some credits," Dugan muttered. "We bought off Fulson's though. That's something."

"But—I have some money. I didn't know—"

Dugan gave him a curious look. "Kid, they didn't teach you much in that school of yours. Well, come on, we'll make out. But you better let me take care of that money."

❊   ❊   ❊

CDSS Vladivostok hurtled toward the orbit of Jupiter. The converted assault troop carrier was crammed with thousands of men jammed into temporary berths welded into the troop bays. There were more men than bunks; many of the convicts had to trade off half the time.

Dugan took over a corner. Corners were desirable territory, and two men disputed his choice. After they were carried away no one else thought it worth trying. Biff used Mark's money to finance a crap game in the area near their berths, and in a few days had trebled their capital.

"Too bad," Dugan said. "If we'd had this much back on Luna, we'd be headed for Sparta. Anyway we bought our way into this ship, and that's worth something." He grinned at Mark's lack of response. "Hey, kid, it could be worse. We could be with BuRelock. You think this Navy ship's bad, try a BuRelock hellhole."

Mark wondered how Bureau of Relocation ships could be worse, but he didn't want to find out. The newscasters back on Earth had documentary specials about BuRelock. They all

said that conditions were tough but bearable. They also told of
the glory: mankind settling other worlds circling other stars.
Mark felt none of the glory now.

Back home Zower would be making an appeal. Or at least
he'd be billing Mark's father for one. And so what? Mark
thought. Nothing would come of it. But something might!
Jason Fuller had some political favors coming. He might pull a
few strings. Mark could be headed back home within a
year . . .

He knew better, but he had no other hope. He lived in
misery, brooding about the low spin gravity, starchy food, the
constant stench of the other convicts; all that was bad, but the
water was the worst thing. He knew it was recycled. Water on
Earth was recycled too, but there you didn't think how it had
been used to bathe the foul sores of the man two bays to star-
board.

Sometimes a convict would rush screaming through the
compartment, smashing at bunks and flinging his fellow prisoners about like matchsticks, until a dozen men would beat him
to the deck. Eventually the guards would take him away. None
ever came back.

The ship reached the orbit of Jupiter and took on fuel from
the scoopship tankers that waited for her. Then she moved to
the featureless point in space that marked the Alderson jump
tramline. Alarms rang; then everything blurred. They sat on
their bunks in confusion, unable to move or even think. That
lasted long after the instantaneous Jump. The ship had covered
light-years in a single instant; now they had to cross another
star's gravity well to reach the next Jump point.

Two weeks later a petty officer entered the compartment.
"Two men needed for cleanup in the crew area. Chance for
Navy chow. Volunteers?"

"Sure," Dugan said. "My buddy and me. Anybody object?"

No one did. The petty officer grinned. "Looks like you're
elected." He led them through corridors and passageways to
the forward end of the ship, where they were put to scrubbing
the bulkheads. A bored Marine watched idly.

"I thought you said never volunteer," Mark told Dugan.

"Good general rule. But what else we got to do? Gets us better chow. Always take a chance on something when it can't be no worse than what you've got."

The lunch was good and the work was not hard. Even the smell of disinfectant was a relief, and scrubbing off the bulkheads and decks got their hands clean for the first time since they'd been put aboard. In midafternoon a crewman came by. He stopped and stared at them for a moment.

"Dugan! Biff Dugan, by God!"

"Horrigan, you slut. When'd you join up?"

"Aw, you know how it is, Biff, they moved in on the racket and what could I do? I see they got you—"

"Clean got me. Sarah blew the whistle on me."

"Told you she wouldn't put up with you messing around. Who's your chum?"

"Name's Mark. He's learning. Hey, Goober, what can you do for me?"

"Funny you ask. Maybe I got something. Want to enlist?"

"Hell, they don't want me. I tried back on Luna. Too old."

Horrigan nodded. "Yeah, but the Purser's gang needs men. Freakie killed twenty crewmen yesterday. Recruits. This geek opened an air lock and nobody stopped him. That's why you're out here swabbing. Look, Biff, we're headed for a long patrol after we drop you guys on Tanith. Maybe I can fix it."

"No harm in trying. Mark, you lost anything on Tanith?"

"No." But I don't want to join the CD Navy, either. Only why not? He tried to copy his friend's easy indifference. "Can't be worse than where we are."

"Right," Horrigan said. "We'll go see the Purser's middie. That okay, mate?" he asked the Marine.

The Marine shrugged. "Okay by me."

Horrigan led the way forward. Mark felt sick excitement. Getting out of the prison compartment suddenly became the most important thing in his life.

Midshipman Greschin was not surprised to find two prisoners ready to join the Navy. He questioned them for a few minutes.

Then he studied Dugan's records on the readout screen. "You have been in space before, but there is nothing on your record—"

"I never said I've been out."

"No, but you have. Are you a deserter?"

"No," Dugan said.

Greschin shrugged. "If you are, we will find out. If not, we do not care. I see no reason why you cannot be enlisted. I will call Lieutenant Breslov."

Breslov was fifteen years older than his midshipman. He looked over Dugan's print-out. Then he examined Mark's. "I can take Dugan," he said. "Not you, Fuller."

"But why?" Mark asked.

Breslov shrugged. "You are a rebel, and you have high intelligence. So it says here. There are officers who will take the risk of recruiting those like you, but I am not one of them. We cannot use you in this ship."

"Oh." Mark turned to go.

"Wait a minute, kid." Dugan looked at the officer. "Thanks, Lieutenant, but maybe I better stick with my buddy—"

"No, don't do that," Mark said. He felt a wave of gratitude toward the older man. Dugan's offer seemed the finest thing anyone had ever tried to do for him.

"Who'll look out for ya? You'll get your throat cut."

"Maybe not. I've learned a lot."

Breslov stood. "Your sentiment for your friend is admirable, but you are wasting my time. Are you enlisting?"

"He is," Mark said. "Thank you, Lieutenant." He followed the Marine guard back to the corridor and began washing the bulkhead, scrubbing savagely, trying to forget his misery and despair. It was all so unfair!

III

Tanith was hot steaming jungle under a perpetual gray cloud cover. The gravity was too high and the humidity was almost unbearable. Yet it was a relief to be there after the crowded ship, and Mark waited to see what would happen to him. He was surprised to find that he cared.

He was herded through medical processing, immunization, identification, a meaningless classification interview, and both psychological and aptitude tests. They ran from one task to the next, then stood in long lines or simply waited around. On the fourth day he was taken from the detention pen to an empty adobe-walled room with rough wooden furniture. The guards left him there. The sensation of being alone was exhilarating.

He looked up warily when the door opened. "Biff!"

"Hi, kid. Got something for you." Dugan was dressed in the blue coveralls of the CD Navy. He glanced around guiltily. "You left this with me and I run it up a bit." He held out a fistful of CoDominium scrip. "Go on, take it, I can get more and you can't. Look, we're pullin' out pretty soon, and . . ."

"It's all right," Mark said. But it wasn't all right. He hadn't known how much friendship meant to him until he'd been separated from Dugan; now, seeing him in the Navy uniform and knowing that Dugan was headed away from this horrible place, Mark hated his former friend. "I'll get along."

"Damned right you will! Stop sniffling about how unfair everything is and wait your chance. You'll get one. Look, you're a young kid and everything seems like it's forever, but—" Dugan fell silent and shook his head ruefully. "Not that you need fatherly advice from me. Or that it'd do any good. But things end, Mark. The day ends. So do weeks and months."

"Yeah. Sure." They said more meaningless things, and Dugan left. Now I'm completely alone, Mark thought. It was a crushing thought. Some of the speeches he'd heard in his few days in college kept rising up to haunt him. *"Die Gedanken, Sie sind frei."* Yeah. Sure. A man's thoughts were always free, and no one could enslave a free man, and the heaviest chains and darkest dungeons could never cage the spirit of man. Bullshit. I'm a slave. If I don't do what they tell me, they'll hurt me until I do. And I'm too damn scared of them. But something else he'd heard was more comforting. "Slaves have no rights, and thus have no obligations."

That, by God, fits, he thought. I don't owe anybody a thing. Nobody here, and none of those bastards on Earth. I do what I have to do and I look out for number one, and rape the rest of 'em.

❊   ❊   ❊

There was no prison, or rather the entire planet was a prison; but the main CD building was intended only for classification and assignment. The prisoners were sold off to wealthy planters. There were a lot of rumors about the different places you might be sent to: big company farms run like factories, where it was said that few convicts ever lived to finish out their terms; industrial plants near big cities, which was supposed to be soft duty because as soon as you got trusty status you could get passes into town; lonely plantations out in the sticks where owners could do anything they wanted and generally did.

The pen began to empty as the men were shipped out. Then came Mark's turn. He was escorted into an interview room and given a seat. It was the second time in months that he'd been alone, and he enjoyed the solitude. There were voices from the next room.

"Why do you not keep him, *hein?*"

"Immature. No reason to be loyal to the CD."

"Or to me."

"Or to you. And too smart to be a dumb cop. You might make a foreman out of him. The governor's interested in this one, Ludwig. He keeps track of all the high-IQ types. Look, you take this one, I owe you. I'll see you get good hands."

"Okay. *Ja.* Just remember that when you get in some with muscles and no brains, *hein?* Okay, we look at your genius."

Who the hell were they talking about? Mark wondered. Me? Compared to most of the others in the ship I guess you could call me a genius, but—

The door opened. Mark stood quickly. The guards liked you to do that.

"Fuller," the captain said. "This is Herr Ewigfeuer. You'll work for him. His place is a country club."

The planter was heavy-set, with thick jowls. He needed a shave, and his shorts and khaki shirt were stained with sweat. "So you are the new convict I take to my nice farm." He eyed Mark coldly. "He will do, he will do. Okay, we go now, *ja?*"

"Now?" Mark said.

"Now, *ja*, you think all day I have? I can stay in Whiskeytown while my foreman lets the hands eat everything and lay around not working? Give me the papers, Captain."

The captain took a sheaf of papers from a folder. He scrawled across the bottom, then handed Mark a pen. "Sign here."

Mark started to read the documents. The captain laughed. "Sign it, goddamnit. We don't have all day."

Mark shrugged and scribbled his name. The captain handed Ewigfeuer two copies and indicated a door. They went through adobe corridors to a guardroom at the end. The planter handed the guards a copy of the contract and the door was opened.

The heat outside struck Mark like a physical blow. It had been hot enough inside, but the thick earthen walls had protected him from the worst; now it was almost unbearable. There was no sun, but the clouds were bright enough to hurt his eyes. Ewigfeuer put on dark glasses. He led the way to a shop across from the prison and bought Mark a pair. "Put these on," he commanded. "You are no use if you are blind. Now come."

They walked through busy streets. The sky hung dull orange, an eternal sunset. Sweat sprang from Mark's brow and trickled down inside his coveralls. He wished he had shorts. Nearly everyone in the town wore them.

They passed grimy shops and open stalls. There were sidewalk displays of goods for sale, nearly all crudely made or Navy surplus or black-market goods stolen from CD storerooms. Strange animals pulled carts through the streets and there were no automobiles at all.

A team of horses splashed mud on Ewigfeuer's legs. The fat planter shook his fist at the driver. The teamster ignored him.

"Have you owned horses?" Ewigfeuer demanded.

"No," Mark said. "I hadn't expected to see any here."

"Horses make more horses. Tractors do not," the planter said. "Also with horses and jackasses you get mules. Better than tractors. Better than the damned stormand beasts. Stormands do not like men." He pointed to one of the unlikely animals. It looked like a cross between a mule and a moose, with wide, splayed feet and a sad look that turned vicious whenever anyone got near it. It was tied to a rail outside one of the shops.

There were more people than Mark had expected. They seemed to divide into three classes. There were those who tended the shops and stalls, and who smiled unctuously when the planter passed; there were others who strode purposefully through the muddy streets; and there were those who wandered aimlessly or sat on streetcorners staring vacantly.

"What are they waiting for?" Mark said. He hadn't meant to say it aloud, but Ewigfeuer heard him.

"They wait to die," the planter said. "*Ja*, they think something else will come to save them. They will find something to steal, maybe, so they live another week, another month, a year even; but they are waiting to die. And they are white men!" This seemed their ultimate crime to Ewigfeuer.

"You might expect this of the blacks," the planter said. "But no, the blacks work, or they go to the bush and live there—not like civilized men perhaps, but they live. Not these. They wait to die. It was a cruel day when their sentences ended."

"Yeah, sure," Mark said, but he made certain the planter had not heard him. There was another group sitting on benches near a small open square. They looked as if they had not moved since morning, since the day before, or ever; that when the orange sky fell dark they would still be there, and when dawn came with its heat and humidity they would be there yet. Mark mopped his brow with his sleeve. Heat lay across Whiskeytown so that it was an effort to move, but the planter hustled him along the street, his short legs moving rapidly through the mud patches.

"And what happens if I just run?" Mark asked.

Ewigfeuer laughed. "Go ahead. You think they will not catch

you? Where will you go? You have no papers. Perhaps you buy some if you have money. Perhaps what you buy is not good enough. And when they catch you, it is not to my nice farm they send you. It will be to some awful place. Run, I will not chase you. I am too old and too fat."

Mark shrugged and walked along with Ewigfeuer. He noticed that for all his careless manner the fat man did not let Mark get behind him.

They rounded a corner and came to a large empty space. A helicopter stood at the near edge. There were others in the lot. A man with a rifle sat under an umbrella watching them. Ewigfeuer threw the man some money and climbed into the nearest chopper. He gunned the engines twice, then let it lift them above the city.

Whiskeytown was an ugly sprawl across a plateau. The hill rose directly up from jungle. When they were higher, Mark could see that the plateau was part of a ridge on a peninsula; the sea around it was green with yellow streaks. The concrete CoDominium administration building was the largest structure in Whiskeytown. There was no other air traffic, and they flew across the town without making contact with any traffic controllers.

Beyond the town were brown hills rising above ugly green jungles. An hours later there was no change—jungle to the left, and the green and yellow sea to the right. Mark had seen no roads and only a few houses; all of those were in clusters, low adobe buildings atop the brown hills. "Is the whole planet jungle?" he asked.

"*Ja*, jungles, marshes, bad stuff. People can live in the hills. Below is green hell, Weem's Beasts, killer things like tortoises, crocodiles so big you don't believe them and they run faster than you. Nobody runs far in that."

A perfect prison, Mark thought. He stared out at the sea. There were boats out there. Ewigfeuer followed his gaze and laughed.

"Some damn fools try to make a few credits fishing. Maybe smart at that, they get killed fast, they don't wait for tax farmers to take everything they make. You have heard of the Loch Ness monster? On Tanith we got something makes Nessie an earthworm."

They flew over another cluster of adobe buildings. Ewigfeuer used the radio to talk to the people below. They spoke a language Mark didn't know. It didn't seem like German, but he wasn't sure. Then they crossed another seemingly endless stretch of jungle. Finally a new group of buildings was in sight ahead.

The plantation was no different from the others they had seen. There was a cluster of brown adobe buildings around one larger whitewashed wooden house at the very top of the hill. Cultivated fields lay around that on smaller hills. The fields blended into jungle at the edges. Men were working in the fields.

It would be easy enough to run away, Mark thought. Too easy. It must be stupid to try, or there would be fences. Wait, he thought. Wait and learn. I owe nothing. To anyone. Wait for a chance—

—a chance for what? He pushed the thought away.

※　※　※

The foreman was tall and cruelly handsome. He wore dirty white shorts and a sun helmet, and there was a pistol buckled on his belt.

"You look after this one, *ja*," Ewigfeuer said. "One of the governor's pets. They say he has brains enough to make supervisor. We will see. Mark Fuller, three years."

"Yes, sir. Come on, Mark Fuller, three years." The foreman turned and walked away. After a moment Mark followed. They went past rammed earth buildings and across a sea of mud. The buildings had been sprayed with some kind of plastic and shone dully. "You'll need boots," the foreman said. "And a new outfit. I'm Curt Morgan. Get along with me and you'll be happy. Cross me and you're in trouble. Got that?"

"Yes, sir."

"You don't call me sir unless I tell you to. Right now you call me Curt. If you need help, ask me. Maybe I can give you good advice. If it don't cost me anything I will." They reached a rectangular one-story building like the others. "This'll be your bunkie."

The inside was a long room with places for thirty men. Each place had a bunk, a locker, and an area two meters by three of clear space. After the ship it seemed palatial. The inside walls were sprayed with the same plastic material as the outside; it kept insects from living in the dirt walls. Some of the men had cheap pictures hung above their bunks: pinups, mostly, but in one corner area there were original charcoal sketches of men and women working, and an unfinished oil painting.

There were a dozen men in the room. Some were sprawled on their bunks. One was knitting something elaborate, and a small group at the end were playing cards. One of the card players, a small man, ferret-faced, left the game.

"Your new man," Curt said. "Mark Fuller, three years. Fuller, this is your bunkie leader. His name is Lewis. Lew, get the kid bunked and out of those prison slops."

"Sure, Curt." Lewis eyed Mark carefully. "About the right size for José's old outfit. The gear's all clean."

"Want to do that?" Curt asked. "Save you some money."

Mark stared helplessly.

The two men laughed. "You better give him the word, Lew," Curt Morgan said. "Fuller, I'd take him up on the gear. Let me know what he charges you, right? He won't squeeze you too bad." There was laughter from the other men in the bunkie as the foreman left.

Lewis pointed out a bunk in the center, "José was there, kid. Left his whole outfit when he took the green way out. Give you the whole lot for, uh, fifty credits."

And now what? Mark wondered. Best not to show him I've got any money. "I don't have that much—"

"Hell, you sign a chit for it," Lewis said. "The old man pays a credit a day and found."

"Who do I get the chit from?"

"You get it from me." Lewis narrowed watery eyes. They

looked enormous through his thick glasses. "You thinking about something, kid? You don't want to try it."

"I'm not trying anything! I just don't understand—"

"Sure. You just remember I'm in charge here. Anybody skips out, I get their gear. Me. Nobody else. José had a good outfit, worth fifty credits easy—"

"Bullshit," one of the card players said. "Not worth more'n thirty and you know it."

"Shut up. Sure, you could do better in Whiskeytown, but not here. Look, Morgan said take care of you. I'll sell you the gear for thirty. Deal?"

"Sure."

Lewis gave him a broad smile. "You'll get by, kid. Here's your key." He handed Mark a magnokey and went back to the card game.

Mark wondered who had copies. It wasn't something you could duplicate without special equipment; the magnetic spots had to be in just the right places. Ewigfeuer would have one, of course. Who else? No use worrying about it. Mark tucked his money into the toe of a sock and threw the rest of his clothes on top of it, then locked the whole works into the locker. He wondered what to do with the money; he had nearly three hundred credits, ten months' wages at a credit a day— enough to be killed for.

It bothered him all the way to the shower, but after that the unlimited water, new bar of soap, and a good razor were such pleasures that he didn't think about anything else.

IV

The borshite plant resembles an artichoke in appearance: tall, spiky leaves rising from a central crown, with one flower-bearing stalk jutting upward to a height of a meter and a half. It is propagated by bulbs; in spring the previous year's crop is dug up and the delicate bulbs carefully separated, then each replanted. Weeds grow in abundance and must be pulled out by hand. The jungle constantly grows inward to reclaim the high ground that men cultivate. Herbivores eat the crops unless the fields are patrolled.

Mark learned that and more within a week. The work was difficult and the weather was hot, but neither was unbearable. The rumors were true: Ewigfeuer's place was a country club. Convicts schemed to get there. Ewigfeuer demanded hard work, but he was fair.

That made it all the more depressing for Mark. If this was the easy way to do time, what horrors waited if he made a mistake? Ewigfeuer held transfer as his ultimate threat, and Mark found himself looking for ways to keep his master pleased. He disgusted himself—but there was nothing else to do.

He had never been more alone. He had nothing in common with the other men. His jokes were never funny. He had no interest in their stories. He learned to play poker so well that he was resented when he played. They didn't want a tight player who could take their money. Once he was accused of cheating, and although everyone knew he hadn't, he was beaten and his money taken. After that he avoided the games.

The work occupied only his hands, not his mind. There were no books to read. There was little to do but brood. *I wanted power,* he thought. *We were playing at it. A game. But the police weren't playing, and now I've become a slave. When I get back I'll know more of how this game is played. I'll show them.*

But he knew he wouldn't, not really. He was learning nothing here.

Some of the convicts spent their entire days and nights stoned into tranquillity. Borshite plants are the source of borloi, and half the Citizens of the United States depended on borloi to get through each day; the government supplied it to them, and any government that failed in the shipments would not last long. It worked as well on Tanith, and Herr Ewigfeuer was generous with both pipes and borloi. Mark tried that route, but he did not like what it did to him. They were stealing three years of his life, but he wouldn't cooperate and make it easier.

His college friends had talked a lot about the dignity of

labor. Mark didn't find it dignified at all. Why not get stoned and stay that way? he thought. What am I doing that's important? Why not go out of being and get it over? Let the routine wash over me, drown in it—

There were frequent fights. They had rules. If a man got hurt so that he couldn't work, both he and the man he fought with had to make up the lost work time. It tended to keep the injuries down and discouraged broken bones. Whenever there was a fight everyone turned out to watch.

It gave Mark time to himself. He didn't like being alone, but he didn't like watching fights, especially since he might be drawn into one himself—

The men shouted encouragement to the fighters. Mark lay on his bunk. He had liquor but didn't want to drink. He kept thinking about taking a drink, just one, it will help me get to sleep—and you know what you're doing to yourself—and why not?

The man was small and elderly. Mark knew he lived in quarters near the big house. He came into the bunkie and glanced around. The lights had not been turned on, and he failed to see Mark. He looked furtively about again, then stooped to try locker lids, looking for one that was open. He reached Mark's locker, opened it, and felt inside. His hand found cigarettes and the bottle—

He felt or heard Mark, and looked up. "Uh, good evening."

"Good evening." The man seemed cool enough, although he risked the usual punishments men mete out to thieves in barracks.

"Are you bent on calling your mates?" The watery eyes darted around looking for an escape. "I don't seem to have any defense."

"If you did have one, what would it be?"

"When you are as old as I am and in for life, you take what you can. I am an alcoholic, and I steal to buy drink."

"Why not smoke borloi?"

"It does little for me." The old man's hands were shaking. He looked lovingly at the bottle of gin that he'd taken from Mark's locker.

"Oh, hell, have a drink," Mark said.

"Thank you." He drank eagerly, in gulps.

Mark retrieved his bottle. "I don't see you in the fields."

"No. I work with the accounts. Herr Ewigfeuer has been kind enough to keep me, but not so kind as to pay enough to—"

"If you keep the work records, you could sell favors."

"Certainly. For a time. Until I was caught. And then what? It is not much of a life that I have, but I want to keep it." He stood in silence for a moment. "Surprising, isn't it? But I do."

"You talk rather strangely," Mark said.

"The stigmata of education. You see Richard Henry Tappinger, Ph.D., generally called Taps. Formerly holder of the Bates Chair of History and Sociology at Yale University."

"And why are you on Tanith?" Prisoners do not ask that question, but Mark could do as he liked. He held the man's life in his hands: a word, a call, and the others would amuse themselves with Tappinger. And why don't I call them? Mark asked himself. He shuddered at the thought that he could even consider it.

Tappinger didn't seem annoyed. "Liquor, young girls, their lovers, and an old fool are an explosive combination. You don't mind if I am not more specific? I spend a good part of my life being ashamed of myself. Could I have another drink?"

"I suppose."

"You have the stigmata about you as well. You were a student?"

"Not for long."

"But worthy of education. And generous as well. Your name is Fuller. I have the records, and I recall your case."

The fight outside ground to a close, and the men came back into the barracks. Lewis was carrying an unconscious man to the showers. He handed him over to others when he saw Tappinger.

"You sneaky bastard, I told you what'd happen if I found you in my bunkie! What'd he steal, Fuller?"

"Nothing. I gave him a drink."

"Yeah? Well, keep him out of here. You want to talk to him, you do it outside."

"Right." Mark took his bottle and followed Tappinger out. It was hot inside and the men were talking about the fight. Mark followed Tappinger across the quad. They stayed away from the women's barracks. Mark had no friends in there and couldn't afford any other kind of visit—at least not very often, and he was always disturbed afterwards. None of the women seemed attractive, or to care about themselves.

"So. The two outcasts gather together," Tappinger said. "Two pink monkeys among the browns."

"Maybe I should resent that."

"Why? Do you have much in common with them? Or do you resent the implication that you have more in common with me?'"

'I don't know. I don't know anything. I'm just passing time. Waiting until this is over."

"And what will you do then?"

They found a place to sit. The local insects didn't bother them; the taste was wrong. There was a faint breeze from the west. The jungle noises came with it, snorts and grunts and weird calls.

"What can I do?" Mark asked. "Get back to Earth and—"

"You will never get back to Earth," Tappinger said. "Or if you do, you will be one of the first ever. Unless you have someone to buy your passage?"

"That's expensive."

"Precisely."

"But they're supposed to take us back!" Mark felt all his carefully built defenses begin to crumble. He lived for the end of the three years—and now—

"The regulations say so, and the convicts talk about going home, but it does not happen. Earth does not want rebels. It would disturb the comfortable life most have. No, if you ship out it will be to another colony. Unless you are very rich."

So I'm here forever. "So what else is there? What do ex-cons do here?"

Tappinger shrugged. "Sign up as laborers. Start their own plantations. Go into government service. You see Tanith as a slave world, which it is, but it will not always be that. Some of you, people like you, will build it into something else, something better or worse, but certainly different."

"Yeah. Sure. The Junior Pioneers have arrived."

"What do you think happens to involuntary colonists?" Tappinger asked. "Or did you never think of them? Most people on Earth don't look very hard at the price of keeping their wealth and their clean air and clean oceans. But the only difference between you and someone shipped by BuRelock is that you came in a slightly more comfortable ship, and you will put in three years here before they turn you out to fend for yourself. Yes, I definitely suggest the government services for you. You could rise quite high."

"Work for those slaving bastards? I'd rather starve!"

"No, you wouldn't. Nor would many others. It is easier to say that than to do it."

Mark stared into the darkness.

"Why so grim? There are opportunities here. The new governor is even trying to reform some of the abuses. Of course he is caught in the system just as we are. He must export his quota of borloi and miracle drugs, and pay the taxes demanded of him. He must keep up production. The Navy demands it."

"The Navy?"

Tappinger smiled in the dark. "You would be surprised at just how much of the CD Navy's operations are paid for by the profits from the Tanith drug trade."

"It doesn't surprise me at all. Thieves. Bastards. But it's stupid. A treadmill, with prisons to pay for themselves and the damned fleet—"

"Neither stupid nor new. The Soviets have done it for nearly two hundred years, with the proceeds of labor camps paying for the secret police. And our tax farming scheme is even older.

It dates back to old Rome. Profits from some planets support BuRelock. Tanith supports the Navy."

"Damn the Navy."

"Ah, no, don't do that. Bless it instead. Without the CD Fleet, the Earth governments would be at each other's throats in a moment. They very nearly are now. And since they won't pay for the Navy, and the Navy is very much needed to keep peace on Earth, why, we must continue to work. See what a noble task we perform as we weed the borloi fields?"

❋   ❋   ❋

Unbearably hot spring became intolerably hot summer, and the work decreased steadily. The borshite plants were nearly as high as a man's waist, and were able to defend themselves against most weeds and predators. The fields needed watching but little else.

To compensate for the easier work, the weather was sticky hot, with warm fog rolling in from the coast. The skies turned from orange to dull gray. Mark had seen stars only twice since he arrived.

With summer came easy sex. Men and women could visit in the evenings, and with suitable financial arrangements with bunkie leaders, all night. The pressures of the barracks eased. Mark found the easier work more attractive than the women. When he couldn't stand it any longer he'd pay for a few minutes of frantic relief, then try not to think about sex for as long as he could.

His duties were simple. Crownears, muskrat-sized animals that resembled large shrews, would eat unprotected borshite plants. They had to be driven away. They were stupid animals, and ravenous, but not very dangerous unless a swarm of them could catch a man mired down in the mud. A man with a spear could keep them out of the crops.

There were other animals to watch for. Weem's Beast, named for the first man to survive a meeting with one, was the worst. The crownears were its natural prey, but it would attack almost anything that moved. Weem's Beast looked vaguely like a mole but was over a meter long. Instead of a prehensile snout, Weem's Beast had a fully articulated grasping member with talons and pseudo-eyes. Men approached holes very carefully on Tanith; the Beast was fond of lying just below the surface and came out with astonishing speed.

It wouldn't usually leave the jungle to attack a man on high ground.

Mark patrolled the fields, and Curt Morgan made rounds on horseback. In the afternoons Morgan would sit with Mark and share his beer ration, and the cold beer and lack of work was almost enough to make life worth living again.

Sometimes there was a break in the weather, and a cooler breeze would blow across the fields. Mark sat with his back to a tree, enjoying the comparatively cool day, drinking his beer ration. Morgan sat next to him.

"Curt, what will you do when you finish your sentence?" Mark asked.

"Finished two years ago. Two Tanith, three Earth."

"Then why are you still here?"

Morgan shrugged. "What else do I know how to do? I'm saving some money; one day I'll have a place of my own." He shifted his position and fired his carbine toward the jungle. "I swear them things gets more nerve every summer. This is all I know. I can't save enough to buy into the tax farming syndicate."

"Could you squeeze people that way?"

"If I had to. Them or me. Tax collectors get rich."

"Sure. Jesus, there's just no goddamn hope for anything, is there? The whole deck's stacked." Mark finished his beer.

"Where isn't it?" Morgan demanded. "You think it's tough now, you ought to have been here before the new governor came. Place they stuck me—my sweet lord, they worked us! Charged for everything we ate or wore, and you open your mouth, it's another month on your sentence. Enough to drive a man into the green."

"Uh—Curt—are there—?"

"Don't get ideas. I'd hate to take the dogs and come find

you. Find your corpse, more likely. Yeah, there's men out in the green. Live like rats. I'd rather be under sentence again than live like the Free Staters."

The thought excited Mark. A Free State! It would have to be like the places Shirley and her friends had talked about, with equality, and there'd be no tax farmers in a free society. He thought of the needs of free men. They would live hard and be poor because they were fugitives, but they would be free! He built the Free State in his imagination until it was more real than Ewigfeuer's plantation.

The next day the crownears were very active, and Curt Morgan brought another worker to Mark's field. They rode up together on the big Percheron horses brought as frozen embryos from Earth and repeatedly bred for even wider feet to keep them above the eternal mud. The newcomer was a girl. Mark had seen her before, but never met her.

"Brought you a treat," Curt said. "This is Juanita. Juanny, if this clown gives you trouble I'll break him in half. Be back in an hour. Got your trumpet?"

Mark indicated the instrument.

"Keep it handy. Them things are restless out there. I think there's a croc around. And porkers. Keep your eyes open." Curt rode off toward the next field.

Mark stood in embarrassed silence. The girl was younger than Mark, and sweaty. He hair hung down in loose blond strings. Her eyes had dark circles under them and her face was dirty. She was built more like a wiry boy than a girl. She was also the most beautiful girl he'd ever seen.

"Hi," Mark said. He cursed himself. Shyness went with civilization, not a prison!

"Hi yourself. You're in Lewis' bunkie."

"Yes. I haven't seen you before. Except at Mass." Each month a priest of the Ecumenical Catholic Church came to the plantation. Mark had never attended his services, but he'd watched idly from a distance.

"Usually work in the big house. Sure hot, isn't it?"

He agreed it was hot and was lost again. What should I say?

"You're lovely" is obvious even if I do think it's true. "Let's go talk to your bunkie leader" isn't too good an idea even if it's what I want to say. Besides, if she lives in the big house she won't have one. "How long do you have?"

"Another two. When I'm eighteen. They still run the sentences on Earth time, I'm eleven, really." There was more silence. "You don't talk much, do you?"

"I don't know what to say. I'm sorry—"

"It's okay. Most of the men jabber away like porshons. Trying to talk me into something, you know?"

"Oh."

"Yeah. But I never have. I'm a member of the church. Confirmed and everything." She looked at him and grinned impishly. "So that makes me a dumb hymn singer, and what's left to talk about?"

"I remember wishing I was you," Mark said. He laughed. "Not quite what I meant to say. I mean, I watched you at Masses. You looked happy. Like you had something to live for."

"Well, of course. We all have something to live for. Must have, people sure try hard to stay alive. When I get out of here, I'm going to ask the padre to let me help him. Be a nun, maybe."

"Don't you want to marry?"

"Who? A con? That's what my mother did, and look, I got 'apprenticed' until I was eighteen Earth years old because I was born to convicts. No kids of mine'll have that happen to 'em!"

"You could marry a free man."

"They're all pretty old by the time they finish. And not worth much. To themselves or anybody else. You proposin' to me?"

He laughed, and she laughed with him, and the afternoon was more pleasant than any he could remember since leaving Earth.

"I was lucky," she told him. "Old man Ewigfeuer traded for me. Place I was born on, the planter'd be selling tickets for me now." She stared at the dirt. "I've seen girls they did that with. They don't like themselves much after a while."

They heard the shrill trumpets in other fields. Mark scanned the jungle in front of him. Nothing moved. Juanita continued to talk. She asked him about Earth. "It's hard to think about that place," she said. "I hear people live all bunched up."

He told her about cities. "There are twenty million people in the city I came from." He also told her of the concrete Welfare Islands at the edges of the cities.

She shuddered. "I'd rather live on Tanith than like that. It's a wonder all the people on Earth don't burn it down and live in the swamps."

Evening came sooner than he expected. After supper he fell into an introspective mood. He hadn't wanted a day to last for a long time. It's silly to think this way, he told himself.

But he was twenty years old, and there wasn't anyone else to think about. That night he dreamed about her.

*   *   *

He saw her often as the summer wore on. She had no education, and Mark began teaching her to read. He scratched letters in the ground, and used some of his money to buy lurid adventure stories—the only reading matter available in the barracks.

Juanita learned quickly. She seemed to enjoy Mark's company, and often arranged to be assigned to the same field that he was. They talked about everything: Earth, and how it wasn't covered with swamps. He told her of blue skies, and sailing on the Pacific, and the island coves he'd explored. She thought he was making most of it up.

Their only quarrels came when he complained of how unfair life was. She laughed at him. "I was born with a sentence," she told him. "You lived in a fine house and had your own 'copter and a boat, and you went to school. If I'm not whinin', why should you, Mr. Taxpayer?"

He wanted to tell her she was unfair too, but stopped himself. Instead he told her of smog and polluted waters, and sprawling cities. "They've got the pollution licked, though," he said. "And the population's going down. What with the licensing, and BuRelock—"

She said nothing, and Mark couldn't finish the sentence. Juanita stared at the empty jungles. "Wish I could see a blue sky some day. I can't even imagine that, so you must be tellin' the truth."

He did not often see her in the evenings. She kept to herself or worked in the big house. Sometimes, though, she would walk with Curt Morgan or sit with him on the porch of the big house, and when she did Mark would buy a bottle of gin and find Tappinger. It was no good being alone then.

The old man would deliver long lectures in a dry monotone that nearly put Mark to sleep, but then he'd ask questions that upset any view of the universe that Mark had ever had.

"You might make a passable sociologist some day," Tappinger said. "Ah, well, they say the best university is a log with a student at one end and a professor at the other. We have that, anyway."

"All I seem to learn is that things are rotten. Everything's set up wrong," Mark said.

Tappinger shook his head. "There has never been a society in which someone did not think there had to be a better deal— for himself. The trick is to see that those who want a better way enough to do something about it can either rise within the system or are rendered harmless by it. Which, of course, Earth does—warriors join the Navy. Malcontents are shipped to the colonies. The cycle is closed. Drugs for the citizens, privileges for the taxpayers, peace for all provided by the fleet—and slavery for malcontents. Or death. The colonies use up men."

"I guess it's stable, then."

"Hardly. If Earth does not destroy herself—and from the rumors I hear the nations are at each other's throats despite what the Navy can do—why, they have built a pressure cooker out here that will one day destroy the old home world. Look at what we have here. Fortune hunters, adventurers, criminals, rebels—and all selected for survival abilities. The lid cannot stay on."

They saw Juanita and Curt Morgan walking around the big

house, and Mark winced. Juanita had grown during the summer. Now, with her hair combed, and in clean clothes, she was so lovely that it hurt to look at her. Taps smiled. "I see my star pupil has found another interest. Cheer up, lad, when you finish here you will find employment. You can have your pick of convict girls. Rent them, or buy one outright."

"I hate slavery!"

Taps shrugged. "As you should. Although you might be surprised what men who say that will do when given the chance. But calm yourself, I meant buy a wife, not a whore."

"But damn it, you don't buy wives! Women aren't things!"

Tappinger smiled softly. "I tend to forget just what a blow it is to you young people. You expect everything to be as it was on Earth. Yet you are here because you were not satisfied with your world."

"It was rotten."

"Possibly. But you had to search for the rot. Here you cannot avoid it."

On such nights it took Mark a long time to get to sleep.

V

The harvest season was approaching. The borshite plants stood in full flower, dull-red splashes against brown hills and green jungles, and the fields buzzed with insects. Nature had solved the problem of propagation without inbreeding on Tanith and fifty other worlds in the same way as on Earth.

The buzzing insects attracted insectivores, and predators chased those; close to harvest time there was little work, but the fields had to be watched constantly. Once again house and processing shed workers joined the field hands, and Mark had many days with Juanita.

She was slowly driving him insane. He knew she couldn't be as naïve as she pretended to be. She had to know how he felt and what he wanted to do, but she gave him no opportunities.

Sometimes he was sure that she was teasing him. "Why don't

you ever come see me in the evenings?" she asked one day.

"You know why. Curt is always there."

"Well, sure, but he don't—doesn't own my contract. 'Course, if you're scared of him—"

"You're bloody right I'm scared of him. He could fold me up for glue. Not to mention what happens when the foreman's mad at a con. Besides, I thought you liked him."

"Sure. So what."

"He told me he was going to marry you one day."

"He tells everybody that. He never told me, though."

Mark noted grimly that she'd stopped talking about becoming a nun.

"Of course, Curt's the only man who even says he's going to—Mark, *look out!*"

Mark saw a blur at the edge of his vision and whirled with his spear. Something was charging toward him. "Get behind me and run!" he shouted. "Keep me in line with it and get out of here."

She moved behind him and he heard her trumpet blare, but she wasn't running. Mark had no more time to think about her. The animal was nearly a meter and a half long, built square on thick legs and splayed feet. The snout resembled an earth wart hog, with four upthrusting tusks, and it had a thin tail that lashed as it ran.

"Porker," Juanita said softly. She was just behind him. "Sometimes they'll charge a man. Like this. Don't get it excited, maybe it'll go away."

Mark was perfectly willing to let the thing alone. It looked as if it would weigh as much as he did. Its broad feet and small claws gave it better footing than hobnails would give a man. It circled them warily, about three meters away. Mark turned carefully to keep facing it. He held the spear pointed at its throat. "I told you to get out of here," Mark said.

"Sure. There's usually two of those things." She spoke very softly. "I'm scared to blow this trumpet again. Wish Curt would get here with his gun." As she spoke there were gunshots. They sounded very far away.

"Mark," Juanita whispered urgently. "There is another one. I'm gettin' back to back with you."

"All right." He didn't dare look away from the beast in front of him. What did it want? It moved slowly toward him, halting just beyond the thrusting range of the spear. Then it dashed forward, screaming a sound that could never have come from an earthly pig.

Mark jabbed at it with his spear. It flinched from the point and ran past. Mark turned to follow it and saw the other beast advancing on Juanita. She had slipped in the mud and was down, trying frantically to get to her feet, and the porker was running toward her.

Mark gave an animal scream of pure fury. He slid in the mud but kept his feet and charged forward, screaming again as he stabbed with the spear and felt it slip into the thick hide. The porker shoved against him, and Mark fell into the mud. He desperately held the spear, but the beast walked steadily forward. The point went through the hide on the back and came out again, the shaft sliding between skin and meat, and impaled animal advanced inexorably up the shaft. The tusks neared his manhood. Mark heard himself whimper in fear. "I can't hold him!" he shouted. "Run!"

She didn't run. She got to her feet and shoved her spear down the snarling throat, then thrust downward, forcing the head toward the mud. Mark scrambled to his feet. He looked wildlly around for the other animal. It was nowhere in sight, but the pinned porker snarled horribly.

"Mark, honey, take that spear of yours out of him while I hold him," Juanita shouted. "I can't hold long—quick, now."

Mark shook himself out of the trembling fear that paralyzed him. The tusks moved wickedly and he felt them even though they were nowhere near him, felt them tearing at his groin.

"Please, honey," Juanita said.

He tugged at the spear, but it wouldn't come free, so he thrust it forward, then ran behind the animal to pull the spear through the loose skin on the porker's back. The shaft came through bloody. His hands slipped but he held the spear and thrust it into the animal, thrust again and again, stabbing in insane fury and shouting, "Die, die, die!"

* * *

Morgan didn't come for another half an hour. When he galloped up they were standing with their arms around each other. Juanita moved slowly away from Mark when Morgan dismounted, but she looked possessively at him.

"That way now?" Morgan asked.

She didn't answer.

"There was a herd of those things in the next field over," Curt said. His voice was apologetic. "Killed three men and a woman. I came as quick as I could."

"Mark killed this one."

"She did. It would have had me—"

"Hold on," Curt said.

"It walked right up the spear," Mark said.

"I've seen 'em do that, all right." Morgan seemed to be choosing his words very carefully. "You two will have to stay on here for a while. We've lost four hands, and—"

"We'll be all right," Juanita said.

"Yeah." Morgan went back to his mount. "Yeah, I guess you will." He rode off quickly.

Tradition gave Mark and Juanita the carcass, and they feasted their friends that night. Afterwards Mark and Juanita walked away from the barracks area, and they were gone for a long time.

* * *

"Taps, what the hell am I going to do?" Mark demanded. They were outside, in the unexpected cool of a late summer evening. Mark had thought he would never be cool again; now it was almost harvest time. The fall and winter would be short, but Tanith was almost comfortable during those months.

"What is the problem?"

"She's pregnant."

"Hardly surprising. Nor the end of the world. There are many ways to—"

"No. She won't even talk about it. Says it's murder. It's that damned padre. Goddamn church, no wonder they bring that joker around. Makes the slaves contented."

"That is hardly the only activity of the church, but it does have that effect. Well, what is it to you? As you have often pointed out, you have no responsibilities. And certainly you have no legal obligations in this case."

"That's my kid! And she's my—I mean, damn it, I can't just—"

Tappinger smiled grimly. "I remind you that conscience and a sense of ethics are expensive luxuries. But if you are determined to burden yourself with them, let us review your alternatives.

"You can ask Ewigfeuer for permission to marry her. It is likely to be granted. The new governor has ended the mandatory so-called apprenticeship for children born to convicts. Your sentence is not all that long. When it ends, you will be free—"

"To do what? I saw the time-expired men in Whiskeytown."

"There are jobs. There is a whole planetary economy to be built."

"Yeah. Sure. Sweat my balls off for some storekeeper. Or work like Curt Morgan, sweating cons."

Tappinger shrugged. "There are alternatives. Civil service. Or learn the business yourself and become a planter. There is always financing available for those who can produce."

"I'd still be a slaver. I want out of the system. Out of the whole damned thing!"

Tappinger sighed and lifted the bottle to drink. He paused to say "There are many things we all want. So what?" Then he drained the pint.

"There's another way," Mark said. "A way out of all this."

Tappinger looked up quickly. "Don't even think it! Mark, you believe the Free State to be some kind of dream world. That is what it is—a dream. In reality, there is nothing more than a gang of lawless men, living like animals off what they can steal. You cannot live without laws."

I can damned well live without the kind of laws they have here, Mark thought. And of course they steal. Why shouldn't they? How else can they live?

"And it is unlikely to last in any event. The governor has brought in a regiment of mercenaries to deal with the Free State."

About what I'd expect, Mark thought. "Why not CD Marines?"

Tappinger shrugged. "Budget. There are not enough CD forces to keep the peace. The Grand Senate will not pay for policing Tanith. So the planters are squeezed again, to pay for their protection."

And that's fine with me, Mark thought. "Mercenaries can't be much use. They'd rather lay around in barracks and collect their pay." His teachers had told him that.

"Have you ever known any?"

"No, of course not. Look, Taps, I'm tired. I think I better get to bed." He turned and left the old man. To hell with him, Mark thought. Old man, old woman, that's what he is. Not enough guts to get away from here and strike out on his own.

Well, that's fine for him. But I've got bigger things in mind.

✽   ✽   ✽

The harvest began. The borshite pods formed and were cut, and the sticky sap collected. The sap was boiled, skimmed, boiled again until it was reduced to a tiny fraction of the bulky plants they had worked all summer to guard.

And Ewigfeuer collapsed on the steps of the big house. Morgan flew him to the Whiskeytown hospital. He came back with a young man: Ewigfeuer's son, on leave from his administrative post in the city.

"That old bastard wants to see you outside," Lewis said.

Mark sighed. He was tired from a long day in the fields. He was also tired of Tappinger's eternal lectures on the horrors of the Free State. Still, the man was his only friend. Mark took his bottle and went outside.

Tappinger seized the bottle eagerly. He downed several swallows. His hands shook. "Come with me," he whispered.

Mark followed in confusion. Taps led the way to the shadows near the big house. Juanita was there.

"Mark, honey, I'm scared."

Tappinger took another drink. "The Ewigfeuer boy is trying to raise money," he said. "He storms through the house complaining of all the useless people his father keeps on, and shouts that his father is ruining himself. The hospital bills are very high, it seems. And this place is heavily in debt. He has been selling contracts. One that he sold was hers. For nearly two thousand credits."

"Sale?" Mark said stupidly. "But she has less than two years to go!"

"Yes," Taps said. "There is only one way a planter could expect to make that much back from the purchase of a young and pretty girl."

"God damn them," Mark said. "All right. We've got to get out of here."

"No," Tappinger said. "I've told you why. No, I have a better way. I can forge the old man's signature to a permission form. You can marry Juanita. The forgery will be discovered, but by then—"

"No," Mark said. "Do you think I'll stay to be part of this system? A free society will need good people."

"Mark, please," Tappinger said. "Believe me, it is not what you think it is! How can you live in a place with no rules, you with your ideas of what is fair and what is—"

"Crap. From now on I take care of myself. And my woman and my child. We're wasting time." He moved toward the stables. Juanita followed.

"Mark, you do not understand," Tappinger protested.

"Shut up. I have to find the guard."

"He's right behind you." Morgan's voice was low and quiet. "Don't do anything funny, Mark."

"Where did you come from?"

"I've been watching you for ten minutes. Did you think you could get up to the big house without being seen? You damned fool. I ought to let you go into the green and get killed. But you can't go alone—no, you have to take Juanny with you. I thought you had more sense. We haven't used the whipping post here for a year, but a couple of dozen might wake you up to—" Morgan started to turn as something moved behind him. Then he crumpled. Juanita hit him again with a billet of wood. Morgan fell to the ground.

"I hope he'll be all right," Juanita said. "When he wakes up, Taps, please tell him why we had to run off."

"Yeah, take care of him," Mark said. He was busily stripping the weapons belt from Morgan. Mark noted the compass and grinned.

"You're a fool," Tappinger said. "Men like Curt Morgan take care of themselves. It's people like you that need help."

Tappinger was still talking, but Mark paid no attention. He broke the lock on the stable and then opened the storage room inside. He found canteens in the harness room. There was also a plastic can of kerosene. Mark and Juanita saddled two horses. They led them out to the edge of the compound. Tappinger stood by the broken stable door.

They looked back for a second, then waved and rode into the jungle. Before they were gone, Tappinger had finished the last of Mark's gin.

❈ ❈ ❈

They fled southwards in terror. Every sound seemed to be Morgan and a chase party following with dogs. Then there were the nameless sounds of the jungle. The horses were as frightened as they were.

In the morning they found a small clump of brown grass, a miniscule clearing of high ground. They did not dare make a fire, and they had only some biscuit and grain to eat. A Weem's Beast charged out of the small clump of trees near the top of the clearing, and Mark shot it, wasting ammunition by firing again and again until he was certain that it was dead. Then they were too afraid to stay and had to move on.

They kept southward. Mark had overheard convicts talking about the Free State. On an arm of the sea, south, in the jungle. It was all he had to direct him. A crocodile menaced them, but they rode past, Mark holding the pistol tightly, while the beast stared at them. It wasn't a real crocodile, of course; but it looked much like the Earthly variety. Parallel evolution, Mark thought. What shape would be better adapted to life in this jungle?

On the third day they came to a narrow inlet and followed it to the left, deeper into the jungle, the sea on their right and green hell to the left. It twisted its way along some forgotten river dried by geological shifts a long time before. Tiny streams had bored through the cliff faces on both sides, and plunged a hundred meters across etched rock faces into the green froth at the bottom. Overhead the orange skies were misty with low cloud patches darting under the haze.

At dark they halted and Mark risked a fire. He shot a crown-ears and they roasted it. "The worst is over," Mark said. "We're free now. Free."

She crept into his arms. Her face was worried but contented, but it had lines that made her seem older than Mark. "You never asked me," she said.

He smiled. "Will you marry me?"

"Sure."

They laughed together. The jungle seemed very close and the horses were nickering in nervous fear. Mark built up the fire. "Free," he said. He held her tightly, and they were very happy.

VI

Mark awoke with a knife at his throat. A big, ugly man, burned dark and with scars crisscrossing his bare chest, squatted in front of them. He eyed Mark and Juanita, then grinned. "What have we got ourselves?" he said. "Couple of runaways?"

"I got everything, Art," someone said from behind them.

"Yeah. Okay, mates, up and at 'em. Move out, I ain't got all day."

Mark helped Juanita to her feet. One arm was asleep from holding her. As Mark stood the ugly man expertly took the gun from Mark's belt. "Who are you?" Mark asked.

"Call me Art. Sergeant to the Boss. Come on, let's go."

There were five others, all mounted. Art led the way through the jungle. When Mark tried to say something to Juanita, Art turned. "I'm going to tell you once. Shut up. Say another word to anybody but me, and I kill you. Say anything to me that I don't want to hear and I'll cut you. Got that?"

"Yes, sir," Mark said.

Art laughed. "Now you've got the idea."

They rode on in silence.

The Free State was mostly caves in hillsides above the sea. It held over five hundred men and women. There were other encampments of escapees out in the jungles, Art said. "But we've got the biggest. Been pretty careful—when we raid the planters we can usually make it look like one of the other outfits did it. Governor don't have much army anyway. They won't follow us here."

Mark started to say something about the mercenaries that the governor was hiring. Then he thought better of it.

The Boss was a heavy man with long colorless hair growing to below his shoulders. He had a handlebar mustache and staring blue eyes. He sat in the mouth of a cave on a big carved chair as if it were a throne, and he held a rifle across his knees. A big black man stood behind the chair, watching everyone, saying nothing.

"Escapees, eh?"

"Yes," Mark said.

"Yes, Boss. Don't forget that."

"Yes, Boss."

"What can you you do? Can you fight?"

When Mark didn't answer, the Boss pointed to a smaller man in the crowd that had gathered around. "Take him, Choam."

The small man moved toward Mark. His foot lashed upward and hit Mark in the ribs. Then he moved closer. Mark tried to hit him, but the man dodged away and slapped Mark across the face. "Enough," the Boss said. "You can't fight. What can you do?"

"I—"

"Yeah." He looked backward over his shoulder to the black man. "You want him, George?"

"No."

"Right. Art, you found him. He's yours. I'll take the girl."

"But you can't!" Mark shouted.

"No!" Juanita said.

The other men looked at the Boss. They saw he was laughing. Then they all laughed. Art and two others took Mark's arms and began to drag him away. Two more led Juanita into the cave behind the Boss.

"But this isn't right!" Mark shouted.

There was more laughter. The Boss stood. "Maybe I'll give her back when I'm through. Unless Art wants her. Art?"

"I got a woman."

"Yeah." The Boss turned toward the cave. Then he turned back to Mark and the men holding him. "Leave the kid here, Art. I'd like to talk to him. Get the girl cleaned up," he shouted behind him. "And the rest of you get out of here."

The others left, all but the black man who had stood behind the Boss's throne. The black man went a few meters away and sat under a rock ledge. It looked cool in there. He took out a pipe and began stuffing it.

"Come here, kid. What's your name?"

"Fuller," Mark said. "Mark Fuller."

"Come over here. Sit down." The Boss indicated a flat rock bench just inside the cave mouth. The cave seemed to go a long way in; then it turned. There was no one in sight. Mark thought he could hear women talking. "Sit, I said. Tell me how you got here." The Boss's tone was conversational, almost friendly.

"I was in a student riot." Mark strained to hear, but there were no more sounds from inside the cave.

"Student, eh. Relax, Fuller. Nobody's hurting your girl friend. Your concern is touching. Don't see much of that out here. Tell me about your riot. Where was it?"

The Boss was a good listener. When Mark fell silent, the man would ask questions—probing questions, as if he were interested in Mark's story. Sometimes he smiled.

Outside were work parties: wood details; a group incomprehensibly digging a ditch in the flinty ground out in front of the caves; women carrying water. None of them were interested in the Boss's conversation. Instead, they seemed almost afraid to look into the cave—all but the black man, who sat in his cool niche and never seemed to look away.

Bit by bit Mark told of his arrest and sentence, and of Ewigfeuer's plantation. The Boss nodded. "So you came looking for the Free States. And what did you expect to find?"

"Free men! Freedom, not—"

"Not despotism." There was something like kindness in the words. The Boss chuckled. "You know, Fuller, it's remarkable how much your story is like mine. Except that I've always known how to fight. And how to make friends. Good friends." He tilted his head toward the black man. "George, there, for instance. Between us there's nothing we can't handle. You poor fool, what the hell did you think you'd do out here? What good are you? You can't fight, you whine about what's right and fair, you don't know how to take care of yourself, and you come off into the bush to find us. You knew who we were."

"But—"

"And now you're all broken up about your woman. I'm not going to take anything she hasn't got plenty of. It doesn't get used up." He stood, and shouted to one of the men in the yard. "Send Art over."

"So you're going to rape Juanita." Mark looked around, for a weapon, for anything. There was a rifle near the Boss's chair. His eyes flickered toward it.

The Boss laughed. "Try it. But you won't. Aw, hell, Fuller,

you'll be all right. Maybe you'll even learn something. Now I've got a date."

"But—" If there was something I could say, Mark thought. "Why are you doing this?"

"Why not? Because I'll lose your valuable loyalty? Get something straight, Fuller. This is it. There's no place left to go. Live here and learn our ways, or go jump over the cliff there. Or take off into the green and see how far you get. You think you're pretty sharp. Maybe you are. We'll see. Maybe you'll learn to be some use to us. Maybe. Art, take the kid into your squad and see if he can fit in."

"Right, Boss. Come on." Art took Mark's arm. "Look, if you're going to try something, do it and get it over with. I don't want to have to watch you all the time."

Mark turned and followed the other man. Helpless. Damn fool, and helpless. He laughed.

"Yeah?" Art said. "What's funny?"

"The Free State. Freedom. Free men—"

"We're free," Art said. "More'n the losers in Whiskeytown. Maybe one day you will be. When we think we can trust you." He pointed to the cliff edge. The sea inlet was beyond it. "Anybody we can't trust goes over that. The fall don't always kill 'em, but I never saw anybody make it to shore."

Art found him a place in his cave. There were six other men and four women there. The others looked at Mark for a moment, then went back to whatever they had been doing. Mark sat staring at the cave floor, and thought he heard, off toward the Boss's cave, a man laughing and a girl crying. For the first time since he was twelve, Mark tried to pray.

Pray for what? he asked himself. He didn't know. I hate them. All of them.

Just when, Mark Fuller, are you going to get some control over your life? But that doesn't just happen. I have to do it for myself. Somehow.

A week went past. It was a meaningless existence. He cooked for the squad, gathered wood and washed dishes, and listened to the sounds of the other men and their women at night. They never left him alone.

The crying from the Boss's cave stopped, but he didn't see Juanita. When he gathered wood there were sometimes women from the Boss's area, and he overheard them talking about what a relief it was that Chambliss—that seemed to be the Boss's name—had a new playmate. They did not seem at all jealous of the new arrival.

Play along with them, Mark thought. Play along until—until what? What can I do? Escape? Get back to the plantation? How? And what happens then? But I won't join them, I won't become part of this! I won't!

After a week they took Mark on hunting parties. He was unarmed—his job was to carry the game. They had to walk several kilometers away from the caves. Chambliss didn't permit hunting near the encampment.

Mark was paired with Art. The older man was neither friendly nor unfriendly; he treated Mark as a useful tool, someone to carry and do work.

"Is this all there is?" Mark asked. "Hunting, sitting around the camp, eating and—"

"—and a little screwing," Art said. "What the hell do you want us to do? Set up farms so the governor'll know where we are? We're doin' all right. Nobody tells us what to do."

"Except the Boss."

"Yeah. Except the Boss. But nobody hassles us. We can live for ourselves. Cheer up, kid, you'll feel better when you get your woman back. He'll get tired of her one of these days. Or maybe we'll get some more when we go raiding. Only thing is, you'll have to fight for a woman. You better do it better'n you did the other day."

"Doesn't she—don't the women have anything to say about who they pair up with?" Mark asked.

"Why should they?"

* * *

On the tenth day there was an alarm. Someone thought he heard a helicopter. The Boss ordered night guards.

Mark was paired with a man named Cal. They sat among rocks at the edge of the clearing. Cal had a rifle and a knife, but Mark was unarmed. The jungle was black dark, without even stars above.

Finally the smaller man took tobacco and paper from his pocket. "Smoke?"

"Thanks. I'd like one."

"Sure." He rolled two cigarettes. "Maybe you'll do, huh? Had my doubts about you when you first come. You know, it's a wonder the Boss didn't have you tossed over the side, the way you yelled at him like that. No woman's worth that, you know."

"Yeah."

"She mean much to you?" Cal asked.

"Some." Mark swallowed hard. His mouth tasted bitter. "'Course, they get the idea they own you, there's not much you can do."

Cal laughed. "Yeah. Had an old lady like that in Baltimore. Stabbed me one night for messing around with her sister. Where you from, kid?"

"Santa Maria. Part of San-San."

"I been there once. San-San, not where you come from. Here." He handed mark the cigarette, and struck a match to light both.

They smoked in silence. It wasn't all tobacco, Mark found; there was a good shot of burl in the cigarette. Mark avoided inhaling, but spoke as if holding his breath. Cal sucked and packed.

"Good weed," Cal said. "You should have brought some when you run off."

"Had to get out fast."

"Yeah." They listened to the sounds of the jungle. "Hell of a life," Cal said. "Wish I could get back to Earth. Some Welfare Island, anyplace where it's not so damned hot. I'd live in Alaska. You ever been there?"

"No. Isn't there—don't you have any plans? Some way to make things better?"

"Well, the Boss talks about it, but nothing happens," Cal

said. "Every now and then we go raid a place, get some new women. We got a still in not long ago, that's something."

Mark shuddered. "Cal?"

"Yah?"

"Got another cigarette?"

"You'll owe me for it."

"Sure."

"Okay." Cal took out paper and tobacco and rolled two more smokes. He handed one to Mark. "Been thinking. There ought to be something better'n this, but I sure don't see what it'll be." As Cal struck his match, Mark shut his eyes so he wouldn't be blinded. Then he lifted the rock he'd found in the darkness and brought it down hard onto Cal's head. The man slumped, but Mark hit him again. He felt something wet and sticky warming his fingers, and shuddered.

Then he was sick, but he had to work fast. He took Cal's rifle and knife, and his matches. There wasn't anything else useful. Mark moved from the rocks onto the narrow strip of flinty ground. No one spoke. Mark ran into the jungle. He did not know where he was going. He tried to think. Hiding out until morning wouldn't help. They'd find Cal and come looking. And Juanita was back there. Mark ran through the squishy mud. Tears came and he fought them back, but then he was sobbing. Where am I going? Where? And why bother?

He ran on until he felt something moving beside him. He drew in a breath to cry out, but a hand clamped over his mouth. Another grasped his wrist. He felt a knifepoint at his throat. "One sound and you're dead," a voice whispered. "Got that?"

Mark nodded.

"Right. Just keep remembering it. Okay, Ardway, let's go."

"Roger," a voice answered.

He was half carried through the jungle away from the camp. There were several men. He did not know how many. They moved silently. "Ready to walk?" someone asked.

"Yes," Mark whispered. "Who are—"

"Shut up. One more sound and we cut your kidneys out.

You'll take a week dying. Now follow the man ahead of you."

Mark made more noise than all the others combined, although he tried to walk silently. They went a long way, or it seemed to be, through knee-deep water and thick mud, then over harder ground. He thought they were going slightly uphill. Then he no longer felt the loom of the trees. They were in a clearing.

The night was pitch-black. How do they see? Mark wondered. And who? He thought he could make out a darker shape ahead of him. It was more a feeling than anything else, but then he touched it. It was soft. "Through that," someone said.

It was a curtain. Another was brought down behind him as he went through, and still another was lifted ahead of him. Light blinded him. He stood blinking.

He was inside a tent. Half a dozen uniformed men stood around a map table. At the end of the tent opposite Mark was a tall, thin man. Mark could not guess how old he was, but there were thin streaks of gray in his hair. His jungle camouflage uniform was neatly pressed. He looked at Mark without expression. "Well, Sergeant Major?"

"Strange, Colonel. This man was sitting guard with another guy. Neither one of them knew what he was doing. We watched them a couple of hours. Then this one beats the other one's brains out with a rock and runs right into the jungle."

Mercenaries, Mark thought. They've come to— "I need help." Mark said. "They've got my—my wife in there."

"Name?" the Colonel asked.

"Mark Fuller."

The Colonel looked to his right. Another officer had a small desk console. He punched Mark's name into it, and words flowed across the screen. The Colonel read for a moment. "Escaped convict. Juanita Corlee escaped with you. That is your wife?"

"Yes."

"And you had a falling out with the Free Staters."

"No. It wasn't that way at all." Mark blurted out his story. The Colonel looked back to the readout screen. "And you are surprised." He nodded to himself. "I knew the schools on Earth were of little use. It says here that you are an intelligent man, Fuller. So far you haven't shown many signs of it."

"No. Lord God, no. Who—who are you? Please."

"I am Colonel John Christian Falkenberg. This regiment has been retained by the Tanith governor to suppress these so-called Free States. You were captured by Sergeant Major Calvin, and these are my officers. Now, Fuller, what can you tell me about the camp layout? What weapons have they?"

"I don't know much," Mark said. "Sir." *Now why did I say that?*

"There are other female captives in that camp," Falkenberg said.

"Here," one of the other officers said. "Show us what you do know, Fuller. How good is this satellite photo map?"

"Christ, Rottermill," a third officer said. "Let the lad be for a moment."

"Major Savage, intelligence is my job."

"So is human compassion. Ian, do you think you can find this boy a drink?" Major Savage beckoned to Falkenberg and led him to the far corner of the tent. Another officer brought a package from under the table and took out a bottle. He handed the brandy to Mark.

Falkenberg listened to Savage. Then he nodded. "We can only try. Fuller, did you see any signs of power supplies in that camp?"

"No, sir. There was no electricity at all. Only flashlights."

"So it is unlikely that they have laser weapons. Rottermill, have any target seekers turned up missing from armories? What are the chances that they have any?"

"Slim, Colonel. Practically none. None stolen I know of."

"Jeremy, you may be right," Falkenberg said. "I believe we can use the helicopters as fighting vehicles."

There was a moment of silence; then the officer who'd given Mark the brandy said, "Colonel, that's damned risky. There's precious little armor on those things."

"Machines not much better than these were major fighting

vehicles less than a hundred years ago, Captain Frazer." Falkenberg studied the map. "You see, Fuller, the hostages have always been our problem. Because of them we have kept Aviation Company back and brought in our troops on foot. We've not been able to carry heavy equipment or even much personal body armor across these swamps."

No, I don't expect you would, Mark thought. He tried to imagine a large group traveling silently through the swamps. It seemed impossible. What had they done when animals attacked? There had been no shots fired. Why would an armed man let himself be killed when he could shoot?

"I expect they will threaten their prisoners when they know we are here," Falkenberg said. "Of course we will refuse to deal with them. How long do you think it will take for them to act when they know that?"

"I don't know," Mark said. It was something he could not have imagined, two years before: men who'd kill and torture, sometimes for no reason at all. No. Not men. Beasts.

"Well, you've precipitated the action," Falkenberg said. "They'll find your dead companion within hours. Captain Frazer."

"Sir."

"You have been studying this map. If you held this encampment, what defenses would you set up?"

"I'd dig in around this open area and hope someone was fool enough to come at us through it, Colonel."

"Yes. Sergeant Major."

"Sir!"

"Show me where they have placed their sentries." Falkenberg watched as Calvin sketched in outposts. Then he nodded. "It seems their Boss has some rudimentary military sense. Rings of sentries. In-depth defense. Can you infiltrate that, Sergeant Major?"

"Not likely, sir."

"Yes." Falkenberg stood for a moment. Then he turned to Captain Frazer. "Ian, you will take your scouts and half the infantry. Make preparations for an attack on the open area.

We will code that Green A. This is no feint, Ian. I want you to try to punch through. However, I do not expect you to succeed, so conserve your men as best you can."

Frazer straightened to attention. "Sir."

"We won't abandon you, Ian. When the enemy is well committed there, we'll use the helicopters to take you out. Then we hit them in the flanks and roll them up." Falkenberg pointed to the map again. "This depression seems secure enough as a landing area. Code that Green A-one."

Major Jeremy Savage held a match over the bowl of his pipe and inhaled carefully. When he was satisfied with the light, he said, "Close timing needed, John Christian. Ian's in a spot of trouble if we lose the choppers."

"Have a better way, Jerry?" Falkenberg asked.

"No."

"Right. Fuller, can you navigate a helicopter?"

"Yes, sir. I can even fly one."

Falkenberg nodded again. "Yes. You are a taxpayer's son, aren't you. Fuller, you will go with Number 3 chopper. Sergeant Major, I want you to put a squad of headquarters assault guards, full body armor, into Number 3. Fuller will guide the pilot as close as possible to the cave where the Boss is holding the women. Number 2 with another assault squad will follow. Every effort will be made to secure the hostages alive. Understand, Sergeant Major?"

"Sir!"

"Fuller?"

"Yes, sir."

"Very good. When the troops are off, those choppers must move out fast. We'll need them to rescue Ian's lot."

"Colonel?" Mark said.

"Yes?"

"Not all the women are hostages. Some of them will fight, I think. I don't know how many. And not all the men are—not everybody wants to be in there. Some would run off if they could."

"And what do you expect me to do about it?"

"I don't know, sir."

"Neither do I. Sergeant Major, we will move this command post in one hour. Until then, Fuller, you can use that time to show Captain Rottermill everything you know about that camp."

It isn't going to work, Mark thought. I prayed for her to die. Only I don't know if she wants to die. And now she will. He took another pull from the bottle, and felt it taken from his hand.

"Later," Rottermill said. "For now, tell me what you know about this lot."

VII

"They've found that dead guard." The radio sergeant adjusted his earphones. "Seem pretty stirred up about it."

Falkenberg looked at his watch. There was a good hour before sunrise. "Took them long enough."

"Pity Fuller couldn't guide that chopper in the dark," Jeremy Savage said.

"Yes. Sergeant Major, ask Captain Frazer to ready his men, and have your trail ambush party alerted."

"Sir."

"I have a good feeling about this one, John Christian." Savage tapped his pipe against the heel of his boot. "A good feeling."

"Hope you're right, Jeremy. Fuller doesn't believe it will work."

"No, but he seems to agree this is her best chance. He's steady enough now. Realistic assessment of probabilities. Holding up well, all things considered."

"For a married man." Married men make the kinds of promises no man can keep, Falkenberg thought. His lips twitched slightly at the memory, and for a moment Grace's smile loomed in the darkness of the jungle outside. "Sergeant Major, have the chopper teams get into their armor."

"Is it always like this?" Mark asked. He sat in the right hand seat of the helicopter. Body armor and helmet gave strange sensations. He sweated inside the thick clothing. The phones in his helmet crackled with commands meant for others. Outside the helmet there were sounds of firing. Captain Frazer's assault had started a quarter of an hour before; now there was a faint tinge of reddish gray in the eastern skies over the jungle.

Lieutenant Bates grinned and wriggled the control stick. "Usually it's worse. We'll get her out, Fuller. You just put us next to the right cave."

"I'll do that, but it won't work."

"Sure it will."

"You don't need to cheer me up, Bates."

"I don't?" Bates grinned again. He was not much older than Mark. "Maybe *I* need cheering up. I'm always scared about now."

"Really? You don't look it."

"All we're expected to do. Not look it." He thumbed the mike button. "Chief, everything set back there?"

"Aye aye, sir."

The voice in Mark's helmet grew loud and stern. "ALL HELICOPTERS, START YOUR ENGINES. I SAY AGAIN, START ENGINES."

"That's us." Bates reached for the starting controls and the turbines whined. "Not very much light."

"HELICOPTERS, REPORT WHEN READY."

"Ready aye-aye," Bates said.

"Aye-aye?" Mark asked.

"We're an old CD Marine regiment," Bates said. "Lot of us, anyway. Stayed with the old man when the Senate disbanded his regiment."

"You don't look old enough."

"Me? Not hardly. This was Falkenberg's Mercenary Legion long before I came aboard."

"Why? Why join mercenaries?"

Bates shrugged. "I like being part of the regiment. Or don't you think the work's worth doing?"

"LIFT OFF. BEGIN HELICOPTER ASSAULT."

"Liftoff aye-aye." The turbine whine increased and the ship lifted in a rising looping circle. Bates moved to the right of the three-craft formation.

Mark could dimly see the green below, with light increasing every minute. Now he could make out the shapes of small clearings among the endless green marshes.

"You take her," Bates said. His hands hovered over the controls, ready to take his darling away from this stranger.

Mark grasped the unfamiliar stick. It was different from the family machine he'd learned on, but the principles were the same. You never really forget, Mark thought. The chopper was not much more than a big airborne truck, and he'd driven one of those on a vacation in the Yukon. The Canadian lakes seemed endlessly far away, in time as well as in space.

Flying came back easily. He remembered the wild stunts he'd tried when he was first licensed. Once a group from his school had gone on a picnic to San Miguel Island, and Mark had landed in a cove, dropping onto a narrow inaccessible beach between high cliffs during a windstorm. It had been stupid, but wildly exciting. Good practice for this, he thought. And I'm scared stiff, and what do I do after this is over? Will Falkenberg turn me in?

There were hills ahead, dull brown in the early morning light. Men huddled in the rocky areas. The Gatling in the compartment behind Mark crackled like frying bacon. The shots were impossibly close together, like a steady stream of noise, and the helicopter raked the Free State with its lash. The small slugs sent chips flying from the rocks. The other choppers opened up, and six tracer streams twisted in crazy patterns intertwining like some courtship dance.

Men and women died on that flinty ground. They lay in broken heaps, red blood staining the dirt around them, exactly like a scene on tri-v. Only it's not fake, Mark thought. They won't get up when the cameras go away. Did they deserve this? Does anyone?

Then he was too busy flying to think about anything else. The area in front of the cave was small, very small—was it large enough for the rotors to clear? A strong gust from the sea struck them, and the chopper rocked dangerously.

"Watch her—" Whatever Bates had intended to say, he never finished it. He slumped forward over the stick, held just above it by his shoulder straps. Something wet and sticky splashed across Mark's left hand and arm. Brains. A large slug had come angling upward to hit Bates in the jaw, then ricochet around in his helmet. The young lieutenant had almost no face. Get her down, Mark chanted, easy baby, down you go, level now, here's another gust, easy baby . . .

Men poured out of the descending chopper. Mark had time to be surprised: they jumped down and ran into the cave even as their friends fell around them. Then something stabbed Mark's left arm, and there were neat holes in the plexiglass windscreen in front of him. The men went on into the cave. They were faceless in their big helmets, identical robots moving forward or falling in heaps . . .

Lord God, they're magnificent. I've got to get this thing down! Suddenly that was the most important thing in his life. Get down and get out, go into the cave with those men. Find Juanita, yes, of course, but go with them, do something for myself because I want to do it—

"BATES, STOP WASTING TIME AND GET TO GREEN A-ONE. URGENT."

God damn it! Mark fumbled with the communications gear. "Bates is dead. This is Fuller. I'm putting the chopper down."

The voice in the phones changed. Someone else spoke. "Are the troops still aboard?"

"No. They're off."

"Then take that craft to Green A-one immediately."

"My—my wife's in there!"

"The Colonel is aware of that." Jeremy Savage's voice was calm. "That machine is required, and now."

"But—"

"Fuller, this regiment has risked a great deal for those hostages. The requirement is urgent. Or do you seriously suppose you would be much use inside?"

Oh, Christ! There was firing inside the cave, and someone was screaming. I want to kill him, Mark thought. Kill that blond-haired bastard. I want to watch him die. A babble filled the helmet phones. Crisp commands and reports were jumbled together as a background noise. Frazer's voice. "We're pinned. I'm sending them back to A-one as fast as I can."

There was more firing from inside the cave.

"Aye-aye," Mark said. He gunned the engine and lifted out in a whirling loop to confuse the ground fire. Someone was still aboard; the Gatling chattered and its bright stream raked the rocks around the open area below.

Where was Green A-one? Mark glanced at the map in front of the control stick. There was gray and white matter, and bright red blood, a long smear across the map. Mark had to lift Bates' head to get a bearing. More blood ran across his fingers.

Then the area was ahead, a clear depression surrounded by hills and rocks. Men lay around the top of the bowl. A mortar team worked mechanically, dropping the shells down the tube, leaning back, lifting, dropping another. There were bright flashes everywhere. Mark dropped into the bowl and the flashes vanished. There were sounds: gunfire, and the whump! whump! of the mortar. A squad rushed over and began loading wounded men into the machine. Then the sergeant waved him off, and Mark raced for the rear area where the surgeon waited. Another helicopter passed headed into the combat area.

The medics off-loaded the men.

"Stand by, Fuller, we'll get another pilot over there," Savage's calm voice said in the phones.

"No. I'll keep it. I know the way."

There was a pause. "Right. Get to it, then."

"Aye-aye, sir."

The entrance to the Boss's cave was cool, and the surgeon had moved the field hospital there. A steady stream of men came out of the depths of the cave: prisoners carrying their own dead, and Falkenberg's men carrying their comrades. The

Free State dead were piled in heaps near the cliff edge. When they were identified they were tossed over the side. The regiment's dead were carried to a cleared area, where they lay covered. Armed soldiers guarded the corpses.

Do the dead give a damn? Mark wondered. Why should they? What's the point of all the ceremony over dead mercenaries? He looked back at the still figure on the bed. She seemed small and helpless, and her breath rasped in her throat. An i.v. unit dripped endlessly.

"I expect she'll live."

Mark turned to see the regimental surgeon.

"We couldn't save the baby, but there's no reason she won't have more."

"What happened to her?" Mark demanded.

The surgeon shrugged. "Bullet in the lower abdomen. Ours, theirs, who knows? Jacketed slug, it didn't do a lot of damage. The Colonel wants to see you, Fuller. And you can't do any good here." The surgeon took him by the elbow and ushered him out into the steaming daylight. "That way."

There were more work parties in the open space outside. Prisoners were still carrying away dead men. Insects buzzed around dark red stains on the flinty rocks. They look so dead, Mark thought. So damned dead. Somewhere a woman was crying.

Falkenberg sat with his officers under an open tent in the clearing. There was another man with them, a prisoner under guard. His face was hidden by the tent awning, but Mark knew him. "So they took you alive," Mark said.

"I seem to have survived." The Boss's lips curled in a sneer. "And you helped them. Fine way to thank us for taking you in."

"Taking us in! You raped—"

"How do you know it was rape?" the Boss demanded. "Not that you were any great help, were you? You're no damned good, Fuller. Your help didn't make a damned bit of difference. Has anything you ever did made any difference?"

"That will do, Chambliss," Falkenberg said.

"Sure. You're in charge now, Colonel. Well, you beat us, so you give the orders. We're pretty much alike, you and me."

"Possibly," Falkenberg said. "Corporal, take Chambliss to the guard area. And make certain he does not escape."

"Sir." The troopers gestured with their rifles. The Boss walked ahead of them. He seemed to be leading them.

"What will happen to him?" Mark asked.

"We will turn him over to the governor. I expect he'll hang. The problem, Fuller, is what we do with you. You were of some help to us, and I don't like unpaid debts."

"What choices do I have?" Mark asked.

Falkenberg shrugged. "We could give you a mount and weapons. It is a long journey to the farmlands in the south, but once there you could probably avoid recapture. Probably. If that is not attractive, I suppose we could put in a good word with the governor."

"Which would get me what?"

"It would depend on him. At the least he would agree to forget about your escape and persuade your patron not to prosecute for theft of animals and weapons."

"But I'd be back under sentence. A slave again. What happens to Juanita?"

"The regiment will take care of her."

"What the hell does that mean?" Mark demanded.

Falkenberg's expression did not change. Mark could not tell what the colonel was thinking. "I mean, Fuller, that it is unlikely that the troops would enjoy the prospect of turning her over to the governor. She can stay with us until her apprenticeship has expired."

"So you're no better than the Boss after all!"

"Watch it," one of the officers said.

"What Colonel Falkenberg means," Major Savage said, "is that she will be permitted to stay with us as long as she wishes. Certainly we lack for women; but there are some slight differences between us and your Free State. Colonel Falkenberg commands a regiment. He does not rule a mob."

"Sure. What if she wants to come with me?"

"Then we will see that she does. When she recovers," Savage said. "Now what is it you want to do? We don't have all day."

What do I want to do? Lord God. I want to go home, but that's not possible. Dirt farmer, fugitive forever. Or slave for at least two more years. "You haven't given me a very pleasant set of alternatives."

"You had fewer when you came here," Savage said.

A party of prisoners was herded toward the tent. They stood looking nervously at the seated officers, while their guards stood at ease with their weapons. Mark licked his lips. "I heard you were enlisting some of the Free Staters."

Falkenberg nodded. "A few. Not many."

"Could you use a helicopter pilot?"

Major Savage chuckled. "Told you he'd ask, John Christian."

"He was steady enough this morning," Captain Frazer said. "And we do need pilots."

"Do you know what you're getting into?" Falkenberg wanted to know. "Soldiers are not slaves, but they must obey orders. All of them."

"Slaves have to obey, too."

"It's five years," Major Savage said. "And we track down deserters."

"Yes, sir." Mark looked at each of the officers in turn. They sat impassively. They said nothing; they did not look at each other, but they belonged to each other. And to their men. Mark remembered the clubs that children in his neighborhood had formed. Belonging to them had been important, although he could never have said why. It was important to belong to something.

"You see the regiment as merely another unpleasant alternative," Falkenberg said. "If it is never more than that, it will not be enough."

"He came for us, Colonel," Frazer said. "When he didn't have to."

"Yes. I take it you are sponsoring him."

"Yes, sir."

"Very well," Falkenberg said. "Sergeant Major, is he acceptable to the men?"

"No objections, sir."

"Jeremy?"

"No objection, John Christian."

"Adjutant?"

"I've got his records, Colonel." Captain Fast indicated the console readout. "He'd make a terrible enlisted man."

"But not necessarily a terrible officer?"

"No, sir. He scores out high enough. But I've got my doubts about his motivations."

"Yes. But we do not generally worry about men's motives. We only require that they act like soldiers. Are you objecting, Amos?"

"No, Colonel."

"Then that's that. Fuller, you will be on trial. It will not be the easiest experience of your life. Men earn their way into this regiment."

"Yes, sir."

"You may go. There will be a formal swearing in when we return to our own camp. And doubtless Captain Fast will have forms for you to fill out. Dismissed."

"Yes, sir." Mark left the command tent. The times are out of joint, he thought. Is that the right line? Whatever. Does anyone control his own life? I wasn't able to. The police, the Marines, the Boss, now these mercenaries—they tell us all what to do. Who tells them?

Now I'm one of them. Mercenary soldier. It sounds ugly, but I don't have any choices at all. It's no career. Just a way out of slavery.

And yet—

He remembered the morning's combat and he felt guilt because of the memory. He had felt alive then. Men and women died all around him, but he'd felt more alive than he'd ever been.

He passed the graves area. The honor guard stood at rigid attention, ignoring the buzzing insects, ignoring everything around them as they stood over the flag-draped figures laid out in neat rows. A cool breeze came up from the sea. Winter was coming, and it would be pleasant on Tanith, but not for long.

The John W. Campbell Jr. Awards
1973–1975

1973   Ruth Berman
George Alec Effinger   Awarded at the 31st World
George R. R. Martin   Science Fiction Convention
*Jerry Pournelle
Robert Thurston   Toronto, Ontario
Lisa Tuttle

1974   Jesse Miller
Tom Monteleone   Awarded at the 32nd World
*Spider Robinson   Science Fiction Convention
Guy Snyder
*Lisa Tuttle   Washington, D.C.

1975   Alan Brennert
Suzy McKee Charnas   Awarded at the 33rd World
Felix Gotschalk   Science Fiction Convention
Brenda Pearce
*P. J. Plauger   Melbourne, Australia
John Varley

indicates winners